HONOR
HARRINGTON
Field of Dishonor

HONOR
HARRINGTON
Field of Dishonor

DAVID WEBER

FIELD OF DISHONOR

This is a work of fiction. All the characters and events portrayed in this book are fictional, and any resemblance to real people or incidents is purely coincidental.

A Baen Books Original

Baen Publishing Enterprises
P.O. Box 1403
Riverdale, NY 10471

ISBN: 0-671-57820-0

Cover art by Gary Ruddell
Map by N.C. Hanger

First hardcover printing, October 1999

Library of Congress Cataloging-in-Publication Data

Weber, David, 1952–
  Field of dishonor / David Weber
       p.   cm.
  ISBN 0-671-57820-0 (HC)
  I. Title.
PS3573.E217F54   1999
813'.54—dc21   99-39177
                                                        CIP

Distributed by Simon & Schuster
1230 Avenue of the Americas
New York, NY 10020

Typeset by Windhaven Press, Auburn, NH
Printed in the United States of America

"It is always a bad thing when political matters are allowed to affect . . . the planning of operations."

Field Marshal Erwin Rommel
160 Ante-Diaspora (1943 C.E.)

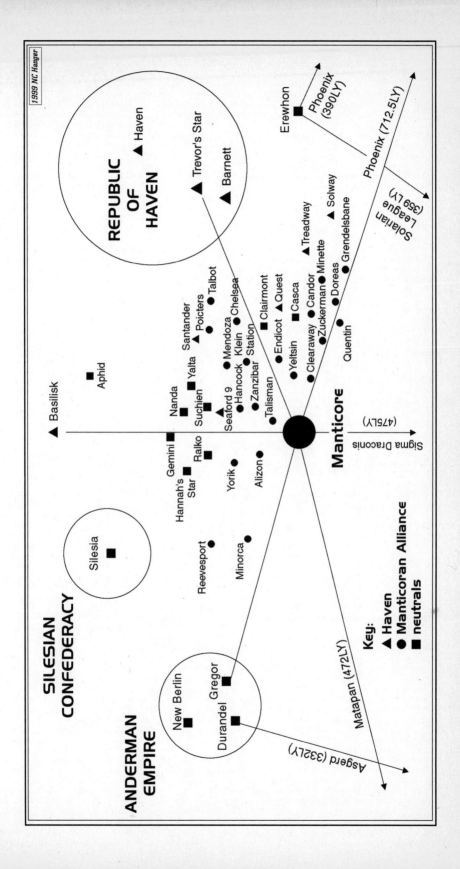

✧ PROLOGUE

It was very quiet in the huge, dimly lit room. The Advanced Tactical Training Course's main lecture hall boasted the second largest holo tank of the Royal Manticoran Navy, and the rising, amphitheaterlike seats facing the tank seated over two thousand at full capacity. At the moment, thirty-seven people, headed by Admiral Sir Lucien Cortez, Fifth Space Lord, and Vice Admiral The Honorable Alyce Cordwainer, the RMN's Judge Advocate General, sat in those seats and watched the tank intently.

The image of a tall, strong-faced woman floated in it, sitting erect and square-shouldered yet calmly in her chair, hands folded on the tabletop before her beside the white beret of a starship's commander. The golden planets of a senior-grade captain gleamed on the collar of her space-black tunic, and she wore no expression at all as she faced the HD camera squarely.

"And what, precisely, happened after the task group's final course change, Captain Harrington?" The voice came from off-camera, and a blood-red caption in the holo tank identified the speaker as Commodore Vincent Capra, head of the board of inquiry whose recommendations had brought the audience here.

"The enemy altered course to pursue us, Sir." Captain Harrington's soprano was surprisingly soft and sweet for a woman of her size, but it was also cool, almost remote.

"And the tactical situation?" Capra pressed.

"The task group was under heavy fire, Sir," she replied in that same, impersonal tone. "I believe *Circe* was destroyed almost as we altered course. *Agamemnon* was destroyed approximately five minutes after course change, and several of our other units suffered both damage and casualties."

1

"Would you call the situation desperate, Captain?"

"I would call it . . . serious, Sir," Harrington responded after a moment's thought.

There was a brief silence, as if her invisible questioner were waiting for her to say something more. But her detached calm was impregnable, and Commodore Capra sighed.

"Very well, Captain Harrington. The situation was 'serious,' the enemy had altered course to pursue you, and *Agamemnon* had been destroyed. Were you in contact with *Nike*'s flag bridge and Admiral Sarnow?"

"Yes, Sir, I was."

"So it was at this time he started to order the task group to scatter?"

"I believe that was his intention, Sir, but if so, he was interrupted before he actually gave orders to that effect."

"And how was he interrupted, Captain?"

"By a report from our sensor net, Sir. Our platforms had picked up the arrival of Admiral Danislav's dreadnoughts."

"I see. And did Admiral Sarnow then order the task group *not* to scatter?"

"No, Sir. He was wounded before he could pass any other orders," the quiet, unshadowed soprano replied.

"And how was he wounded, Captain? What were the circumstances?" The off-camera voice was almost irritated now, as if frustrated by Harrington's clinical professionalism.

"*Nike* was hit several times by enemy fire, Sir. One hit took out Boat Bay One, CIC, and Flag Bridge. Several members of the Admiral's staff were killed, and he himself was severely injured."

"He was rendered unconscious?"

"Yes, Sir."

"And did you pass command of the task group to the next senior officer?"

"I did not, Sir."

"You retained command?" Harrington nodded wordlessly. "Why, Captain?"

"In my judgment, Sir, the tactical situation was too serious to risk confusion in the chain of command. I was in possession of knowledge—the fact that Admiral Danislav had arrived—which might not be known to Captain Rubenstein, the next senior officer, and time was very limited."

"So you took it upon yourself to assume command of the entire task group in Admiral Sarnow's name?" Capra's question was sharp—not condemnatory, but with the air of making a crucial point—and Harrington nodded once more.

"I did, Sir," she said, without even a flicker of emotion as she admitted violating at least five separate articles of war.

"Why, Captain?" Capra pressed. "What made the situation time critical enough to justify such an action on your part?"

"We were approaching our preplanned scatter point, Sir. Admiral Danislav's arrival gave us the opportunity to lead the enemy into a position from which he could not escape interception, but only if we remained concentrated and offered him a target worth pursuing. Given the damage I knew Captain Rubenstein's com facilities had suffered, I judged there was too great a risk that the task group would scatter as previously planned before Captain Rubenstein could be fully apprised of the situation and assert tactical control."

"I see." There was another lengthy moment of silence, broken only by what might have been the soft, off-camera sound of shuffling paper. Then Capra spoke once more.

"Very well, Captain Harrington. Please tell the Board what happened approximately fourteen minutes after Admiral Sarnow was wounded."

The first, faint trace of emotion crossed Captain Harrington's calm face. Her almond-shaped eyes seemed to harden with a cold, dangerous glitter and her mouth tightened. But only for an instant. Then all expression vanished once more, and no hint of whatever had glittered in her eyes colored that dispassionate soprano when she replied with a question of her own.

"I assume, Sir, that you're referring to the actions of CruRon Seventeen?"

"Yes, Captain. I am."

"It was at approximately that time, Sir, that CruRon Seventeen scattered and detached from the remainder of the task group," Harrington said, and her voice was colder and even more emotionless than before.

"On whose responsibility?"

"That of Captain Lord Young, Sir, acting squadron CO following Commodore Van Slyke's death earlier in the action."

"Did you instruct him to detach?"

"No, Sir, I did not."

"Did he inform you of his intentions before he detached his squadron?"

"No, Sir, he did not."

"So he acted entirely on his own initiative and without orders from the flagship?"

"Yes, Sir, he did."

"Did you instruct him to return to formation?"

"Yes, Sir, I did."

"More than once?"

"Yes, Sir."

"And did he obey your instructions, Captain?" Capra asked quietly.

"No, Sir," Harrington replied like a soprano-voiced machine. "He did not."

"Did the *remainder* of CruRon Seventeen return to its station when so instructed?"

"Yes, Sir, they did."

"And Captain Lord Young's own ship—?"

"Continued to withdraw, Sir," Honor Harrington's recorded image said very, very softly, and an echo of that hard, frightening glitter gleamed in her eyes as the HD tank froze.

There was a moment of complete and utter silence, and then the tank blanked. The lights came up, and all eyes turned to the JAG Corps captain standing behind the speaker's lectern as she cleared her throat.

"That completes the relevant portion of Lady Harrington's statement to the Board of Inquiry, ladies and gentlemen." Her crisp alto carried well, with the easy courtroom manner of the experienced lawyer she was. "The entire statement, as well as all other testimony taken before the Board is, of course, available. Would you care to review any further portions of it before we proceed?"

Admiral Cordwainer glanced at Cortez and crooked an eyebrow, wondering if the Fifth Space Lord had caught the same nuances she had. Probably. She might be a jurist by training, more alive to the things that weren't said—and the *way* they weren't—than most people, but Sir Lucien Cortez was a line officer who'd seen combat, and it had showed in his eyes and the tightening of his lips as he listened to Lady Harrington's cold, bloodless recitation of events.

But Cortez shook his head, and the JAG looked back at the woman behind the lectern.

"If there are any questions, we can view the rest of the transcript following your brief, Captain Ortiz," she said. "Carry on."

"Yes, Ma'am." Ortiz nodded and glanced down, tapping keys to scroll through the notes in her memo pad, then looked back up. "This next portion is the real reason I asked ATC to make the main tank available to us, Ma'am. What you're about to see is a recreation of the relevant portion of the actual engagement, drawn from the sensor logs of all surviving units of Task Group Hancock-Zero-Zero-One. There are holes in the data, due to the task group's heavy losses, but we've been able to fill most of them by interpolating captured data from

Admiral Chin's dreadnoughts. Using that information, ATC's computers have generated the equivalent of a combat information center display at a time compression of—" Ortiz glanced back at her memo pad "—approximately five-to-one, beginning shortly before Admiral Sarnow was wounded."

She pressed buttons, and the lights dimmed once more. There was a brief blur of light in the stupendous HD tank; then everything snapped into sharp focus once more, and Cordwainer felt Cortez stiffen beside her as the glowing icons of a battle display burned before them.

The larger portion of the two-level projection displayed the inner system of the red dwarf star called Hancock, as far out as the eleven-light-minute hyper limit. The widespread light codes of planets and the green dot of the fleet repair base that was the heart of Hancock Station blazed within it, but three brighter, flashing light codes drew the eye like magnets. Not even ATC's huge tank was able to display individual warships on such a scale, but only one of the flashing lights was the bright green of friendly units; both of the others glared the sullen crimson of hostiles, and funnel-like cores of light joined each of them to exploded-view projections which *could* display individual ships and their formations.

The JAG was no trained tactician, but it didn't take one to understand Cortez's sudden tension. One crimson smear—the larger, by far—hung all but motionless, barely halfway from the hyper limit to Hancock Station, and the icons of the projection linked to it identified a blood-chilling number of superdreadnoughts of the People's Navy. But the second enemy force was far closer to the repair base, closing on it rapidly even as it slowly overhauled Task Group H-001, and the handful of green dots representing Manticoran units was horribly outnumbered—and even more horribly outgunned—by the glaring red dots of the warships pursuing them. The heaviest Manticoran units were six battlecruisers, three of them already circled by the flashing yellow bands of combat damage, and six superdreadnoughts led the Peeps charging up their wakes.

Cordwainer winced as the glittering sparkles of missiles streaked back and forth between the two formations. The Peeps poured fire into TG H-001 on at least a three-for-one ratio. It was hard to be certain—the compressed time scale reduced missile flight times drastically and made any real estimate of numbers impossible—but it looked as if the Manticorans were scoring at least as many actual hits. Unfortunately, the Peeps could *take* a great many more hits.

"The task group has already lost two battlecruisers at this point," Captain Ortiz's detached, invisible voice said from out of the darkness. "The Peeps have lost much more heavily thanks to Admiral Sarnow's initial ambush, but it's important to note that the Admiral has lost both his senior divisional commanders and Commodore Van Slyke. In short, there are no surviving flag officers, other than Admiral Sarnow himself, in the task group at this time."

Cordwainer nodded silently, listening to Cortez's harsh breathing beside her, and winced as another Manticoran ship—this one a light cruiser—vanished from the display with heart-stopping suddenness. Two of the damaged battlecruisers took more hits, as well. The yellow band around one of them— she squinted her eyes to make out the name HMS AGAMEMNON beside its icon—was tinged with the red of critical damage, and she shuddered as she tried to imagine how it must feel to know eight or nine times your own firepower had you in killing range.

"We're coming up on the task group's final course change," Ortiz said quietly, and the JAG watched TG H-001's vector suddenly angle away from its previous course by at least fifteen degrees. She bit her lip as the Peep dreadnoughts turned to cut the chord of the angle, and the tank suddenly froze.

"This is the point at which Admiral Sarnow made his final bid to draw the enemy away from the repair base and its personnel," Captain Ortiz said, and the tank flickered once more. The exploded-view formation displays burned unchanged, but the system-scale display shrank into a tiny fraction of its former volume to make room for three new projections. Not of battle codes and warships, this time, but of command decks and Manticoran officers eerily frozen in midmotion, as if awaiting the restoration of the time stream.

"We're now approaching the actions significant to the board of inquiry's determinations," Ortiz went on. "A perusal of Admiral Sarnow's pre-battle briefings and discussions with his squadron commanders and captains will, I feel, make it abundantly evident that all of them understood his intention to divert the enemy from the base by any means possible, specifically including the use of his own ships as decoys. At the same time, in fairness to Lord Young, I should perhaps also point out that those same discussions had also covered the Admiral's intention for his force to scatter and evade independently once it became evident that further diversion had become impossible, although execution of such an evolution was, of course, contingent upon express orders from the flagship."

She paused a moment, as if awaiting comment, but there was none, and her voice resumed.

"From this point on, the time scale drops to one-to-one, and the command deck projections—drawn from the relevant ships' bridge recorders—are synchronized with the events in the tactical display. For the record, this—" one of the projections flashed brighter "—is the flag deck of HMS *Nike*. This—" another projection flashed "—is *Nike*'s bridge deck, and this—" the third projection flashed "—is the bridge deck of the heavy cruiser HMS *Warlock*." She paused again to invite questions, then the entire complex light sculpture in the tank sprang back to life as if she'd touched it with a magic wand, and this time the silence was shattered by the wail of alarms, the beep of priority signals, and the frantic background crackle of battle chatter.

The command deck projections were frighteningly lifelike. They weren't things of cool, lifeless light; they were *real*, and Cordwainer knew she was leaning forward on the edge of her comfortable chair as their reality swept over her. Nor was she alone. She heard someone groan behind her as at least four Peep missiles scored direct hits on the heavy cruiser *Circe* and the ship blew apart under their bomb-pumped x-ray lasers, but her eyes were riveted to *Nike*'s bridge and a woman who was nothing at all like the cool, detached captain whose testimony they'd already viewed.

"Formation Reno, Com—get those cruisers in tighter!"

Honor Harrington's snapped order crackled with authority, and the entire task group shifted like a machine in the tactical display, realigning itself instantly. The change made the formation's missile defenses far more effective—even Cordwainer could tell that—yet the observation was peripheral, almost unimportant, as she watched Harrington ride her command chair like a valkyrie's winged steed. As if it were inevitable she should be there—impossible that she should be anywhere else in the universe. She was the heart and core of the frantic, disciplined activity of her ship's bridge, yet there was nothing frantic about her. Her face was cold—expressionless not with detachment but with purpose, a killer's total, focused concentration—and her brown eyes flashed frozen flame. Cordwainer could *feel* the tendrils of her concentration reaching out to every officer on her bridge like a maestro gathering a superbly trained orchestra into her hands and driving its musicians to perform on a plateau they could never have reached without her. She was in her element, doing the one thing she'd been born to do and carrying the others with her as she fought her ship and her ship led the embattled task group.

The white-faced, sweating man in HMS *Warlock*'s command chair was a nonentity beside Harrington, something so small, so trivial, it barely registered, but a corner of the JAG's eye watched Admiral Sarnow and his staff. Her intellect recognized the admiral's skill and a purpose at least as focused as Harrington's, his uncanny ability to carry the entire complex tactical situation in his head, the authority radiating from him, yet even he seemed strangely distant. Not diminished, but . . . pushed back, set at one remove beside the icy, brighter than life fire of *Nike*'s captain. His was the task group's brain, Cordwainer thought, but Harrington was its soul, and something deep inside her was amazed by her own thoughts. Such dramatic metaphors were alien to her, clashed with all her jurist's cold, analytical training, yet they were the only ones that fit.

"We've lost *Agamemnon*, Skipper!" someone snapped from *Nike*'s bridge, and Cordwainer bit her lip as another green icon vanished, but her eyes were fixed on Harrington's face, watching the slight tick at the right corner of her mouth as her ship's division mate died.

"Close us up on *Intolerant*. Tactical, tie into her missile defense net."

Acknowledgments rattled back, but her eyes were fixed on the com screen linking her to Admiral Sarnow's flag bridge, and there was something else in those eyes. A bitter something, raw as poison, as her admiral looked back at her. The price the task group was paying was too high for a mere diversion from a base it couldn't save, and both of them knew it. Their ships were dying for nothing, and Sarnow opened his mouth to order them to scatter.

But he never gave that order. A shout from his staff jerked him around, and new green light codes pocked the holo tank's system and tactical displays. Forty—fifty!—new ships appeared on the hyper limit, Manticoran ships led by ten dreadnoughts, and Sarnow watched tautly as they swept around onto an intercept course and began to accelerate.

He turned back to his link to Captain Harrington, his eyes bright . . . and in that instant *Nike* heaved and twisted like a mad thing as x-ray lasers smashed through her armor and gouged deep into her hull. Displays flashed and died on her bridge as her combat information center was blown apart, but her flag bridge was a holocaust.

Cordwainer rocked back in her seat, hands clenching in fists of shock, as the flag bridge's after bulkhead exploded with an ear-shattering roar. White-hot chunks of battle steel screamed across it, smashing through computers, displays, command consoles, and flesh with gory abandon while a hurricane of outraged atmosphere screamed through the rents in *Nike*'s hull. The JAG had never seen combat. She was an imaginative, keenly intelligent woman, yet nothing less than reality could have prepared her for the horror and chaos of that moment, for the appalling fragility of human beings before the elemental destruction they commanded, and her stomach heaved as Admiral Sarnow was blown out of his command chair, legs horribly mutilated, skinsuit soaked in sudden blood.

She ripped her eyes from the smoke and the wail of alarms, the shouts of the survivors and the screams of the dying, and saw the shock in Honor Harrington's face. The awareness of what had happened to her admiral and her ship. Cordwainer saw it all in that moment—the recognition of what it meant and the instant, instinctive decision that went with it. No inkling of it shadowed Honor's voice as she acknowledged the torrent of damage reports, but the JAG knew. Harrington was Sarnow's flag captain, his tactical exec, but authority passed with the admiral. She had no legal choice but to inform the next senior officer he was in command, yet she made herself lean back in her command chair as the damage reports ended . . . and said nothing.

The task group raced onward, flailed with fire, and hit after hit screamed in on HMS *Nike*. Whether the Peeps had realized she was the flagship or simply that she was the largest and most powerful of their enemies was immaterial; their missiles ripped at her like a whirlwind of flame, and *Nike* writhed at its heart. The heavy cruisers *Merlin* and *Sorcerer* clung to her flanks, joining their defensive fire with hers and *Intolerant*'s, but they couldn't stop it all, and the holo of Harrington's command deck shuddered and jerked again and again and again as the hits got through. Her ship twisted in agony, but a new icon glowed ahead of the task group in the display, a brilliant crosshair that even Cordwainer recognized: the point at which it would become mathematically impossible for the pursuing Peeps to evade the freshly arrived Manticoran dreadnoughts still beyond their own onboard detection range.

Minutes oozed past, slow and terrible, written in thunder and the death of human beings, twisting the hushed audience's nerves in pincers of steel, and the bleeding survivors of TG H-001 swept toward that crosshair, paying in blood and courage to lure their enemies to their doom. Debris and atmosphere streamed from *Nike*'s wounded hull as the enemy battered her slowly toward destruction, and Cordwainer crouched in her chair, watching the blazing purpose in Harrington's eyes, seeing the anguish as her people died, and urged her silently on, straining with her to reach her objective.

And then it happened.

A single missile targeted HMS *Warlock*. It evaded the so far unwounded heavy cruiser's point defense, racing in to attack range. It detonated, and two lasers slashed into the ship. The damage was sudden and shocking, if minuscule compared to what other ships had suffered, but a shrill, terrified tenor voice wrenched all eyes from *Nike*'s command deck to Captain Lord Pavel Young.

"Squadron orders! All ships scatter! Repeat, all ships scatter!"

Cordwainer snapped her gaze back to the tactical display, watching in horror as Heavy Cruiser Squadron Seventeen obeyed its orders. Its units arced away from the main formation—all but HMS *Merlin*, who clung grimly to *Nike*'s flanks, fighting desperately to beat aside the fire screaming in upon her flagship—and chaos struck the fine-meshed, interlocking network of the task group's missile defenses. The light cruiser *Arethusa* blew apart under a direct hit, more hits battered the suddenly exposed target of HMS *Cassandra*, lacerating the battlecruiser's hull, knocking out her entire port sidewall and leaving her naked and vulnerable, and Honor Harrington's voice rose through the chaos like a cold, clear trumpet.

"Contact *Warlock*! Get those ships back in position!"

Cordwainer's head turned back to *Warlock*'s bridge in automatic reflex as Harrington's com officer relayed her orders . . . and Pavel Young said nothing. He only stared at his com officer, unable—or unwilling—to respond, and his executive officer's face hardened in disbelief.

"Orders, Sir?" the exec asked harshly, and Young wrenched his wild eyes back to his own display, face white and stark with terror, and watched the Peeps savage the ships his desertion had exposed to their fire.

"*Orders, Sir?!*" the exec half-shouted, and the muscles of Captain Lord Pavel Young's face ridged as he clamped his jaw and hunkered down in his command chair and stared at his display in silence.

"No response from *Warlock*, Ma'am." Stunned surprise echoed in the voice of Harrington's com officer as *Nike* quivered to yet another hit, and the captain's head whipped up.

The com officer flinched back from her, for her face was cold and focused no longer. Shock and fury and something more—something raw and ugly with hate—blazed in her eyes, and her voice was a lash.

"Give me a direct link to Captain Young!"

"Aye, aye, Ma'am." Her com officer stabbed buttons, and a screen at Harrington's knees lit with Young's sweat-streaked face.

"Get back into formation, Captain!" Harrington snapped. Young only stared at her, his mouth working soundlessly, and Harrington's soprano was harsh with hatred and contempt.

"Get back into formation, damn you!" she barked . . . and the screen went dead as Young cut the circuit.

Harrington stared at the blank com for one shocked second, and even as she stared, her ship heaved and shuddered to fresh hits. Frantic damage reports crackled, and she wrenched her eyes from the screen to her com officer.

"General signal to all heavy cruisers. Return to formation at once. Repeat, return to formation at once!"

The system tactical display shifted and changed once more as four of the five fleeing cruisers reversed course. They socketed back into the task group formation, locking back into the point defense net. All of them but one. HMS *Warlock* continued to flee, racing away from the rest of the formation while Young's exec shouted curses at him from the holo of his command deck and Young returned a screaming torrent of invective raw with panic, and then the entire holo tank went blank and the lights came up once more.

"I believe," Captain Ortiz said into the dead, stunned silence, "that that concludes the relevant portion of the evidence." A JAG Corps commander raised his hand, and Ortiz nodded to him. "Yes, Commander Owens?"

"Did *Warlock* return to formation at all, Ma'am?"

"She did not." Ortiz's voice was flat, its very neutrality shouting her own opinion of Pavel Young, and Owens sat back in his chair with a cold, hard light in his eye.

Silence returned, hovering for long, still moments, and then Vice Admiral Cordwainer cleared her throat and looked at Sir Lucius Cortez.

"I don't think there's any question that Lady Harrington exceeded her own authority in failing to pass command, Sir Lucius. At the same time, however, there can be neither doubt about nor excuse for Lord Young's actions. I endorse Admiral Parks' recommendation without reservation."

"Agreed." Cortez's voice was grim, his eyes and mouth even tighter than what they'd just seen seemed to justify, then he shook himself. "As for Lady Harrington's actions, Admiral Sarnow, Admiral Parks, the First Space Lord, Baroness Morncreek, and Her Majesty herself have all endorsed them. I don't think you need to concern yourself over them, Alyce."

"I'm relieved to hear that," Cordwainer said softly. She drew a deep breath. "Shall I have Data Services begin officer selection for the court-martial board?"

"Yes. But let me add something—something for everyone here." The Fifth Space Lord stood and turned to the white-faced JAG officers seated behind the two admirals, and his expression was stern. "I wish to remind you—all of you—that what you have just seen is privileged information. Lady Harrington and Lord Young have not yet even returned from Hancock, and neither this briefing nor anything else which you have heard, seen, or read concerning this case is for public consumption until the formation of the court itself is announced by my office. Is that clear?"

Heads nodded, and he jerked a nod of his own, then turned once more and walked slowly from the silent, shaken amphitheater.

✧ CHAPTER ONE

THE TALL, GLASS-FRONTED CLOCK in the corner ticked slowly, end-lessly, its swinging pendulum measuring off the seconds and minutes in old-fashioned mechanical bites, and Lord William Alexander, Chancellor of the Exchequer and the Manticoran government's second ranking member, watched its mesmerizing motion. A modern chrono glowed silently and far more precisely on the desk at his elbow—the clock face was actually divided into the twelve standard hour increments of Old Earth's day, not Manticore's twenty-three-plus-hour day—and he wondered, not for the first time, why the man whose office this was surrounded himself with antiques. Lord knew he could afford them, but why was he so *fascinated* by them? Could it be because he longed for a simpler, less complicated time?

Alexander hid a small, sad smile at the thought and glanced at the man behind the desk. Allen Summervale, Duke of Cromarty and Prime Minister of the Star Kingdom of Manticore, was a slender man whose fair hair had turned silver long since, despite all prolong could do. It wasn't age which had bleached his hair or cut those deep, weary lines in his face; it was the crushing responsibilities of his job, and who could blame him if he hungered for a world less complex and thankless than his own?

It was a familiar thought, and a frightening one, for if anything ever happened to Cromarty, the burdens of his office would fall upon Alexander's shoulders. He could conceive of nothing more terrifying . . . nor understand what in his own character had driven him to place himself in such a position. Which was only fair, for he couldn't even imagine what had compelled Cromarty to shoulder the office of prime minister for over fifteen years.

"He didn't say *anything* about his reasons?" Alexander asked finally, breaking the ticking silence that gnawed at his nerves.

"No." Cromarty's voice was a deep, whiskey-smooth baritone, a potent and flexible political weapon, but it was frayed by worry now. "No," he repeated wearily, "but when the leader of the Conservative Association requests a formal meeting rather than a com conference, I know it has to be something I'm not going to like."

He smiled crookedly, and Alexander nodded. Michael Janvier, Baron High Ridge, was not high on either man's list of favorite people. He was cold, supercilious, and filled with a bigot's awareness of his own "lofty" birth. The fact that both Alexander and Cromarty were far more nobly born than he seemed beside the point to him, a mere bagatelle, something to be resented, perhaps, but not something a Baron of High Ridge need concern himself with.

That was typical of the man, Alexander thought sourly. Alexander seldom considered his own birth—except, perhaps, to wish from time to time that he'd been born to a less prominent and powerful family, free to ignore the tradition of public service his father and grandfather had bred into his blood and bone—but it was the core of High Ridge's existence. It was all that really mattered to him, a guarantor of power and prestige, and the narrow-minded defense of privilege lay at the heart of his political philosophy, such as it was. Indeed, it was the rallying point of the entire Conservative Association, which explained why it had virtually no representation in the House of Commons, and it went far to explain the Association's xenophobic isolationism. After all, anything that might cause stress and change in the Manticoran political system was one more dangerous force to conspire against their exalted lot!

Alexander's mouth twisted, and he slid further down in his chair, reminding himself not to curse in the Prime Minister's office. And, he thought, to strangle his own dislike when High Ridge finally turned up. If only they didn't need him and his reactionaries! Their own Centrist Party held a clear sixty-vote majority in the Commons, but only a plurality in the Upper House. With the alliance of the Crown Loyalists and the Association, the Cromarty Government could poll a narrow majority in the Lords; without the Association, that majority disappeared, and that made High Ridge, insufferable as he was and loathsome as he might be, critically important.

Especially now.

The com unit on Cromarty's desk hummed for attention, and the duke leaned forward to key it.

"Yes, Geoffrey?"

"Baron High Ridge is here, Your Grace."

"Ah. Send him in, please. We've been expecting him." He released the key and grimaced at Alexander. "Expecting him for the past twenty minutes, in fact. Why in *hell* can he never be on time?"

"You know why," Alexander replied with a sour expression. "He wants to be sure you realize how important he is."

Cromarty snorted bitterly, and then the two of them stood, banishing their honest expressions with false smiles of welcome as High Ridge was ushered through the door.

The baron ignored his guide. Of course, Alexander thought. That was what peasants existed for—to bow and scrape for their betters. He shoved the thought deep and nodded as pleasantly as he could to their tall, spindly visitor. High Ridge was even more slender than Cromarty, but on him it was all long, gangling arms and legs, and a neck like an emaciated soda straw. He'd always reminded Alexander of a spider, except for the vulpine smile and cold little eyes. If central casting had sent him to an HD producer for the role of an over-bred, cretinous aristocrat, the producer would have sent him back with a blistering memo about stereotypes and typecasting.

"Good evening, My Lord," Cromarty said, extending his hand in greeting.

"Good evening, Your Grace." High Ridge shook hands with an odd, fastidious gesture—not, Alexander knew, something assumed for the occasion but simply his normal mannerism—and seated himself in the chair before the Prime Minister's desk. He leaned back and crossed his legs, placing his seal of possession upon the chair, and Cromarty and Alexander resumed their own seats.

"May I ask what brings you here, My Lord?" the duke asked politely, and High Ridge frowned.

"Two things, actually, Your Grace. One is a rather, um, disconcerting bit of information which has reached my ears."

He paused, one eyebrow cocked, enjoying his own sense of power as he waited for the duke to ask what he meant. It was another of his more irritating little tricks, but, like all of the others, the realities of political survival required his host to swallow it.

"And that bit of information is?" Cromarty inquired as pleasantly as possible.

"I'm told, Your Grace, that the Admiralty is considering pressing charges against Lord Pavel Young before a court-martial," High Ridge said with an affable smile. "Naturally I realized there could be no foundation to the rumors, but I thought it wisest to come directly to you for a denial."

Cromarty's was a politician's face, accustomed to telling people what he wanted it to tell them, but his lips tightened and his eyes smoldered as he glanced at Alexander. His political second in command looked back, and his expression was equally grim—and angry.

"May I ask, My Lord, just where you heard this?" Cromarty asked in a dangerous voice, but High Ridge only shrugged.

"I'm afraid that's privileged, Your Grace. As a peer of the realm, I must safeguard my own channels of information and respect the anonymity of those who provide me with the facts I require to discharge my duty to the Crown."

"Assuming a court-martial were being contemplated," Cromarty said softly, "that fact would be legally restricted to the Admiralty, the Crown, and this office until the decision was made and publicly announced—a restriction designed, among other things, to protect the reputations of those against whom such actions are contemplated. The individual who provided it to you would be in violation of the Defense of the Realm Act and the Official Secrets Act, and, if a serving member of the military, of the Articles of War, not to mention the oaths he—or she—has personally sworn to the Crown. I insist that you give me a name, My Lord."

"And I respectfully refuse, Your Grace." A corner of High Ridge's lip curled in disdain at the very thought that laws applied to him, and a dangerous, fulminating silence hovered in the office. Alexander wondered if the baron even realized just how fragile was the ice upon which he stood. Allen Summervale would tolerate a great many things in the name of politics; violation of DORA or the Official Secrets Act wasn't one of them, especially not in time of war, and High Ridge's refusal to identify his informant constituted complicity under the Star Kingdom's law.

But the moment passed. Cromarty's jaw ridged, and his eyes glittered ominously, but he shoved himself further back in his chair and made himself inhale deeply.

"Very well, My Lord. I won't press you—this time," he said in a hard voice that, for once, made no effort to conceal his opinion of the other. Not that High Ridge seemed to notice; the threatening qualifier rolled off the armor of his arrogance like water, and he smiled again.

"Thank you, Your Grace. I'm still waiting for you to deny the rumor, however."

Alexander's fist clenched under the cover of the edge of

Cromarty's desk at the man's sheer gall, and Cromarty regarded the baron with icy eyes for several long seconds of silence. Then he shook his head.

"I can't deny it, My Lord. Nor will I confirm it. The law applies even to this office, you see."

"Indeed." High Ridge shrugged off the pointed reminder and tugged delicately at the lobe of one ear. "If, however, there were no truth to it, I feel certain you *would* deny it, Your Grace. Which, of course, suggests that the Admiralty does, indeed, intend to prosecute Lord Young. Should that be the case, I wish to register the strongest protest, not simply for myself, but for the entire Conservative Association."

Alexander stiffened. Pavel Young's father was Dimitri Young, Tenth Earl of North Hollow and the Conservative Association's whip in the House of Lords. He was also, as everyone in this room knew, the most powerful single man in the Association. He was the king-maker, ruler of the Association's back rooms, armed with a deadly nose for scandal and intrigue, which made the private files he was reputed to maintain a terrifying political weapon.

"May I ask the basis for your protest?" Cromarty asked sharply.

"Of course, Your Grace. Assuming the information in my possession is accurate—and I think it is, given your refusal to deny it—this is only one more step in the Admiralty's unwarranted persecution of Lord Young. The Navy's persistent efforts to make him some sort of whipping boy for the tragic events on Basilisk Station have been an insult and an affront which, I believe, he has borne with remarkable equanimity. This, however, is a far more serious situation, and one that no one with a decent respect for justice can allow to pass unchallenged."

Gorge rose in Alexander's throat at High Ridge's sanctimonious tone. He made a strangled sound, but Cromarty shot him a quick warning glance and he clenched his jaw and made himself stay in his chair.

"I strongly disagree with your characterization of the Admiralty's attitude towards Lord Young," the Prime Minister said sharply. "And even if I didn't, I have no power—or legal right—to intervene in the affairs of the Judge Advocate General's Corps, particularly not over something as speculative as a court-martial which hasn't even been officially announced yet!"

"Your Grace, you're Prime Minister of Manticore," High Ridge replied with an indulgent smile. "*You* may lack the power to intervene, but Her Majesty certainly doesn't, and you're her first minister. As such, I earnestly advise you to recommend to her that this entire proceeding be dropped."

"I cannot and will not undertake such an action," Cromarty said flatly, yet something inside him sounded an alarm, for High Ridge simply nodded, and his expression showed a strange sense of triumph, not alarm or even irritation.

"I see, Your Grace. Well, if you refuse, you refuse." The baron shrugged and his smile was unpleasant. "With that out of the way, however, I suppose I should turn to my second reason for calling upon you."

"Which is?" Cromarty asked curtly when the baron paused once more.

"The Conservative Association," High Ridge said, eyes gleaming with that same, strange triumph, "has, of course, made a very careful study of the Government's request for a declaration of war against the People's Republic of Haven."

Alexander stiffened once more, eyes widening in horrified disbelief, and High Ridge glanced at him, then went on with a sort of gloating exultation.

"Naturally, the Havenite attacks on our territory and warships must be viewed with the gravest concern. Given recent events within the People's Republic, however, we believe that a more . . . reasoned response is in order. I fully realize the Admiralty desires to act promptly and powerfully against the Havenites, but the Admiralty often suffers from the shortsightedness of a military institution and overlooks the importance of restraint. Interstellar political problems have a way of working themselves out over time, after all, particularly in a position such as this. And, from the Association's viewpoint, the Admiralty's unmerited hostility towards Lord Young is a further indication that its judgment is . . . not infallible, shall we say?"

"Get to the point, My Lord!" Cromarty snapped, all pretense of affability abandoned, and High Ridge shrugged.

"Of course, Your Grace—to the point. Which is, I fear, that I must regretfully inform you that if the Government pushes for a declaration of war and unrestricted military operations against the People's Republic at this time, the Conservative Association will have no choice but to go into opposition as a matter of principle."

✧ CHAPTER TWO

THE TENSION IN HMS *NIKE*'S sole operational boat bay was a cold, physical thing, yet it was but a thin echo of Honor Harrington's inner turmoil. Her shoulder felt light and vulnerable without Nimitz's warm weight, but bringing him here would have been a mistake. The empathic treecat's personality was too uncomplicated for him to hide his feelings as the moment's formality required. For that matter, there was no real reason *she* had to be here, and she made herself stand motionless, hands folded behind her, and wondered why she'd truly come.

She turned her head, almond eyes dark and still, as Captain Lord Pavel Young entered the bay. He was immaculate as ever in his expensive uniform, but his set face was leached of all expression and he looked straight ahead, ignoring the silent, armed Marine lieutenant at his heels.

His expressionless mask slipped for an instant as he saw Honor. His nostrils flared and his lips thinned, but then he inhaled deeply and made himself continue across the boat bay gallery toward her. He stopped before her, and she straightened her shoulders and saluted.

An ember of surprise guttered in his eyes, and his hand rose in reply. It wasn't a gesture of respect the way he did it. There was defiance and hatred in it, but also a tiny trace of what might almost be gratitude. She knew he hadn't expected to see her. That he hadn't *wanted* to see her here to watch his humiliation, but she felt strangely drained of triumph. He'd been her worst living enemy for thirty T-years, yet all she saw when she looked at him was his pettiness. The vicious, small-souled egotism that had believed his birth truly made him superior to those about him and would eternally protect him from any consequence of his own actions.

He was no longer a threat . . . only a vile mistake the Navy was about to correct, and all that really mattered to Honor now was that she put him behind her forever.

And yet—

She lowered her hand from the salute and stepped aside as the junior-grade captain with the balance scale shoulder patch of the Judge Advocate General's Corps cleared his throat behind her.

"Captain Lord Young?" the stranger said, and Young nodded. "I am Captain Victor Karatchenko. You are instructed, by order of the Judge Advocate General, to accompany me ground-side, Sir. I am also required to officially notify you that you are under close arrest, pending trial by court-martial for cowardice and desertion in the face of the enemy." Young's face tightened at the measured words. In shock, perhaps, but not in surprise. This was his first official notice, yet he'd known what the board of inquiry had recommended.

"You will be in my custody until we reach the appropriate planetary authorities, Sir," Karatchenko continued, "but I am not your counsel. Accordingly, you are advised that client privilege does not apply and that anything you say to me may constitute evidence which I can be called upon to give at your trial. Is all of this understood, Sir?"

Young nodded, and Karatchenko cleared his throat again.

"Forgive me, Sir, but you're required to answer verbally for the record."

"I understand." Young's tenor sounded flat and rusty.

"If you will accompany me, then, Sir." Karatchenko stood aside and gestured to his cutter's docking tube. Another Marine officer waited at its far end. Young looked at him with empty eyes for a moment, then stepped into the tube. Karatchenko paused just long enough to salute Honor before he followed, and the gallery-side hatch closed behind them. Humming machinery evacuated the sealed tube, and a red zero-pressure light glowed. The cutter undocked, and Honor watched through the armorplast as it drifted out of *Nike*'s bay on its thrusters.

She drew a deep, deep breath and turned her back upon it. The boat bay officer and his ratings came to attention, and she walked past them and out of the gallery without a word.

Captain Paul Tankersley looked up as Honor stepped into the lift.

"So he's gone, is he?" She nodded. "Good riddance," he snorted, then cocked his head. "How did he take the official news?"

"I don't know," Honor said slowly. "He didn't say a word. Just stood there." She shivered and shrugged irritably. "I should be dancing a jig, I suppose, but it all seems so . . . so *cold*, somehow."

"And better than he deserves." Tankersley's expression was as sour as his voice. "At least he'll get a fair trial before they shoot him."

The lift began to move, and Honor shivered again as Paul's words sent a fresh chill through her. She'd hated Pavel Young almost as long as she could remember, yet Paul was right about his probable fate. God knew he was guilty as charged, and the Articles of War provided only one sentence for cowardice in the face of the enemy. Tankersley watched her for a moment, then frowned and touched the override to stop the lift in mid-movement.

"What is it, Honor?" His deep, resonant voice was gentle, and she looked at him with a fragile smile that vanished almost instantly. "Damn it," Tankersley went on more harshly, "that man tried to rape you at the Academy, tried to ruin your career in Basilisk, and then did his dead level best to get you killed in Hancock! He ran away—tried to take his entire squadron with him—when you needed him, and God only knows how many of your people that *did* kill! Don't tell me you're feeling *sorry* for him!"

"No." Honor's soprano was soft enough he had to strain to hear it. "I'm not sorry for him, Paul. I just—" She paused and shook her head. "I'm afraid for myself. *Of* myself. He's finally crashing and burning after all these years, all this hatred. There's been some sort of—well, of a link between us all that time, however much I hated it. I've never understood how his mind works, but he's always been there, like some sort of evil twin. A . . . a *part* of me, somehow. Oh," she waved a hand, "you're right. He deserves it. But I'm the one who gave it to him, and I *can't* feel sorry for him, however hard I try."

"Damn straight you can't!"

"No, that's not the point." Honor's headshake was sharper. "I'm not saying he deserves sympathy, only that whether he deserves it or not shouldn't affect whether or not I *feel* any." She looked away. "He's a human being, not just a piece of machinery, and I don't want to hate anyone so much that I don't even care if the Fleet executes him."

Tankersley studied the left side of her sharp, gracefully carved profile. Her left eye was a sophisticated prosthesis, yet artificial or not, he could see the pain in it, and hatred stirred deep within him, dull but made fierce by his love for her.

He started to speak sharply, angry with her for her feelings, but he didn't. He couldn't. If she hadn't felt them, she wouldn't have been the woman he loved.

"Honor," he sighed instead, "if you don't care what happens to him, then you're a bigger person than I am. I *want* him shot, not just for what he's tried to do to you over the years, but because of what he is. And if the tables were reversed, if he could have gotten *you* in front of a court-martial, *he* damned well *would* dance a jig! If you don't feel the same way, then the only thing wrong with you is that you're better than he is."

She turned back to meet his eyes, and he smiled almost sadly. Then he slid an arm about her. There was an instant of tautness, almost resistance, the habit of too much loneliness, too many years of command and self-discipline, and then she yielded and leaned against him. He was shorter than she, but she pressed her cheek into the top of his beret and sighed.

"You're a good man, Paul Tankersley," she said softly, "and I don't deserve you."

"Of course you don't. No one *could* deserve me. But you come closer than most, I suppose."

"You'll pay for that, Tankersley," she growled, and he squirmed away with a yelp as she pinched his ribs hard. He cowered against the lift wall, grinning hugely, and she chuckled. "That's only a down payment," she warned him. "Once I get *Nike* tucked in with *Hephaestus*, you and I are going to spend some sparring time in the gym. And if you survive that, I've got some *seriously* exhausting plans for later!"

"I'm not scared of you!" Tankersley said defiantly. "Nimitz isn't here to protect you now, and as for tonight—piffle!" He snapped his fingers, then drew himself up to his full height and twirled an imaginary mustache with an epic leer. "Fritz has been prescribing extra vitamins and hormone shots. I'll reduce you to palpitating putty, begging for mercy!"

"Now you'll *really* pay!" Honor swatted him with a grin, and he gave her an aggrieved look and adjusted the hem of his tunic fastidiously while she turned to release the override switch. She watched the position indicator begin to move once more—then went up on her toes with a most uncaptainly squeak as a wicked pinch to her posterior repaid her assaults on his person.

She started to turn on him, but the lift was still moving, and the panel flashed warning of imminent arrival. She snapped back to face the door, head still turned to glower down at him, and he grinned back unrepentantly.

"We'll see who pays who, Lady Harrington," he murmured smugly from the corner of his mouth, and then the doors opened.

Admiral Sir Thomas Caparelli, First Space Lord of the Royal Manticoran Navy, rose courteously as Francine Maurier, Baroness Morncreek, walked through the door. Admiral Sir Lucien Cortez stood beside him, and both of them waited until Morncreek had seated herself. The baroness was a small, slender woman, over seventy but still young and almost dangerously attractive in a dark, feline way thanks to the prolong treatment. She was also First Lord of the Admiralty, the civilian head of their service, and at the moment her face was tense.

"Thank you for coming, gentlemen," she said as her subordinates resumed their own seats. "I assume you've deduced the reason for this meeting?"

"Yes, Milady, I'm afraid we have." Caparelli towered over Morncreek, even seated, but there was no question who was in charge. "At least, I believe we have."

"I expected you would." Morncreek crossed her legs and leaned back, then looked at Cortez. "Has the court's board been selected yet, Sir Lucien?"

"It has, Milady," Cortez said flatly.

Morncreek waited, but the admiral said nothing more. Officially, no one outside his own Bureau of Personnel, which included the Judge Advocate General's Corps, was supposed to know who would sit in judgment on Pavel Young until the court actually convened. For that matter, no one was even supposed to know a court had been recommended. The fact that they did know, that information Cortez was sworn to keep privileged had become common knowledge among those "in the know," infuriated not just the admiral but most of the rest of the Navy. Cortez had no intention of feeding any more leaks, and since recent events had proved *no* secret was leak proof, his sole defense was a stubborn refusal to divulge information to anyone without a clear need to know it.

Morncreek knew exactly what the Fifth Space Lord was thinking, and why, but her mouth tightened and her dark eyes hardened.

"I'm not asking out of morbid curiosity, Admiral," she said coldly. "Now tell me who's on it."

Cortez hesitated a moment longer, then sighed.

"Very well, Milady." He drew a memo pad from his pocket, keyed its display, and passed it across to her. He still didn't mention any names aloud, however, and Caparelli hid a sour smile. He didn't really object to Lucien's hanging onto his secrets, but it was a bitter sign of just how bad things had become that Cortez had brought the memo along despite his obvious intention not to discuss the court's membership with anyone.

"We had to throw out three initial selections because the officers in question are out-system, Milady," Cortez said as Morncreek scanned the names, and she and Caparelli both nodded. By long tradition, the Bureau of Personnel's computers randomly selected the members of a court-martial sitting on a capital offense from all serving officers of sufficient rank. Given the Manticoran Navy's current deployments, they were hitting well above the average if only three of the initial choices had been unavailable.

"The members of the court, in order of seniority, are listed there. Admiral White Haven—" Cortez glanced sideways at Caparelli "—will be senior officer, assuming he returns from Chelsea in time. We anticipate that he will. The other members are all in-system now and will remain here."

Morncreek nodded, then winced as she read the other names.

"Should any of those listed become unavailable for any reason, we've selected three alternates, as well. They're listed on the next screen, Milady."

"I see." Morncreek frowned and rubbed the fingers of her right hand together as if they were covered in something sticky. "I see, indeed, Sir Lucien, and there are times I wish our procedures were a little more . . . discretionary."

"I beg your pardon, Milady?"

"The problem," Morncreek said with slow precision, "is that our scrupulously fair selection process has just presented us with one hell of a dogfight. I don't know about Captain Simengaard or Admiral Kuzak, but all four of the others are going to have their own axes to grind."

"With all due respect, Milady," Cortez said stiffly, "these officers all know their duty to be fair and impartial."

"I'm sure they do." Morncreek's smile was wintry. "But they're also, unfortunately, human beings. You know better than I how White Haven has been shepherding Lady Harrington's career. I happen to agree with you that he'll do his utmost to remain impartial and unbiased, but neither that nor the fact that her record has amply justified his support will prevent his inclusion on the court from infuriating Young's partisans. As for these other three—" She shuddered. "Given the current situation in the Lords, this court-martial has a frightening potential to turn into a fight between political factions, not an impartial legal proceeding."

Cortez bit his lower lip. Clearly, he wanted to dispute Morncreek's gloomy assessment; equally clearly, he was afraid she was right, and Caparelli shoved himself deeper into his own chair. He didn't know who else was on the list, and, frankly, he didn't *want* to know. He had fuel for enough nightmares without adding that to it.

The People's Republic of Haven's recent attack on the Star Kingdom of Manticore had been driven back in disarray by a combination of skill and old-fashioned, barefaced luck. The People's Navy had suffered shattering losses to both arms of its opening offensive, and the Royal Manticoran Navy's quick ripostes had taken half a dozen of the Peeps' forward bases. Unfortunately, the People's Navy still outnumbered the RMN by a terrifying margin, and events on the PRH's capital planet had produced a blizzard of political dispute and infighting on Manticore.

No one knew where the People's Republic was headed. Available reports suggested that the Navy had attempted a coup following its initial defeats, but if it had, it certainly hadn't done so very effectively. The attack that wiped out the entire Havenite government—and the heads of most of the prominent Legislaturalist families which had run it—had been as brilliant as it was savage, but there'd been no effective follow-through, and it had provoked the formation of a Committee of Public Safety in the People's Quorum. That committee now controlled the central organs of the PRH, and it was moving with merciless dispatch to assure that no military coup could succeed.

The result was chaos within the Havenite military. No one yet knew how many officers had been arrested, but the arrest—and execution—of Admiral Amos Parnell, the PN's chief of naval operations, and his chief of staff had been confirmed. There were also confused reports of resistance and infighting as the new committee pressed ahead with its purge of "unreliable" senior officers, and one or two of the Republic's member systems seemed to have seized the chance to rebel against the hated central government.

Every strategic bone in Caparelli's body cried out to ram the Star Kingdom's current advantage home. The enemy was in disorder, savaging himself internally, some, at least, of his star systems in open rebellion and his senior officers more than half paralyzed lest any act of initiative be misconstrued as treason against the new regime. God only knew how many

of them might actually come over to Manticore's side if the
RMN pressed a heavy offensive now!

The thought of watching such a chance slip through his
hands turned Caparelli's stomach, but he hadn't been allowed
to do anything about it. In fact, he might *never* be allowed to,
and the reason was politics.

Duke Cromarty's majority in Parliament had disappeared with
the defection of both the Conservative Association and Sir
Sheridan Wallace's "New Men" to the side of the Opposition.
The Government's support in the Commons was solid; in the
Lords, it was well short of a majority . . . and there'd been
no formal declaration of war.

Caparelli's teeth ground together in acid frustration. Of course
there hadn't! The People's Republic had *never* declared war
during its half-century of conquest; such formal niceties would
only have served to warn its victims. The Star Kingdom,
unfortunately, didn't do things that way. Without a formal,
legal declaration, carried in both houses, the Constitution
empowered the Cromarty Government only to defend the
integrity of the Star Kingdom. Anything more aggressive
required the declaration of a state of war, and the Opposition leaders insisted the letter of the law be obeyed.

Their solidarity was unlikely to last, for their philosophies
and motives were too fundamentally contradictory, but for the
moment those motives were reinforcing one another, not
clashing.

The Liberals hated the very thought of military operations.
Once their initial panic had passed, they'd responded with a
spinal reflex opposition to all things military that never consulted the forebrain at all. They knew better than to publicly
restate their long-standing position that Manticore's military
buildup was an unnecessary provocation of Haven—even they
saw the suicide potential in that, given the public reaction
to recent events—but they'd found another way to justify
resistance to sanity. They'd decided what was happening inside
the People's Republic represented the birth of a reform movement committed to the overthrow of "the old, militaristic
regime" in recognition of "the uselessness of resorts to brute
force," and they wanted "to help the reformers achieve their
goals in a climate of peace and amity."

Their allies in Earl Gray Hill's Progressive Party no more
believed in the pacifism of this Committee of Public Safety
than Caparelli did. *They* wanted to let the PRH stew in its
own juice—after all, if the Republic self-destructed, there'd be
no need for further military operations—which made them even

stupider than the Liberals. Whoever the brains behind the Committee of Public Safety was, he'd acted with dispatch and energy to secure control. Unless someone from outside toppled him, he was going to hang onto it, and sooner or later he'd finish crushing the last domestic resistance and turn his attention back to Manticore.

Then there was the Conservative Association—reactionary, xenophobic, isolationist to the core . . . and pigheaded enough to make the Progressives look smart. The Conservatives believed (or claimed to believe) that the Republic's initial, shattering reverses would lead the new leadership to abandon any further thought of attacking the Manticoran Alliance lest still worse befall them, which overlooked both the tonnage imbalance and the fact that the People's Navy had to be lusting to avenge its humiliation. And last, and most contemptible, were the New Men, whose sole motive was a cynical bid to secure greater parliamentary clout by selling their votes to the highest bidder.

It was insane. Here they were, with a golden opportunity to strike deep and hard, and the politicians wanted to throw it away . . . and leave *his* Navy to suck up the losses when the bill came due!

He dragged his mind back from its increasingly well-worn path of angry resentment and cleared his throat.

"Just how bad *is* the situation, Milady? I spoke with Duke Cromarty yesterday and assured him the Navy would support him, but—" Caparelli broke off as Morncreek looked at him sharply, then he shrugged. "I thought you knew he'd commed me, Milady."

"Well, I didn't. Nor did he happen to mention it when we spoke this afternoon. Exactly what sort of 'support' did you promise him?"

"Nothing at all on the domestic side, Milady." Caparelli was careful to avoid words like "coup," and Morncreek relaxed a bit. "I simply assured him we would continue to obey the lawful orders of Her Majesty and her ministers if he instructed me to continue operations. We can do that without a declaration, but not for very long, I'm afraid. If I completely suspend all current construction and divert every dollar I can from our essential infrastructure, I could probably sustain operations for another three months or so. After that, we'd need a special appropriation—assuming we don't have a formal declaration to free the Exchequer's hands—and I don't see how we can expect to get that if we can't get the declaration in the first place."

He paused with a shrug, and Morncreek nibbled gently on a fingernail, then sighed.

"The next time the Prime Minister coms you directly, Sir Thomas, I would appreciate your informing *me* of the fact," she said, but there was as much weariness as frost in her voice. "I suppose the Duke could order you to continue offensive operations, as long as the money holds out, without a declaration, but I assure you there'd be a furor in Parliament that would make the Gryphon Crisis look like a pillow fight! A point," she added grimly, "I intend to emphasize in my next discussion with His Grace."

"Yes, Ma'am." Caparelli fought an urge to rise and come to attention; Lady Morncreek might be petite and attractive, but the snap of her authority was unmistakable. "I understand, Ma'am. And I assure you we only touched very briefly on what I suppose I might call the tactical situation in Parliament. In light of what you've just said, could you give us a feel for just what it is we're looking at there?"

"We're looking at something that couldn't get a lot worse," the First Lord said bluntly. "The Duke is fighting for every vote in the Lords—God only knows what promises he's going to have to make, or to whom—and even if he puts a new majority together, it's going to be incredibly fragile."

"Stupid bastards," Cortez muttered, then flushed crimson as he realized he'd spoken aloud. "Forgive me, Milady," he began quickly, "I only—"

"You only said what I'm thinking, Sir Lucien." Morncreek waved away his apologies and looked back at Caparelli. "It *is* stupid, and one of the great flaws of our system. Oh," she gestured irritably as Caparelli's jaw started to drop, "I'm not saying the fundamental system is unsound. It's served us well for the last four or five T-centuries, after all. But the House of Lords doesn't have to stand for election. That can be a tremendous strength when it comes to resisting popular pressure for unwise policies, but it can also be an equally tremendous weakness. An MP in the Commons knows what will happen in the next general election if he hog-ties the Government at a time like this; the Lords don't have to worry about that, and they've got a marked tendency to create single-viewpoint cliques around their own pet theories of the way things *ought* to be.

"At the moment, there's a distinct sense of euphoria, of having dodged the pulser dart, coupled with a desire to hide under the blankets till the threat goes away. Of course, it's not *going* to go away, but they don't want to face that.

Eventually, they'll have to, and I pray to God they do it before it's too late, but even if they do, their positions will have hardened. The strain of our own military buildup's polarized our politics, and too many of the Opposition buy into the theory that opposing the use of force—for *whatever* reason—is inherently 'noble' and not a gutless renunciation of the will—and ability—to resist aggression or any other sort of organized evil! As long as someone else gets on with fighting the war, they can enjoy the luxury of continuing to oppose it to prove their moral superiority, and I'm afraid too many of them are going to do just that.

"Which brings us right back to Young's trial. I realize neither you nor Sir Lucien had any voice—or any legal right to one—in its selection, but I can't imagine a more dangerous board. This thing has the potential to blow the entire situation wide open at the very moment the Duke's turning over every rock on Manticore for the votes he needs for that formal declaration."

"Well, I know where he can get one of them," Caparelli said sourly. Morncreek raised an eyebrow, and he gave a wry smile. "Lady Harrington would certainly cast her vote in favor."

"I wish she could," Morncreek sighed, "but that, too, is out of the question. She's never taken her seat in the House, and this isn't the time for her to do it. The Duke feels that, even without the trial, admitting her to the Lords just now would almost certainly backfire. The Opposition would scream that he was only doing it to steal another vote, and given the irregularity with which she was raised to the peerage in the first place—"

The First Lord shook her head, and Caparelli had to nod in agreement. God, what he wouldn't give never to have to deal with politics again!

"So what do you want us to do, Milady?" he asked.

"I don't know." Morncreek rubbed her temple in a quick, nervous gesture. "And I'm pretty sure the Duke doesn't know yet, either. That was why he wanted me to find out who was on the court—for which I apologize. I realize it's a technical violation, but under the circumstances he had no choice."

Caparelli nodded his understanding, and the baroness rubbed her temple again, then sighed.

"The Prime Minister hasn't told me how he intends to handle it," she said at last, "but he really has only two options: push forward quickly, or put the brakes on. Getting it out of the way as quickly as possible might be the best tactic, but that could turn around on us, even if the court votes to convict.

On the other hand, the longer we delay, the more the Opposition will try to extort out of the Duke by playing on his fear of its outcome. And the whole situation is further complicated by the fact that Young is legally entitled to a speedy trial *and* the possibility that if we delay until after we bribe, blackmail, and extort the votes for a declaration the Opposition will seize on the delay as a cynical political maneuver by the Government. Which," she admitted with a tight smile, "is exactly what it *would* be, after all."

She sighed again and shook her head.

"Captain Harrington seems to have a penchant for setting the Kingdom on its ear, one way or the other." She made the observation wryly, but Caparelli felt compelled to reply.

"In all fairness to Lady Harrington, Milady, this is *not* her fault. I fully realize how unpopular she is with the Opposition's leadership, but she's never done a millimeter less than her duty. Moreover, the charges against Lord Young were filed by Vice Admiral Parks on the recommendation of a formal board of inquiry. And, I might add, only because they were amply justified—even required—by Lord Young's own actions."

"I know, Sir Thomas, I know." Morncreek uncrossed her legs and stood, and her smile was penitent. "Please don't construe my last remark as a criticism of Captain Harrington or her record. It's just that some people have a positive gift for being at the center of things, and for the last few years, she's the one who's had it. I admire and respect her accomplishments, but I can't help wishing she'd been a little less . . . visible since Basilisk."

" 'Visible,' " Caparelli repeated softly, as if tasting the word, then surprised himself with a grin. "Now *that*, Milady, is certainly a fair description of Captain Harrington." His grin faded, and he cocked his head. "Shall I call her in and discuss the situation with her, Milady? In light of the political pressures, it might be wise to warn her to be on her guard. God knows the media will be waiting to pounce on anything she says!"

Morncreek considered the offer carefully, then shook her head.

"No, Sir Thomas. Oh, she needs to be warned, but this is much more a political matter than a naval one. I'll see her at the palace in the morning, and I can discuss it with her myself. I owe her that, and I'm afraid—" she smiled crookedly "—that sort of thing comes with my job."

✧ CHAPTER THREE

HONOR WATCHED THE LANDING PAD grow beneath her cutter and reminded herself this wasn't the first time she'd been to Mount Royal Palace. She reminded herself of that quite sternly, and that her status had changed since her first visit, as well. Then she'd been a commoner; now she was not only a decorated captain of the list but a knight and a peer of the realm—none of which lightened her nervousness at all.

She smiled wryly at her own tension and glanced at her executive officer. Commander The Honorable Michelle Henke looked perfectly at ease . . . as well she might; unlike her captain, Mike was simply dropping by to visit the head of the senior branch of her own family. Nimitz looked up from Honor's lap, twitching his fluffy tail as if to chide her inner turmoil, and she reached down to stroke his ears. The movement caught Henke's eyes, and the commander looked up with an impish grin.

"Nerves, eh?" Her husky, almost furry contralto was rich with fond amusement, and Honor shrugged.

"Unlike some people, I'm not accustomed to rubbing elbows with royalty."

"Odd. I would've thought you'd be getting used to it by now," Henke replied deadpan.

Honor snorted, but she had to admit (and not as modestly as she would have liked) that Mike had a point. Most officers spent their entire careers without ever receiving their monarch's personal thanks, yet this would be the fourth time for Honor—and the third in barely five T-years. It was almost as frightening as it was flattering, but it was more than that, as well. She'd met her ruler as a person, as the individual behind the symbol of her crown, and she'd found that person worthy of her loyalty.

Elizabeth III had been Queen for almost eleven Manticoran years—over eighteen T-years—since her father's tragic death in a grav-skiing accident. She was the sixteenth monarch in direct descent from Roger I, founder of the House of Winton, and she had all of her dynasty's dignity and poise. She also had an intense and personal charisma all her own, despite a sometimes prickly personality. Honor had heard about her temper and the personal determination, one might even say obstinacy, which would have done any of her Sphinxian subjects proud. It was rumored she held grudges till they died of old age, then had them stuffed and mounted, but Honor could live with that. The Queen was equally loyal to those who served her kingdom well. Some political analysts argued that her fiercely direct personality hampered delicate political and diplomatic maneuvers, but she compensated with inexhaustible energy and absolute integrity, and she'd made resistance to Havenite encroachment her life's work.

All of that was true and important, yet it was almost inconsequential to Honor. Elizabeth III was the woman to whom she'd sworn her loyalty as an officer and her fealty as a countess. She *was* the Star Kingdom of Manticore to Honor Harrington. Not an infallible, superior being to be venerated, but a living, sometimes quirky, occasionally exasperating human being who nonetheless represented all Honor insisted her kingdom be. Honor was sworn to lay down her life in the Crown's service, and while she had no particular inclination toward martyrdom, it was a vast relief to know Elizabeth Adrienne Samantha Annette Winton was worthy of that oath.

The cutter slid into a smooth hover, then descended in a soft whine of counter-grav. The hatch opened, and Honor rose and set Nimitz on her shoulder. By tradition so old it actually predated the Navy's acceptance of treecats on active duty, 'cats accompanied their adopted humans when they answered a royal summons. Seven of Manticore's last nine monarchs, including Elizabeth herself, had been adopted on visits to Sphinx, almost as if the 'cats had known they were coming and lain in wait for them. Indeed, there was a standing joke— on Sphinx, at least—that the Crown ruled only in consultation with the 'cats. Honor smiled politely whenever someone told the hoary old chestnut, but she sometimes suspected there was an element of truth in it. Certainly Nimitz was never shy about registering approval or disapproval of *her* actions!

She smothered a smile at the familiar thought, then led Henke through the hatch. Normally, Henke would have exited first, since her birth would have taken precedence over her junior rank under these special circumstances, but Honor was a countess as well as a captain. It was odd, yet this was the first time she'd truly realized that she'd overtaken her oldest friend's social rank as well as her military one. She wasn't certain she liked it, but there was no time to reflect upon it as the honor guard snapped to attention. The mustachioed major at its head wore the scarlet facings of the Queen's Own Regiment and the shoulder flash of the Copper Walls Battalion, the component drawn from Honor's homeworld, and obvious delight at the honor paid a fellow Sphinxian warred with expressionless discipline as he flashed a salute.

Honor and Henke returned it, and he returned his hand to his side with parade ground precision.

"Lady Harrington. Commander Henke. I am Major Dupre, your escort." His clipped Sphinx accent was like a breath of home, and he stepped crisply to the side to gesture toward the pad exit.

"Thank you, Major," Honor replied, and headed in the indicated direction with Henke in tow and butterflies dancing in her middle.

The walk took longer than Honor had expected, and she suddenly realized they weren't following the route she'd taken on her previous visits. In fact, they weren't headed for the hideously incongruous block of the Crown Chancery at all. Honor was just as happy—the architect who'd designed the Chancery a T-century before had suffered from a terminal case of the "functional" school that clashed horribly with the older, more graceful sections of the palace—but the unexpected diversion gave her butterflies bigger wings. The Queen had received her in the Blue Hall on each of her previous visits. The official throne room was roughly the size of a soccer field, with a soaring ceiling guaranteed to intimidate anyone, but the thought of meeting her sovereign in closer, less formal proximity was oddly terrifying.

She scolded herself. She had no right to think anything of the sort was in the offing. It was presumptuous, if nothing else, and—

Major Dupre made a sudden turn towards the very oldest part of the palace, and Honor cleared her throat.

"Excuse me, Major, but where, exactly, are we going?"

"King Michael's Tower, Milady." Dupre seemed surprised, as if anyone should have known where she was, but Honor heard Henke inhale behind her. She looked over her shoulder, but Mike had recovered from her surprise—if that was what it had been—and returned her gaze with a brown-eyed innocence her cousin Paul couldn't have bettered.

Honor spared her bland-faced exec a fulminating look, then turned back to the square finger of native stone looming before them. It wasn't much of a "tower" by the standards of a counter-grav civilization, but it thrust up with a certain imposing grace, and something prodded at the back of her mind. It was elusive, whatever it was, and she scrolled through her mental files, trying to ferret it out. Was it something she'd read somewhere?

The Manticoran media had reached a sort of gentleman's agreement with the Crown almost at the Kingdom's founding. In return for an official policy of public availability to the press and restraint in invoking the Official Secrets and Defense of the Realm Acts, the royal family's personal life was effectively off-limits, but there'd been something in the *Landing Times* about—

And then she remembered. King Michael's Tower was Queen Elizabeth's private retreat, open only to her closest political allies and intimates.

Her head started to whip back around to Henke, but it was too late; they were already at the tower entrance. The uniformed sentries snapped to attention as the door swung open, and Honor made herself swallow her questions and follow Dupre without comment.

The major led them down an airy, sunlit hall to an old-fashioned, straight-line elevator that had to be part of the tower's original equipment and punched a destination. The elevator didn't even use internal grav lifters, but the car rose surprisingly smoothly for such an obsolete device, and the doors opened onto another spacious hall in the tower's upper stories. There were no sentries in evidence, but Honor knew sophisticated security systems were observing their every move and schooled her face into a calm she was far from feeling as she accompanied the major to a closed door of age-darkened wood. He rapped once, sharply, on the carved panel, then opened it.

"Your Majesty," he announced in a carrying voice, "Lady Harrington and Commander Henke."

"Thank you, Andre," someone said, and the major stood aside for Honor and Henke to pass him, then closed the door silently behind them.

Honor swallowed and walked forward across a sea of rich, rust-red carpet. Details of comfortable but simple furnishings registered on the periphery of her brain, but her eyes were on the two women in old-fashioned, overstuffed armchairs that faced her across a coffee table.

There would have been no possible way to mistake the woman on the right, even without the treecat on her shoulder. Her warm-tinted mahogany skin was lighter than Michelle Henke's, but it was darker than most Manticorans', and the similarity between her features and Henke's was even more remarkable in person. She wasn't as pretty as Mike, Honor thought, but there was even more character in her face, and her eyes were sharp, direct, and intense.

Queen Elizabeth rose as the two officers approached her, and Honor went to one knee. As a commoner, she would have been expected only to bow; a deeper and more formal acknowledgment of her liege lady was required from a peer, but the Queen chuckled.

"Get up, Dame Honor." Even her voice sounded like Mike's, Honor thought, with that same husky timbre. She looked up, flustered and a bit uncertain, and the Queen chuckled. "This is a private audience, Captain. We can save the formalities for another time."

"Uh, yes, Your Majesty." Honor flushed as her voice stumbled, but she managed to rise with something like her normal grace, and the Queen nodded.

"Better," she approved. She held out her hand, and Honor felt every centimeter of her height—and all of them off balance—as she automatically took it. Elizabeth's grip was firm, and the cream and gray 'cat on her shoulder cocked its head at Nimitz. The Queen's companion was smaller and slimmer than Nimitz. Fewer age bars ringed its tail, but its eyes were just as bright and green, and Honor felt the very fringe of a deep and subtle exchange between it and Nimitz. Then the 'cats nodded to one another, and Nimitz gave a soft "bleek" and relaxed on her own shoulder.

She looked at the Queen, and Elizabeth smiled wryly.

"I was going to introduce Ariel, but it seems he's already introduced himself." Her tone was so droll Honor's lips twitched, and much of her uncertainty fell away. The Queen released her hand and turned to Henke.

"Well, well! If it isn't Cousin Mike!"

"Your Majesty." Henke shook hands in turn—much more naturally than her captain had, Honor noted—and Elizabeth shook her head again.

"So formal, Captain Henke?"

"I—" Henke began, then paused. "What did you say?" she demanded after a moment, and the Queen chuckled.

"I said 'Captain,' Mike. You *are* familiar with the rank?"

"Well, of course I am, but—" Henke bit off what she'd

started to say, and the Queen laughed aloud at her expression and looked at Honor.

"I can only put Mike's flattering deference down to your influence, Dame Honor. I seem to recall at least one occasion on which she kicked me in the shin. Both shins, in fact."

"Only after you dumped sand down my swimsuit," Henke said. "*Wet* sand. And *I* seem to recall Mother sending us both to bed without supper. Which," she added, "was grossly unfair, since you were the one who'd started it!"

Honor managed—barely—not to quail at her exec's astringent tone. Mike might be the oldest daughter of a cadet branch of the royal family, and Honor had always envied her comfortable assurance with the most loftily born of aristocrats, but this—!

"Ah, but I was a guest!" Honor relaxed as the Queen grinned with obvious delight. "It was your responsibility to be a gracious host to your future monarch."

"Sure it was. But don't go changing subjects on me. What's this 'Captain Henke' business?"

"Sit down, both of you." The Queen pointed at a couch and waited until they had obeyed. Nimitz swarmed down into Honor's lap as soon as she was seated, and Ariel flowed down into the Queen's lap with equal alacrity.

"Good," she said, then nodded to the woman in the second armchair. "I don't believe either of you have met Baroness Morncreek?" she asked.

Honor looked at the woman who'd replaced Sir Edward Janacek as First Lord of the Admiralty and castigated herself for not having recognized her before. The totally unexpected informality of the occasion offered a fair excuse, but she should have known who Morncreek was without being prodded. She realized the others were awaiting her reply and gave herself a mental shake.

"No, Your Majesty. I'm afraid I've never had the privilege."

"I hope you still think it's a 'privilege' when we're done, Captain." There was a wry, almost bitter note in the Queen's voice, but it vanished so quickly Honor wasn't certain she'd actually heard it. "At any rate, Mike," Elizabeth went on, "I think I'll let Lady Morncreek explain. Francine?"

"Of course, Your Majesty," Morncreek murmured, then turned to Henke. "Despite Her Majesty's somewhat unconventional and premature way of expressing herself, Commander Henke, she's essentially correct. As of this afternoon, you're a junior-grade captain." Henke's jaw dropped, and Morncreek smiled. "In addition, you'll be receiving formal orders detailing you as commanding officer of Her Majesty's light cruiser *Agni* within the week. Congratulations, Captain."

Henke stared at her, then wheeled to her cousin.

"Was this your idea, Beth?" she demanded almost accusingly, but the Queen shook her head.

"Blame Dame Honor, not me, Mike. I know how you hate trading on the family name, but Lady Morncreek tells me it's customary to promote the executive officer of a captain who distinguishes herself in action. Of course, if it really bothers you, I can probably get them to take it back."

"Don't you dare!"

"I thought you'd feel that way," the Queen murmured. "Once it was explained there was no wicked and unworthy nepotism involved, of course."

Henke gave her a quelling glance, then looked back at Morncreek.

"Thank you, Milady," she said in a much more serious voice.

"You're welcome, Captain."

"And now, Dame Honor, it's your turn," the Queen said, and Honor straightened. "We'll take care of the formalities— including the award of a richly deserved thank you—later in the Blue Hall, but I've decided to appoint you to the rank of Colonel of Marines, as well."

Honor's eyes widened in surprise as great as Henke's. Appointment as a colonel of Marines was a way for the Crown to show special approval of a captain too junior for promotion to flag rank, and very few officers ever received the honor. It wouldn't change her actual authority in any way, but she would receive a colonel's salary in addition to her regular pay, and the appointment was an unequivocal indication of royal favor.

"Thank you, Your Majesty," she managed, and the Queen shook her head.

"Don't thank me, Dame Honor," she said in an entirely serious voice. "If any officer ever deserved it, you do."

Honor's face heated, and she made a small, uncomfortable gesture. Elizabeth only nodded as if she'd expected no other reaction, for which Honor was grateful, but then she leaned back in her chair with a sigh.

"And now that we've given you the good news, ladies, it's time to consider some a little less pleasant," she said. Honor felt Henke stiffen on the couch beside her, and Nimitz raised his head in her lap. The Queen said nothing else for a few seconds, then shrugged.

"How much do you know about the situation in the Lords, Dame Honor?"

"Very little, Your Majesty." Honor knew her tone was guarded and wished it weren't. The Queen raised her eyebrows, and Honor stifled a shrug of her own. "We've only been in-system about fourteen hours, Your Majesty, and I'm afraid I'm not much of a student of politics. To be perfectly honest, I don't like them very much."

"Hard to blame you, in light of your experiences," the Queen said. "And I'm afraid what's going on right now won't make you any fonder of them. Unfortunately, you're squarely in the middle of a major political crisis, and I need you to understand exactly what's happening."

"*I'm* in the middle of a crisis, Ma'am?" Honor blurted, and the Queen nodded.

"You are. Through no fault of your own, I hasten to add, but you are. Let me explain."

Elizabeth crossed her legs and stroked Ariel's spine with a frown.

"The problem, Dame Honor, is that the House of Lords has chosen to irritate me immensely. At the moment, the Opposition parties have united in a solid front against the Centrists and Crown Loyalists, which leaves Duke Cromarty short of a working majority in the upper chamber. Which, in turn, means our entire military policy is frozen until he can beg, borrow, or steal the votes to regain control. I'm sure I don't have to tell you what that means in terms of fighting the war?"

"No, Your Majesty." Honor was stunned by the revelation, yet not even shock could quite keep the sour disgust out of her voice. The Queen smiled wryly, but it was a fleeting smile that vanished quickly, and she continued in a level voice.

"I need that majority restored, Dame Honor. I need it badly. At the moment, the Peeps are in wild disarray, but that won't last, and I can't do a thing about it as long as the Opposition blocks a formal declaration of war. And I'm very much afraid rumors of Lord Young's court-martial are already having an impact on their resistance."

Honor leaned back against the couch cushions, and puzzlement and the beginning of apprehension darkened her eyes.

"Too many members of the Opposition dislike you, Captain," the Queen said quietly. "It's not your fault. Your service has been exemplary—more than that, it's been outstanding, and I suspect you're even more popular in the Commons than you are *un*popular in the Lords. In fact, you're something of a hero to the population in general, but your very success has embarrassed the Opposition's leadership. You underscored their mistakes and made them look stupid in Basilisk, and as for what happened in Yeltsin—"

She shrugged, and Honor bit her lip. For the first time, she genuinely regretted striking Reginald Houseman. He'd deserved it, but she'd let her temper get away from her, and now it seemed his prominent family's connections to the Liberal Party were going to bring that home to roost. And not just for her, she thought miserably as she recognized the worry in her Queen's voice.

"Don't distress yourself, Dame Honor." Elizabeth's voice was gentle, and Honor made herself meet her eyes. "I didn't interfere when you were reprimanded because I make it a rule to leave the Navy to the Admiralty. And, frankly, because you *were* out of line. On the other hand, I understand how it happened, and, speaking as a woman and not your Queen, I only wish you'd hit him harder. Nor should you feel that you've created the situation in the Lords. You didn't. But smacking Houseman did make you anathema to the Liberals, and now the charges against Lord Young have made you even more unpopular with the Conservatives. To be blunt, too many of the idiots opposing Duke Cromarty also dislike *you*, and because of who Lord Young is, his father and his cronies are seizing on that emotional reaction to you in an effort to protect him."

She paused, and silence stretched out for long, endless seconds. Honor bore it as long as she could, then cleared her throat and broke it.

"What can I do, Your Majesty?" she asked.

"You can understand what's happening," Elizabeth said simply. She saw the sick pain in Honor's eyes and shook her head quickly. "No, I'm not going to quash the charges against Young!" Honor inhaled in deep, painful relief, but the Queen wasn't quite done. "What I'm afraid of is that his trial, by the nature of things, is going to make the present political crisis even worse."

Fresh worry flared in Honor's eyes, and the Queen waved to Morncreek, who leaned toward Honor across the coffee table.

"As of this moment, Captain Harrington, the Admiralty has assembled a court to try Lord Young on the charges and specifications laid against him by Admiral Parks. Officially, I can have no opinion on those charges until the court reaches its verdict, but since I have no voice in that decision, I'll tell you, personally and off the record, that my reading of the evidence supports only a guilty verdict. The problem is that the charges carry a death sentence, which means the Earl of North Hollow is pulling every lever in sight to save his son's life, and the Conservatives as a whole seem to think they can turn the trial to advantage against the Duke. They're already screaming behind the scenes, and I expect that to get nothing but worse—and more public—once the charges are officially announced and the media gets hold of them. And while I can't tell you who's on the court, the political struggle in the Lords is likely to spill over onto it . . . and vice versa. Are you with me so far?"

Honor nodded, trying to hide her dread that Young was somehow going to evade the consequences yet again. She watched Baroness Morncreek's face with almost painful intensity, unaware of how sick her own expression was, and felt Henke squeeze her shoulder gently.

"We are *not* going to let him walk, Dame Honor," Morncreek said, "but we're sailing into a minefield here. We have to approach it far more cautiously than it deserves because of the other ramifications. The most important thing of all is for you to be extremely careful. The press is going to hound you for comment from the instant we release the official account of the Battle of Hancock, and it is imperative, absolutely imperative, that you say *nothing* about the trial, the charges, or the events which led up to them. It's grossly unfair to you, and I apologize from the bottom of my heart, but you must keep as low a profile as possible until after the verdict is in."

"Of course, Ma'am." Honor bit her lip again, then made herself ask, "But if you'll forgive me for asking, just what impact do you expect all of this to have on the trial's outcome?"

"I hope it won't have one, but I can't guarantee it," Morncreek said honestly. "We don't know enough about the tactics they're likely to pursue. At the moment, the Conservatives are pushing for outright dismissal of all charges. That much, at least, I can promise you won't happen." Morncreek glanced at the Queen, and her lips firmed. "In addition, although it's highly irregular for me to say this, I can also promise you Young will never again serve on active duty. Whatever the trial's outcome, no First Lord—not even Admiral Janacek—will ever take him off half-pay again, politics or no. Beyond that, however, things are so up in the air that even I can't guess where they're headed. And that, to be perfectly honest, is why I'm here today. Because we *don't* know . . . and because I damned well owe you a personal explanation of what may be forcing our hand!"

There was too much frustration in Morncreek's voice for Honor to doubt her sincerity, and she nodded slowly. Dark, bitter anger had replaced her earlier numbness where Young was concerned, but she understood. The same forces which had saved him so many times before were rallying to his defense once more, and the timing meant not even the Crown could guarantee their defeat. She wanted to weep in sheer, sick loathing, but she only nodded once more, and the Queen met her eyes compassionately.

"I want you to know, Dame Honor, that I am deeply and sincerely sorry. I've already informed both Duke Cromarty and Admiral Cordwainer that I want this trial to proceed on the basis of the current charges and with the full rigor of the Articles of War. But I have to be aware of my responsibilities to the realm, as well. I can't—literally *cannot*—allow the enormous debt the Kingdom owes you to outweigh the need for a viable military response to the threat Haven poses."

"I . . . understand, Your Majesty. And please don't apologize." The very idea of hearing her Queen apologize to her was repugnant to Honor, and she made herself smile.

"Thank you," Elizabeth said softly. She held Honor's eyes for a long moment, then shook herself. "At any rate, I intend for this entire Kingdom to know how *I* regard you. That's the reason for your appointment as Colonel of Marines, of course, but I want you to understand something, Dame Honor. When we walk into the Blue Hall in a few minutes and I express my thanks as Queen of Manticore for your actions in Hancock, it won't be a formality. Nor will I ever allow myself to forget how much I owe you."

✧ CHAPTER FOUR

SOFT MUSIC FROM REAL, LIVE MUSICIANS drifted through the dim, intimately lit restaurant on the delicious smells of a hundred worlds' cuisine. Cosmo's, the most exclusive night spot in the city of Landing, boasted that no one had ever ordered a dish its kitchen couldn't supply. That was no small claim, given the stupendous volume of shipping (and the passengers who went with it) which passed through the central terminus of the Manticore Wormhole Junction, but Honor could believe it.

She'd been to Cosmo's exactly once before, when her mother had settled for that after Honor refused the Academy graduation gift she'd initially had in mind. Honor had been too goggle-eyed with curiosity to pay much attention to the food then; this time around she was not only older but here in the role of hostess, and she'd discovered that the chefs' handiwork was even better than Cosmo's owners claimed.

It certainly ought to be, considering its price tag—not that she begrudged a penny of it. Willard Neufsteiler hadn't said so yet, but his 'cat-with-a-celery-stick expression told her she could afford it.

Neufsteiler had represented Honor's financial interests for almost five T-years, and she was profoundly grateful she'd fallen into his hands. He had a few quirks that could be irritating, like his childlike delight in delaying the disclosure of good news to tease her, but he was scrupulously honest, and he had an uncanny investment sense. Honor's prize money from Basilisk Station had made her a millionaire; Neufsteiler's management had made her a *multi*-millionaire several times over. Which meant the least she could do was buy him an occasional supper, even at Cosmo's prices, and put up with his version of a sense of humor.

She raised her wineglass at the thought, using it to hide her smile. But she wasn't here simply to hear Willard's report, and her eyes circled the table, lighting with a deeper warmth as they brushed over Paul Tankersley before settling on the newest pair of replacements to report aboard *Nike*.

The battlecruiser's attached Marine battalion had suffered heavier losses in Hancock, proportionate to its numbers, than any other department. Both Lieutenant Colonel Klein and Major Flanders, his exec, had been killed in action, and Klein's senior company commander was on indefinite medical leave for his wounds. Captain Tyler, the ranking survivor, had done well, considering her relative inexperience, but everyone knew she was only acting CO. Yet the Admiralty had been in no hurry to relieve her or even to replace the other casualties. Intellectually, Honor found it hard to blame Their Lordships. Her Marines weren't likely to be dropped into combat while *Nike* was under repair, after all, and the Navy had other things on its mind. But it had been hard not to resent the effect on her people's morale and training schedules.

That much, at least, was about to change, she thought with intense satisfaction, because the Admiralty had shown unusually good sense when it finally picked Klein's successor.

Colonel Tomas Santiago Ramirez had been a major the last time Honor saw him. He'd commanded HMS *Fearless*'s Marines at Yeltsin's Star, and she suspected that the job he'd done then had something to do with his rapid promotion since. Whether it did or not, he certainly deserved his new rank, and Honor was delighted to see him again.

The colonel was an émigré from San Martin, which explained his almost fearsomely imposing presence. He, his sisters, and his mother had fled San Martin via the Trevor's Star terminal of the Manticore Worm Hole Junction even as the Havenite occupation fleet moved in, crushing the out-classed San Martin Navy and killing his father in the process. Ramirez had been only twelve at the time, but people reached physical maturity early on San Martin, and the colonel reflected the gravity to which he'd been born.

The first adjective to occur to anyone on first sight of him was "big," but "enormous" was a better choice. His height wasn't much above average, but he was huge-boned and squat with lumpy muscle, a man whose beer-barrel neck tapered sharply to merge with his head. Paul Tankersley sat beside him at the table, and the difference between them was instructive. Paul was a chunky, powerful man, despite his relative shortness, but Ramirez's shoulders were twice as broad as his, and the colonel's upper arms were thicker than most men's thighs. At a hundred and eighty-three centimeters, he massed over a hundred and fifty kilos, and if there were three excess grams of fat anywhere about his person, twenty T-years of Marine phys-ed had been unable to find them.

His new exec was another matter. Major Susan Hibson, another veteran of the Blackbird Raid and the Second Battle of Yeltsin, was as dark skinned and haired as Ramirez, but she was almost petite, with startling, sea-green eyes in a face which was much tougher than the colonel's. It was a good face, with finely chiseled features, but there was no softness in it. It wasn't harsh; it simply warned all comers that the woman who wore it had never had the slightest interest in figuring out how to back up for anyone.

It was the first time Ramirez and Hibson had served together since Yeltsin's Star, and Honor was delighted to see them both. Between them, this pair would blow any rust off of *Nike*'s Marines in record time.

She lowered her glass, and their waiter reappeared like an alert genie to refill it. He circled the table, checking all the others, as well, then disappeared again without a word. Good as he was, he could have taken a few lessons in total unobtrusiveness from her own steward, but perhaps he was supposed to be seen to make certain the customers were aware of the service for which they were paying.

She smiled at the thought and toyed with the notion of calling him back to order a cup of cocoa, but even her sweet tooth had been momentarily sated by the baklava they'd just finished. Besides, offering Paul such an opening to twit her over her beverage of choice might not be the smartest thing she could do.

She decided against it, not without regret, and offered Nimitz another stick of celery. The maître d' hadn't turned a hair when she arrived with the 'cat. He couldn't see many of them here on Manticore, but he'd simply snapped his fingers to summon a waiter with a highchair that worked equally well for infant humans or adult treecats and had it placed at Honor's elbow. Nimitz had settled himself into it with the dignity of a monarch assuming his throne, and his table manners, always excellent on formal occasions, had been even better than usual. As a rule, Honor tried to keep his celery intake to a minimum. Much as he loved it, he had the wrong enzymes to digest Terran cellulose, but this time he'd earned it, and she rubbed his ears as he crunched blissfully away.

"I still can't believe how much he likes that stuff." Neufsteiler shook his head. "You'd think he'd get tired of it eventually, Dame Honor."

"The average life expectancy of a Sphinx treecat is about two hundred and fifty years," Honor told him, "and there's no record of *any* 'cat ever getting tired of celery."

"Really?" Amusement glinted in Neufsteiler's voice, and Honor shook her head.

"Really. I scold him about it, but it never fazes him. And, in a way, I suppose I'm actually grateful for it."

"Grateful?" Paul Tankersley chuckled. "I have to say I'd never have suspected it from the way you go on at *me* for slipping him his fix!"

"That's because you spoil him," she said severely. "And I didn't actually mean to say I was grateful for *his* addiction. I was speaking of treecats in general."

"Why?" Neufsteiler asked.

"Because it was celery that first brought humans and 'cats together."

"This I've got to hear!" Tankersley laughed and sat back in his chair. "Assuming, of course, that you're not pulling my leg," he added. Nimitz paused in his chewing to give him a haughty look, and Honor smiled.

"No, I'm serious. Humans didn't go out of their way to study 'cats when they first arrived on Sphinx. The first colonists had other things on their minds; they hardly even realized treecats existed, and none of the survey teams ever guessed how intelligent they really are. Personally, I think that's because of their size. No one's ever encountered another intelligent species with such a low body mass, and no one expected to . . . which is probably why the survey crews never looked closely enough to realize they're tool-users."

"I'd never heard that, Ma'am," Colonel Ramirez sounded surprised. His voice was as deep as one might have expected from that enormous chest, but his San Martin accent softened its rumble with almost musical overtones. "I don't doubt you, of course, but I've always been fascinated by treecats. I've read everything I could find on them, and I've never seen a hint of that."

"I don't doubt it, Tomas." Honor glanced around the table, then shrugged and looked back at Ramirez. "In fact, I'd be surprised if you've found much about their social organization, either. Am I right?"

"Well, yes, Ma'am, now that you mention it." Ramirez rubbed his chin. "I *have* found a fair amount on their physiology, and the literature on their adoption bonds with humans is fairly extensive. Not that it explains very much. Every 'expert' seems to have a different explanation for just how it works."

"And the best any of them can offer is a 'hypothesis,' right?" Honor asked, and Ramirez nodded. "Well, the truth is that most people who know much about 'cats aren't talking. I wouldn't go so far as to call it a conspiracy of silence, but the xenologists who drop by to study them either get adopted themselves or else don't seem to learn very much before they get bored and leave. Those who do get adopted usually wind up working for the Sphinx Forestry Commission, and treecats are a protected species, which means the planetary authorities—including Forestry's xenologists—discourage people from bugging them. In fact, almost all Sphinxians tend to be extremely protective where the 'cats are concerned. We just don't talk about them very much, except with people we trust. Which, in turn, tends to keep the available off-planet literature on them in the schoolgirl primer category, but they're definitely tool-makers. Oh, we're talking very simple implements, about on the order of Neolithic man's, but you should see the flint hand-axes and other artifacts some of the Sphinx 'cat communities turn out. Of course, they're not very interested in ornaments or personal possessions without some specific utility. And those who adopt humans—like Mister Greedy Guts over there—don't really need tools. They've got people to do the heavy work for them."

Nimitz made a sound suspiciously like a quelling sniff, and she chuckled and handed him another stick of celery. The bribe was accepted with becoming graciousness, and she returned her attention to her guests.

"The thing is, even after over three local years—almost sixteen T-years—on Sphinx, the colonists had made even less contact with the 'cats than the survey crews had. They were smart enough to stay out of sight and out of mind while they adjusted to the sudden intrusion of humans, and the settlers had more than enough other things to worry about. But that changed once they had their greenhouses in and started growing something besides staple food crops. Personally, I suspect the 'cats had been making reconnaissances of the homesteads right along—believe me, you *don't* see a 'cat in the wild unless he wants you to—and no one had ever considered the need to lock a greenhouse. Until, that was, every single head of celery started vanishing swiftly and silently away in the dark of night."

"You're kidding me. They were *stealing* the stuff?" Neufsteiler laughed, and Honor nodded.

"Absolutely, though I doubt they thought of it that way. 'Cats don't have much sense of individual property. It took me years to explain the concept to Nimitz, and he still thinks it's one of humanity's sillier notions. But the Great Vanishing Celery Mystery caused a sensation, let me tell you! You wouldn't *believe* some of the theories the settlers came up with to explain the traceless disappearance of that plant and only that plant. Not that anyone came particularly close to the truth. I mean, think about it. Can you conceive of anything less likely—or more ridiculous on the face of it—than that a bunch of carnivorous, extraterrestrial arboreals should be staging commando raids on greenhouses in the dead of night just to steal *celery*?"

"No, I don't suppose I can." Ramirez's deep voice rippled with amusement. Nimitz went to some lengths to ignore it, and Hibson laughed.

"I doubt even a Marine would think of that one, Ma'am," the major agreed.

"Neither did anyone on Sphinx—until the night a ten-year-old girl couldn't sleep and caught one of them in the act."

"So she blew the whistle on them?" Neufsteiler chuckled, but Honor shook her head.

"Nope. She didn't tell a soul."

"Then how did the settlers find out what was going on?" Paul demanded.

"Oh, now, that's another story. If you're real nice to me, I may even tell it someday."

"Ha! I bet you don't *know* the rest of it!"

"Nice try, Paul, but you're not going to goad me into telling. I will tell you one thing, though."

She paused, eyes laughing while he glared at her in exasperation. But she knew his sense of curiosity too well, and he capitulated with a sigh.

"All right, I'll ask. What will you tell me?"

"The little girl in question?" Honor raised her eyebrows, and he nodded. "Her last name was Harrington," she told him smugly. "You might say 'cats run in the family."

"I might also say her present-day descendant's questionable sense of humor will lead her to an evil end if she doesn't come clean."

"We'll see about that. Maybe you can think of something to bribe me with."

"Maybe I can, at that," he murmured so wickedly Honor blushed.

"You're really not going to tell us, are you?" Neufsteiler asked. Neither he nor the two Marines seemed to notice

Honor's blush, and she shook her head at the prize agent with a grateful if teasing smile. "Then maybe *I* shouldn't tell you why I wanted to see you."

"Ah, but you and I have a fiduciary relationship. Unlike you, I can sue."

"And probably would, too." Neufsteiler shook his head at her perfidy, but he grinned, as well, and produced a small sheaf of hardcopy. "Take a look at this," he suggested, and slid it across the table to her.

Honor unfolded the sheets of printout, ran her eye down the neat columns of figures . . . and froze.

"*You're joking!*" she gasped, but Neufsteiler shook his head with a broad smile.

"I most assuredly am not, Dame Honor. The first quarterly income from your estates on Grayson came in just about the time the prize court made its official award on those dreadnoughts you and Admiral Danislav captured in Hancock. As of—" he glanced at his chrono "—six hours ago, your net worth was exactly what it says on that report."

Honor stared at him in disbelief, almost numb, then slid the report to Tankersley. He glanced at the bottom line and pursed his lips silently.

"I wouldn't exactly say the major merchant cartels have to start worrying about you," he said after a moment, "but I've got some bottom land on Gryphon I'd like to show you."

Honor smiled at him, but the reaction was almost automatic, and shock still rippled through her. She came of yeoman stock. Her parents were undeniably well off, thanks to the performance of their medical partnership, but the majority of yeoman families were land-rich and money-poor, especially on Sphinx. It had been hard enough for her to accept that her prize money from Basilisk had made her a millionaire, but this—!

"You're sure there's not some mistake, Willard?" she asked hesitantly.

"Dame Honor," he said patiently, "a dreadnought is valued at somewhere in the neighborhood of thirty-two billion dollars, and the prize court awards three percent of the value of a surrendered enemy ship to the task force which captured it, assuming the Navy buys the prize into service. Of that total, the flag captains of said task force split twelve percent among themselves, and there were only four flag captains in Hancock at the time Admiral Chin surrendered. The Admiralty survey judged two of her five surviving dreadnoughts too badly damaged for repair, but the Navy bought the other three in.

Now, three percent of ninety-six billion dollars is two-point-eight-eight billion, and twelve percent of that is three hundred forty-five million, plus change. Which means, dear lady, that *your* share comes to a paltry eighty-six million four hundred thousand dollars—exclusive of the lighter vessels surrendered with them. Of course, they only added another six million to your total award, so I suppose we don't have to worry about them. Believe me, those figures are correct. In fact, if you look at page three, you'll see that the most junior enlisted person serving under you will receive almost fifty thousand dollars."

Honor hardly even heard the last remark. She'd known she was bound to receive a hefty award, but she'd never imagined one *this* hefty. Why, it almost quadrupled her total net worth! The thought of that much money was frightening, and especially since prize money was untaxable. She got to keep every penny!

She shook her head numbly.

"What in God's name am I going to *do* with all this?" she asked almost plaintively, and Neufsteiler chuckled.

"I'm sure you'll think of something, Milady. In the meantime, you can leave it in my hands, if you wish. I've got my eye on several promising opportunities, but I don't want you to rush into anything. Give yourself a few days to adjust to the idea, then let me show you some annual reports and projected returns before you decide where to put it."

"I—" Honor shook herself again and grinned crookedly. "I think that sounds like an excellent idea, Willard."

"So do I. After all, I get five percent of net for managing your interests. Although," Neufsteiler managed to produce a mournful expression, "the Exchequer *does* get a cut from my share."

"Poor fellow." Honor's eyes twinkled as she came back on balance. "I guess that means you're going to stick me with the check after all."

"The first lesson a banker learns, Milady."

"Well, in that case I—"

Honor broke off as someone called her name. She twisted around, and her face lit as she recognized the three men walking toward her table.

"Alistair!" She shoved up out of her chair and reached out to shake hands. "And Andy and Rafe, too! What are you three doing here?!"

"Well, we checked with Captain Henke, and she told us where you were, Ma'am," Andreas Venizelos explained, "so Captain McKeon said he'd pick up the cover charge to come looking for you." Honor laughed, and Venizelos grinned. "It was only right, Ma'am. He *is* the senior officer, after all."

"A point you'd better remember, Commander," McKeon observed darkly.

"Aye, aye, Sir!" Venizelos snapped a sharp salute, and Honor laughed again, her eyes bright and happy as her waiter did his materialization trick again, producing chairs for the new arrivals.

"Don't worry about it, Alistair. I just discovered that I've become a woman of substance, and this is my party. Are you three hungry?"

"Not really. We ate before we went looking for you aboard *Nike*." Some of the humor faded from McKeon's eyes, and he shook his head. "I wish to hell you'd be a little more careful. Just once I'd like to see you take a ship over without getting it—and you—shot to bits."

"So would I," she said softly as she heard the concern in his voice. Then she shook herself. "Before I completely forget my manners, let me make the introductions. I think all three of you know Colonel Ramirez and Major Hibson?"

McKeon nodded and extended his hand, first to Ramirez and then to Hibson. "I see congratulations are in order," he said, indicating their rank insignia. "Looks like the Corps recognizes talent when it sees it."

"It certainly does," Honor agreed, and gestured to Paul. "This fellow is Captain Paul Tankersley, *Hephaestus'* newest deputy constructor, and this is Willard Neufsteiler, my agent. Paul, Willard, these are Captain Alistair McKeon, Commander Andreas Venizelos, and Lieutenant—no," she corrected herself, "Lieutenant *Commander* Rafe Cardones." She gave Cardones an approving smile and tapped the new half ring on his cuff as Tankersley reached across the table to shake hands with the new arrivals in turn. "Congratulations, Rafe!"

"Thank you, Ma'am—I mean, Dame Honor." Cardones colored slightly, and Honor swallowed a chuckle. Rafael Cardones was very young for his rank. He'd earned it the hard way, but there were still traces of the awkward puppy of a junior-grade lieutenant she'd first met five T-years before.

"Well!" She leaned back and looked from face to face. "May I ask what brings all three of you here together looking for me?"

"Oh, this and that." McKeon accepted a wineglass from the waiter and waved it at his two companions. "Andy and I are assigned to Home Fleet, and both our ships are currently docked at *Hephaestus*, so it seemed like a good opportunity to pay you a call."

"And you, Rafe?"

"Me?" Cardones grinned. "I'm *Nike*'s new tac officer, Ma'am."

"You are? That's wonderful, Rafe! But when did that happen?"

"About six hours ago, Ma'am."

"Well, welcome aboard, Guns!" She slapped his forearm with a grin, then frowned. "But no one said anything about Commander Chandler leaving. I'm delighted to see you, but I hate losing her."

"You're not, Ma'am. Things are still pretty confused at the moment, but I brought Captain Henke a general list of transfers and replacements when I reported aboard. From what I understand, BuPers is bumping Commander Chandler over from Tactical to replace Captain Henke when they move her to *Agni*. I'm afraid you're stuck with both of us, Skipper."

"I can stand it," Honor told him, and turned to McKeon and pointed to the four gold cuff bands on his sleeves. "They told me you were getting your fourth ring, Alistair. I think that shows remarkably good judgment on someone's part. Congratulations."

"I think some of your reputation rubbed off on me," McKeon said wryly, enjoying the delicate blush on her cheeks.

"So what did they give you?"

"*Prince Adrian*." McKeon's pleasure was obvious, and Honor nodded in approval. *Prince Adrian* might be smaller than one of the newer *Star Knights*, but the two-hundred-forty-thousand-ton heavy cruiser was still a powerful unit. She was, in fact, an outstanding prize for a junior-grade captain . . . and no more than Alistair deserved.

"Is Scotty still with you?"

"Indeed he is," McKeon said, then chuckled.

"What?" Honor asked.

"Someone else came aboard right after he did. I believe you know him. Senior Chief Petty Officer Harkness."

"*Harkness* made senior chief?!"

"Word of honor." McKeon raised his hand solemnly. "Took him thirty-odd years to make chief and keep it, but it looks like Scotty's been some sort of stabilizing influence."

"You're not telling me he's turned over a new leaf!"

"No, just that he hasn't happened across a Marine in a bar or fallen afoul of a customs inspection yet. On the other hand, it may just stick this time."

"I'll believe it when I see it." Honor shook her head in fond memory, then looked at Venizelos. "And what did our lords and masters give *you*, Andy?"

"Nothing so splendid as a heavy cruiser, Ma'am, but I'm

not complaining." Venizelos grinned. "I took over *Apollo* from Captain Truman when the yard finished her repairs."

"Outstanding, both of you." Honor raised her glass in silent toast, and a rare sense of complete satisfaction filled her as she contemplated their well-deserved good fortune. And her own, she thought, glancing at Paul.

"Thank you," McKeon said, returning her salute with his own glass, then leaned back in his own chair. "And now that we've run you to ground and told you what *we've* been up to, I want to hear the real story about what happened in Hancock. From what I've already heard," he shot her a knowing grin, "it sounds like you've been up to your old tricks again, Dame Honor!"

✧ CHAPTER FIVE

"I GUESS IT'S TIME I WAS GOING." Michelle Henke sighed. Her left shoulder bore the horseshoe-shaped name patch of her new command, and the ribbon of the CGM gleamed white and blue on the left breast of her space-black tunic. That tunic was barely a shade darker than her skin, but her coloring made the new white beret of a starship commander stand out even more sharply, and the four equally new gold pips of a junior-grade captain flashed back splinters of light from her collar. Honor wished she'd been able to pass her own junior-grade pips on to her friend. It was an unofficial tradition when an exec was promoted, but Honor had skipped that rank on her own way up. Yet new insignia or old, Mike looked better than merely perfect; she looked *right*.

"I guess it is." Honor reached out to adjust the scarlet-and-gold shoulder flash of the Navy's snarling, rampant manticore on Henke's right sleeve. "I'm glad for you, Mike. I hate seeing you go—I'd hoped we'd have more time together—but God knows you deserve it."

"I told you when you came aboard that I wouldn't be content with anything less than a cruiser of my own, didn't I?" Henke shrugged and smiled. "You should know I always get my way."

"I suppose you do," Honor agreed. "Let me walk you to the boat bay."

Henke nodded, and Honor glanced at Senior Chief Steward James MacGuiness as she lifted Nimitz to her shoulder. Her steward's face was expressionless, but one eyelid dipped minutely, and she returned the tiny wink with a casual nod and followed Henke out the hatch.

They stepped past the Marine sentry who guarded the quarters of *Nike*'s captain and made their way to the lift. The passage was deserted, as it usually was in officer's country, but Honor noted the way Henke's eyes flitted about. *Nike*'s entire wardroom had joined Honor in hosting a congratulatory dinner the night before, yet it was traditional for a ship's senior officers to "accidentally" bump into a departing exec and wish her well in her new post, as well, especially when she was leaving to assume command of a ship of her own.

Only there wasn't a sign of them today, and a shadow darkened Henke's eyes. She looked as if she were about to speak, then shrugged and stepped into the lift. Honor punched their destination code and stood beside her, engaging in inconsequential conversation. She kept her voice light, jollying Henke out of her disappointment, and actually got her friend to laugh as the two of them watched the location display flicker. The lift moved swiftly and silently, but the trip took an unusually long time, for they were headed for Boat Bay Three. Of all *Nike*'s boat bays, Three was least conveniently placed in relation to the captain's quarters, but unrepaired battle damage meant both forward docking facilities were still unserviceable.

They reached their destination, the lift door opened, and Honor waved Henke out with a flourish. Henke laughed and responded with a regal bow, but then her head snapped up in shock as the opening notes of the fanfare of the Saganami March suddenly rippled pure and golden over the boat bay speakers.

She spun to face the boat bay gallery, eyes wide, and a command cut through the majestic strains of the Royal Manticoran Navy's anthem.

"Preeeesent *arms!*" it barked, and hands slapped pulser stocks with crisp precision as the Marine honor guard obeyed. Colonel Ramirez and Major Hibson were there, but they stood to one side, watching as Captain Tyler, the senior Marine to survive the Battle of Hancock, whipped her dress sword up in salute. She and her people were a solid block of gorgeous green-and-black dress uniforms, but the gallery bulkheads were lined with Navy officers and ratings, all stiffly at attention to form a black-and-gold double line to the side party waiting at the mouth of the boarding tube.

Henke turned back to Honor, eyes bright.

"You set me up!" she accused under cover of the anthem, and Honor shook her head.

"Not me. It was the crew's idea. I just had Mac warn them you were on your way."

Henke started to say something more, then swallowed and turned back to the gallery. She squared her shoulders and marched down its length between the rigid lines with Honor at her heels. They reached the boarding tube, and Commander Chandler snapped a parade-ground salute.

Henke returned it, and the diminutive redhead who'd replaced her as *Nike*'s exec extended her hand as the music died.

"Congratulations, Captain Henke," she said. "We'll miss you. But on behalf of *Nike*'s officers and crew, I wish you Godspeed and good hunting."

"Thank you, Commander." Henke's contralto was huskier than usual, and she swallowed again. "You've got a good ship and good people, Eve. Take care of them. And—" she managed a smile "—try to keep the Skipper out of trouble."

"I will, Ma'am." Chandler saluted once more, then stepped back, and bosun's pipes twittered in formal salute to a departing starship's commander. Henke gripped Honor's hand once more, hard, and stepped into the tube without another backward glance.

Pavel Young turned from the window as the soft chime sounded. He paused a moment to twitch his uniform straight, then pressed the admittance key and watched the door to his quarters open.

The Marine sentry in the hall beyond wasn't the symbol of respect she would have been aboard ship. She was Young's keeper, the formal symbol of his disgraced status, and her cool, impersonal expression shouted her own judgment upon him. His mouth tightened at the fresh reminder, and his seething anger and humiliation surged up stronger than ever as the counter-grav life-support chair hummed past her into his sitting room.

The man in the chair was barely ninety T-years old, not even early middle age in a society with prolong, but his color was bad and he filled the chair in a billow of obesity that always made Young more aware than he liked of his own thickening middle. There were limits to how much even modern medicine could limit the consequences of a lifetime's catastrophic self-indulgence.

The chair purred into the center of the room, and the Tenth Earl of North Hollow leaned back in it to regard his eldest son from fat-pouched eyes.

"So," he wheezed. "Put your foot in it this time, didn't you?"

"I acted as I felt best under the circumstances, Father," Young said stiffly, and the earl's snort sent a ripple through his mountainous girth.

"Save it for the court, boy! You fucked up—don't try to pretend you didn't. Not with me. Especially not"—his piggy little eyes hardened— "if you expect me to get you out of this with your hide!"

Young swallowed hard. He'd thought he was already as frightened as he could get; the suggestion that this time his father might not be able to save him proved he hadn't been.

"Better." The earl moved his chair over to the window and glanced out, then pivoted back to face his son. "I can't believe you were stupid enough to fuck up this way with that bitch in charge," he grunted. Like Young himself, he seldom used Honor Harrington's name, but Young flushed under the scathing contempt in his voice, for this time it wasn't aimed at her. "Damn, boy! Hasn't she made enough problems for you without *this*?" The earl waved a slablike hand at the closed, guarded door. "What the hell were you using for brains?!"

Young bit his lip, and fresh anger burned like sick fire. What did his father know about it? He hadn't seen *his* ship at the middle of a missile storm!

"Twelve minutes. That's what made the difference," that high, wheezy voice went on. "All you had to do was stick it out for twelve more *minutes*, and none of this would've happened!"

"I made the best decision I could, Sir," Young said, and knew it was a lie. He could feel the terrible echoes of unthinking, paralyzing panic even now.

"Bullshit. You ran for it." Young flushed crimson, but the earl ignored it and continued, as if speaking to himself. "Should never've sent you into the Navy in the first place. Suppose I always knew you didn't have the stomach for it."

Young stared at him, unable to speak, and North Hollow sighed.

"Well, that's all air out the lock, now." He seemed to realize his son was still stiffly at attention and jabbed a sausage-shaped finger at a chair. "Oh, sit down, boy. Sit down!" Young obeyed with machinelike rigidity, and his father sighed again. "I know I wasn't there, Pavel," he said more gently. "And I know things like this happen. The important thing now is how we get you out of it. I've got a few irons already in the fire, but before I can do anything effective I've got to know exactly what happened. Not just the official record—what *you* were thinking. *Really* thinking," he added with a sharp, piercing look. "Don't bullshit me now, boy. There's too much at stake."

"I realize that, Father," Young said in a low voice.

"Good." The earl reached out to pat his knee and settled his chair to the carpet. "Then suppose you start with everything you can remember. Save the justifications for the court and just tell me what happened."

✧   ✧   ✧

Admiral of the Green Hamish Alexander, Thirteenth Earl of White Haven, stared at his younger brother and heir across the snowy white tablecloth while their grim-faced host, Admiral Sir James Bowie Webster, Commander in Chief Home Fleet, watched them both.

"I can't believe this," White Haven said at last. His own flagship had been back in Manticore orbit for less than an hour when Webster "invited" him aboard HMS *Manticore* for supper. Now he shook his head like a man in a bad dream. "I knew things were screwed up, but Caparelli's dispatches never suggested it was *this* bad!"

"We didn't know how bad it was going to get when he sent you your last download and ordered you home, Hamish." William Alexander shrugged almost apologetically. "We knew we'd lost Wallace and his cronies, but we didn't know the Conservative Association was going to sign on with the Opposition, too."

"Damn it, Willie, we've got to hit the Peeps *now*! They're falling apart before our eyes—they didn't even fire a shot when I moved on Chelsea!—but if they get their feet back under them . . ." The earl let his voice trail off, and his brother shrugged.

"You're preaching to the converted, Hamish. The Duke's calling in every favor from the last fifty years, but the Opposition's standing firm for now. I think the Liberals have truly convinced themselves they're looking at a genuine reform movement on Haven. As for the Progressives—! I doubt Gray Hill and Lady Descroix would recognize a principle if it bit them, but they've persuaded the Progressive rank and file that the Peeps will simply self-destruct if we just let them alone."

"That's horseshit, Willie!" Webster put down his cup so angrily coffee slopped over the brim. "Goddamn it, don't *any* of them read history?!"

"No, they don't." William's own anger was apparent in his over-controlled voice. "It's not 'relevant.' "

"Idiots!" White Haven grunted. He shoved himself up out of his chair and took a quick, frustrated turn around Webster's dining cabin. "This is a classic situation. The Havenite government's been a disaster in waiting for decades, but this new Committee of Public Safety is a whole 'nother animal. I don't care what their propaganda says, they're no more reformers than the Conservative Association is, and they're ruthless as hell. Your own sources report they've already shot over a dozen admirals! If we don't smash them before they finish consolidating, we're going to be up against something ten times as dangerous as Harris and his stooges ever were."

"At least they may shoot enough of their commanders to give us an edge." William sounded like a man trying to convince himself the cloud really had a silver lining, and his brother snorted harshly.

"You never did read your Napoleon, did you, Willie?" Alexander shook his head, and White Haven grinned crookedly. "When Napoleon built the army that conquered most of Europe, he did it by turning lieutenants, sergeants—even corporals!—into colonels and generals. His troops used to say there was a field marshal's baton in every knapsack, that *anyone* could rise to the heights once the old regime was out of the way. Well, the Legislaturalists are gone now. Sure, the new regime's costing itself a lot of experience by killing off the old guard, but it's also offering non-Legislaturalists their first real chance at the top. Damn it, all we need is a Peep officer corps with a genuine stake in the system and the chance to rise on merit!"

"And that doesn't even consider the other new motivating factor," Webster threw in. William looked at him, and the admiral shrugged. "Come back with your shield or on it," he said. "Anyone who disappoints the new regime will go the same way Parnell went." An expression of genuine regret crossed his features, and he sighed. "The man was an enemy, and I hated the system he represented, but damn it all, he deserved better than that."

"He certainly did." White Haven dumped himself back into his chair and reached for his own coffee cup. "He was good, Jim. Better than I thought. I had him cold in Yeltsin. He never had a clue we were there, or in such strength, before we opened up on him, and he *still* managed to get almost half his fleet out of it. And then his own government shot him for 'treason'!" The earl sipped coffee, then shook his head sadly and drew a deep breath.

"All right, Willie. Jim and I understand the Duke's problems, but what, exactly, do you expect *me* to do? Everyone knows I support the Centrists, and not"—he managed a tired smile—"just because my baby brother's in the Cabinet. I doubt I can change too many minds you and he can't already get to."

"Actually," William said uncomfortably, "I'm afraid you're going to be more central to the situation than you think."

"Me?" White Haven said skeptically. He glanced at Webster, but his friend only shrugged his own ignorance, and they both looked back at William.

"You," Alexander sighed, and leaned back in his chair. "I'm not supposed to know this, but the court's been appointed for Pavel Young, Hamish."

"And about fucking time!" Webster snorted, but something in Alexander's voice sounded warning bells deep in White Haven's brain, and his eyes sharpened. William met them levelly and nodded.

"You're on it. In fact, you're its senior member."

"Oh, *Jesus*!" Webster groaned in sudden understanding. White Haven said nothing for a long moment as he gazed at his brother, and then he spoke very carefully.

"Willie, I'm willing to do a great many things for Allen Summervale, but I draw the line at this. You tell the Duke that if I'm appointed to sit on a court—even Pavel Young's—I'm going to listen to the evidence and make my decision on that basis and *only* that basis."

"No one's asking you to do anything else!" William snapped. Blue eyes flashed into matching eyes of Alexander blue, and White Haven raised a hand in apology. His brother glared at him a moment longer, then sighed. "Sorry, Hamish. Sorry. It's just that—"

He broke off and closed his eyes briefly. When he opened them once more, his face was calm.

"Look, we're not trying to influence you, but the last thing any of us need—including you—is for you to get blindsided, all right?"

" 'Blindsided'?" White Haven repeated, and William nodded.

"I know the selection process is supposed to avoid any possibility of favoritism in the selection of a court-martial's board, but this time it's boomeranged on us big time, Ham. You're on the court, all right—and so are Sonja Hemphill, Rex Jurgens, and Antoinette Lemaitre."

White Haven winced, and Webster swallowed an oath of disbelief. Silence lingered once more until the earl broke it.

"Who're the other two?" he asked.

"Thor Simengaard and Admiral Kuzak."

"Um." White Haven frowned and crossed his legs while he rubbed an eyebrow. "Theodosia Kuzak's as apolitical as they come," he said after a moment. "She'll look at the evidence, and only the evidence. Simengaard's more problematical, but I expect if he listens to his prejudices he'll come down against Young. Of course, I haven't seen any of the evidence yet—for that matter, I don't officially know what the charges are—but I don't think he'd care for Young on general principles."

"Which still leaves the other three," William pointed out, "and North Hollow is pulling out all the stops. Unless I miss my guess, he's going to talk High Ridge into making the Conservatives' continued support for the Opposition contingent on the outcome of the trial, and that'll bring the Liberals and Progressives in on it, too. They smell blood, maybe even the chance to bring the Duke's Government down despite the Crown's support. They won't pass up the chance, and if getting his son off is the price tag—" He broke off with an eloquent shrug.

"Does he really have *that* much clout, Willie?" Webster put in.

"Hell, Jim! You should know that as well as I do, after so long as First Space Lord! The old bastard is the Association whip in the Lords. Worse, he knows where every political body on Manticore is buried. You think he won't exhume every one of them to save his son's neck?" Alexander's lip curled, and Webster nodded slow agreement.

"How do you expect him to come at it, Willie?" White Haven asked.

"We don't know yet. At the moment, he's demanding we drop the charges in their entirety, but he has to know that's not going to happen. Her Majesty's made her own position clear and, Opposition or not, that's going to carry weight in a lot of minds. He's got Janacek in his corner as an advisor, though, and that worries us. Janacek may be a hide-bound, reactionary old bastard, but he knows the Navy side of the street as well as North Hollow knows the political one. At the moment, I think they're just trying to stake out an initial bargaining position, but between them, they're going to come up with something more effective. You can count on that."

"And I get to serve as president of the court. Wonderful." White Haven unfolded his legs and slid further down in his chair.

"And you get to serve as president," his brother confirmed. "I don't envy you—and I'm not even going to try to suggest what you ought to do. Aside from the fact that you'd take my head off for it, no one knows enough yet *to* suggest anything. But this is shaping up as the nastiest fight I can remember, Ham, and it's not going to get better."

"An understatement if I ever heard one." White Haven studied the toes of his polished boots and brooded, then managed a sour grin. "I suppose it's no more than my just desserts, Jim," he said almost whimsically, and both the others looked at him in surprise.

"What do you mean?" Webster asked.

"Didn't I suggest sending Sarnow to Hancock with Harrington as his flag captain?"

"It seemed like a good idea to me, too, Hamish. And judging from the after-action reports, it was a damned good job we *did* send them out."

"Agreed." White Haven pushed himself a bit higher in his chair and frowned. "By the way, how's Sarnow doing?"

"He looks like hell," Webster said candidly, "but the medics are pleased. He lost both legs right at the knee, and his internal injuries are nothing to sneeze at, but they say the quick heal's taken hold nicely. You couldn't prove it by me, but that's what they say. Of course, he's going to be on the sick list for months once they start regenerating his legs."

"At least they can," White Haven murmured, and Webster and his brother looked at one another in silence. The earl sat wordless for several seconds, then gave another sigh. "All right, Willie, I'm warned. Tell the Duke I'll do my damnedest to hold down the political fallout, but if the evidence supports the charges, tell him there's no way I'm letting Young walk, either. If that makes the situation worse, I'm sorry, but that's the way it is."

"I know that, jerk." William smiled sadly at his older brother and reached out to squeeze his forearm in a rare physical display of affection. "Hell, I knew that before I came up here!"

"I imagine you did," White Haven agreed with a tiny smile. He glanced at the bulkhead chrono and pushed himself back to his feet. "All right," he said more briskly, "I'm warned. And now, much though it grieves me to walk out on such august personages, I haven't seen Emily in almost four months, and it's just about dawn at White Haven. So if you'll excuse me—?"

"We'll walk you to the boat bay," Webster said.

✧ CHAPTER SIX

HONOR HARRINGTON PROWLED HER quarters moodily, movements quick and abrupt, hands shoved deep into her tunic pockets, and her slouched shoulders were tight with a frustration that had no way to strike back. Nimitz watched her from his bulkhead perch above her desk, flicking the very tip of his prehensile tail, but MacGuiness had staged a strategic withdrawal after a single abortive attempt at conversation. Honor knew he had, and why, and it only increased her anger and frustration. Not that she blamed *him.*

She sighed and flopped down on the padded seat beneath her enormous cabin view port. Her quarters were on *Nike*'s outboard side as the wounded battlecruiser nuzzled up against HMSS *Hephaestus'* ungainly, mothering bulk, and there was always plenty to see from Manticore orbit. The port offered her an unobstructed panorama of pinprick stars, orbital warehouses and transfer platforms, and the glittering motes of passing traffic. The capital planet's huge solar power receptors were distant, brilliant jewels of reflected sunlight, and Thorson, Manticore's moon, gleamed white as *Hephaestus'* geosynchronous orbit swept it across Honor's field of view. Under normal circumstances, she could have sat and watched for hours, wrapped in the semi-hypnotic delight of the universe's unending ballet, but not even that gorgeous starscape could lighten her mood today.

She grimaced and ran harried fingers through her hair. The Admiralty had released the official after-action report on the Battle of Hancock two days after her dinner at Cosmo's, and she'd been forced within hours to order George Monet, her com officer, to refuse all nonofficial com access as the only way to stem the tidal wave of interview requests. It was even worse than after Basilisk or Yeltsin's Star, but not even Basilisk had included such nasty political overtones as this one, she thought despairingly. News of Pavel Young's court-martial had been released at the same Admiralty press conference, and the scent of blood was in the water.

Honor didn't like newsies. She disliked the way they over-simplified and trivialized the news almost as much as she detested their sensationalism and the way they trampled on the most rudimentary concepts of courtesy to pursue a story. She was willing to concede they had a function, and the teeth Parliament had given the Privacy Act of 14 A.L. normally prevented the brutal intrusiveness societies like the Solarian League tolerated, but any vestige of restraint had vanished on this one. Young's court-martial had provoked a feeding frenzy that suggested most editors were willing to risk the near certain (and expensive) loss of an invasion of privacy suit as long as their reporters got the story.

The media were after all of *Nike*'s people, rabid for any shred of a firsthand account to flesh out the Admiralty's bare-bones report of the battle and the incidents leading to what prom-ised to be a spectacular trial, but they'd gone after *Nike*'s captain with special fervor . . . and not just about events in Hancock. Every detail of Honor's past—and Young's, she conceded—had been exhumed and plastered across every newsfax in the Kingdom, along with equally detailed, usually inaccurate, and almost invariably tasteless analyses and specu-lation. Every documented incident, every *rumor*, of the hos-tility between her and Young had become front-page news. Some of the services had even gone clear back to her child-hood on Sphinx, and one particularly obnoxious team of reporters had cornered her parents in their surgical offices. They'd gotten in by claiming to be patients, then badgered both Doctors Harrington—and any other staff member who came in range—with personal questions until her mother lost her temper, screened the police, and had them charged with privacy violation. Honor had been livid when she heard about it, nor had she cooled off much since, and her own situa-tion was even worse. Half the capital planet's news corps had infested *Hephaestus*, lurking like Sphinx spider lizards in passages and spacedock galleries on the off chance that she might set toe aboard the space station.

The whole thing appalled her. Not just because of the over-powering omni-intrusiveness, but because of the incredibly partisan way the story was being reported. The media were treating it like a gladiatorial circus, as if Young's court-martial somehow crystallized the Kingdom's anxieties. All the last half-T-century's growing fear of the People's Republic, the sense of defiance and victory stemming from the opening battles, and the uncertainty of the ongoing political crisis seemed to have focused on Young's trial . . . and on her. Reporters, analysts, academics, the person in the street—all of them were choosing up sides, and Honor Harrington was right in the middle.

She wasn't surprised by the way Opposition newsfaxes and the services controlled by the Hauptman Cartel were inveighing against her, but the pro-Government 'faxes and commentators who'd made themselves her champions were almost worse. Hearing herself referred to as "this Kingdom's most courageous naval hero" was agonizingly embarrassing, but at least half of them seemed to have seized upon her as some sort of shining paladin with whom to bludgeon the "obstructionist Opposition." Political analysts of all stripes opined that the Young court-martial would make or break the Cromarty Government's chance to secure a declaration of war, and there'd actually been mass demonstrations—with people waving placards with *her* picture on them!—outside Parliament.

It was a nightmare, and she'd become a virtual prisoner on *Nike* since the moment the story broke. She'd promised her Queen she wouldn't discuss the charges against Young; even if she hadn't, Pavel Young was the last thing she would willingly have discussed under *any* circumstances. Talking about her own accomplishments like some vainglorious twit was almost equally repugnant, and even if it hadn't been, she'd always hated—and feared—cameras.

Honor was still grappling with the novel concept that she might be attractive. Paul Tankersley had made enough progress in convincing her she'd outgrown the sharp-faced homeliness of her adolescence that she could accept, intellectually, that he was right, that hers was a face which improved with maturity. But the early age at which the current generation of the prolong treatment was first applied meant the improvement process had taken decades, and he'd only been working on her for a few months. That wasn't much set against a lifetime's ugly-duckling mentality, and she was still far from accepting his judgment that she was "beautiful," even if Nimitz's ability to tap Paul's emotions proved *he* believed it. Honor couldn't remember a single photo of herself, flatpix or dimensional, that she liked, and she still felt herself go stiff and wooden whenever anyone pointed a camera her way.

It wasn't *fair*, she thought bitterly, and kicked a hassock clear across the cabin without even rising from her seat. She shouldn't have to put herself in solitary to avoid a flock of self-important, officious busybodies who wanted to turn her into a central player in a political confrontation that threatened the Kingdom's very survival just to increase their viewership! And the ones who were portraying her as some sort of Machiavellian manipulator out to "get" Pavel Young, as if this were all somehow *her* fault, *her* idea—!

Nimitz's hiss was a soft, angry sibilance, echoing her own fury. He reared up on his true-feet, ears flat, ivory claws unsheathed, and she looked up in quick repentance. She rose and lifted him down, crooning to him as she hugged him to her breasts, and his dangerous, quivering tension eased. He made another sound—more grumpy than angry this time—and she nipped one pricked ear gently, then chuckled as he put up a long-fingered true-hand to pat her cheek. He stroked her face, his hostility toward those who were making her life a misery pouring into her through their telepathic link, and she cuddled him tighter, burying her nose in his soft, clean-smelling fur while she tried not to feel fresh resentment for his sake, as well as her own.

The reporters hounding her were hounding him, too. They might not realize it (assuming they would have cared if they had), but his empathic sense made him particularly sensitive to the predatory pack mentality that went with the media's pursuit. That was one reason for her self-imposed immurement. Another of the shouted "press conferences" that had ambushed her at *Nike*'s main docking tube yesterday would have driven the 'cat into a fury with decidedly unpleasant consequences . . . especially for the newsies.

Treecats were direct and uncomplicated souls who didn't quite grasp the concept of measured response, and, despite their small size, they were formidably armed. Nimitz had more experience dealing with humans than most of his kind, but she'd still found herself busy restraining a double armful of hissing, snarling, bare-clawed 'cat as she fought her way out of the shouting throng and fled back down the tube. Nor had that been all, for Eve Chandler and Tomas Ramirez had doubled the sentries on the station ends of all *Nike*'s docking tubes the minute the story broke. Honor's Marines knew Nimitz, and they'd recognized his distress and covered her retreat with more energy than tact. In fact, one reporter who'd attempted to force his way aboard in pursuit had suffered abrasions, contusions, and a certain amount of dental damage when he "accidentally" collided with a pulse rifle's butt. Honor supposed she should reprimand whoever that rifle had belonged to. Fortunately for her sense of duty, the confusion had been too intense for the gallery surveillance systems to tell her which Marine it had been . . . and if there'd been any witnesses, she had no intention of finding them.

She eased Nimitz back onto his perch and took another turn around the cabin. This was ridiculous. She was the captain of a Queen's ship, not a felon hiding from the police! She should be able to come and go without—

A soft, clear chime sounded, and she wheeled toward the hatch with something all too much like one of Nimitz's snarls. The chime sounded again, and she drew a deep breath and forced her instant, uncharacteristic anger back under control. After all, she told herself with a tired smile, it wasn't like the newsies could get aboard *Nike* . . . as at least one of them could testify.

Her smile deepened, and she ran her hands through her hair once more, settling its disordered, barely shoulder-length curls back into some sort of order, and keyed the intercom.

"Yes?" Her soprano was cool and courteous, almost normal sounding.

"Captain Tankersley, Ma'am," her Marine sentry announced, and Honor's eyes lit with sudden, relieved gladness.

"Thank you, Private O'Shaughnessy," she said, unable to keep her pleasure out of her voice, and opened the hatch.

Tankersley stepped through the opening, then paused and braced himself as he saw her coming. Her long, graceful stride was far quicker than usual, and the hatch barely had time to cycle shut behind him before his arms closed about her and she sighed in profound relief.

She felt the vibration of his chuckle as she pressed her cheek into the soft warmth of his beret, and her own lips quirked. She was a full head taller than he, and she supposed they looked a bit ridiculous, but that couldn't have mattered less to her at the moment.

"You should see the mob camped in the gallery," he told her, hands caressing her spine and shoulders as he held her tightly. "I think there are even more of them now than there were yesterday."

"Thanks a lot," she said dryly, and gave him a quick, answering squeeze before she stood back and drew him down on the couch beside her. He studied her expression for a moment, then laughed softly and cupped the right side of her face in his palm.

"Poor Honor. They're really giving you hell, aren't they, love?"

"An understatement if I ever heard one." Her reply was tart, but his presence had lightened her mood enormously. She caught his hand in both of hers and leaned back against the couch cushions while Nimitz leapt from his perch to the couch arm. The six-limbed 'cat flowed down from there to drape himself across Paul's lap, resting his chin on Honor's thigh, and his buzzing purr rose as Tankersley's free hand stroked his spine.

"Have you been following the circus?" Paul asked after a moment.

"Not likely!" she snorted. He smiled in understanding and squeezed her hand, but his eyes were serious.

"It's getting uglier," he warned. "North Hollow's publicity shills and a certain, loathsome subspecies of parliamentary staffers are getting into it—always as 'anonymous' sources, of course. They're trying to present the whole thing as some sort of personal vendetta on your part, coupled with the strong implication that Cromarty is pushing it to punish the Conservative Association for breaking with the Government over the declaration. Which, of course, the Conservatives did only as a matter of high moral principle."

"Wonderful." Honor closed her eyes and inhaled deeply. "I don't suppose they're mentioning anything *Young* ever did to *me*?"

"Some of the services are," Tankersley conceded, "but Young's partisans certainly aren't. You know Crichton, the Palmer Foundation's pet military analyst?" Honor nodded with a grimace, and Tankersley shrugged. "He's claiming *Young's* the real victim because the Admiralty has been trying to get him ever since Basilisk. According to his version—for which, I trust, he charged High Ridge and North Hollow an arm and a leg each—poor old Young, having been saddled with a defective ship in Basilisk, was turned into a scapegoat by the Admiralty and the Cromarty Government when he was forced to withdraw for repairs. It seems Young didn't do it to get *you*, nor did his earlier inefficiency on the station contribute in any way to the problems you faced. What *really* created the dangerous situation in Basilisk was the Admiralty's culpable negligence in assigning only two ships, one on the verge of imminent breakdown, to the picket in the first place."

"Oh, for God's sake!" Honor snapped. "*Warlock* didn't have any real problems—and downsizing the picket was *Janacek's* policy!"

"Sure, but you don't expect them to admit the *Conservatives* created the mess, do you? Especially not when everyone on the Opposition side of the aisle still blames *you* for how the Government amended the Act of Annexation after the station blew up in your face! You certainly do have a penchant for ticking off politicos, don't you, love?"

There was too much tender amusement in his voice for her to protest or resent the statement. Especially when she knew it was true.

"Look, Paul," she said instead, "if it's all the same to you, I'd really rather not discuss it. As a matter of fact, I'd prefer not even *thinking* about it—or Young."

"Fair enough." His instant response sounded so penitent she smiled and caught his face between her hands to kiss him. He leaned into it, savoring the taste of her lips, then drew back with a smile of his own.

"Actually, I didn't mean to discuss it at all when I arrived. What I meant to do was issue an invitation."

"An invitation?"

"Absolutely. You need to get out of this cabin, Honor. In fact, you need to get off *Nike* and leave it all behind for a while, and I, in my ever efficient fashion, have found just the place for you to go. And one with no press, too."

"Where?" Honor demanded. "The weather station on Sidham Island?"

Tankersley laughed and shook his head. Sidham Island, well above Sphinx's arctic circle, was probably the most barren, desolate, and generally godforsaken piece of technically inhabited real estate on any of the Manticore binary system's three habitable planets.

"No, I don't think we're quite that desperate yet. But it *is* an island. How do you feel about a jaunt to Kreskin Field?"

"Kreskin Field?" Honor twitched upright, eyes suddenly intent. Kreskin Field was the main air facility for Saganami Island, site of the RMN's Naval Academy.

"Exactly," Tankersley said. "I can file the flight plan down in my name, and you know the Academy will cover for you as long as you keep a low profile. The press won't even know you're there, and, frankly, you need to smell some sunshine. Besides," he jerked a thumb at the sailplane etched into a heat-twisted golden plaque on the cabin bulkhead, "haven't you been telling me for months how handy you are in primitive aircraft?"

"I have *not*," she said indignantly.

"Really?" He scratched his chin in manifest thought. "Must have been Mike, then. But I distinctly remember someone telling me rather boastfully that you hold the all-time Academy sailplane record. Are you saying you don't?"

"Of course I do, you snot." She jabbed for his ribs, but he was expecting it, and his elbow blocked hers neatly.

"I find that hard to believe," he sniffed. "It's always been my observation that small, compact people are better in the air when they can't rely on counter-grav to hold them up."

It was Honor's turn to laugh. Paul was one of the very few people in the universe who could tease her about her height without irritating her.

"Is this a challenge, Captain Tankersley?"

"Oh, no, not a *challenge*. Just a friendly little match to see who's really best. Of course, I do have a certain advantage. Not only am I one of those small, compact people, but I bet I've been up more recently than you."

"Practicing beforehand, huh? Don't you know that spoils the fun?"

"Spoken like a true barbarian. Interested?"

"Sailplanes or powered?" she demanded.

"Oh, sailplanes are so . . . so *passive*. Besides, if we used them, *you*'d have the advantage, not me. No, I talked to Kreskin and they've got a pair of Javelins standing by for us."

"Javelins?" Honor's eyes lit with pure delight, and Tankersley grinned at her. The Javelin advanced trainer was a deliberate technical anachronism: an old-fashioned, variable geometry airfoil jet aircraft with no counter-grav but incredible power. It was small, sleek, and fast, and the Academy instructors had always insisted flying it was even better than sex. Honor couldn't quite agree with that now that she'd met Paul . . . but she was willing to admit it was the next best thing.

"Javelins," Tankersley confirmed. "And," he added enticingly, "they've agreed to midair refueling if we decide we want to stay up a while."

"How in the world did you swing that much flight time? There's always a waiting line for the Javelins!"

"Ah, but I was able to conjure with the name of a famous naval officer. When I told Kreskin Flight Control who I'd be flying wing on—after, of course, swearing them to strictest secrecy—they could hardly wait to roll out the red carpet." Honor blushed, and he flipped the tip of her nose with an affectionate finger. "So how about it, Dame Honor? Game?"

"Bet your life I am!" She scooped Nimitz up with a laugh and set him on her shoulder. "Come on, Stinker—we've got an appointment to pin back someone's ears!"

✧ CHAPTER SEVEN

HONOR SLAMMED THE THROTTLES WIDE and rode the rudder pedals as she hauled the stick back into a near-vertical climbing turn. Twin, screaming turbines shook the airframe, and the artificial nerves in her rebuilt left cheek shivered with electric fire as acceleration squeezed like a fist. The sensation was strange but not really painful, and she watched the icons of the Heads-Up-Display on her flight helmet's visor shift as her vision tunneled.

Paul was "it" in their game of gun-camera tag at the moment, and her lips drew back in an acceleration-flattened smile as she shot away from his aircraft. She'd caught him napping this time, and she waited, watching the HUD and counting seconds. His nose flipped up and he committed to a pursuit curve . . . and she reversed her turn, slammed the stick forward, and pitched into an even steeper dive that had her floating against her harness straps as she howled down toward the distant sea.

No simulator, no small craft with its grav generators or pinnace with its inertial compensator and impeller drive, could match the sheer, wild delight of a moment like this. Honor's flight computers were simpleminded and minimal, for the Javelin had been designed to be one thing and one thing only: a pilot's aircraft—and her whoop of triumph was an eagle's shriek as she pulled out.

She roared into the north with wings swept for maximum speed and Paul in pursuit, and Saganami Island, site of the RMN's naval academy for over two and a half Manticoran centuries, grew below the aircraft's needle nose like a sunstruck emerald, rich with memories as she shot toward it at Mach six.

Honor was no stranger to salt water. She'd been born within sight and smell of Sphinx's Tannerman Ocean—in spite of which, Ms. Midshipman Harrington had found the Academy took some getting used to. The twenty-five percent lower gravity had made her feel wonderfully light on her feet, but Saganami Island lay at the mouth of Silver Gulf. The deep, glittering inlet which linked Jason Bay and the Southern Ocean was just twenty-six degrees below the capital planet's equator, and Manticore was near the inner edge of its primary's liquid-water zone while Sphinx lay barely inside its outermost limit. The fact that the Academy was on an island had helped, yet she'd taken weeks to adjust to the unending, enervating warmth.

Once she had, of course, she'd gone overboard in enjoying it. She could still remember the hideous sunburn she'd managed to inflict upon herself despite all warnings. Once had been enough, especially when poor Nimitz—still grappling with his own adaptation to the change in climate—had been forced to endure it with her via their link. Chastened but wiser for the experience, she'd explored her new environment with more caution and soon found that sailing tropical waters was just as much fun as roaming the colder, rougher seas of home. And the updrafts had made hang gliding almost as glorious as, if less excitingly treacherous than, those of Sphinx's Copper Wall Mountains. She and Nimitz had spent endless hours of precious free time soaring above the gulf's magnificent blue waters with a fine disdain for the emergency counter-grav units native Manticorans insisted on hauling along just in case.

Her disdain for counter-grav had worried some of the instructors, but hang gliding was a planetary passion on her homeworld. Most Sphinxians made it a point of honor (as silly, she admitted, as most points of honor) to eschew artificial assists, and Honor had been a qualified glider since age twelve—which might have helped explain her finely developed kinesthetic sense. Honor *always* knew where she was in the air, with an unerring instinct a Sphinx albatross might have envied . . . and one that had baffled the Saganami instructors.

The RMN maintained a vast marina of small sailing craft, and every midshipman, regardless of eventual specialization track, was required to qualify not only in sailplanes and old-fashioned airfoil aircraft but in even more old-fashioned seamanship as well as counter-grav. Critics might sniff at the requirement as a throwback to the bad old days when starship captains navigated the grav waves of hyper space as much by instinct as instruments, but the Academy clung to the tradition, and Honor, like most of the Navy's better shiphandlers, firmly believed it had taught her things and given her a confidence no simulator could—which didn't even consider how much *fun* it was!

At the same time, she had to admit that her own natural ability in the air, and her confidence and delight in proving it, had landed her in trouble more than once.

She hadn't *meant* to be wicked, but Ms. Midshipman Harrington's tendency to ignore her instruments and rely on her instincts had reduced certain instructors to frothing incoherence. Senior Master Chief Youngman, who ruled the marina with an iron hand, hadn't given her much trouble once they got to know one another. Youngman was from Gryphon, but she'd often vacationed on Sphinx to enjoy what she called *real* blue-water sailing. Once she'd checked Honor's abilities in person, she'd made her an assistant instructor.

Flight school had been another matter. With the benefit of hindsight, Honor shared Lieutenant Desjardin's appalled reaction to her blithe assertion that she didn't *need* instruments, but a much younger and brasher Honor had been furious when he grounded her for a full month for ignoring weather warnings and instruments alike on a night sailplane flight in her first term. Then there'd been her mock dogfight with Mike in their second form that, she admitted, really had gotten just a *bit* out of hand. And, of course, there'd been that unscheduled aerobatics display above the regatta. She hadn't known Commandant Hartley was winning at the moment she crossed his sloop in the run up to the ancient "Cuban Eight," but she still thought he'd been more miffed than the offense had required. It hadn't been her fault Kreskin Control had failed to designate the regatta's course restricted airspace. And it wasn't as if she'd inflicted any actual damage, after all; she'd cleared his masthead by a good forty meters, and *he* was the one who'd decided to go over the side.

She giggled as she remembered Hartley's thunderous rakedown, though neither it nor the legend-inspiring heap of black spots that went with it had seemed humorous at the time, then checked her HUD again as a threat warning pinged. Paul was still much too far away to tag her with a camera lock, but he was closing the range. She watched his icon trade altitude for still more speed, arrowing down to intercept her flight path, and smiled as she adjusted her fingers on the stick and reached for the air brakes. He was good, all right, but she'd been airborne long enough to get the touch back, and she doubted he was expecting . . . *this!*

She chopped the throttles, popped the brakes, and slammed forward against her harness. The suddenly extended spoilers slowed her as if she'd just dropped anchor, the wings automatically configured forward as her velocity fell toward a stall, and then she made it still worse by yanking up into a climbing loop. The Javelin hung on the brink of a spin, warning hooters bellowing . . . until she snapped the brakes closed and went back to full burner on her screaming turbines. Sheer, incredible power pulled the Javelin through, and Paul's plane was suddenly in front of her as she half-rolled to complete the Immelmann. She'd had to bleed too much speed to get behind him, though, and he almost outran her . . . until he pitched up in a sudden climb of his own.

Honor grinned wolfishly and followed him into a climbing scissors with the throttles wide open. She felt herself graying out and bared her teeth as she hung on to him. Their aircraft were identical, but a Javelin could exceed any pilot's physical limits, and her gee tolerance was higher than his. She used it ruthlessly, clinging to his tail, wracking in tighter than he could manage, and then her own camera pipper suddenly ringed his icon on the HUD.

She squeezed the trigger, pinging him with a radar "tag" and capturing him on the scoring chip, then broke to port, flipped around on a wing-tip, and went screaming back the way she'd come with a triumphant laugh.

"Sailor to Yard Dog. You're going to have to do better than *that* if you want to play with the big kids!"

The luxurious waiting room was hushed. Brilliant sunlight puddled on the parquet floor in warm, liquid gold, but Honor hardly noticed. The joyous exuberance of her flight with Paul seemed a distant, half-forgotten memory as she sat stiff and silent and tried to pretend she was as calm as she looked. Not that she was fooling anyone who knew her, for Nimitz couldn't keep still. He kept getting up from his nest in the armchair beside hers, prowling around and around in a circle as if searching for some softer spot in the cushion before he curled down once more.

It would have helped if she'd been permitted to speak to any of the dozen or so other officers present. Most were acquaintances and many were friends, but the Admiralty yeoman seated beside the door was there to do more than see to their needs and comfort. Witnesses in a Royal Navy court-martial were forbidden to discuss their testimony before they gave it. By tradition, that meant no conversation at all was permitted as they waited to be called, and the yeoman's presence was a reminder of their responsibilities.

She leaned further back, pressing the back of her skull against the wall behind her chair and closing her eyes, and wished they'd get on with it.

Captain Lord Pavel Young marched into the huge, still chamber with his eyes fixed straight ahead. The Judge Advocate General's Corps captain appointed as defense counsel stood waiting for him as his escorting Marines marched him across the scarlet carpet. One entire wall of the enormous room consisted of floor-to-ceiling windows. Rich wood paneling shone in the light streaming in, and Young tried not to blink against the brilliance lest the involuntary reaction be misconstrued. He relaxed ever so slightly in relief as he reached his own chair, but the turn away from the sunlight also faced him toward the long table with its six blotters and carafes of ice water. He felt the silent, watching audience behind him, knew his father and brothers were there, yet he couldn't tear his eyes from the table. A gleaming sword—*his* sword, the mandatory sword of mess dress uniform—lay before the central blotter, the symbol of his honor and authority as a Queen's officer delivered to the court for judgment.

A door opened, and he stood rigid at attention as his court-martial board entered in reverse order of seniority. The junior members stood by their chairs, waiting while the president of the court crossed to his own place, before all six sat simultaneously.

Admiral White Haven leaned forward, looked both ways down the table, then picked up the small, silver-headed hammer and struck the bell before him with two crisp strokes. The musical notes seemed to hover in the sun-laden air, and feet rustled and chairs scraped as everyone else was seated. White Haven laid the hammer aside, opened the old-fashioned folder before him, laid his hands on it as if to hold it down, and looked out across the courtroom.

"This court is now in session."

His baritone voice fell into the background silence and filled it, and his eyes dropped to the hardcopy documents before him.

"This tribunal has been assembled, pursuant to the procedures and regulations laid down in the Articles of War and Manual for Courts-Martial, by order of Lady Francine Maurier, Baroness Morncreek, First Lord of Admiralty, acting for, by the authority of, and at the direction of Her Majesty the Queen, to consider certain charges and specifications laid against

Captain Lord Pavel Young, Royal Navy, commanding Her Majesty's Starship *Warlock*, and arising from his actions during an engagement with enemy forces in the System of Hancock."

He paused and turned the top sheet, laying it carefully to one side, and raised his ice-blue eyes to Young. There was no expression at all on his face, yet Young knew that dispassion was a lie. White Haven was one of the bitch's partisans, one of those who thought she could do no wrong, and he tasted rancid hate as he stared back at the admiral.

"The accused will stand," White Haven said quietly. Young's chair scuffed softly on the carpet as he pushed it back and obeyed, standing behind the defense table to face the court.

"Captain Lord Young, you stand accused before this court upon the following specifications.

"Specification the first, that on or about Wednesday, the twenty-third day of Sixth Month, Year Two Hundred and Eighty Two After Landing, while acting as commodore of Heavy Cruiser Squadron Seventeen in the System of Hancock consequent to Commodore Stephen Van Slyke's death in action, you did violate the Twenty-Third Article of War, in that you did quit the formation of Task Group Hancock-Zero-Zero-One, thereby breaking off action against the enemy, without orders so to do.

"Specification the second, that you did subsequently violate the Twenty-Sixth Article of War, in that you did disobey a direct order from the flagship of Task Group Hancock-Zero-Zero-One by disregarding repeated instructions to return to formation.

"Specification the third, that in direct consequence of the actions alleged in the first and second specifications of these charges, the integrity of the missile defense net of Task Force Hancock-Zero-Zero-One was compromised by the withdrawal of the units under your command, thereby exposing other units of the task group to concentrated enemy fire, which, in consequence of your actions, inflicted severe damage and heavy loss of life upon them.

"Specification the fourth, that the actions and consequences alleged in the first, second, and third specifications of these charges constitute and did result from personal cowardice.

"Specification the fifth, that the actions alleged in the first and second specifications of these charges constitute desertion in the face of the enemy as defined under the Fourteenth, Fifteenth, and Nineteenth Articles of War, and, as such, an act of high treason under the Articles of War and the Constitution of this Star Kingdom."

Young knew he was pale as White Haven finished reading and turned the fresh sheet with that same, maddening deliberation, but he stiffened his knees. His pulse hammered and his belly was a hollow, singing void, yet humiliation and hatred for the woman who'd brought him here lent him strength.

"Captain Lord Young, you have heard the charges," White Haven said in that deep, quiet voice. "How do you plead?"

"Not guilty to all specifications, My Lord." Young's tenor was less ringing than he would have liked, without the note of defiance he tried to put into it, but at least it didn't quaver.

"So noted," White Haven replied. "Be seated, Captain."

Young lowered himself into his chair once more, folding his hands on the table and gripping them hard together to still their trembling, and White Haven nodded to the prosecutor, who rose in turn.

"My Lords and Ladies of the Court," she began formally, "it is the intention of the prosecution to prove that the accused did, in fact, commit the offenses listed in the specifications against him. The prosecution further intends to demonstrate . . ."

Young tuned the words out by a deliberate act of will, staring down at his folded hands and feeling hate and fear swirl at his core like acid. Even now, he couldn't have said which of those emotions was stronger. For all his father's vocal, confident relief at how the court-martial's board had broken down, it would take only four of the six to convict. And if he was convicted, he would die. That was the only possible sentence for the last two crimes of which he stood accused.

Yet overwhelming as the terror that woke was, his hate swirled up to match it, fueled by the humiliation and degradation of the charges. Even if he was exonerated, the taint would always remain. The unspoken whisper "coward" would follow him wherever he went, whatever he did, and it was all Harrington's fault. Harrington, the bitch who had humiliated him at the Academy by rejecting his advances and shaming him before his friends. Harrington, who had beaten him into bloody, sobbing, puking wreckage the night he caught her alone to punish her as she deserved. Who had survived every attempt by him, his family, and its allies to derail her career. Who'd covered herself with glory and made him look like a fool on Basilisk Station, and then emerged from Hancock as the unwashed herd's heroine when she herself had violated the Articles of War by refusing to pass command to the unwounded senior officer! Damn it, she was junior to *him*, yet it was her orders—her *illegal* orders—he was accused of disobeying!

Bile choked him, and his hands clenched into white-knuckled fists before he could unlock them. He felt the sweat of hatred and fear prickling on his scalp and in his armpits, and drew a deep breath. He forced himself to sit square and straight in his chair while the audience and the ghouls of the media hung on the prosecutor's every word, and the muscles of his jaw clenched.

Her time would come. Somehow, somewhere, whatever happened to him, the bitch's time would come, and she would pay for every humiliation she'd ever inflicted upon him.

" . . . concludes the prosecution's opening statement, My Lords and Ladies," Captain Ortiz said finally. White Haven nodded for her to be seated, then looked out over the audience behind Young.

"This court wishes to remind all present that the accused enjoys the presumption of innocence until and unless the validity of the charges and specifications are demonstrated to the complete satisfaction of a majority of the court. This is not, however, a civil court, and the members of the court are not judges in the civilian sense of the word. We, as the prosecutor and defense counsel, are charged with an active role in determining the facts of the charges and specifications set forth against the accused. Further, we are charged with considering the impact of those facts not merely upon the accused but upon the discipline and fighting capability of the Queen's Navy. Should a member of the court address a question or questions to any witness, it will reflect not a violation of judicial impartiality, but the responsibility of the court to discover and weigh all facets of the truth.

"In addition, the court is aware of the intense public interest which has focused upon this case. It is, in fact, that interest which has led the Admiralty to open these proceedings to the public and allow the presence of the media. The court, however, admonishes the media that this is a court of military law, and that the media's representatives are present upon sufferance and not of right. This court will tolerate no abuse of its patience nor any violation of the Defense of the Realm Act, and the media is so warned."

He swept the press gallery with stern blue eyes, and the silence rang like crystal. Then he cleared his throat and raised a finger at the prosecutor.

"Very well, Ms. Prosecutor. You may call your first witness."

"Thank you, My Lord." Captain Ortiz rose once more and looked at the sergeant-at-arms. "My Lord, the prosecution calls as its first witness Captain the Countess Dame Honor Harrington."

✧ CHAPTER EIGHT

THE COURT-MARTIAL BOARD FILED INTO the conference room set aside for its deliberations. Not a word was exchanged as its members passed the Marines flanking the room's single door, and the soft click as that door closed behind them was almost deafening.

Earl White Haven seated himself at the head of the table, looking down its length at Admiral of the Green Theodosia Kuzak at its foot. Their juniors took chairs flanking the polished slab of native golden wood, two on each side, and he let his cool, expressionless eyes study them as they settled.

Of them all, he knew Kuzak best. For reasons of her own, the red-haired admiral had nourished a reputation as a strict, humorless disciplinarian almost from Academy graduation, and her green eyes and severe features could produce a poker face that went well with that perception. Except, he thought fondly, for those who knew the woman behind them. He and Theodosia had been friends literally since childhood—and once, briefly, they'd been much more. It had been a difficult time in White Haven's life, a time when he'd been forced to accept at last that his wife's injuries were real and permanent. That no medical miracle would let her leave her life support chair ever again. The accident hadn't been his fault, but he hadn't been there to prevent it, either, and he'd been wracked by guilt and almost unbearable grief as he watched her turn into a frail and fragile ghost of the beautiful woman he'd loved. The woman he still loved, and with whom he could never again have a physical relationship. Theodosia had understood he could no longer be strong. That he'd needed comfort—no more and no less—from someone whose integrity he knew he would never have cause to question . . . and he hadn't.

81

Rear Admiral of the Green Rexford Jurgens, at Kuzak's left, was a very different proposition. He was a blocklike, chunky man with sandy hair and a permanently belligerent expression, but his belligerence was more pronounced than usual today, and his light brown eyes were like shutters. He didn't look like a man facing a decision; he looked like one who'd already decided and prepared himself to defend his position against all comers.

Admiral of the Red Hemphill, next in seniority after Kuzak, was harder to read, even after all the years she and White Haven had spent as adversaries. As fair-skinned as Kuzak, Sonja Hemphill was a handsome woman, golden haired and with striking blue-green eyes, but where Theodosia's face often hid the real Theodosia, the determination that was Hemphill's driving force tightened her features and made her look almost as opinionated as she actually was. Though twenty years younger and far junior to White Haven, she'd made her name early in the R&D community, and she was a leading advocate of the *jeune ecole's* material-based "new tactical thinking," whereas the earl was the acknowledged leader of the historical school. He respected both her personal courage and her abilities in her own areas of competence, yet they'd never liked one another, and their professional differences only made their natural antipathy worse. Their clashes had assumed mythic stature over the last fifteen T-years, and there were other worries this time: she was also a cousin of Sir Edward Janacek and heir to the Barony of Low Delhi, and, like Jurgens, her spiritual home was the Conservative Association.

The third female member of the board, Commodore Lemaitre, was a complete contrast to Theodosia Kuzak, and not just physically. She was dark haired, dark skinned, and whippet thin, with intense brown eyes, and she radiated taut, barely leashed energy. Another member of the *jeune ecole*, Lemaitre was nonetheless an excellent tactical theorist, though she'd never commanded in action. She was also, despite an abrasive personality, a superior administrator. White Haven suspected her support for the *jeune ecole* stemmed less from a rigorous analysis of its merits than from her family ties to the antimilitary Liberal Party and its fundamental distrust for all things traditional, yet sheer ability had her on the fast track for a rear admiral's star. Unfortunately, she knew it did, and she lacked the one thing which made Hemphill endurable. Sonja might be a hard driver and more than a bit ruthless, and she was oppressively confident of the merits of her own pet technical and tactical theories, yet she was willing to admit she herself was fallible. Lemaitre wasn't. She was totally convinced not only of her own rectitude but of the superiority of any ideology she chose to honor with her support, and he'd seen her nostrils flare when Captain Harrington took the stand.

Captain The Honorable Thor Simengaard was the board's junior officer, and also its largest. His family had migrated to Sphinx two T-centuries before, but they'd come from Quelhollow, an ancient world, settled before Old Earth's Final War and the galaxy-wide ban on the practice of genetically engineering colonists for their new homes. The massively thewed Simengaard stood just over two meters tall, with hair so intensely black it hurt the eye. His dark coppery complexion made his startling, topaz eyes appear even brighter, and his mild, homely features masked a stubbornness more than equal to Jurgens' more obvious belligerence.

It would not, White Haven thought, be a pleasant task to preside over these personalities.

"All right." He broke the silence at last, and five pairs of eyes swiveled to him. "We all know the pertinent regs, and I trust we've all reviewed the JAG's procedural notes and the specific wording of the articles cited in the charges?" He let his gaze circle the table until they'd all nodded. Even the way some of them did that only shouted that they'd already made up their minds, whatever the regs said about considered judgments, and he leaned back in his chair, resting his elbows on its arms and intertwining his fingers above his lap as he crossed his legs.

"In that case," he went on quietly, "let's get to it. We've all heard the evidence, but before I open discussion of the charges, let's admit that our decision—whatever it may be— is going to set off a political warhead."

Lemaitre and Jurgens stiffened, and White Haven smiled without humor. Bringing politics into a court-martial decision was forbidden. Indeed, each officer had been required to affirm under oath that his or her decision would be *apolitical*, rendered solely on the basis of the evidence, and he was certain Kuzak and Simengaard had so sworn in good faith. He was equally certain Jurgens hadn't, and Lemaitre's expression was informative, to say the least. Hemphill, though. . . . He wasn't certain about Sonja. She simply looked back at him, and if her lips were tight, her aqua eyes were unflinching.

"I'm not suggesting that any one of us would use his or her vote for partisan purposes," he went on. One must, after all, be polite. "Nonetheless, each of us is a fallible human, and I'm certain all of us have considered the political ramifications."

"May I ask exactly what your point is, Sir?" Commodore Lemaitre asked stiffly. White Haven turned his cool, blue eyes on her, then shrugged.

"My point, Commodore, is that each of us should realize that our fellows are as aware of the political dimension as we are ourselves."

"It sounds to me, Sir, as if you *are* suggesting someone might cast a partisan vote," Lemaitre returned, "and I, for one, resent the imputation."

White Haven carefully said nothing about shoes that fit, but he smiled faintly, holding her eyes until she flushed and looked down at her blotter.

"You are, of course, free to place whatever interpretation you wish upon my remarks, Commodore," he said after a moment. "I will simply repeat that this will be a politically sensitive decision, as we all know, and add to that the fact that it should not be allowed to shape our perception of the evidence. That warning, and the need to issue it, comes with my other responsibilities as president of this court. Is that understood?"

Heads nodded again, though Jurgens looked as if he'd swallowed a fish bone. Lemaitre, however, didn't nod, and White Haven's gaze sharpened.

"I asked if that was understood, Commodore," he repeated softly. She twitched as if he'd pinched her, then nodded angrily. "Good," he said, voice still soft, and looked at the others. "In that case, is it your pleasure to cast your initial ballots without debate, ladies and gentlemen, or to open the floor to preliminary discussion of the charges and evidence?"

"I don't see any need for ballots, Sir." Jurgens spoke up instantly, as if he'd been primed and waiting, and his irritated voice was almost theatrically brusque. "The entire body of the charges is based on an illegal interpretation of the Articles of War. As such, they can have no merit."

There was a moment of absolute silence. Even Hemphill and Lemaitre seemed stunned, and Kuzak's poker face slipped enough to let contempt leak through. White Haven only nodded, lips pursed, and swung his chair gently from side to side.

"Perhaps you'd care to elaborate on that point, Admiral," he said after a moment, and Jurgens shrugged.

"The specifications allege that Lord Young broke off the action on his own initiative and then refused orders to return to formation. Whether or not that's an accurate description of his actions, and whether they showed good judgment or bad, doesn't affect the fact that he had every legal right to do so. Admiral Sarnow had been wounded and incapacitated, and all other flag officers of the task group had already died in action. As the acting commander of a heavy cruiser squadron, it was his responsibility to take the actions *he* felt were called for in the absence of orders to the contrary from competent authority. He may well have shown execrable judgment, but the judgment was legally *his* to make, and any other interpretation is nonsense."

"That's insane!" Thor Simengaard's deep, rumbling voice was a snarl of blunt disgust. "Tactical command hadn't been shifted from *Nike*—and he certainly had no way to know Sarnow had been wounded!"

"We're not discussing what Lord Young did or did not know." Jurgens glared at the captain, but, despite his junior status, Simengaard didn't even flinch. "We're discussing the *facts* of the case," the rear admiral went on, "and the facts are that Lord Young was senior to the woman who instructed him to return to formation. As such, he was not bound to obey her orders, and she, in fact, had no authority to give them."

"Are you suggesting she gave the *wrong* orders, Admiral?" Theodosia Kuzak asked in a cool, dangerous tone, and Jurgens' shoulders twitched again.

"With all due respect, Admiral, whether they were right or wrong has no bearing on their *legality*."

"And the fact that Admiral Sarnow, Admiral Danislav, Admiral Parks, an independent Captain's Board, and the General Board of Admiralty have all endorsed them in the strongest terms *also* has no bearing on the case?" Kuzak's quiet, measured voice dripped vitriol, and Jurgens flushed.

"Again, with all due respect, it does not," he said flatly.

"Just a moment, ladies and gentlemen." White Haven's raised hand cut off Kuzak's reply, and the members of the board looked back down the table at him. "I anticipated that this point might arise," he continued once he had their undivided attention, "and I asked the Judge Advocate General to address it for me." He laid a memo pad on the table and keyed it alive, but his eyes held Jurgens' rather than looking down at the small screen.

"This particular situation has never before arisen, but according to Vice Admiral Cordwainer, the precedents are clear. An officer's actions must be judged by two standards. First, by the situation which actually obtained at the moment of those actions; second, by the situation he *believed* obtained, based on the information available to him. Admiral Jurgens is correct that, in fact, Admiral Sarnow had been incapacitated. By the same token, however, Lord Young was under the impression that the admiral remained in command, and that Lady Harrington, as Admiral Sarnow's flag captain, was fully empowered to give him orders. As such, his refusal to obey her repeated order to return to formation constituted defiance of his legal, acting superior *to the best of his own, personal knowledge*. That, according to Admiral Cordwainer, is the reason the specifications were written as they were. He stands charged not with disobeying Captain Harrington, his junior, but with disobeying orders from the flagship which, so far as he then knew, had every legal right to issue those orders."

"Gobbledygook!" Jurgens snorted. "Lawyer's double-talk! What he knew or didn't know can't change the facts!"

"What he knew or didn't know *are* the facts of the matter, Sir," Simengaard returned sharply.

"Don't be absurd, Captain!" Lemaitre spoke up for the first time, dark eyes flashing. "You can't convict an officer who acted within the law simply because some *other* officer withheld critical information from him. It was Captain Harrington's duty to transfer command when Admiral Sarnow was wounded. The fact that she didn't do so makes *her* culpable, not him!"

"And just whom, do you suggest, should she have transferred command *to*, Commodore?" Kuzak asked. "The next surviving officer in the chain of command after Sarnow was Captain Rubenstein, but by his own sworn affidavit, his communications had been so badly damaged as to make it impossible to exercise tactical control from his ship."

"Then she should have transferred it to Captain Trinh," Lemaitre shot back. "*Intolerant*'s com facilities were unimpaired, and he was next in seniority to Captain Rubenstein."

"*Intolerant* was also under heavy fire, as was the entire task group," Kuzak replied in cold, dispassionate tones. "The tactical situation was as close to desperate as any I've ever reviewed. Any confusion in command at that moment could have led to catastrophe, and Dame Honor couldn't even know the extent of Trinh's current knowledge of the situation. Under the circumstances, she showed eminently sound judgment in refusing to risk disordering the task group's command at such a moment. Moreover, her actions led the enemy directly into the arms of Admiral Danislav's relieving force and left forty-three enemy ships no option but to surrender to him. Captain Young's actions, on the other hand, speak volumes about what *he* would have done in her place."

Kuzak's upper lip curled, and Lemaitre and Jurgens both flushed. It showed more clearly on Jurgens' pale, freckled complexion, but the commodore's face turned darker than ever.

"Even if Captain Harrington were a paragon of all the military virtues—a point I am not prepared to grant, Ma'am—she had still arrogated to herself a command authority which was not legally hers." Lemaitre bit off each word with furious precision. "Lord Young was not legally—*legally*, Ma'am!—bound to accept that authority, particularly when he was in fact senior to her. The details of the tactical situation can have no bearing on the law."

"I see." Kuzak regarded the commodore dispassionately for a moment, then smiled thinly. "Tell me, Commodore Lemaitre— when was the last time *you* exercised tactical command in a combat situation?"

Lemaitre's dark complexion paled. She opened her mouth to reply, but White Haven's knuckles rapped sharply on the table, swinging the disputants back toward him once more, and his face was hard.

"Allow me to point out, ladies and gentlemen, that Lady Harrington's actions have been approved at the highest level. She is not, has not been, and will not *be* charged with any wrongdoing."

His deep, measured voice was as hard as his expression, and Lemaitre clenched her jaw and looked away. Jurgens snorted derisively, but Sonja Hemphill sat in masklike silence.

"Having said that, this court undoubtedly has the right to consider any bearing her actions may have had on Lord Young's. Since this set of circumstances has never before arisen, we, like many a court-martial, are faced with the need to set precedent. The Judge Advocate General's brief makes it clear that an officer's understanding of the situation *is* an acceptable basis for determining the probity of his actions. Admittedly, it's a meterstick which is usually appealed to by the defense, not the prosecution, but that doesn't mean it applies in only one direction. Whether or not it's applied in this case, and how, lies in our hands. From that perspective—and that perspective *only*—Lady Harrington's actions and how Lord Young understood them are germane. This board will restrict itself to considering them in that light."

"Is that an order, Sir?" Jurgens asked through gritted teeth.

"It is the direction of the president of the court," White Haven returned coldly. "If you disagree with it, you are, of course, entitled to note your disagreement and take written exception to it. You are even—" he showed his own teeth in a humorless smile "—entitled to withdraw yourself from the court, if you so desire."

Jurgens glared at the earl but said nothing more. White Haven waited a moment, then leaned back in his chair once more.

"Shall we return to the discussion at hand?" he suggested, and Kuzak nodded sharply.

"The operable points, in my view," she said, "are, first, that the flagship had not passed command and that, in consequence, Dame Honor was, so far as Young then knew, legally empowered to give the orders she gave him. Second, that, without orders from *anyone*, he unilaterally withdrew his squadron from the support of the task group at a critical juncture. And, third, that he refused orders from the task group flagship to return to formation, even though all other ships then under his command did so. I believe the record is amply clear. He panicked; he ran; and he didn't *stop* running even after the other units of his command had done so."

"So you're saying the specifications are valid in every jot and tittle, are you?" Jurgens' tone was much more caustic than any a rear admiral should address to an admiral, and Kuzak regarded him as she might have a particularly disgusting form of insect life.

"I believe that's substantially what I said, Admiral Jurgens." Her voice was cold. "If you'd prefer for me to be plainer, however, I believe his actions were as contemptible as they were gutless, and that if any officer ever deserted in the face of the enemy, Pavel Young is certainly that man. Is that clear enough for you, *Admiral*?"

Jurgens turned purple and half-rose from his chair, and White Haven cleared his throat.

"We'll have no personal exchanges, ladies and gentlemen. This is a court-martial, not a shouting match. Formality may be relaxed to allow free discussion and decisions without respect to rank, but the rudiments of military courtesy will be observed. Please don't make me repeat that warning."

Jurgens sank back slowly, and the silence that followed was both fragile and sullen. White Haven let it linger a moment, then continued.

"Does anyone wish to bring forth any additional points for the court's consideration?" No one replied, and he gave a tiny shrug. "In that case, ladies and gentlemen, I suggest we vote on the specifications. Please indicate your votes on the forms before you."

Styluses scratched and paper rustled as the forms were folded and passed to the head of the table. He gathered them in a small heap, then opened them one by one, and his heart sank as he found what he'd expected.

"The vote is: guilty on all specifications, three; innocent on all specifications, three." He looked up with a thin smile. "It would seem we're going to be here a while, ladies and gentlemen."

✦ CHAPTER NINE

HONOR HARRINGTON LEANED BACK in her waiting room chair, eyes closed, and tried to pretend she was asleep. She doubted she was fooling anyone . . . and she *knew* she wasn't fooling Paul Tankersley. Nimitz was a soft, warm weight in her lap, and the 'cat's empathic sense linked her to Paul's emotions as he sat beside her. She'd felt his growing concern as the endless hours stretched longer and longer, and his matching worry had only made her own worse, but she was grateful for his willingness to leave her in peace, without the well-meant efforts at reassurance someone else might have inflicted upon her.

It was taking too long. From the moment she'd learned who was on the court, she'd feared only one thing, and every agonizing tick of the wait deepened that fear. The memory of the Queen's warning about the political considerations she had no choice but to face burned like acid in an open wound. A hung verdict would be almost worse than an acquittal, she thought wretchedly. A way for Young to walk, to flaunt the protection of his family's influence yet again, and she didn't know if she could endure that.

The conference room didn't *really* stink of sweat and stale hate, White Haven thought, but it still felt as if the air conditioner had packed it in. Not that he blamed it. The psychic ferocity of the last several hours had been more than enough to overwhelm any inanimate object unfortunate enough to be exposed to it.

He sat back in his chair, tunic hanging over its back, and rubbed his aching eyes, trying not to show his depression as the debate lapsed once more into stormy silence. Not that "debate," with its implications of discussion and reasoned argument, was the right word. There was no sign that any of the court's members—himself included, he admitted wearily—would yield even a fraction. Mindful of his position as president of the court, he'd let Kuzak and Simengaard carry the battle to Jurgens and Lemaitre. Sonja Hemphill had said even less than he—in fact, she'd said virtually nothing, despite her seniority—but the other two had more than compensated, and she'd voted in lockstep with them. They'd balloted on the charges eight more times with no change at all, and a dull, sick headache hammered in his temples.

"Look," he said finally, "we've been arguing for hours, and no one has even addressed the actual evidence or testimony." His voice sounded as tired as he felt, despite his effort to put energy into it. "Does anyone here question the facts as presented by the prosecution?"

No one replied, and he lowered his hand with a sigh.

"That's what I thought. And that means we're deadlocked not on what Lord Young did or didn't do, not on what Lady Harrington did or didn't do, but on the parameters we apply to our decision. We haven't moved a millimeter."

"And I don't believe we're *going* to . . . Sir." Jurgens voice had grown hoarse, but he met White Haven's eyes defiantly. "I contend, and will continue to contend, that Lord Young acted within the scope of the Articles of War, and that makes nonsense of this entire proceeding."

"I agree," Commodore Lemaitre said. Kuzak and Simengaard looked murderous, but White Haven raised a hand once more before either could speak.

"That's as may be, Admiral Jurgens," he said, "but I seriously doubt another board will share your view. If we return a hung verdict, the Admiralty will have no choice but to impanel another court—one whose decision will almost certainly be against Lord Young."

"In your own words, Sir, that's as may be," Jurgens replied. "I can only vote my conscience, based on my own understanding of the relevant law."

"Regardless of the political consequences to the war effort, Admiral. Is that it?" White Haven could have bitten his tongue off the instant he spoke, but it was too late, and Jurgens' eyes flamed as the words were finally said.

"I took an oath to decide this case based on the evidence and my understanding of the Articles of War, Sir," he said almost spitefully. "The political ramifications are beside the point. Since politics have been brought up, however, I will say that this entire *trial* is about politics. Its sole purpose is to convict Lord Young on a capital charge simply to help a cabal of politicians and senior officers wring political advantage from satisfying Captain Harrington's personal thirst for vengeance!"

"*What?!*" Thor Simengaard half rose, glaring across at his superior, and his huge fists gripped the table edge as if to reduce it to splinters.

"It's common knowledge, Captain," Jurgens snarled. "Harrington has hated Young ever since they were at the Academy together. Now she's the mob's darling, finally in a position to finish him off through this farce of a court-martial, and certain senior officers"—he kept his eyes fixed on Simengaard, refusing to look at White Haven—"are prepared to adopt any sort of legal mumbo-jumbo to give her his head on a platter and mobilize public opinion against the Opposition. Well, I, for one, won't be a party to it!"

A thick, inarticulate sound guttered in Simengaard's throat, but Lemaitre's sharp voice cut across it.

"I believe you've raised an excellent point, Admiral Jurgens." She turned her own glare on Simengaard. "And I might add that the Government's choice of Captain Harrington as their standard bearer in this matter is disturbing. *Highly* disturbing. Her record clearly demonstrates that she's hot-tempered and vindictive—and not simply where Lord Young is concerned, Captain. I need hardly remind you that she *assaulted* a Crown envoy in Yeltsin, nor that she attempted to murder POWs in her charge in that same system. Her tendency to insubordination and arrogance is clearly established, as well. I remind you of her testimony before the Weapons Development Board—testimony that was a direct attack upon Admiral Hemphill as its then chairwoman!"

Sonja Hemphill winced and raised a hand, only to let it fall as Lemaitre went on spitting out her exhausted anger.

"The woman is a menace! And I don't care who may have endorsed her actions in Hancock! No one is above the law, Captain Simengaard—*no one!*—and it is my intention, following this court-martial, to request the Judge Advocate General, on my own authority, to thoroughly investigate her conduct with an eye to possible charges of mutiny arising from her brazen usurpation of command authority in Hancock!"

"I'll endorse that request, Commodore," Jurgens snapped, and Simengaard and Kuzak exploded almost in unison.

White Haven slumped in his chair, aghast at what his slip of the tongue had unleashed. Rank was forgotten as the four officers leaned across the table, shouting at one another in a tidal wave of fury. Only Sonja Hemphill sat silent, her expression sick, as the solemnity of a court-martial disintegrated.

The earl shook his head like an exhausted fighter, and then he rose to his feet and slammed both fists on the table like white-knuckled sledgehammers.

"Silence!"

His bellow shook the room, and the disputants jerked around as one to stare at him. The naked fury on his face stunned them wordless, and he braced himself on the polished conference table as he glared at them all.

"Sit down!" he snapped. They hesitated, and his lips drew back in a snarl. *"Now!"* he barked, and the explosive syllable drove them back into their chairs like a blow.

"You will all now listen to me," he went on in an icy, over-controlled voice, "because I will say this only once. I will have the next person who raises his or her voice in this room, on either side of the discussion, for any reason, regardless of rank, up on charges for conduct unbecoming! *Is that clear?"* Crackling silence answered for them, and he inhaled deeply and forced himself back down in his own chair.

"This is a court-martial. Whatever our views or disagreements, we will conduct ourselves as senior officers of Her Majesty's Navy and not as a bunch of juvenile hooligans. If you cannot maintain the rudiments of common civility in the give and take of normal conversation, then I will impose formal parliamentary rules of procedure and recognize each of you, individually."

Kuzak and Simengaard looked abashed and ashamed, and Lemaitre looked frightened and sullen. Only Jurgens returned the earl's glare measure for measure, and there was no give in his face.

"With all due respect, Admiral White Haven," the effort it took to keep his voice level was obvious, "there's no point in further deliberation. This is a hung court. Whatever certain members of the board want, they're not going to get a vote to convict. In my opinion, you, as president of the court, have only one option."

"Indeed, Admiral Jurgens? And what might my single option be?" The calm in White Haven's voice was deadly.

"To announce that we are unable to reach a verdict and recommend that all charges be dropped."

"Dropped?" Simengaard strangled his incredulous response just short of a shout, and Jurgens jerked a nod without ever looking away from White Haven.

"Dropped." He didn't try to hide his triumph. "As you yourself have pointed out, Admiral, the political situation is critical. A decision to retry Lord Young would only make that crisis worse. As president, you have the right to make whatever recommendation you like, but the *decision* will be made at a higher level, and I doubt very much that Duke Cromarty will thank the Admiralty for pursuing the matter. Under the circumstances, the most constructive thing you can do is advise against a retrial. Such a recommendation from within the Service would give the Government an out, a graceful way for it to drop the charges so that Duke Cromarty—and the Opposition—can put this all behind them and get on with the war."

White Haven's clenched jaw ached with fury at the vicious satisfaction in Jurgens' tone. The man had taken the gloves off at last. He was no longer even pretending, for this was the end to which he'd worked from the beginning.

"A moment, Admiral White Haven." Theodosia Kuzak's frozen-helium voice quivered with the effort it cost her to restrain her own temper, and her eyes were jade ice as she looked at Jurgens.

"Admiral Jurgens, you've seen the evidence. You *know*, as well as anyone else in this room, that Pavel Young panicked. That he ran. That by pulling out he exposed his comrades—other members of the Queen's Service—to enemy fire, and that scores, probably hundreds, of them died as a result. You *know* that. Forget about any enmity for or by Lady Harrington. Forget about the letter of the law or his 'understanding of the situation.' He betrayed his oath and his comrades, and they know he did it, and this court is charged with far more than merely determining his guilt or innocence. Fine, narrow distinctions of law and clever legal tactics may have their place in a civilian court, but this is a *military* court. We're also charged with protecting the Queen's Navy. With insuring its discipline and safeguarding its morale and fighting power. You know—you *must* know—what the larger consequences will be if the Fleet discovers we refuse to punish arrant cowardice! Are you telling us that, knowing all that, you're still willing to use specious legalisms and political pressure to save *scum* like Young from a firing squad? My God, man! Can't you see what you're *doing*?"

Jurgens looked away from her and hunched his shoulders, and she turned to Lemaitre and Hemphill.

"Can't *any* of you see?" She was no longer furious. She was pleading with them. "Are all three of you prepared to just sit there and see this disgrace to our uniform and honor *walk away*?"

Commodore Lemaitre shifted in her chair and joined Jurgens in refusing to meet Kuzak's gaze, but Sonja Hemphill raised her head. She looked all around the table, then locked almost defiant eyes with her fellow admiral.

"No, Admiral Kuzak," she said softly. "I'm *not* prepared to see that."

Jurgens' head whipped up. He and Lemaitre both turned on Hemphill, their faces incredulous, and Jurgens started to suck in air to speak. But Hemphill ignored them to swivel her gaze to White Haven, and the corners of her tight mouth twitched with the ghost of a smile as she saw the matching astonishment in his eyes.

"I will not vote to convict Lord Young of the capital charges against him, Sir." Her voice was low, but her words were crisp in the stillness. "Whether he was legally within his rights to refuse Lady Harrington's orders or whether he was bound by his understanding of the situation to accept them is immaterial to that decision."

She paused, and White Haven nodded slowly. That simple statement might well be construed as abandonment of her sworn impartiality, but at least she'd had the honesty to admit the truth. Unlike Jurgens or Lemaitre.

"At the same time, I will not allow a man like Lord Young to escape punishment," she went on in that same level voice. "Whatever the legal right or wrong of his actions, they were inexcusable. Accordingly, I have a . . . compromise to suggest."

Someone knocked on the waiting room door. Honor twitched in her chair, astonished to realize she actually *had* managed to nod off, then opened her eyes. She turned her head, and an expressionless Admiralty yeoman wearing a court-martial brassard looked back at her from the doorway

"The Court will reconvene in ten minutes, ladies and gentlemen," the yeoman announced. He withdrew, and she barely heard him knocking on another door through the sudden thunder of her pulse.

There were fewer spectators than before, but witnesses freed from their formal segregation once they'd testified made up some of the numbers, and the entire audience seemed to be in motion as it flowed out to find places. Not even the usual advantage of Honor's height let her see clearly, and she clung painfully tight to Paul's hand. She hated that sign of weakness, but she couldn't stop herself, and Nimitz was taut and quivering on her shoulder. They inched their way down the central aisle, and suddenly she was almost afraid to look at the judges already reassembled in their places behind the long table.

She and Paul found chairs and sat, and she drew a deep, deep breath. She raised her eyes to the court—and gasped as relief stabbed like a knife.

Admiral White Haven sat square-shouldered and silent, Pavel Young's sword lying on his blotter, and the hilt was toward him.

She felt herself begin to tremble, heard the sudden, rising murmur of voices as others noted the sword's position, and a harsh, choking sound came from her right. She turned toward it, and her mouth tightened as she saw the monstrously obese man in the counter-grav life-support chair. The Earl of North Hollow's fat face was pasty white, his eyes shocked. Both of Young's younger brothers sat with their father, flanking his chair, and their faces were almost as pale as his. Something deep inside her said she should feel pity for North Hollow, that however loathsome Young might be, he was the earl's *son*. But she couldn't. Perhaps worse, she didn't even want to.

There was a fresh stir, and then the sharp, musical notes of the bell as White Haven struck it once more with the small hammer.

"This court is in session," the admiral announced, and nodded to the Marines flanking the side door. One of them vanished through it, and the entire courtroom held its breath. Then the door reopened, and Pavel Young marched through it, flanked by his guards.

Young's bearded face worked. His fight to keep it blank was obvious, but his cheeks twitched and sweat gleamed on his forehead. The wait had been agonizing for her, Honor thought; it must have been a foretaste of Hell for him, and she was shocked by how glad that made her feel.

Young hardly even saw her. His eyes were locked straight ahead, as if keeping them there could delay the inevitable moment just a few more seconds. But then he reached the defense table and turned toward the judges, and he could delay no longer. His gaze dropped to the sword, and his heart stopped.

The point was toward him. The point was *toward* him, and a sudden wave of terror engulfed him as that single, horrible fact penetrated.

He felt himself trembling and tried to stop it, but he couldn't. Nor could he keep his head from turning, stop himself from looking over his shoulder. His eyes met his father's, raw with panic and desperate appeal, and his father's expression of frightened, furious impotence drove a dagger of terror into his belly. He wrenched his gaze away, and not even the hatred as he saw his one-time executive officer sitting beside Harrington—sitting there holding the bitch's *hand!*—could penetrate the ice about his soul.

"The prisoner will face the court."

White Haven's cold voice cut through the stillness, and Young's head snapped around in sheer, mechanical reflex. He swallowed, trying not to sway in numb despair, and White Haven cleared his throat.

"Captain Lord Young, you have been tried by court-martial on the specifications named against you. Are you prepared to hear its verdict?"

He swallowed again. And then a third time, trying to moisten his kiln-dry mouth as the proceedings' drawn out, formal agony flayed his nerves. It was like some exquisite torture, yet he was trapped within it, and some last flicker of pride gave him the strength.

"Yes." The word came out hoarse but clear, and White Haven nodded.

"Very well. On the first specification of the charges, that you did violate the Twenty-Third Article of War, this court, by vote of four to two, finds you guilty as charged." Someone groaned behind him—his father, he thought—and his own hands clenched at his sides as White Haven's voice rolled out, deep and dispassionate as doomsday.

"On the second specification of the charges, that you did violate the Twenty-Sixth Article of War, this court, by vote of four to two, finds you guilty as charged.

"On the third specification of the charges, that your actions did expose other units of the task group to severe damage and casualties, this court, by vote of four to two, finds you guilty as charged.

"On the fourth specification of the charges," even through his sick despair, Young heard White Haven's voice shift, "that your actions constituted and did result from personal cowardice, this court, having voted three for conviction and three for acquittal, has been unable to reach a verdict."

There was a louder, more incredulous chorus of gasps, and Young twitched in disbelief. *Unable to reach a verdict?* That—

"On the fifth specification," White Haven continued in that same, flat tone, "that your actions did constitute desertion in the face of the enemy as defined by the Fourteenth, Fifteenth, and Nineteenth Articles of War, this court, having voted three for conviction and three for acquittal, has been unable to reach a verdict."

Pavel Young felt the stir of shocked hope. A hung verdict. They'd reached a *hung verdict* on the only two charges that really counted, the only ones that could send him before a firing squad! Electricity sparkled up and down his nerves, and the sound of his own breathing was harsh in his nostrils.

"Inability to reach a verdict," White Haven said flatly, "does not constitute an acquittal, but the accused enjoys the presumption of innocence. Accordingly, the court has no option at this time but to dismiss the fourth and fifth specifications of the charges against you."

Honor Harrington sat stiff and still in her chair, paralyzed by a horror that had matched each surge of Pavel Young's relief. Again. He'd done it *again*. The first three specifications weren't even enough to get him out of uniform—not with his family's power. Half-pay, letters of censure, yes. As Lady Morncreek had promised, he would be beached forever, never to serve on active duty again, but it wouldn't matter. He'd evaded execution and beaten the system where it truly counted, for the Admiralty would never refile charges in such a politically divisive trial and climate, and she wanted to vomit as the sudden relaxation of his shoulders told her he'd realized the same thing.

Admiral White Haven was still speaking, yet it was merely noise without meaning. She could only sit there, frozen in a moment of petrified sickness. But then, suddenly, the meaningless noise became words once more, and she felt Paul's hand tighten on hers like a talon.

" . . . the duty of this court," White Haven was saying, "to decide the penalty which attaches to the crimes of which you stand convicted, and it is the view of a two-thirds majority of the court, irrespective of the votes on specifications four and five of the charges against you, that your conduct in course of the Battle of Hancock demonstrates a culpable negligence and lack of character which exceed any acceptable in an officer of Her Majesty's Navy. This court therefore rules, by vote of four to two, that the accused, Captain Lord Pavel Young, shall be stripped of all rank, rights, privileges, and prerogatives as a captain in the Royal Manticoran Navy and dishonorably dismissed the Service as unfit to wear the Queen's uniform, judgment to be executed within three days of this hour.

"This court stands adjourned."

The clear, sweet notes of the bell sang once more. They

struck through Honor like bolts of cleansing silver lightning, but they were something very different for Pavel Young. They were almost worse than execution. A deliberate dismissal, as if he were too far beneath contempt—too *petty*—even to shoot. The knowledge that he'd been spared execution only to endure the disgrace of a formal expulsion from the Service and a lifetime as an object of disdain.

He swayed in an ashen-faced horror immeasurably more agonizing for his momentary belief that he'd escaped destruction. The dead, stunned silence of the whipsawed spectators was pregnant with the first as yet unspoken whispers of his shame, and his soul writhed in anticipation of the rising background murmur. And then he jerked as a shrill, electronic wail sounded behind him.

He couldn't place it. For a heartbeat, two—three—he heard it with no recognition at all, and then he wheeled in sudden understanding.

The medical alert screamed, tearing at his nerves, and he stared, unable to move, as the Earl of North Hollow slumped flaccidly forward in his wailing life-support chair.

✧ CHAPTER TEN

"MY GOD."

Paul Tankersley's murmur mingled bemusement with incredulity, and Honor turned her head on the pillow of his shoulder to see why it did. The RMN took pains over its battlecruiser captains' comfort, which meant her sleeping cabin aboard *Nike* was larger and considerably more palatial than his quarters aboard *Hephaestus*. Now they lay comfortably intertwined in her wide bed, still just a bit sweaty, still just a little flushed, and glowing with shared pleasure.

Not that pleasure was what had provoked Paul's comment. He'd expressed himself eloquently, if wordlessly, on that topic already; now he watched the most recent broadcast from the city of Landing with something very like awe.

"I can't believe it," he said after a moment. "*Look* at that, Honor!"

"I'd rather not." She closed her eyes and inhaled his strong, warm scent, savoring the texture of his long hair trapped between her right cheek and his shoulder. "I'm just as glad they're chasing someone else, but I'm not all that interested in Young. He won't be bothering *me* again. Frankly, that's all I really care about, where he's concerned."

"That's just a tad narrow of you, my love," Paul mock-scolded. "This is an historical moment. How many men, do you suppose, get cashiered and inherit an earldom in three minutes flat?"

Honor made a face of distaste and opened her eyes just as the screen of her bedside terminal cut from file footage of the latest demonstrations outside Parliament to a well-lit HD set. The flat screen lacked the rich dimensional detail of a proper HD, and the sound was down, but she recognized

Minerva Prince and Patrick DuCain of the syndicated *Into the Fire*, and their guests. Sir Edward Janacek and Lord Hayden O'Higgins were both retired first lords of admiralty, but they held very different convictions and, just as the choice of guests mirrored the political fracture lines, so did today's backdrop: two enormous holos, one of Pavel Young and one of Honor herself, glaring at one another. She didn't need the sound to guess the topic, but Paul twitched the volume up anyway, and she grimaced.

"—what extent, in your opinion, does this affect the balance in the Lords, Sir Edward?" the heavyset DuCain asked, and Janacek shrugged.

"That's very difficult to say, Pat. I don't believe the situation's ever arisen before, after all. Certainly Lord Young—excuse me, Earl North Hollow—*must* be admitted to the Lords. The result of the court-martial will be something of a political embarrassment to him, but he *is* a peer, and the law is clear. That means the balance between the parties will remain unchanged, and, frankly, given the court's blatantly partisan vote, I hardly think—"

"*Partisan?*" Lord O'Higgins interrupted. "Hogwash! That was hardly a one-party court, Ed, and it voted to cashier him by a two-thirds margin!"

"Of course it was partisan!" Janacek snapped back. "Whatever the vote, it was impaneled—under an officer who's both the Chancellor of the Exchequer's brother *and* one of Captain Harrington's strongest supporters—solely to embarrass the Opposition. There were numerous irregularities in Hancock, and not simply on Lord Young—Earl North Hollow's—part. Indeed, some of us are convinced the wrong captain was tried in the first place, and if you think for one moment the Opposition will take this insult lying down, you're sadly mistaken. Duke Cromarty and his Government can play party politics in a time of crisis if they wish, but be assured that the Opposition will call them to account for it!"

"Are you suggesting the court's membership was rigged, Sir Edward?" Minerva Prince demanded. Janacek started to reply, then closed his mouth tightly and cocked an eyebrow in knowing fashion.

"Poppycock!" O'Higgins snorted. "Sir Edward can suggest what he likes, but he knows as well as I that human interference in the selection of officers for courts-martial is impossible! The Admiralty computers select them at random, and the defense is entitled to examine the electronic records of the entire selection process. If there were any sort of chicanery, why didn't Young or his counsel move to strike the board's suspect members *then*?"

"Well, Sir Edward?" DuCain asked, and Janacek shrugged irritably.

"Of course it wasn't 'rigged,'" he admitted. "But the decision to proceed with the trial at all under such polarized, prejudicial circumstances reflects both utter disregard for reasoned judicial process and the worst sort of reckless, petty party politics. It can only be seen as—"

"Why is it, Sir Edward," O'Higgins interrupted again, "that anything the Government does is 'petty party politics,' but anything the Opposition tries to pull is high-minded statesmanship? Wake up and smell the coffee before plain old arrogance and stupidity cost you the twelve Commons seats you still hold!"

"Should we understand that you support the Government's position on the trial and the declaration of war, then, Lord O'Higgins?" Prince asked, cutting off any response from Janacek, and O'Higgins shrugged.

"Certainly I support Duke Cromarty's position on the declaration. But I can't support his position on the Young courtmartial because the Government hasn't *taken* one. That's the point I keep trying to get through to my somewhat dense colleague. This was a military trial, under military law, on charges recommended by a formal board of inquiry convened immediately after the battle. More than that, one of the three supposedly pro-Young members of the court *must* have concurred in the guilty verdicts and Young's sentence."

"What d'you mean, 'pro-Young'?" Janacek demanded hotly. "Are you suggesting there was some sort of plot to get him off?"

"*Heavens*, no! Surely you don't think I'm suggesting that some sort of *deal* was struck, do you?"

"What sort of deal, Lord O'Higgins?" DuCain cut in once more, with more haste than grace, before a puce-faced Janacek could explode.

"I find it remarkable that Young was convicted on all specifications *except* those which carried a death sentence," O'Higgins replied in a colder, much more serious tone. "I find it especially remarkable given that the grounds for his dismissal from the Service were stated in almost precisely the language which would have been used if those capital charges had been sustained. I'm only a private citizen these days, but, to me, that combination suggests that someone who voted against the charges still believed he was guilty of them. If so, I'm disturbed that whoever it was refused to vote his or her conscience and convict, since that tends to indicate the triumph of politics over evidence. But at least they wanted him out of the Service and had the moral courage to see to it that happened. And thank God for it! If anyone who'd demonstrated this level of cowardice escaped with a mere slap on the wrist, the Navy—"

"That's monstrous!" Janacek snapped. "My God—your own precious court-martial refused to convict him of cowardice! Isn't it enough for you that he's been smeared and dishonored? That his father *died* of a stroke when he heard the verdict? How much longer do you intend to hound him?!"

"Until Hell freezes over, if necessary," O'Higgins said coldly. "He's the most contemptible example of—"

"How *dare* you?!" Janacek exploded. "I'll have you—"

"Gentlemen! Gentlemen, *please!*" Prince waved her hands in manicured distress, but DuCain only sat there, fighting a losing battle against laughter, as both ex-first lords ignored the anchorwoman to tear into one another. And then, suddenly, the shouting guests and their hosts vanished as the program's director cut to a commercial break.

Honor shook her head slowly, then turned to glare at Paul. Her undutiful lover was convulsed with laughter, and she snatched the control unit from his hand. The terminal went blank as she switched it off and tossed the remote onto the bedside table.

"Oh, that's just too hilarious for words, Paul!" she snapped. "Aren't they *ever* going to let this thing rest?"

"S-s-sorry!" Paul gasped, fighting to control his laughter, and his eyes were truly repentant. "It's just—" He shrugged helplessly, lips quivering with a rebellious smile.

"Maybe it *is* funny, in a macabre sort of way," Honor sighed, "but I hate it. *Hate* it! And I still can't poke my nose off the ship without some stupid reporter trying to pounce!"

"I know, love." His face had sobered, and he squeezed her tight. "But you're stuck in the repair slip where they can lurk for you, at least until *Hephaestus* turns *Nike* loose. So I'm afraid you're just going to have to put up with it until this whole thing blows over."

"If it ever does," Honor said dourly.

"Oh, it will. It's barely been a full day, you know. I'd think a lot of the sensationalism should die down once they formally bust Young out."

"You hope, you mean. There's still his investiture into the Lords, and the little matter of the declaration of war. I—"

Honor broke off as the sleeping cabin hatch hissed open

and Nimitz flowed into the compartment. He leapt onto the foot of the bed and sat up on his rearmost limbs, head cocked, and Honor frowned as he turned his bright green eyes on her. Neither she nor Paul were bothered by their nakedness, for while Nimitz was clearly pleased for them, human amatory adventures simply didn't interest treecats—which meant he was here for some other reason.

She concentrated on the link between them. The empathic 'cats had always been able to sense human emotions, but as far as she knew, no other human had ever been able to sense a 'cat's emotions in return. *She* certainly hadn't been able to do so, not with any reliability, until two T-years ago, and her sensitivity to Nimitz's feelings was still growing. The change was just a bit disturbing, after almost forty years together, but it was a pleasant sort of disturbance . . . though she hadn't reported it to anyone else.

Paul had figured it out, and so, she suspected, had Mike Henke, James MacGuiness, and her parents. No one else had, and she trusted those five to keep her secret. She wasn't certain why that was important to her, but it was.

Now Nimitz sat patiently, gazing into her eyes while she worked on divining his message. It wasn't easy when all they could pass back and forth were emotions and a few extremely vague images, but she'd been practicing, and suddenly she chuckled out loud.

"What?" Paul asked.

"I think we'd better get dressed," Honor replied.

"Why?" Paul sat up on his elbows, eyebrows raised, and she grinned as she rose and reached for the silk kimono her mother had given her.

"Mac's about to make up his mind to disturb us, and I'd hate to shock him."

"Mac," Tankersley said wryly, "knows all about us, my love. He's certainly covered for us often enough."

Honor's grin turned into a smile of agreement. Her steward was twice her age and often seemed to regard her as a reckless adolescent without the sense to check the lock pressure before she stepped into it. But while he might fuss and fidget and certainly wasn't above manipulating her (always for her own good, of course), he was also the very soul of discretion. She knew he kept track of Paul's visits and acted to intercept any disturbance, for which she was profoundly grateful. He was also pleased for her, and that was even more important.

"I'm fully aware he knows about us," she said now. "That's the problem. He's afraid we might be, um, occupied, and if he screens me and I have to accept audio only, he's going to be sure he interrupted. So put some clothes on, exhibitionist!"

"Orders, orders, orders," Paul grumbled. He reached for a robe of his own and stood, then gathered his hair behind his head, and she watched with a touch of envy. Her own hair was finally long enough to gather in a ponytail—in fact, she *had* to do so whenever she wore a helmet—but Paul's hair hung down in a longer, thicker tail than any she could attain, though she was working on fixing that. Burying her face and fingers in his hair was so delightful she intended to make it a mutual exercise.

She chuckled and watched herself in a mirror as she ran a brush over her own silky mop. It was less curly than it had been; or, rather, its *ends* were just as curly as ever, but the strands were settling into a sort of elegant wave as they grew longer. She was glad of it, too. For a time she'd been afraid she'd have to wear it the same way Mike wore hers, and the ancient style called an "Afro" for reasons lost in the mists of etiology would have been just a bit too overpowering on someone Honor's size.

She grinned again at the thought and slid the brush into its storage space. She'd just put it away and rebelted her kimono when her terminal beeped.

"See?" she said smugly to Paul, and pressed the acceptance key. "Hi, Mac. What can I do for you?"

MacGuiness smiled from her screen at her cheerful tone, his relief that he hadn't, in fact, intruded at a delicate moment obvious.

"I'm sorry to disturb you, Ma'am, but Commander Chandler has passed two messages for you."

"Ah?" Honor cocked an eyebrow, and mental gears meshed as she dropped into her captain's persona. "What sorts of messages, Mac?"

"I believe the first is simply an update on the dockmaster's repair schedule, Ma'am. I haven't viewed it, of course, but Commander Chandler assured me it could wait until supper. I'm afraid the other is a bit more pressing, however. I believe it's from Admiral White Haven."

"Admiral White Haven?" Honor's spine stiffened, and MacGuiness nodded. "Does it carry any special priority?"

"No, Ma'am. But since it was from a flag officer—" MacGuiness shrugged slightly, and she nodded. Any admiral's message automatically carried a priority no lesser mortal could match.

"Understood, Mac. They're in the system?"

"Queued in your message bin, Ma'am."

"Thank you. I'll get right on them."

"Of course, Ma'am."

MacGuiness cut the circuit and vanished. Honor punched the playback key, and the screen relit with Eve Chandler's face.

"Mac tells me you're not available, Ma'am," *Nike*'s exec said, "and this isn't urgent enough to disturb you, but I thought you'd like to know we've finally got the go ahead to pull Graser Six for complete replacement."

Chandler's tone was almost gloating, and Honor's smile matched it. Graser Six had suffered serious collateral damage from the hit that took out Graser Eight, but *Hephaestus'* surveyors had argued that it could be repaired "good as new." Repair would have the virtue of saving something like fourteen million dollars—if they were right; if they were *wrong*, HMS *Nike* might just find her starboard broadside ten percent short the next time she went into action. Ivan Ravicz, Honor's senior engineer, was adamant on the need for replacement, and she and Chandler had gone to the mat with Vice Admiral Cheviot in his support. It hadn't been easy, but Honor's arguments had been bolstered by Paul's behind the scenes coaching, and it sounded as if they'd paid off.

"The dockmaster's promised to start on it first thing tomorrow," Chandler went on. She glanced down at something as if checking notes, then shrugged. "That's about it, except that he also says they'll have Boat Bay One back up by Wednesday. That's almost a week ahead of schedule, and it kills two birds for us. It'll simplify our boat traffic enormously, and with pressure in the bay galleries again, we won't have to worry about the integrity of the emergency seals on CIC. That means the yard dogs can work unsuited in the compartment, which should cut a few days off the schedule for that, too." She looked back up at her com's pickup and smiled. "They're still not as fast as Hancock Base was, Ma'am, but they're learning! Chandler, clear."

"Well, well, well! It's about time we got some *good* news around here," Honor said with undisguised pleasure as the screen blanked once more.

"Beg pardon?" Paul poked his head out a hatch behind her in a cloud of steam. "Were you talking to me?"

"Yes, I suppose I was." Honor gave him a smile over her shoulder. She hadn't even noticed him leaving the sleeping cabin, but it was typical of him. He never intruded into the internal affairs of her command, and he had a habit of finding somewhere else to be whenever she had to tend to anything that might remotely be considered privileged information.

"What about?" he asked now.

"According to Eve, we're getting replacement on Graser Six after all."

"You are? Outstanding! May I assume my own humble contributions to your case had something to do with it?"

"I wouldn't be surprised, but the important thing is that Admiral Cheviot finally told those useless bean counters in Survey to get their fingers out and listen to the *real* Navy for a change."

"Now, now, Honor! You shouldn't talk that way about Survey. After all, *I* used to do survey work, and you bluff, simple-minded spacedogs simply aren't equipped to understand the pressures they face. Of course, *my* recommendations were always unencumbered by anything so unworthy as the impact of cost considerations on efficiency ratings, but few individuals possess my resolute and fearless character. Most survey specialists toss and turn all night, bathed in cold sweat, clutching empty bottles of cheap rotgut in their palsied hands as futile protection against nightmares about their next cost accountability inspection." He shook his head sadly. "The last thing they need is some captain with an ironclad case for spending money on his ship."

"Poor babies. I weep for them."

"Bless you, my child. Such sympathy becomes you." Paul could manage an amazingly unctuous tone when he wanted to, and she grinned as he raised a hand in benediction. But then a buzzer sounded from the far side of the hatch, and he yelped in alarm. "Shut-off warning on the hot water! Gotta run!"

He disappeared back into the head before the sensors which had noted his absence shut down the shower, and Honor chuckled and punched for the next message in the queue. The screen flickered once more, and the Earl of White Haven's face appeared before her.

"Good afternoon, Dame Honor," he said formally. "I've just received notification that the Fifth Battlecruiser Squadron will be reassigned to Home Fleet when its repairs are completed. I realize you don't have your orders to that effect yet, but, in fact, you're being attached to Task Force Four."

Honor sat straighter and her eyes lit. After its losses in Hancock, she'd been half afraid BCS Five would be disbanded. Now she knew it wouldn't be, and assignment to TF Four would put it under White Haven's direct command.

"Your official notification should come through in the next day or so," the admiral continued, "and my understanding is that Admiral Mondeau will be taking over from Admiral Sarnow.

Of course, you'll need at least another couple of months to complete your repairs, and the Admiralty is still looking for replacement ships to bring you up to strength, so I don't anticipate her momentary arrival, but I've spoken to her, and she intends to retain *Nike* as the squadron flag. That means you're going to be one of my flag captains, and I thought I'd screen to welcome you aboard."

Honor's satisfaction turned into a broad grin. Two back-to-back stints as flag captain—and to two different admirals, at that—was an enormous professional compliment, and she looked forward to serving under White Haven's command. She didn't put much stock in the media's chewed-over reports that he was some sort of secret patron of hers. That sounded too much like an Opposition-sponsored rumor intended to attack the court-martial's verdict, but she respected him enormously. And the fact that he was one of the Navy's star commanders should guarantee the squadron a place at the heart of the action, once the House of Lords got off its collective backside and voted to declare war on the Peeps.

"In the meantime, however," the admiral went on, "I would very much appreciate it if you could join me for supper this evening. There are a few points I want to discuss with you as soon as possible. Please com back by fourteen hundred to confirm. White Haven, clear."

The screen blanked, and Honor sat back on the bed and rubbed the tip of her nose. His tone had changed there at the very end. She couldn't quite put her finger on just what that change had been or what it might mean, but it had been there. A bit of . . . caution? Worry? Whatever it was hadn't seemed to be aimed at *her*, yet he clearly had something more than supper on his mind.

She sighed and shook her head, then rose and shed her kimono. Whatever it was could wait. Right now, she had a man in her shower, which was entirely too good an opportunity to waste.

✧ CHAPTER ELEVEN

BOSUN'S PIPES TWITTERED, THE SIDE party snapped to attention, and the young lieutenant at its head saluted as Honor stepped into HMS *Queen Caitrin*'s boat bay. She managed not to smile, retaining her cool, calm captain's expression while Nimitz preened on her shoulder, as if all the stir were in his personal honor, yet satisfaction of her own flickered when she saw the officer waiting beyond the side party. The stupendous superdreadnought dwarfed her own command, but Earl White Haven's flag captain had come down in person to greet her.

"Welcome aboard, Lady Harrington." Captain Frederick Goldstein had the professional stature one might have expected of Admiral White Haven's flag captain. He was not only one of the RMN's most respected captains, but one of its most senior, as well. Rumor had him on the next short list for flag rank, and he smiled in genuine welcome.

"Thank you, Sir," she said, gripping his hand, and his smile grew.

"I imagine you're just as happy to get out of *Nike* without meeting a newsie," he suggested, and it was Honor's turn to smile.

"I'm afraid they *have* gotten to be more than a bit of a pain, Sir."

"Just between us, Dame Honor, they always have been. And, also just between us, let me take this chance to congratulate you on Hancock. That was well done, Captain. Very well done."

"Thank you, Sir," Honor said again with quiet sincerity. An officer like Goldstein knew exactly what Hancock must have been like, and that made a compliment from him more precious than any amount of civilian adulation. "I wish I could take the credit," she added, "but it was Admiral Sarnow's battle plan, and we had good people to make it work. And we were lucky, too."

"I don't doubt it." Goldstein's eyes approved her tone as much as her words. "I know Mark Sarnow, and I know what sort of squadron he must've put together. But it took sense, and guts, to take advantage of what he gave you and keep going when it all fell in your lap. Some people wouldn't have—like a certain officer whose name we won't mention."

Honor bobbed her head in silent acknowledgment, and Goldstein motioned for her to accompany him from the boat bay gallery. He was shorter than she, which forced her to shorten her stride slightly as they walked down the passage, but he moved with brisk, quick energy and waved her into the lift ahead of him. The trip was a lengthy one—not surprisingly, given *Queen Caitrin*'s size—but it didn't seem that way. Goldstein had been White Haven's flag captain ever since the earl had shifted his flag to *Queen Caitrin* before the battles of Third Yeltsin, Chelsea, and Mendoza, and he laid them out for her in clear, concise detail in response to her questions. The first of those engagements had dwarfed Hancock's scale, yet he managed to distill its essence into a few, crisp sentences. Not that he used brevity to depress her pretension in asking. Indeed, he made all three battles come alive in a way no official after-action report could have, and he did it without lecturing or condescending. It was a professional discussion between equals, despite the difference in their ages and seniority, and Honor felt more than a little regret when they reached Admiral White Haven's cabin at last and Goldstein bade her farewell with another handshake. But it wasn't until the admiral's Marine sentry had announced her that she suddenly wondered *why* he'd excused himself. He was the admiral's flag captain, and she was about to join the task force in the same capacity for another admiral. Surely this would have been an excellent opportunity for them to get to know one another . . . unless there was some reason White Haven wanted to see her alone?

An eyebrow crooked at the thought, but she smoothed it quickly as the hatch slid open and she found herself face to face with the admiral himself.

"Dame Honor." White Haven held out his hand in welcome. "It's good to see you again. Please, come in."

Honor obeyed the invitation, and memories of their last meeting replayed in her mind. That had been after the Second Battle of Yeltsin, and she had to suppress a smile as she remembered his lecture on the virtue of restraining her temper. Not that she hadn't deserved it, but since then she'd heard a few tales about times when he'd lost *his* temper which gave a certain "do as I say, not as I do" air to his admonition. On the other hand, one of the more famous episodes had singed every hair on then-Admiral Sir Edward Janacek's head, and White Haven had spent four T-years dirt-side on half-pay when Janacek became First Lord, so perhaps his warning had come from hard experience.

"Have a seat," White Haven went on, waving her toward an armchair. His steward appeared almost as silently as MacGuiness could have managed, offering her a glass of wine, and she accepted it with a murmured thanks.

The tall, dark-haired admiral sank into a facing chair and leaned back, then raised his own wineglass in Honor's direction.

"To a job very well done, Dame Honor," he said, and this time she blushed. It was one thing when a fellow captain, however senior, complimented her, but only nine active-duty officers in the entire Royal Navy were senior to Earl White Haven. She nodded her silent thanks, unable to think of a verbal response that wouldn't sound either stuffy or foolish, and his answering smile was almost gentle, touched with understanding and a trace of compassion.

"Not to embarrass you, Dame Honor, but I've seen how the newsies are chewing you up over this whole court-martial business. It's become more important to them, somehow, than what you and your people did in Hancock. That's more than a little disgusting, but it's also how politics often seem to work. The Fleet, however, knows better . . . as do I. I wish I could say I was surprised by your performance, but I know your record, and Hancock was no less than I would have expected of you. That's one reason I specifically requested BatCruRon Five's assignment to TF Four, and I'm delighted the Admiralty saw fit to grant that request."

"I—" Honor paused and cleared her throat, half-stunned by the immensity of the implied compliment. "Thank you, Sir. I appreciate it, and I hope you'll continue to be pleased."

"I'm sure I will." He paused to sip wine, then sighed. "I'm sure I will," he repeated, "but I'm also afraid the politics aren't quite behind us yet. To be frank, that's the real reason I invited you tonight, and, if you'll forgive me, I might as well dispose of the main business before Captain Goldstein returns."

Honor's eyebrows rose. She couldn't stop them, and White Haven gave a dry chuckle.

"Oh, yes. He and the officers of my staff will be joining us for supper, but I thought it would be just as well to make the explanations in private. You see, you're about to go on extended leave."

"I beg your pardon, Sir?" She must have misunderstood. Her ship was under repair, new personnel were coming aboard to replace casualties, and she had a brand new executive officer. No captain with all that on her plate had any business taking an extended leave. A day or two here and there to visit her parents or stretch her legs ground-side might make sense, but leaving Eve Chandler to deal with so many responsibilities in her absence would be inexcusable. Nor, for that matter, had she even requested leave!

"I said you're going on leave. In fact, I suggest—unofficially, of course—that you visit your holdings on Grayson for, oh, a month or two."

"But—" Honor closed her mouth and gave White Haven a sharp look. "May I ask why, Sir? Unofficially, of course."

"Certainly you may." The admiral met her gaze without evasion. "I might say you've more than earned it, which would be true. But saying it will be extremely convenient for the Government has the added virtue of being frank."

"Am I that big an embarrassment, Sir?" The question came out more bitterly, she knew, than any captain should speak to an admiral of White Haven's seniority, but this was too much. Was she going to be run entirely out of the Star Kingdom by the Government after all she'd already endured from the Opposition? Pent up frustration surged high inside her, fanned to the brink of explosion at receiving her marching orders from an officer she respected so highly, and Nimitz stiffened on her shoulder, surprised by the sudden spike of her emotions, but White Haven didn't even frown.

"I suppose it may seem that way, Dame Honor, and I'm sorry." His deep voice was as level as his eyes, and the understanding in it made her ashamed of her own anger— which only made it worse. She reached up and lifted Nimitz down into her lap, trying to soothe his ear-flattened indignation with physical caresses while she fought her own bitterness and tried to damp its echoes in the treecat, and White Haven went on in that same unflinching tone.

"The truth is that you *are* an embarrassment, though certainly not through any fault of your own. In fact, the exemplary way you've done your duty, coupled with what's going on elsewhere, is what *makes* you an embarrassment."

He leaned further back and crossed his legs, and Honor felt her anger begin to ebb as she realized how serious his expression was.

"The situation in the People's Republic is getting worse, not better," he said quietly. "We're picking up reports of some sort of purge, complete with mass executions, against the Legislaturalists who survived the Harris Assassination. To date, we have confirmation that they've shot over a hundred captains and flag officers, as well, and at least twice that many other senior officers have simply disappeared. Some of their middle-level commanders are actually resorting to armed resistance, no doubt in self-preservation, and at least eight star systems have declared their independence from the central government. That hasn't kept this Committee of Public Safety's chairman, a Mr. Pierre, from securing control of most of the major fleet bases, though, and there are disturbing indications that some sort of revolutionary fervor is sweeping the Haven System itself. The Dolists are no longer simply sitting around passively collecting their Basic Living Stipends. Pierre's managed to get them genuinely involved for the first time in living memory, and several other systems, mostly among those the Peeps have controlled longest and brought most thoroughly under central control, are experiencing the same thing."

The admiral paused for a moment, watching her expression, and nodded as her lips tightened.

"Exactly, Dame Honor. Our analysts are hopelessly divided on what it all means, of course. The coup—or whatever it was—completely blindsided us, and the various think tanks are all scrambling to build new models. In the meantime, no one knows what's really going on, or where it's likely to lead. Some of us, including myself and Duke Cromarty, believe we're seeing the evolution of something far more dangerous than the old regime ever was. Pierre's shown excellent tactical sense by concentrating on the major bases and most heavily populated systems first. If his committee, or junta, or whatever we want to call it, can secure its position there, which is exactly what it seems to be doing, it can always snap back up weaker, break-away systems later, especially if it brings genuine popular support to bear on the problem."

He paused, and Honor nodded slowly, fingers gentle on Nimitz's ears.

"And shooting admirals lets them put their own people in command positions when they start doing that," she murmured.

"Precisely. It means they'll have reliable fleet commanders—officers who owe their new positions solely to the committee's patronage—when they get back around to us, as well." White Haven shrugged. "It's costing them in terms of experience, at least in the short run. For your private information—and this is classified data, Dame Honor—several of their better flag officers have fled the Republic. Some have even come over to us, and, according to them, their Navy had nothing to do with the Harris assassination. For myself, I'm inclined to believe them, which, in turn, raises some very interesting questions about Mr. Pierre and his fellows, particularly in light of how quickly they moved to prevent a 'military coup.'

"But the key point is that until what's happening becomes so obvious no one can dispute it, the members of our own factions are free to assume whatever best suits their own prejudices. To be completely honest, that's probably true of myself and Duke Cromarty, as well, but Cromarty doesn't have the luxury of debating Havenite affairs over brandy at his club. He has to act in the real world, and that, I'm afraid, is where you come in."

"Me, Sir?" Honor was frowning, but in concentration now, not frustration. White Haven's frankness had soothed away her anger, and listening to his analysis was like hearing a fleet commander laying out her units' missions and ops plans.

"You. Raoul Courvosier once told me you dislike politics, Dame Honor. I wish he were here to explain this to you himself, but he's not, and this time you're in them right up to your neck."

Honor felt a familiar pain at the reminder of Admiral Courvosier's death, but there was something else under the hurt. She'd never imagined that Courvosier had discussed her with anyone else, especially not to the extent that remark suggested. Her surprise showed, and White Haven smiled sadly.

"Raoul and I were close friends, Dame Honor, and he always considered you one of his most outstanding students. As a matter of fact, he once told me he regarded you as the daughter he'd never had. He was extremely proud of you, and I don't think he'd be disappointed—or surprised—by how amply you've justified his confidence."

Honor blinked on sudden tears. Courvosier had never told her that. He wouldn't have, of course, yet the bitterest hurt when she'd lost him in Yeltsin had been her deep, undying regret that she'd never told him how much *he* meant to *her*, either. But if that was truly how he'd seen her, perhaps it meant he'd already known. That he'd always known.

"Thank you, Sir," she said finally, her voice husky. "For telling me that. The Admiral meant a great deal to me, too."

"I know he did," White Haven said quietly, "and I wish with all my heart that he were here today. But the point at hand, Captain, is that whether you like politics or not, this time you have to play by the politicos' rules."

"Yes, Sir." Honor cleared her throat and nodded. "I understand, Sir. Just tell me what you want me to do."

White Haven smiled his approval and uncrossed his legs, leaning forward to brace his elbows on his knees.

"At the moment, the Opposition parties, each for its own reasons, want to leave Haven to its own devices. They've chosen to endorse the analysts who believe the Peeps are genuinely trying to reform themselves—or at least that they'll self-destruct if we refuse to provide a foreign threat for them to rally against. That's an attractive proposition. In fact, it's downright seductive. Unfortunately, I believe, as does Duke Cromarty, that it's the *wrong* proposition. That we have to hit them now, while they're still divided and before their Committee of Public Safety fully consolidates its power.

"The Opposition disagrees, which is the reason so many disparate political groups have rallied to Young's defense. They're looking for *anything* to tie up the Lords and avoid a declaration of war until Haven collapses. The notion that Young's court-martial was politically motivated is bullshit, but it's highly emotional bullshit, and politics is a game of perceptions. They know that, and they're using the uproar over the verdict to paralyze substantive action on any other issue. Unfortunately, in order to defend Young, they have to attack *you*, and, quite frankly, your record gives many of them more than sufficient reason—by their lights, at least—to want your scalp."

"So you want me out of reach of the media," Honor said flatly.

"Exactly, Dame Honor. I know you've been avoiding interviews, but the newsies aren't going to give up as long as the Opposition keeps the issue alive. In a way, the fact that you've been essentially sequestered aboard *Nike* actually plays into the Opposition's hands. They can speculate on what you've got to hide, why you don't want to meet the media and 'present your side,' but if you *do* make yourself available, you give them the opportunity to twist whatever you say to suit their own purposes."

"But won't sending me to Grayson only make that even worse, Sir? I mean, won't it look like I'm running away?"

"It may. On the other hand, you're also Steadholder Harrington."

He paused again, cocking an eyebrow, and Honor nodded. White Haven had been present when Benjamin Mayhew named her to the position.

"You and I know Protector Benjamin understood when he asked you to assume the office that your duties as a naval officer would limit your ability to be physically present on Grayson," the admiral continued. "The Protector has been in touch with Duke Cromarty, however, and he's officially requested permission to summon you to attend the Conclave of Steadholders, which convenes on Grayson in three weeks. I'm sure Her Majesty would give you special leave to attend in any event, but under the present circumstances the opportunity is heaven-sent. It's an incontestably genuine request for your presence from an allied head of state to whom you owe personal fealty and in whose system a decisive battle just took place. If the Opposition's spokesmen try to make it look like some sort of retreat on your part, the Government will crucify them."

"I see." Honor was nodding once more, her eyes thoughtful. It was neat, she thought, and the fact was that she really ought to have returned to Grayson for a visit already, much as the idea secretly terrified her. She'd done her best to stay abreast of events in "her" steading and paid careful attention to all the proclamations and appointments she'd approved on her regent's recommendation, but she had no desire to be any more of an absentee noble than she could avoid. Besides, it was her responsibility to know what she was doing . . . and she didn't. Not really.

"I thought you'd understand." White Haven didn't try to hide his approval. "Actually, there's another advantage to the timing, as well, though."

"Another advantage, Sir?"

"Yes. Her Majesty has called to Duke Cromarty's attention the fact that you've never formally taken your seat in the House of Lords."

"Well, yes, Sir, I know. But—" Honor paused, unable to express her own ambivalent feelings. She was a member of the Manticoran peerage, but she'd never been fully comfortable with the idea, particularly when her only real claim to that status was her Grayson title. No Manticoran had ever before been seated in the Lords on the basis of foreign holdings, and she'd been more than pleased to let things slide for as long as the Crown was prepared to forget about seating her there.

"A problem, Dame Honor?" White Haven asked, and she drew courage from the gentle, understanding irony of his tone.

"Sir, I'd just as soon *not* take my seat. As you say, I don't like politics. I usually don't understand them very well, either, and I don't like the idea of voting on things I can't understand. I try to avoid making decisions about things I'm not qualified to judge, Sir. And, frankly, given the irregularity of my title, I'd feel presumptuous if I tried."

White Haven cocked his head and studied her expression for a moment, then smiled faintly.

"I don't think that's going to be a very viable option, Captain. And I remind you that membership in the House of Lords will require you to make far fewer decisions than your position as Steadholder Harrington will."

"I realize that, My Lord." Honor returned his gaze with serious eyes. "As a matter of fact, if I'd realized all the office of steadholder entails, Protector Benjamin would never have talked me into accepting it. But he did. That means I'm stuck with it, and I can only say that I'm more grateful than I could ever express that he found such an outstanding regent for me. And at least he understood from the outset that I could never remain on Grayson full-time—that I'm going to *have* to delegate my authority there."

White Haven allowed his smile to become an equally faint frown. "Should I understand, then, that you intend to be no more than a figurehead? That you're going to delegate your Grayson responsibilities to someone more qualified than yourself?"

"No, Sir, you should not." Honor felt herself flush at the carefully metered sting in his voice. "I accepted the position, and whether I knew what I was doing at the time or not is beside the point. It's mine now, and any officer who's ever commanded a Queen's ship understands responsibilities. I have no choice but to learn my duties to Grayson and discharge them to the very best of my ability, and I intend to do so." White Haven's eyes softened, and she went on in a quieter voice. "But the prospect frightens me, Sir, and I'd rather not assume still more responsibility and make still more decisions in our own House of Lords at the same time."

"I'd say that indicates you'd vote a great deal more responsibly than many of our present peers," White Haven said seriously, and her blush turned darker. The earl's title dated back to the Star Kingdom's founding, yet her own ennoblement meant that, technically, she was his equal. It made her feel uncomfortable, like a little girl dressing up as an adult woman, and she squirmed in her chair.

"The operative point, however," White Haven went on after a moment, "is that Her Majesty wants you seated there, and she isn't especially pleased with Duke Cromarty for having delayed this long. I understand she expressed herself quite, um, forcefully on the subject."

Honor's blush turned scarlet at the thought, and he chuckled.

"You may as well give in gracefully, Captain. Unless *you* want to explain your reservations to Her Majesty?"

Honor shook her head quickly, and White Haven laughed out loud.

"In that case, I think we can treat the subject as closed. At the same time, it would be wiser to wait until the declaration's clinched before we throw another log on the fire, and sending you off to Grayson will let us delay until after Young's seated and the votes are counted."

Honor stared down at Nimitz's ears and nodded. Personally, she would have preferred delaying it permanently. White Haven smiled at the crown of her bent head and reclaimed his wineglass, sipping at it to give her a moment to adjust to the news, and silence stretched out between them, only to be shattered by the quiet buzz of the admittance signal from the cabin hatch.

"Ah!" White Haven glanced at his chrono and spoke briskly as Honor looked up. "Captain Goldstein and company, right on schedule. Never forget, Dame Honor, that admirals demand strict punctuality on all social occasions."

Honor smiled at the change of subject. "I believe they mentioned something to that effect at the Academy, My Lord."

"I always knew the Academy was good for something, Milady." White Haven smiled back and stood as the signal buzzed once more. "And now that we've got the political claptrap out of the way, I hope you're prepared to tell us all firsthand what happened in Hancock." His smile turned into a grin. "What *really* happened. I think you'll find you're among friends here."

✧ CHAPTER TWELVE

"I'M GOING TO BE FEELING MIGHTY sorry for myself for the next couple of months," Paul Tankersley murmured as the shuttle approached the waiting heavy cruiser. "Especially at night," he added wickedly.

Honor blushed and looked around quickly, but no one was close enough to overhear. The dozen diplomats with whom they shared the Foreign Office shuttle had chosen seats near the front of the passenger compartment, more than willing to leave the two naval officers alone. Now they sat chatting quietly among themselves while the cruiser grew in the visual display, and she sighed in relief, then grimaced at him.

"You're as bad as my mother," she scolded. "Neither of you have a scrap of self-restraint. Or even common decency, for that matter."

"I know. That's why I liked her so much. In fact, if she were just a little taller—"

Tankersley broke off with a chuckle as Honor's elbow dug into his ribs, but her right cheek dimpled uncontrollably. She and Paul had found time for only a single, one-day visit to Sphinx, but her parents—and especially her mother—had greeted him with open arms. Allison Harrington was an emigrant from the Sigma Draconis System's Beowulf, and Beowulf's sexual mores were very different from straight-laced Sphinx's. Her daughter's total lack of a sex life had baffled Doctor Harrington almost as much as it worried her, and she would have been ready to welcome any male with approximately the right number of appendages. When she saw the quality of the male Honor had actually found and realized how deeply they loved one another, she'd none too figuratively clasped him to her bosom. Indeed, at one point Honor had almost feared Allison's half-T-century of acculturation might slip and result in an offer that would have shocked even Paul. It hadn't happened, but she couldn't help wishing a bit wistfully that she could have seen his reaction if it had.

"You just stay away from Sphinx till I get back, Paul Tankersley," she said severely. Nimitz looked up from her lap with a soft, bleeking laugh, and Tankersley laid a hand on his breast and tried to look innocent.

"Why, Honor! *Surely* you don't think—"

"You don't want to know what I think," she interrupted. "*I* saw how the two of you snuck off into the corner. Just what were you whispering about, anyway?"

"Oh, lots of things," Paul said brightly. "She did surprise me a couple of times, though—and not just with that bare-bottomed baby holo of you. Did you know Beowulfans don't believe in tubing babies?"

Honor felt herself blush again, much more brightly, but this time she couldn't quite smother a gurgle of embarrassed delight. One of the diplomats glanced over his shoulder, then turned away again, and Paul's eyes brimmed with laughter as he looked up at her.

"Yes," she said after a moment, "I believe I did know that."

"Really?" He grinned at her refusal to rise to the holo bait and shook his head. "Hard to believe an itty-bitty little thing like that carried you to term. Seems like an awful lot of work to me."

"Are you casting aspersions on my size? Or just suggesting it was wasted effort?"

"Oh, heavens, *no*! Neither of those would be tactful—or safe, now that I think about it." Paul's grin broadened, then faded into a more serious expression. "But, seriously, that must have been quite a chore on Sphinx."

"It was," Honor agreed. "Beowulf's gravity's higher than Manticore's, but it's still about ten percent lower than Sphinx's. Daddy was more than ready to have me tubed, only Mother wouldn't hear of it. He was still in the Service at the time, and they didn't even have the cash to fit the house with grav plates, either, but she's a stubborn little thing."

"I knew you got it from somewhere," Paul murmured. "But what I can't understand is why she was so insistent. It certainly isn't what I would have expected out of someone from Beowulf."

"I know."

Honor frowned and rubbed the tip of her nose, considering how best to explain the apparent incongruity. Beowulf led the explored galaxy in the life sciences and boasted its most advanced genetic engineering facilities, especially in applied eugenics. The rest of humanity had virtually abandoned the entire field for over seven hundred T-years late in the tenth century of the Diaspora, after the specialized combat constructs, bio weapons, and "super soldiers" of Old Earth's Final War had wreaked unbelievable carnage on the mother world. Some historians insisted that only the Warshawski sail and the relief expeditions mounted by other members of the recently formed Solarian League had saved the planet at all, and the Sol System had needed almost five T-centuries of recovery before it regained its preeminent place in the galaxy.

Yet when the rest of humanity recoiled in horror from what it had unleashed, Beowulf did nothing of the sort. Probably, Honor thought, because Beowulfans had never gone as overboard with the concept of "improving the breed" from the beginning. The oldest of Old Earth's daughter colonies, Beowulf had evolved its own bio-sciences code well before the Final War, and that code had prohibited most of the excesses other worlds had embraced. Nor had there been as much pressure on the Beowulfan medical establishment to join the general retreat as one might have expected, for it had been researchers from Beowulf who'd tackled and defeated, one by one, the hideous diseases and genetic damage the Final War had inflicted on Old Earth's survivors.

Yet even today, almost a thousand T-years later, Beowulf maintained its code. Perhaps it was even more rigorous than it had been then, in fact. The Star Kingdom of Manticore, like most planets with decent medical science, made no legal or ethical distinction between "natural born" children and embryos brought to term in vitro. There were compelling arguments in favor of tubing, as the process was still known, not least because of the way the fetus could be monitored and the relative ease with which defects could be corrected. And, of course, it had immense appeal for career women, especially for servicewomen like Honor herself. But Beowulf rejected the practice.

"It's sort of hard to explain," she said finally. "Personally, I think it has a lot to do with the fact that they maintained their eugenics programs when everyone else rejected them. It was . . . oh, a sort of gesture to reassure the rest of the galaxy that they weren't going to do any wild tinkering with human genotypes. And they don't, you know. They've always favored a gradualist approach. They'll work right up to the natural limits of the available genetic material, but they won't go a millimeter beyond that in humans. I suppose you might argue that they crossed the line when they came up with the prolong process, but they didn't really *change* anything in the process. They only convinced a couple of gene groups to work a bit differently for two or three centuries. On the other hand, their insistence on natural childbearing is more than just a gesture to the rest of us, too. Mother says the official reason is a desire to avoid 'reproductive techno dependency,' but she smiles a lot when she says it, and once or twice she's admitted there's more to it."

"What?" Paul asked as her voice trailed off.

"She won't say—except to assure me that I'll understand when it's my turn. She gets almost mystic about it." Honor shrugged, then grinned and squeezed his hand. "Of course, she may decide to make an exception in our case, given the schedules we're likely to be looking at for the next few years."

"She has," Paul said quietly. Honor's eyebrows rose, and he smiled. "She says the next time you and I visit, she's bringing out her bottles. Something—" he lifted his nose with a superior sniff "—about not letting high-class sperm get away from you."

Honor's eyes rounded in amazement, then softened. She hadn't realized just how much her mother approved of Paul, and her hand tightened on his.

"I think that's a marvelous idea," she said softly, and leaned over to kiss him despite the diplomats' presence, then straightened in her chair and smiled wickedly. "Not that I ever had any intention of letting any 'high-class sperm' escape, of course."

A docking tractor reached out to draw the shuttle into the heavy cruiser *Jason Alvarez*'s boat bay. The small craft rolled on gyros and thrusters, aligning itself with the docking arms, then settled into the buffers without so much as a jar, and Honor sat very still, watching the brightly garbed clutch of civilians rise and begin fussing with carry-on baggage while *Alvarez*'s traffic control crews ran the personnel tube out to the hatch. The moment was here, and she suddenly realized how little she wanted it to be.

Nimitz gave a soft little croon in her lap, and Paul's arm slipped about her shoulders to squeeze briefly. She looked at him, blinking suddenly misty eyes while her hands stroked the treecat's fluffy coat.

"Hey, it's only a couple of months!" Paul whispered.

"I know." She leaned against him for a moment, then inhaled deeply. "You know, I always felt just a little smug when I watched people snuffling on each other in departure lounges. It always seemed so silly. Now it doesn't."

"Serves you right for being so heartless all those years, then, doesn't it?" Paul brushed the tip of her nose with a finger, and she clicked her teeth at it. "That's better. Besides, I object to being snuffled on. It leaves tear stains on my tunic. That's why I never let any of my women do it."

"I bet you don't, cad." She gave a quiet chuckle and stood, lifting Nimitz to her padded shoulder. The Star of Grayson glittered in golden beauty on its crimson ribbon against the space-black of her tunic's breast. It was normal wear with dress uniform—in Grayson service, anyway—and she adjusted its unaccustomed weight before her hands fluttered over her person, checking her flawless appearance. It was completely automatic after so many years, and Paul smiled at the sheer reflex action.

"I knew I couldn't keep any secrets from you. Except, of course, for the important ones."

"If you think stashing away a harem is *un*important, you're in for a sad surprise, friend!" Honor warned him, and he laughed.

"Oh, that!" He waved a dismissive hand, then stood beside her and opened the overhead luggage compartment to withdraw a large, expensive-looking shoulder bag. It was black, made of natural leather and polished to a mirror-bright gloss. It was also, she noticed in surprise, badged in gold with the coat of arms she'd selected as Steadholder Harrington: side-by-side representations of the western hemispheres of Sphinx and Grayson, joined by the stylized key that was the patriarch's sigil of a steadholder, under a vac helmet crest. The helmet looked very little like modern equipment, but it was the symbol which had denoted naval service for almost two thousand T-years.

"What's that?"

"This, my love," he grinned teasingly, "is one of the aforesaid *important* secrets. I'd like to pretend it was a going-away present, but I've been working on it for quite a while now. As a matter of fact, I didn't think it would be ready before you left, but they put a rush on it for me."

"On *what*?" she demanded, and he chuckled. He set the bag on the seat she'd vacated and unsealed it, and her eyes widened.

It was a vac suit. More to the point, it looked exactly like a Fleet skinsuit . . . except for its tiny size and provision for six limbs.

"Paul!" she gasped. "That *can't* be what it looks like!"

"Ah, but it is!" He fished around under the suit and came up with the equally undersized helmet. He burnished it with his forearm, then extended it to her with a bow and a flourish. "For His Nibs," he explained unnecessarily.

Honor took the helmet and turned it in disbelieving hands while Nimitz peered down at it from her shoulder. The 'cat realized what he was looking at, and she felt his own surprise and the glow of his pleasure through their link.

"Paul, I never even considered— I mean, why didn't *I* think of this? It's *perfect*!"

"And so it should be," he said smugly. "As to why you never thought of it, well, far be it from me to suggest that you can be a bit slow at times, but—" He shrugged with Gallic perfection.

"And tactfulness, too," Honor marveled. "Gosh, what did I ever do to deserve you?"

"Just getting into your good graces so you won't clobber me when I start dropping underwear on the carpet, dear." He chuckled at the look she gave him, then turned more serious. "Actually, I thought of it the first time I saw that life-support module you keep for him in your cabin. I started out with BuShips, you know, before I got sidetracked into shipboard assignments. One of my first chores out of the Academy was a stint as junior project officer on the redesign of the old skinsuits when the new higher pressure storage vacuoles came in, so I started doodling on my terminal in my off time. I had the design run up by the time we got back from Hancock."

"But it must have cost a fortune," Honor said slowly. "That module alone cost me an arm and a leg."

"It wasn't cheap," Paul agreed, "but my family's always been involved in shipbuilding and chandlering. I took it to Uncle Henri—he's not really related, but he runs our R&D section— and he took over from there. Gave me a pretty hard time about my design, too," he added meditatively. "I'd guess he'd improved it by a couple of hundred percent by the time he finished playing with it. After that—" he shrugged "—the actual fabrication was a snap."

Honor nodded, but her expression was uneasy, and she frowned as she turned the helmet more slowly. She'd been surprised to discover how wealthy Paul's family was. She shouldn't have been, perhaps, given his relationship to Mike Henke, but that was on the commoner side of Mike's family. Yet despite his breezy dismissal of the suit's price tag, she knew how much a regular life-support module ran, and this had to be far more costly.

"It's gorgeous, Paul, but you shouldn't have done something so expensive without warning me."

"Oh, don't worry about that! Uncle Henri thought it was going to turn into some sort of expensive toy, too. Until Marketing got wind of it, that is." Honor looked surprised, and Paul grinned. "You're not the only person with a treecat, Dame Honor. We supply about a third of the modules people buy for them, and the people who sell the other two-thirds are going to be very unhappy when we start marketing *skinsuits* for them! You have no idea how flattering it is to be considered a prodigy after all these disappointing years."

"I bet." Honor's frown melted into a smile, and she raised the helmet for Nimitz to examine more closely. He sniffed at it delicately, whiskers quivering, then shoved his head into its armorplast transparency, and she laughed as he flicked his ears at her through it.

"Thank you," she said warmly. She touched Paul's cheek with her free hand. "Thank you very much. From both of us."

"A mere nothing." He made an airy gesture and held out his hands. She gave the helmet back, and he placed it atop the suit, sealed the bag, and arranged the strap on her shoulder.

"There. All ready to go." He waved her toward the hatch, and she looked up, surprised to see that everyone else had already left. He hooked elbows to accompany her to the hatch, and his eyes twinkled. "It's even got its own thrusters. They're not as flexible as a standard skinsuit's, but they're fitted with bio-feedback actuators. Judging from some of the aerobatics I've seen Nimitz pull off, he shouldn't have too much trouble once he gets the hang of them. They're disabled and uncharged, right now, of course, and the software's set up for flexible modification once the two of you figure out which muscle group works best to initiate what maneuver. There's a tether line for training him under zero gee, too, and the manuals are in the bag. Be sure you read them clear through before you start fooling around with it."

"Aye, aye, Sir."

"Good." They reached the hatch and he drew her head down to convenient kissing height and brushed his lips across hers. "Have a good trip."

She smiled wordlessly, determined not to sniffle, and he propelled her gently into the personnel tube. She reached for the outboard grab bar and swung across the gravity interface, then paused and turned, floating in free fall, as a throat cleared itself behind her.

"Um, one thing I didn't mention." She cocked her head,

and her eyebrows lowered as she recognized his unholy amusement.

"Oh?"

"Well, it's just that I'm *so* pleased it was available before your trip rather than after." Her eyebrows swept even lower, and he smiled sweetly. "You see, this way *you* get to explain it to Nimitz. Uncle Henri went to considerable pains to failsafe its operation, but there's one thing he couldn't get around."

"Like what?" she demanded suspiciously.

"Let's just put it this way, love. I certainly hope Nimitz is in a tolerant mood when you start to explain the plumbing connections."

Senior Captain Mark Brentworth finished greeting the last of the Manticoran dignitaries in *Alvarez*'s boat bay gallery, then snapped back around to the personnel tube as someone cleared his throat in warning. A tall, slender captain in black and gold sailed down the tube, graceful as a bird after the diplomats' clumsier efforts. A long, sinuous shape clung to her shoulder, and Brentworth's eyes lit with pleasure.

His right hand made a tiny gesture, and the side party's senior petty officer produced an old-fashioned, lung-powered bugle in place of his electronic bosun's pipe. More than one of the Manticoran diplomats wheeled in surprise as the crisp, golden notes rang through the gallery and the honor guard of Grayson Marines snapped from parade rest to rigid attention.

"Preeeeeee-sent *arms*!" their commander barked. Pulse rifles came up in perfect unison, the side party saluted, and Brentworth removed his cap and bowed with a flourish as Honor Harrington stepped out of the tube to a second bugle fanfare.

She stood motionless, as startled as the diplomats, and only decades of discipline kept her surprise off her face.

"Steadholder Harrington." Brentworth's voice was deep as he straightened and tucked his cap under his arm. "I am honored, and privileged, to welcome you aboard my ship in the name of the people of Grayson, My Lady."

Honor gazed at him, wondering what the proper response was, and decided to settle for a gracious half-bow of her own.

"Thank you, Captain Brentworth. I'm delighted to be here, and—" she smiled and extended her right hand "—she looks like a wonderful ship, Mark."

"Thank you, My Lady. I'm rather proud of her myself, and I look forward to showing you around her at your convenience."

"I'll hold you to that." She squeezed his hand firmly, privately surprised by how right he looked in a captain's uniform. And in command of this ship, as well. The last time she'd seen him, he'd been a commander, but she suspected his promotion owed little either to his family or the desperate nature of Grayson's need for senior officers.

Brentworth held her hand longer than mere protocol demanded, and she deliberately turned her head to the right to show him her left profile as she recognized his scrutiny. The last time he'd seen *her*, her ruined left eye had been covered by a black eye patch and the entire side of her face had been a frozen, nerve-dead mask. She saw his eyes warm in relief as she returned his smile and the left corner of her mouth moved naturally. Or what would look natural to him, she reminded herself. He'd only seen her smile a time or two before her injury.

He released her hand and stepped back with a gesture that made it courteously but firmly clear that she took precedence over the various middle and high-ranking diplomats who'd preceded her aboard.

"I'm looking forward to your tour, My Lady. In the meantime, please allow me to escort you to your quarters. Your steward should have your gear settled in by now."

✧ CHAPTER THIRTEEN

THE MAN WHO HAD BEEN Pavel Young stopped short as he faced the unexpected mirror. He stared across his new office, frozen while the door sighed shut behind him, and his hollow-eyed face looked back, white with strain above his exquisitely tailored tunic. His *civilian* tunic.

Something happened inside him. His shoulders twitched with an almost electric shock. His nostrils flared, and he crossed the room quickly, his mouth twisted in shame too fresh to lose its fury, and hooked his fingers under the mirror's frame.

It was bracketed to the wall, not simply hung, and pain lanced up his arm as a fingernail tore. But he welcomed the hurt. It was an ally, fanning his hate-filled strength, and he grunted with effort as he drove his fingertips into the small gap like splitting wedges of flesh. Expensive wood paneling yielded with a pistol-sharp crack as the mirror ripped out of the wall, and he staggered back and hurled it from him. It sailed across the palatial office, spinning end-for-end with a soft, whirring sound, then hit the opposite wall with a shattering smash. Mirror-backed fragments of glass pattered across the carpet, ringing and rolling like splintered diamonds on the bare wood beyond the carpet's edges, and madness glittered in his eyes.

A voice from the outer office exclaimed in muffled alarm as the mirror's destruction shook the room. The door opened abruptly, and a distinguished looking man with hair of iron gray looked in. His face revealed nothing, but his eyes widened as he saw the wild-eyed, panting Eleventh Earl of North Hollow standing in the center of the room. The earl was still bent forward in a throwing posture, shuddering as he sucked in huge gulps of air and glared fixedly at the shattered mirror.

129

"My Lord?" The iron-haired man's soft, courteous voice was touched with the tiniest edge of caution, but North Hollow ignored it. The other man cleared his throat and tried again, a bit louder. "My Lord?"

The earl shook himself. He closed his eyes and rammed his fingers through his hair, then drew a deep breath and turned to the newcomer.

"Yes, Osmond?"

"I heard the mirror fall." North Hollow's mouth twitched at Osmond's choice of verb, and Osmond paused. "Shall I call a cleaning crew, My Lord?" he suggested delicately.

"No." North Hollow's voice was harsh. He drew another deep breath, then turned and walked deliberately behind his desk. He seated himself in the expensive new chair that had replaced his father's life-support chair, and shook his head. "No," he said more calmly. "Leave it for now."

Osmond nodded, expression still bland, but his thoughts were wary. The newest Earl North Hollow could scarcely be blamed for feeling the strain, but there was something dangerous about him. The glitter in his eyes was too bright, too fixed, before he lowered them to the data console before him.

"That will be all, Osmond," North Hollow said after a moment, gaze still fixed on the console, and the other man withdrew without a sound. The door whispered shut behind him, and North Hollow slumped in his chair and scrubbed his face with his palms.

The mirror had brought it all back . . . again. Five days. Five hideous days and five nights more terrible still had passed since the Navy completed his dishonor. He closed his eyes, and the scene played itself out once more against the blood-red haze of his lids. He couldn't stop it. He didn't even know if he *wanted* to stop it, for agonizing as it was, it fed the hate that gave him the strength to go on.

He saw the iron-faced admiral once more, his eyes shouting out the disgust his regulation expression hid, as he read the court-martial's sentence aloud. He saw the watching ranks of black and gold while the snouts of HD cameras peered pitilessly down from vantage points and hovering air cars. He saw the junior-grade lieutenant marching forward, the brisk, impersonal movement of his gloved hands belied by the contempt in his eyes as they ripped the golden planets of a senior-grade captain from the collar of his mess dress uniform. The braid on his cuffs followed. It had been specially prepared for the event, tacked to his sleeves with a few fragile stitches that popped and tore with dreadful clarity in the silence. Then it was the medal ribbons on his chest, his shoulder boards, the unit patch with his last ship's name, the gold and scarlet Navy flash from his right shoulder.

He'd wanted to scream at them all. To spit upon their stupid concept of honor and reject their right to judge. But he couldn't. The shock and shame had cut too deep, the numbed horror of it had frozen him, and so he'd stood rigidly at attention, unable to do anything else, as the lieutenant removed the beret from his head. The white beret of a starship's commander, badged with the Kingdom's arms. Gloved fingers ripped the badge from it and returned it to his head, replacing it with contemptuous dismissal, as if he were a child unable even to dress himself, and *still* he stood at attention.

But then it was his sword, and he swayed ever so slightly. His eyes closed, unable to watch, as the lieutenant braced the needle-sharp point against the ground, holding it at a forty-five-degree angle, and raised a booted foot. He couldn't see it, but he heard that foot fall, heard the terrible, brittle snap of breaking steel.

He stood before them, no longer a Queen's officer. He stood in a ridiculous black suit, stripped of its finery, its badges of honor, and the breeze picked at the scraps of gold and ribbon which had meant so much more than he'd known before he lost them. The wind rolled them over the manicured grass while the broken halves of his shattered sword glittered at his feet in the brilliant sunlight.

"About *face!*" The admiral's voice had snapped the command, but it no longer applied to him. His eyes had opened again, against his will. It was as if some outside force were determined to make him watch his final shame as those solid ranks turned their backs upon him in perfect unison.

"Forward, *march!*" the admiral snapped, and the officers who had not been found wanting obeyed. They marched away from him, with a precision Marines could not have bettered, timed by the slow, measured beat of a single drum, and left him alone and abandoned on the field of his dishonor. . . .

His eyes popped open, escaping the substance of his night-mares—for a time. His mouth twisted with a foul, bitter curse, and his fists were white knuckled on the desk before him as the hate poured through him.

He was a man who was used to hate. It had always been a part of him, racing through his veins. When some arrogant commoner challenged his rightful authority, when some spiteful superior denied him the recognition which was his just due, the hate had been there, boiling like lye. And the hate had been there when he crushed some upstart inferior, as well. He'd tasted it when he used his power to punish those who dared defy him, but then it had burned sweet, like intoxicating wine.

This hate was different. It didn't burn; it blazed. It was a furnace within him, consuming him. This time his whole world had turned upon him, chewed him up and spat him out like so much carrion at the feet of the bitch who'd delivered him to destruction, and every cell of his being cried out for vengeance. Vengeance upon that slut Harrington, but not just upon her. He would—he *must*—destroy her and everyone else who had betrayed him, yet he needed even more. It had to be done right, in a way that returned their contempt sneer for sneer, that spat upon their precious codes and putrid honor.

His teeth grated, and he made himself sit still, trembling, until the raw fury receded. It didn't go away. It simply shrank back to something that let him move and think, speak without spewing the curses that seethed within.

He pressed a key on his com console, and his father's— no, *his*—senior aide answered instantly.

"Yes, My Lord?"

"I need to see Sakristos and Elliott, Osmond. And you. Immediately."

"Of course, My Lord."

The circuit went dead, and North Hollow tilted his chair back. He folded his hands in front of him, lips curled in an ugly smile, and nodded slow agreement with his thoughts as he waited.

The door opened again within minutes to admit Osmond and another, younger man. They were accompanied by an elegantly groomed red-haired woman of stunning beauty, and something hungry flickered in the back of North Hollow's eyes as he gazed at her.

"Sit." He pointed at the chairs facing his desk, and a trickle of pleasure seeped through him as they obeyed. It wasn't the same as the Navy, but there was another sort of power here. The power of his name and the political machine he'd inherited was like a subtle aphrodisiac, and he rolled it across his tongue as he considered his underlings.

He let them sit for several seconds, let them absorb their obedience even as he absorbed his authority over them, then pointed at Osmond.

"Where are we in our negotiations with Baron High Ridge?"

"The Baron has agreed to sponsor your maiden speech, My Lord. He's expressed some small concern over the Jordan matter, but I took the liberty of assuring him his fears were groundless."

North Hollow nodded with a grunt of pleasure. High Ridge had been reluctant to personally sponsor North Hollow's first speech in the Lords. The baron was as well known for the religious fervor with which he protected his family name and political position as for his reactionary intolerance, and he'd been afraid the dishonor the Navy had smeared across North Hollow would besmirch him, as well . . . but not as frightened as he'd been when he discovered the earl's father had passed his arsenal of secret files to his son with his title. North Hollow could have destroyed a score of political careers—and the family names of the men and women those careers belonged to—and High Ridge's was among them.

The baron's involvement in the Jordan Cartel had been hidden behind more than a dozen layers of dummy shareholders, but the last Earl of North Hollow had discovered it. High Ridge's shares had been no more or less than bribes, providing the cash to bail out the family fortunes at a critical moment. Worse, he'd sold them in a single block, using inside information to get out just before the Admiralty announced the suspension of all Navy contracts with the cartel while charges of fraud and substandard building practices were investigated. That large a stock transaction, coming just before the actual announcement, had been a major factor in sparking the frantic sell-off that brought the cartel down in the Kingdom's worst financial failure in over a T-century. Thousands had been hurt, hundreds had been completely wiped out, and none of the investigators had ever been able to determine who'd ordered that first, fatal sale.

None of them except those who'd worked for North Hollow's father.

"The Baron did ask me what subject you intend to speak upon, however, My Lord." Osmond's voice broke in on the earl's reverie, and North Hollow snorted.

"I intend to speak about the declaration," he said in a sarcastic, "what else?" tone. Osmond simply nodded, and the earl's eyes swiveled to the younger man beside his aide. "That's why I wanted to see you, Elliott."

His chief speech-writer cocked his head and poised his fingers attentively over the keys of a stenographer's memo pad.

"I want this handled carefully," North Hollow went on. "I do *not* want to attack the Government." The red-haired woman on Osmond's other side raised her eyebrows, and North Hollow snorted again. "I have no intention of breaking with the rest of the party, but if I sound as if I want some sort of vengeance for what the Government's done to me, I'll only undermine my own influence."

Elliott nodded, fingers flicking keys, and North Hollow pretended not to notice the way Osmond's shoulders relaxed ever so slightly.

"As a matter of fact, I don't want to sound anti-Navy, either," the earl continued. "We'll settle up with those bastards later. For now, I want to strike an 'in sorrow, not in anger' note. And—" he paused, studying the three staffers narrowly "—I intend to speak in favor of the declaration."

Elliott's eyes widened and darted up to the earl's face before he could snatch them back down again, and North Hollow saw the shock in them. Osmond stiffened in his chair, half-opening his mouth as if to protest, then snapped it closed again. Only Georgia Sakristos seemed unsurprised. She leaned back in her chair, crossing sleek legs, and her blue eyes gleamed with a certain detached amusement as Elliott finally found his voice again.

"I— Of course, My Lord, if that's what you want. But, forgive me for asking, have you discussed any of this with Baron High Ridge?"

"I have not. I will, of course—after we deliver the draft of the speech to him. At the moment, however, you three are the only ones who know. No one outside this room *will* know until I tell you differently. I intend for this speech to come as a complete surprise when I deliver it."

"But, My Lord," Osmond began in his most diffident voice, "this represents a complete break with the Association's position."

"It does." North Hollow smiled thinly. "But the Peeps are going to attack us again as soon as they get organized whether we declare war or not. Should they do that while the party still opposes a war vote, it'll only validate the policy Cromarty and his cronies have been advocating all along. And, of course, *in*validate the Opposition's."

He paused, watching Osmond's face, and the aide nodded slowly.

"I don't expect the Government to embrace me—not, at least, until the . . . public relations situation dies down. Nor do I expect to play any overt role in the actual tactics of arranging the accommodation. But opening the door by advocating a partnership with the Government despite what it's done to me will be an investment in political capital. Hell, half the Association already realizes we're backing an untenable position.

If I give them a way out—especially one that lets whatever deal they strike look like a patriotic gesture—they'll kneel down in line to kiss my ass."

"And the Government will owe you, too, whether it wants to admit it or not," Sakristos murmured.

"Exactly." North Hollow's smile turned even more unpleasant. "I'm too new to the Lords to retain the whip's position, but I don't plan to be that way forever. Not that the whip is what I want. It'll take a few years, but Baron High Ridge will have to step down eventually. When he does, I intend to be ready."

Even Sakristos' face showed surprise this time, and all three of North Hollow's subordinates sat back, eyes narrow as they worked through the permutations. The earl's father had never wanted the party's top position. He'd preferred to act more discreetly, brokering deals as the power behind the throne, but it seemed the new earl was cut from different cloth.

Different cloth, perhaps, but with the same secrets in his vault and the same organization behind him, and narrow eyes began to gleam with ambition of their own as they visualized the ways those secrets could be used to ease other contenders aside. North Hollow let them contemplate the possibilities, then pointed at Elliott once more.

"Does that give you a feel for the sort of speech I need?"

"Uh, yes. Yes, My Lord. I think I understand."

"How soon can you have a draft for me?"

"By tomorrow afternoon, My Lord?"

"Not soon enough. I'm due to take my seat in three days. Give it to me before you go home tonight."

Elliott swallowed, then nodded.

"In that case, you'd probably better get on it. Osmond, I want you to draw up a list of reliable newsies. Set up an exclusive interview with someone we can trust to ask the right questions, then get to work on the answers. I want to go over the preliminary list with you, with dossiers on each possibility, by tomorrow morning."

"Of course, My Lord."

North Hollow nodded dismissal but waved Sakristos back into her chair when she rose with the two men. Osmond and Elliott filed out of the office without seeming to notice, and Sakristos crossed her legs once more.

The door closed, and North Hollow smiled at his father's chief dirty tricks specialist.

"Yes, My Lord?" she said politely.

"Pavel. It's still Pavel to you . . . Elaine."

"Of course, Pavel." Sakristos smiled back, but it was hard, even for her, for she knew the new earl's reputation. His father had promised to remove her name from his vault before he passed it on—that had been part of the *quid pro quo* that ensured her loyalty—but Pavel's use of the name "Elaine" proved he hadn't. She'd been afraid of that, given the suddenness of the old earl's death, and a shiver ran through her at the confirmation of her worst fear. Dimitri Young had been too wrecked by dissipation to do more than ogle her, but Pavel's smile told her he wanted more of her than the last earl had . . . and he had the weapons to demand it. He could do far worse than ruin her career; he could send her to prison for so long not even prolong would preserve her looks until she was released.

"Good." North Hollow's smile turned ugly for just a moment, touched with a greasy hunger that revolted her, then vanished. "At the moment, however, I have another job for you. I've got some . . . unfinished business with the Navy, and you're going to help me take care of it."

"If you wish, Pavel," she said as coolly as she could. "From a political viewpoint, however, Mr. Osmond would—"

"I'm not thinking about politics," he interrupted. "You're my direct action specialist, aren't you, 'Georgia'?" She could almost taste the gloating pleasure with which he used her assumed name, but she forced her expression to remain politely attentive.

"Yes, My Lord, I am," she said calmly.

"Well, that's what I want. Direct—*very* direct—action. Now, here's what I have in mind. First—"

✧ CHAPTER FOURTEEN

HONOR'S GRAVITY BOOTIES SHUFFLED on the deck, and she wore a huge smile as she turned in place with the anchor end of Nimitz's tether. The 'cat had always loved zero gee; now he circled her on buzzing suit thrusters, chittering with delight over his helmet com. Her earbug carried his comments to her, but she didn't really need it. The sheer exuberance echoing through their link was far more eloquent.

His headlong progress slowed abruptly as he snapped his long, sinuous body end-for-end and shot up in a perfect loop. Paul's "Uncle Henri" must be a genius, she thought, listening to the spatter of applause from their audience. He'd configured the thrusters' computers to react to every range of movement possible to a 'cat; all she'd had to do was watch Nimitz and figure out how to coordinate his normal zero-gee aerobatics with the suit's greater capacity.

He flowed through a slow roll and altered direction, and she ducked as he buzzed her head. She felt the wash of his thrusters as he passed and sent a flash of warning disapproval over their link. He hadn't quite grasped the need to respect his thruster safety zone, but she felt his repentance and moderated the strength of her scold. And, she reminded herself, at least the thrusters' minuscule size gave them a much smaller danger zone than a full-size suit's.

He executed another loop, then launched himself straight toward her, and the thrusters died as his four rearmost limbs reached for her padded shoulder. She staggered under the impact—even in free fall, he retained the momentum and inertia of his nine-plus standard kilos, plus the suit's mass—but, over all, she was impressed by how gently he'd landed. He was a natural, which probably shouldn't have been a surprise, given

his species' treetop environment on Sphinx. Not that she
intended to trust him without a tether outside the safe con-
fines of a ship any time soon.

She toggled the remote hand unit to lock the thrusters on
safe and reached up to unseal his helmet, but he rose high
enough to evade her hand and bleeked reprovingly at her. His
gauntleted true-hands found the pressure releases, and she
heard the soft "shussh" of an opening seal. He let the
armorplast bowl hang down his spine and groomed his whiskers
fastidiously.

"Good job, Stinker." She drew a celery stalk from her belt
purse, and he stopped grooming and seized it greedily, happier than even his aerobatics had made him. It wasn't a case
of response-reward training—Nimitz had no need for that sort
of thing—but he'd certainly earned his treat.

Gravity returned suddenly. Not the 1.35 *g* of her homeworld,
but the much lighter gravity of Grayson, and she looked over
her unencumbered shoulder. Captain Brentworth stood beside
the gym's control panel, grinning at her.

"Agile little devil, isn't he?" *Alvarez*'s captain said.

"He is that," Honor agreed. She reached up and ran a
fingertip over one tufted ear, and Nimitz paused—briefly—in
his chewing to push back against her touch. Then he got back
to important matters with a juicy crunch.

Honor laughed and lifted him down into her arms. Skinsuits
might be far lighter than older styles of vac gear, but their
internalized storage vacuoles made them much more massive
than they looked, and Nimitz's suited weight was too much
for comfort even in this gravity. The 'cat didn't care about
the change; he only curled comfortably in her embrace and
clutched his celery tight, and her smile turned into a grin.
Nimitz was comfortable enough with the suit now, but he'd
bristled indignantly when she first introduced him to the
plumbing connections Paul had warned her of.

She started to bend over to remove the gravity booties, but
one of Brentworth's crew was already there. The barely
postadolescent electronics tech went down on one knee, offering
the other knee as a raised platform, and she smiled as she
lifted one foot to the proffered support. He unsealed the booty
and laid it aside, then repeated the process on her other foot.

"Thank you," she said, and the youngster—he couldn't have
been over twenty T-years old—blushed.

"My pleasure, My Lady," he got out, and she managed not
to chuckle at the near-awe in his tone. Not that she'd been
particularly amused when she first encountered the reverence

in which Brentworth's crew held her. They watched her almost worshipfully, with a deference they normally would have offered only to the Protector himself. It had annoyed her immensely— not least because she hadn't had a clue how she should react. But there was nothing sycophantic about it, so she'd settled for just being herself, however they cared to treat her, and it seemed to have been the right tack. Awe had turned into something much more like respect, and they no longer looked as if they wanted to genuflect whenever they met her in a passage.

Still, she thought, it might have been easier all around if she weren't the only woman in *Alvarez*'s complement of eight hundred. She'd never encountered *that* situation before, either, but up until three T-years ago Grayson women had been legally barred from military service . . . or from owning property, serving on juries, or managing their own money, for that matter. It would be a while yet before they started serving on warships.

She nodded again to the youngster who'd helped with the booties, then settled Nimitz's weight more evenly in her arms and headed for the hatch, and Brentworth fell into step beside her.

The Grayson captain studied her profile in silence as they headed down the passage. She looked better than he'd dared hoped, but now that she'd been aboard a couple of days he was beginning to realize the repairs hadn't been quite as complete as he'd first thought. The left side of her mouth moved with an ever so small hesitation. It gave her smile a slight lopsided effect, more a matter of timing than anything else, and hard though she tried to overcome it, certain consonants still came out just a bit slurred. Grayson's pre-Alliance medical establishment could never have matched the near-miraculous job Manticore's had done, but he couldn't suppress a twinge of regret.

She turned her head and caught his expression, and he blushed as one of her crooked smiles showed she'd followed his thoughts. But she only shook her head at him, and he smiled back.

This was a very different woman from the one he'd seen defending Yeltsin's Star. She'd been driven and grim, then— unfailingly courteous but with cold, naked steel in her one good eye while ghosts of pain and loss twisted deep inside her. She had, he thought, been the most dangerous person he'd ever met as she placed her two damaged ships between the battlecruiser *Saladin* and a planet full of people who weren't even allied to her Kingdom. People who'd done their best to

humiliate and denigrate her for daring to insult their prejudices by wearing an officer's uniform. She'd gone up against
a warship more than twice as massive as both her own
wounded ships for that planet, and she'd lost nine hundred
of her people stopping it.

That memory still shamed him . . . and explained the
reverence with which *Alvarez*'s crew regarded her. He felt it
himself, but he knew her better than most, for he'd been on
HMS *Fearless*'s bridge as her liaison officer when she did it,
and he snorted in sudden laughter.

"What?" she asked, and he grinned.

"I was just thinking, My Lady."

"About?" she prompted.

"Oh, about how amused you probably would have been
when your steward came aboard."

"Mac?" One eyebrow rose. "What about him?"

"Well, it's just that he's a man, My Lady." The other eyebrow rose in sudden understanding, and she began to chuckle
wickedly. "Absolutely," Brentworth agreed. "It came as, er,
something of a shock to some of our people. I'm afraid we're
not quite as liberated as we'd like to think just yet."

"Lord, I can imagine!" Honor's chuckle turned into soft
laughter. "And I can imagine the way Mac reacted to it, too!"

"Oh, no, My Lady! He took it perfectly in stride—just looked
at them like a Sunday school teacher who'd caught a bunch
of adolescents telling dirty stories in the head."

"That's exactly what I meant. He saves the same sort of
look for me when I'm late for supper."

"Does he?" Brentworth laughed, then nodded slowly. "Yes,
I can just see him doing it. He's really attached to you, My
Lady."

"I know." Honor smiled fondly, then shook her head. "By
the way, Mark, there's something I've been meaning to mention
to you. You're a senior captain yourself, now. There's no reason
you have to go on 'My Ladying' me all the time. My name
is Honor."

Brentworth almost missed a stride in sheer shock. Grayson
society was barely beginning to evolve the proper modes for
a society of sexual equality; indeed, he suspected much of
the planet was still too bemused by the changes Protector
Benjamin had mandated to realize just how sweeping they truly
were. The use of an unmarried, unrelated woman's Christian
name would have been an unthinkable insult to her under
the old mores, even if the woman in question hadn't been a
steadholder. Especially *this* steadholder!

"I— My Lady, I don't know if—"

"Please," she interrupted. "As a personal favor. You don't have to do it in public if you'd rather not, but all these 'My Ladies' and 'Steadholders' are suffocating me. Do you realize there's not a single person aboard this ship who would *dream* of calling me by name?"

"But you *are* a steadholder!"

"I haven't been one all my life," she replied a bit tartly.

"Well, no, I know that, but—"

Brentworth broke off to struggle with his emotions. One part of him was immensely flattered, but it wasn't as simple as she seemed to think. As he'd said, she was a steadholder, and the first and *only* woman to hold that high office in Grayson's thousand-year history. She was also the only presently living holder of the Star of Grayson and the person who'd saved his planet. And last but not least, he admitted, there was her sharp-edged, intriguing beauty.

She didn't look a bit like a Grayson woman, and she was ten T-years older than he was, but his body had been fully mature, too old to respond to the prolong therapies when Manticore made them available to his people. That meant she looked ten T-years *younger* than him . . . and his hormones were disrespectfully aware of her apparent youth.

Her strong, triangular face, with its exotically slanted eyes, owed nothing to classical beauty, but that didn't matter. Nor did the fact that she was easily fifteen centimeters taller than most Grayson men, and other, deeper changes made her attractiveness even more noticeable. She was . . . happier, more relaxed, than he'd ever imagined she could possibly be, and she seemed far more aware of her femininity. She'd never worn a trace of makeup in Yeltsin, even before she'd been wounded; now understated, skillfully applied cosmetics enhanced the graceful strength of her face, and the hair which had been close-cropped fuzz fell almost to her shoulders, instead.

He realized he'd stopped dead while he wrestled with her request and looked up to meet her eyes as she stood quietly, waiting. The cybernetic left one looked exactly like the natural one, he thought inconsequentially, and then he looked still deeper and saw the loneliness within them both. It was a loneliness she was used to, one he was still learning to bear himself. It came to every starship's captain, but that made it no less lonely, and as he recognized it, his mind suddenly settled.

"Very well . . . Honor." He reached out and touched her arm, something else no well brought up Grayson male would ever have done, and smiled. "But only in private. High Admiral

Matthews would take my head off if anyone suggested I was offering you *lese majesty* in public!"

GNS *Jason Alvarez* settled into Grayson orbit, and Honor leaned back in the admiral's command chair on the heavy cruiser's flag bridge. It felt a bit presumptuous to seat her fundament in such an exalted perch, but Mark had insisted, and she had to admit she hadn't argued very hard.

There was only a skeleton watch on the flag bridge with her while Mark handled the final maneuvers from his own command deck, but the displays were live, and she watched them with appreciation and a sense of awe as she realized how much Grayson had achieved since her last visit.

Grayson was as beautiful as ever—and as deadly. The Church of Humanity Unchained had come here fleeing what it had regarded as Old Earth's soul-corrupting technology only to discover it had marooned itself on a planet with higher concentrations of heavy metals than most toxic waste dumps. Had it been up to her, she would have abandoned the planetary surface completely in favor of orbital habitats, but Grayson's stubborn people had rejected that policy. They'd moved as much as possible of their *food* production into orbit, once they regained space capability, but they themselves clung to the world they had made their own with such titanic toil. The enormous constructs floating in orbit with *Alvarez* were even more numerous than they'd been before Grayson joined the Alliance and gained access to modern industrial capacity, but they were still farms and pastures, not retreats.

And, she thought, that really shouldn't be a surprise. She didn't think Graysons knew *how* to retreat. They weren't the religious fanatics who peopled their fratricidal sister planet of Masada, but they had a core of stubbornness which perhaps only a Sphinxian could fully appreciate. And for people descended from antitechnology, religious fundamentalist loonies, they'd shown an incredible flexibility and technical ingenuity, as well.

A surprising percentage of their orbital constructs were fortifications, small, perhaps, but heavily refitted now that they had modern technology to work with. And newer, bigger forts were under construction to augment the ones left over from the long Grayson-Masada cold war. She hadn't seen any schematics or blueprints, but she was willing to bet their designs were impressively innovative, too. The Graysons hadn't simply bought off-the-shelf Manticoran designs. They still required advice and technical assistance, but they'd studied their defensive requirements and made their own decisions with formidable self-confidence, just as they had with *Alvarez* herself. The heavy cruiser mounted barely half as many energy weapons as a Manticoran cruiser would have, yet those she *did* mount were far heavier, easily a match for most battlecruisers' beams. She couldn't hit as many targets, but the ones she did hit were going to know they'd been nudged. It was a radical departure in warship design, yet it made uncompromising sense, given the increased power of modern energy weapons. And now that she'd seen it, Honor wondered how many other aspects of Manticore's own building policies had been shaped by an unconscious acceptance of outdated conventionality.

And the sheer scale of the Graysons' efforts was even more astonishing than their sense of innovation. The planet's entire population was barely two billion, only a quarter of it male, and she doubted that even a tiny fraction of its women had yet been integrated into its workforce, yet they'd already put in—with a great deal of Manticoran assistance, to be sure— not one, or even two, but *three* modern orbital shipyards. The smallest was easily eight kilometers across, and it was growing steadily . . . all of that despite the fact that they were simultaneously building a modern navy from the keel out.

She shook her head, marveling silently, as the visual display showed her a quartet of orbiting battlecruisers. They were units of the new *Courvosier* class, and tears prickled as she watched them. The Grayson Navy had chosen its own way to acknowledge its debt to Admiral Courvosier and the other Manticorans who'd fallen in its home world's defense. Somehow, she thought, the admiral would have found it a fitting tribute . . . once he stopped laughing. But—

Her thoughts broke off as the flag bridge hatch whispered open, and she turned her head to smile a welcome at Mark Brentworth.

"All tucked neatly into orbit, Captain?" she asked, conscious of the understrength bridge watch's ears, and he nodded.

"Yes, My Lady," he returned just as formally. He crossed to her side and looked down into her visual display, then tapped the image of one of the battlecruisers. "That's the *Courvosier* herself. You can recognize her by the missing graser bay amidships. They left it out to free up mass for her flag accommodations and a full-scale fleet CIC. The other three should be *Yountz*, *Yanakov*, and *Madrigal*; together they form the First and Second Divisions."

"They're gorgeous," Honor said, and she meant it. They were easily the size of her own *Nike*, perhaps even a bit bigger, and their design mirrored *Alvarez*'s concentration on fewer but more powerful weapons.

"We think so," Brentworth admitted. He reached past her to manipulate controls, and the view in the display shifted to a more distant objective. "And this, My Lady, is what your kingdom gave the Grayson Navy," he said quietly.

Honor inhaled sharply at the sight. She'd heard about it, of course, but this was the first time she'd actually seen it. When Admiral White Haven ambushed the powerful Havenite fleet that had attacked Yeltsin, eleven of its superdreadnoughts had been forced to surrender intact. Not undamaged, by any means, but in repairable condition, and White Haven and Admiral D'Orville, his immediate Manticoran subordinate, had handed them directly over to Grayson.

It had been a generous gesture—in more ways than one. On a personal level, White Haven and D'Orville had given up an almost unimaginable prize money award, and, on another level, some Royal Navy officers argued that the ships should have been retained for Manticore's own desperate need. But Queen Elizabeth had endorsed White Haven's decision without a moment's hesitation, and Honor was in complete agreement with her Queen. The Grayson Navy, for all its gallantry and willingness, had yet to build its first ship of the wall. That had made it little more than a spectator in the titanic clash which had raged across its system, but Grayson deserved those ships—and even a political illiterate like her grasped the enormous diplomatic benefit in giving them to the GSN. It told the Graysons how highly Manticore valued its alliance with them—and said exactly the same thing to all the Star Kingdom's *other* allies.

But even though she'd known about it, she hadn't been emotionally prepared to see those wounded leviathans lying quietly under the guns of Grayson's orbital forts. They dwarfed those forts to Lilliputian dimensions, yet their very presence was proof the navy which had built them was far from invincible. Repair ships swarmed about them as the furious business of repair and refit went on, and it looked like one of them was already nearing its recommissioning under the Grayson flag.

"We're going to rename that one *Manticore's Gift*," Brentworth said quietly, and shrugged as Honor looked up at him. "It seemed appropriate, My Lady. I don't know what they've decided to call the others, and they won't be true sisters when we're done with them. We're upgrading their electronics to Manticoran standards and putting the new inertial compensators into each of them, but we're also retaining any weapons that survived. I imagine we'll refit all of them to the same standard once we have time; for right now, we're concentrating on simply getting them back into service as quickly as possible."

"If *Manticore's Gift* is as close to ready as she looks, you people must be setting new records," Honor said, and he smiled at her sincerity.

"We're certainly trying to, My Lady. As a matter of fact, our biggest problem just now is figuring out how to crew them. You do realize that the Navy's total tonnage is something like a hundred and fifty *times* what it was before the Alliance? The first batch of our officers is just finishing accelerated training at your Saganami Island, and the scale of our orbital work's always given us a lot more trained spacers than our planetary population might suggest, but we're recruiting heavily from Manticore's merchant fleet. Not," he grinned suddenly, "without some screaming about 'poaching' from your own Admiralty. Of course, we've promised to give them back as soon as we can."

"I'm sure that helped." Honor laughed. "But, tell me, are you recruiting mixed crews?"

"Yes, My Lady, we are." Brentworth shrugged again. "There was some opposition, but those SDs made too big a hole in our personnel. We'd managed to keep up with our own construction, barely, and some of our more conservative types wanted to do the same with them—until they saw the numbers. I'm afraid we're still restricting 'our' female personnel to the capital ships, though."

"Really? Why?"

"Because," Brentworth replied with a slight blush, "the Office of Shipbuilding insisted on separate accommodations for them, and only ships of the wall have the mass for that." Honor blinked in astonishment, and his blush darkened. "I know it sounds silly, My Lady, and High Admiral Matthews argued himself blue over it, but the whole concept is still too new to us. I'm afraid it's going to be a while before we stop doing silly things."

"Don't sweat it, Mark," Honor said after a moment. "Nothing says there's any reason for Grayson to mirror-image Manticoran practice. And one thing you *don't* want to do is destabilize yourself making changes too quickly."

Brentworth cocked his head, as if a bit surprised to hear her, of all people, say that, and she chuckled.

"Oh, I was furious over the way you treated our female personnel when we first arrived here, but you people have done an unbelievable job so far, and I know it hasn't been easy for you. I assure you, no one from the Star Kingdom—with the possible exception of a few idiots in the Liberal Party—is keeping any sort of scorecard. *I'm* certainly not. Your Navy and I got to know one another too well for that sort of nonsense."

Brentworth started to reply, then closed his mouth and nodded with a smile before he stood back from her chair and gestured at the hatch.

"In that case, Lady Harrington, may I invite you to accompany me? Certain members of that Navy, including High Admiral Matthews, Admiral Garret, and my father, should be arriving in Boat Bay Two to welcome you back in about fifteen minutes."

✧ CHAPTER FIFTEEN

THERE WERE NO REMOTE ORDER terminals in Dempsey's Bar. Patrons were served by real, live waiters and waitresses—a factor, given civilian labor costs on the Navy's busiest orbital shipyard, which explained much about Dempsey's price levels. It also helped explain why Dempsey's patrons were willing to *pay* those prices, but it wasn't the entire story.

The bar and its adjoining restaurant were the gathering place of choice for virtually all off-duty personnel for many reasons. One was familiarity. Dempsey's Restaurants, Inc., had been the original flagship corporation of the Dempsey Cartel, second only to the Hauptman Cartel in wealth and power, and virtually every city in the Kingdom boasted at least one Dempsey's of its own. They were everywhere, and everyone knew them, and if the chain couldn't match the eminence of one-of-a-kind establishments like Cosmo's, or emulate the frenetic activity of "cutting edge" night spots, that was fine with its managers, because they didn't want those things. What they *did* want was visibility and familiarity coupled with a level of service, comfort, and quality guaranteed to attract and hold the loyalty of their patrons (even at Dempsey's prices), and that was precisely what they had achieved.

This particular Dempsey's lay at the very hub of HMSS *Hephaestus*'s core, yet its designers had gone to great lengths to create a ground-side environment. They couldn't avoid the legally mandated color codings for emergency life support and other disaster-related access and service points, but they'd paid through the nose for permits to build double-high compartments, then used the extra height to accommodate dropped ceilings that hid the snake nests of pipes and power conduits which covered deckheads elsewhere. Sophisticated holo projections outside the casement "windows" displayed ever-changing planetary panoramas, and it was Monday, which meant the bar was "on" Sphinx. The cold, blue skies of autumn soared over the spires of Yawata Crossing, Sphinx's second largest city, and traffic and pedestrian noises drifted in through open windows on artfully cool breezes that smelled of live greenery and sidewalk-cafe cooking. Dempsey's holos never repeated themselves, either. Unlike the constructs less discerning owners might have used, they were broadcast from or recorded at other units of the chain on Manticore, Sphinx, and Gryphon, which gave them specific locations and complete spontaneity. Diners could—and did— sit for hours watching ground-side places they often knew well, and Manticore and Sphinx were close enough to *Hephaestus* to allow near real-time transmission.

Background holos, however nice, might have seemed a relatively minor element in producing the near-fanatic loyalty of Dempsey's *Hephaestus*-based regulars when Manticore itself was barely twenty minutes away by shuttle. But for more than a single person, that twenty-minute trip demanded coordination of duty schedules which was often difficult and frequently worse. A spur of the moment evening ground-side with a lover or a few close friends was a near impossibility . . . except at Dempsey's, where they brought ground-side to *you*.

Colonel Tomas Santiago Ramirez discovered his glass was empty and paused in conversation with Paul Tankersley to raise a summoning hand. His chair creaked with his movement, and he grimaced wryly at its complaint. He was used to such sounds of strain, and it was hard to blame the furniture. It hadn't been designed with him in mind.

Paul saw his grimace and hid a smile of sympathy. He and Ramirez had taken to one another almost from the first, and acquaintance had turned quickly into friendship. The colonel was a voracious reader and a man of catholic tastes, with a dry, understated sense of humor he took great pains to hide. His guard tended to come down once he got to know someone, and he and Paul had fallen into the habit of getting together for wide-ranging conversations, liberally fueled by excellent beer. Ramirez's émigré origins gave him a different, often subtly provocative viewpoint on things native Manticorans took for granted, and Paul enjoyed their discussions immensely. It didn't hurt that the colonel was devoted to Honor, but Paul suspected they'd have become friends even if he hadn't been.

Ramirez was also just as tough as his physique suggested, yet he was simultaneously one of the gentlest men Paul had ever met . . . except where the People's Republic of Haven was concerned. No one could have called the colonel soft, but it was as if all his hostility had been distilled and directed toward a single goal: the destruction of the People's Republic and all its works. It might have been inaccurate to call his hatred for the Peeps obsessive, but not by very much.

His exec was another matter. Susan Hibson didn't share her boss's implacable vindictiveness toward Haven, but only an idiot would ever take liberties with her . . . and *no one* would take them twice. She was no martinet, and her people were devoted to her, but they feared her, as well. It wasn't that she didn't suffer fools gladly; she didn't suffer them at all, and God help anyone who dared to suggest there was anything, however impossible, *her* Marines couldn't do.

Perhaps, Paul thought, the difference between Hibson and Ramirez had something to do with their sizes. The major was thirty-five centimeters shorter than her superior, barely squeaking past the Corps' minimum height requirement, and she was built for speed, not power. Her colonel could afford his gentleness because someone built like a suit of battle armor never *needed* an attack-dog mentality, but Susan Hibson looked too small and delicate for a "proper" warrior. The Marines, unlike the Navy, were expected to get down in the mud and the blood, and Paul had no doubt Hibson had been forced to prove herself in her chosen profession—not simply to others, but to herself—for years.

The summoned waiter appeared at Ramirez's elbow, and the colonel smiled at his companions.

"The same again for everyone?" His voice was deep, but its curiously liquid consonants gave it an almost musical lilt. San Martin was one of the worlds whose ethno-preservationist colonists had managed to hang onto their native language, and Ramirez had never lost his accent.

Murmurs of agreement met his question, but Alistair McKeon shook his head with a smile.

"No more beer for Mr. Tremaine," he announced. Lieutenant (Senior Grade) Scotty Tremaine made an indignant sound, and McKeon chuckled. "We adults have to look after the infants among us. Besides, he's going on watch soon."

"With all due respect, Sir, that's a load of, um, unfounded prejudice. We younger, fitter types have the metabolism to handle alcohol without impairing our faculties. Unlike," the sandy-haired lieutenant added, "some old—I mean, certain distinguished senior officers."

"You, young man, spend entirely too much time with people like Senior Chief Harkness." McKeon's tone was austere, but his eyes twinkled, and Tankersley swallowed a laugh. He'd come to know the people around this table well and liked them all, not just Ramirez, but he'd been more than a little surprised by McKeon's and Tremaine's off-duty informality.

Most captains he'd known never socialized with their juniors, much less joked with them, but McKeon managed it without ever undermining his authority or suggesting that he played favorites. Paul wasn't certain how the captain managed that, and he was fairly sure he couldn't have done it himself, but Tremaine's own personality probably had something to do with it.

"Not guilty, Sir," the lieutenant said now. "I'm just reminding you of scientifically demonstrated facts."

"Of course you are." McKeon smiled again, then shrugged. "All right. One more beer for Mr. Tremaine. After that, he's on sodas."

His voice held a slight but unmistakable undertone of command, and Tremaine accepted it with a nod and a smile of his own. The waiter tapped their orders into his pad and departed, and Hibson drained the last swallow from her current stein and sighed.

"I have to say I'm glad things are finally settling down dirtside," she said, picking up the thread of their earlier conversation, "but I can't help wishing Burgundy had pulled it off."

"Amen to that," Ramirez rumbled with an uncharacteristic frown, and McKeon nodded, but Tankersley shook his head.

"I don't think I do, Susan," he disagreed. The others looked at him in surprise, and he shrugged. "I don't give a good goddamn what happens to Pavel Young, as long as it's unpleasant, but refusing to admit him to the Lords would only have made the situation still worse."

"I hate to admit it, but you're probably right," McKeon said after a moment. He shook his head. "Who would have believed that little shit would actually *support* the declaration? I hate agreeing with him on anything, and I don't believe for a minute that he's really changed, but the son-of-a-bitch *has* been useful. And I imagine refusing to seat him would have made things worse for the Captain in the long run, too, now that you mention it."

Paul nodded seriously, but the corners of his mouth tried to smile. All of his companions knew he was Honor's lover, and all of them were unabashed partisans of hers, as well, but they all—every one of them, including McKeon, who commanded his own ship—referred to her only as "the Captain" or "the Skipper."

"I think you're right, too, Sir," Scotty Tremaine said with unwonted seriousness, "but I'm still not clear on exactly what happened or what it was all about. I mean, Young did inherit an earldom. Doesn't that automatically make him a member of the House of Lords?"

"Yes and no, Scotty." Paul gazed down into his empty glass, turning it slowly on the table before him, then looked up and relinquished the empty as the waiter returned. He took a sip of his fresh beer and pursed his lips.

"Young—or North Hollow, now—is, indeed, a peer of the realm," he continued. "Unless he'd been attainted for treason—which he would have been, had he been convicted of cowardice in the face of the enemy—he's legally his father's heir. But the Constitution gives the Lords the right to refuse to seat someone, peer or no, as unfit for membership. It hasn't been done in something like a hundred T-years, but the right to exclude is still there, and not even the Queen can override it if a two-thirds majority of the Lords chooses to exercise it. That's what Burgundy was after when he introduced his motion to consider North Hollow's 'demonstrated lack of character.' "

Tremaine nodded, and Tomas Ramirez used his own stein to hide his grimace of distaste. He was a loyal subject of Queen Elizabeth, but he'd never quite accepted the notion of birth as an automatic guarantor of privilege. San Martin had enjoyed, if that was the word, its own hereditary elites before its conquest by the Peeps, but an explicit aristocracy had never been part of them.

He was willing, if pressed, to admit that Manticore's nobility had done well by the Star Kingdom over the centuries. And, certainly, *any* political system had its own built-in faults. After all, it was designed to govern humans, and humanity could be counted upon to screw anything up periodically. But ever since he'd become aware of the hatred between Pavel Young and the Captain, and especially since he'd learned how it had all started, he'd been even more skeptical than ever about this notion of inherited political power. Like McKeon, he had no faith in Young's apparent conversion, either. The bastard was up to something. The thought that he might get away with whatever he was after was nauseating, and the way some of the other Lords were still trying to prevent effective operations against the Peeps hadn't done a thing to change Ramirez's mind about the institution itself, either.

Of course, the Captain herself was a noble now, he reminded himself, and there were others who'd earned their titles the hard way—or proven they deserved them, however they'd gotten them. People like the Dukes of Cromarty and New Texas, or Earl White Haven and Baroness Morncreek. And there were others who at least recognized their responsibilities and did their best to meet them, like the Duke of Burgundy and the five other peers who'd joined his motion to exclude North Hollow. But the combination of stupidity and self-interest which was making it so hard for Cromarty to obtain his declaration—and so easy for Young to play statesman—sickened the colonel.

"—and the Government couldn't support Burgundy," Tankersley was going on to Tremaine. "I'm pretty sure they would have loved to do just that, at least until North Hollow started pushing support for the declaration. But with the Opposition ready to scream partisan politics, supporting Burgundy and the other nonaligned peers would have—"

Ramirez tuned it out and looked around the bar. He couldn't disagree with Tankersley, but that didn't mean he had to like it. And hearing someone who loved the Captain being forced to explain why the Government had no choice but to *support* the admission to the highest legislative body in the Kingdom of a piece of garbage who hated her did bad things to his digestion.

His eyes swept the patrons about him, and a tiny flaw in his surroundings caught at his attention. He couldn't put his finger on exactly what it was, but something drew his gaze back to a fair-haired civilian standing with one elbow on the bar nursing a frosted glass. The colonel's eyes narrowed, something like a ghost of elusive memory plucking at the corner of his mind, but he couldn't quite lay hands on it and pin it down. Perhaps it was nothing at all. Or, more likely, it was simply the way the man was standing. There was an almost theatrical gracefulness to his pose, and he was gazing more or less towards Ramirez's table as he, too, surveyed the crowd. Their eyes met for just a moment, the stranger's bland and incurious; then he turned back to the bartender to order a refill, and the colonel shrugged and returned his attention to his companions.

"—why Burgundy never had a chance, really," Tankersley was finishing up. "It's too bad. They don't call him 'the conscience of the Lords' for nothing, but once North Hollow actually made himself valuable to the Government, there were too many factors against him."

"I see." Tremaine sipped his own beer, making it last since he wasn't going to be getting another one, then shrugged. "I see, but I still don't like it, Sir. And I'm with the Skipper—he's up to something dirty. D'you think this pro-war talk of his was just to force the Government to support seating him?"

"That's certainly one explanation that makes sense, but—"

Tankersley broke off and looked up. Ramirez turned his head to follow the direction of his gaze, and smile wrinkles crinkled about the colonel's eyes as he recognized the sturdy-looking red-haired woman approaching their table. She wore the uniform of a Marine sergeant-major, and the streaks of gray in her hair proclaimed that she was old enough to have received one of the earlier generations of the prolong treatment.

"Well, well! If it isn't Gunny Babcock," Ramirez said, and the woman smiled at him. The Royal Manticoran Marines no longer used the official rank of gunnery sergeant. They'd lost it when they merged with the Royal Army three hundred T-years before and hadn't reinstated it when they split back off a hundred years after that. But the senior Marine noncom aboard any ship was still referred to as "gunny," and Iris Babcock had been the battalion sergeant-major attached to HMS *Fearless* with Ramirez and Hibson.

"Good evening, Colonel. Captain. Major." Babcock nodded respectfully to the senior officers around the table, and her smile turned into something like a grin as Scotty Tremaine flipped her an impudent salute. The Navy was less punctilious about military protocol in off-duty situations, and the Corps had learned to put up with them. Besides, only a convinced misanthrope could have produced an appropriate glower at Tremaine.

"To what do we owe the honor, Gunny?" Ramirez asked, and the sergeant-major nodded at McKeon once more.

"I'm sergeant-major to Major Yestachenko in Captain McKeon's Marine detachment now, Colonel. I was just on my way back to *Prince Adrian* when I noticed all of you over here. I haven't seen you or Major Hibson since your promotions, and I thought I'd pay my respects in passing."

Ramirez nodded. Dempsey's was a civilian establishment. It wasn't uncommon for officers and noncoms, or even enlisted personnel, from the same commands to run into one another here, and there was an unofficial protocol for what happened when they did. He started to reply when Tankersley's chrono chirped, and the naval officer looked down at it with a grimace.

"Damn," he said mildly. "Looks like I have to be going, folks. Places to be and people to see, I'm afraid." He finished off his drink and rose, smiling at the others. "It's been fun, and I'll see you all later."

He nodded to Babcock, who came to a sort of parade rest in reply, then turned toward the exit. The others watched him go, and Ramirez saw Babcock smile at his back. So, the colonel thought. The sergeant-major was another of the Captain's well-wishers.

But then Babcock's smile vanished. It didn't fade; it disappeared into a sudden, bleak expression Ramirez had seen on her face only once before, when they broke into the cell blocks of Blackbird Base and discovered what the Masadans had done to their Manticoran POWs. It happened like magic, in a single beat of the heart, and the raw hatred in her eyes stunned the colonel with its abrupt, brutal impact.

"Gunny?" The single word came out softly, questioningly, before he could stop himself, and Babcock shook herself. Her eyes dropped down to meet his for a moment, then rose once more, and he turned to look over his own shoulder. She was staring at the man at the bar, the one who'd looked elusively familiar, and Ramirez's brows lowered in a frown.

"What is it, Gunny?" His voice was firmer and more authoritative. "Do you know that man?"

"Yes, Sir, I do," Babcock's reply was grim and stark.

"Well, who is he?" Ramirez felt the others looking at them both in surprise. Surprise both at Babcock's reaction and his own tone as that nagging sense of almost recognition tugged at him again.

"Denver Summervale, Sir," Babcock said flatly, and air hissed between Ramirez's teeth as the pieces suddenly clicked. He felt Hibson tense beside him, and McKeon frowned at him across the table.

"What's going on, Tomas?" the captain asked. "Who *is* that guy?"

"You wouldn't know, Sir," Ramirez replied. He forced his fists to unclench and turned his back deliberately upon Summervale's presence. "He wasn't one of yours; he was ours."

"Not for a long time now, Sir," Susan Hibson said quietly.

"He was ours for too *damned* long, Ma'am," Babcock grated, then shook herself. "Excuse me, Ma'am."

"Don't apologize, Gunny. Not for that."

"Would one of you please explain what's going on?" McKeon asked, and Ramirez smiled without humor.

"Captain The Honorable Denver Summervale was once a Marine officer, Sir," he said. "He's also some sort of cousin of Duke Cromarty. Thirty-odd years ago, he was court-martialed and dismissed from the Queen's Service after he killed a brother officer in a duel."

"In a duel?" McKeon looked back toward the bar, and Babcock made a grating sound of disgust.

"If you can call it that, Captain," she said flatly. "The officer he killed was a lieutenant—*my* lieutenant. I was his platoon sergeant. Mr. Tremaine here reminds me a lot of him, only he was even younger." McKeon's eyes snapped back to the sergeant-major, and she met his gaze levelly. "He was just a kid. A nice kid, but so new he squeaked. Only it turned out his family had enemies, and *Captain* Summervale goaded him into a duel. It was a farce, a put-up job, and I couldn't get Mr. Thurston to realize it."

The sergeant-major's bleak face was cold with almost as much self-hatred as loathing for Summervale. It was the face of someone who'd failed a junior officer she was supposed to look after.

"It wasn't your fault, Gunny," Ramirez said. "I've heard the stories, and everyone knew Summervale's reputation. Lieutenant Thurston should have realized what was going on."

"But he didn't, Sir. He actually believed he'd accidentally impugned Summervale's honor, and that made him hesitate. That bastard was a good second faster off the mark, and he put that bullet exactly where he'd been damned well *paid* to put it."

"That was never proven," Ramirez said quietly, and Babcock's snort was just short of insubordinate. The colonel ignored it. "It *wasn't* proven," he went on in that same quiet voice, "but I think you're right. And so did the Corps when they cashiered him."

"Too late for Mr. Thurston," Babcock half-whispered, then shook herself again. "I'm sorry, Sir. I shouldn't have spoken that way. It just . . . sort of took me by surprise after all these years."

"Like Major Hibson says, don't apologize. I knew about Summervale, but I didn't know you'd been in Thurston's platoon at the time." Ramirez turned to glance over his shoulder again just as Summervale paid his bill and left, and the colonel's eyes narrowed in speculation.

"I haven't heard anything much about him or what he's been up to for the last several years," he mused aloud. "Have you Susan? Gunny?"

"No, Sir," Babcock replied, and Hibson shook her head silently.

"Odd." Ramirez rubbed an eyebrow, frowning down into his drink, and made a mental note to report Summervale's presence to Marine Intelligence. They liked to keep track of their own bad apples, even after they were officially "theirs" no longer. "It's probably just a coincidence," he went on thoughtfully, "but I wonder what a paid duelist, who has to know how any Marine who recognizes him is going to react, is doing aboard *Hephaestus*?"

✧ CHAPTER SIXTEEN

HONOR HARRINGTON SQUARED HER shoulders and tried not to feel absurd as she strode down the arched, ancient hallway in a swishing rustle.

In three decades as a Queen's officer, Honor had never worn a skirt. In fact, she'd never worn one at *all*, and she'd been pleased (whenever she considered it) that they'd gone out of style—again—fifty Manticoran years ago. They were worse than useless in zero gee and almost equally impractical for most other things she did with her time, yet they also showed a stubborn refusal to die once and for all. They were actually making a modest comeback in the Star Kingdom even now . . . among idiots with the money to replace entire wardrobes and a need to be on the cutting edge of every fashion trend, anyway.

Unfortunately, Grayson women didn't wear trousers. Period. Which had led to something very like panic among the protocolists when she arrived without a single gown to her name.

She'd started out by refusing even to consider wearing one, but it was hard enough for half the Graysons she met to deal with the concept of a female steadholder in the first place. The notion of seeing not merely a woman but a woman in *trousers* in the sacred precincts of Steadholder Hall had threatened more conservative thinkers with heart failure. Even the "Modernists" had viewed the idea with sufficiently mixed feelings for Protector Benjamin, the man who'd seized avidly upon Honor's achievements to initiate Grayson's mammoth social reforms, to beg her to reconsider.

That was the point at which she'd finally given in—if less than graciously. It all seemed so silly, and she felt like an actress dressed for some historical costume drama. Worse, she'd seen the graceful way Grayson women managed their flowing, traditional skirts and knew perfectly well she couldn't match it. But Admiral Courvosier had lectured her once on the importance of diplomacy, and she supposed this was a time for a negotiated surrender.

So now she made her way down the echoing stone hall towards the huge, closed portals, Nimitz cradled in her arms (her gown lacked the padded shoulder protection of her naval uniforms), while floor-length fabric swirled about her legs. There was something oddly sensual about the sensation, but she felt totally out of place in the unfamiliar garment and had to keep reminding herself to shorten her long stride to something more decorous. And, she thought with a wry twist of her lips, she probably looked as ridiculous as she felt.

She was wrong about that. Her gown was the work of Grayson's finest designer, and she had too little experience with civilian fashions to realize quite how daring it was by local standards. Its unadorned white native spider silk set off the dark, jewel-toned green of her hip-length vest—suede, not the traditional brocade—and together they made the most of her tall, muscular slenderness, dark hair, and pale complexion. They clung to her, flowed with her movements, enshrouding her as tradition decreed but without trying to pretend there wasn't a female body at their heart or to hide the athletic grace of her movements. She wore no jewels (that much tradition, at least, she was still prepared to reject), but the Star of Grayson glittered golden on her breast. She'd felt odd about that, too, for Manticoran dress codes proscribed decorations for civilian dress, but she wasn't a civilian on Grayson, whatever she might wear. A steadholder not only wielded a personal feudal authority which would have stunned most Manticoran aristocrats but commanded the Army units based in his (or her) steading, as well. As such, medals were worn on all official occasions . . . and Honor Harrington, off-worlder or no, was the sole living holder of Grayson's highest award for valor.

She swept down the hall in a swirl of white, uncovered brown hair loose over her shoulders, cream-and-gray treecat in her arms, and that, too, might have struck some observers as odd. On most non-Manticoran planets, bringing a "pet" to such a ceremony would have made things even worse, yet the people of this world knew Nimitz, and no one had even suggested leaving him behind. Not on Grayson.

The hall seemed to stretch forever, lined with troopers from the Steadholders' Guard, not regular Army personnel, who went to one knee as she passed, and tension shivered in her middle.

She rehearsed the formalities to come in her mind as she went, yet she felt no calmer to know she had her lines down pat. Protector Benjamin had invested her with her steading before she returned to Manticore for medical treatment, but that had been only an acknowledgment of things to come. The Steading of Harrington had existed only on paper. Now it had people, towns, the beginnings of industry. It was real, and that made it time for her to formally face the Conclave of Steadholders, the final arbiter of her fitness for her office. To accept her role as the protector and ruler of people—of *her* people—and assume a direct authority over their lives and well-being such as no Manticoran noble had ever known. She knew that, and she'd done her best to prepare herself for it, but deep inside she was still Honor Harrington, a yeoman's daughter from Sphinx, and that part of her wanted nothing in the galaxy more than to turn and run for her life.

She reached the enormous iron-strapped double doors of the Conclave Chamber at last. Those ponderous barriers dated back almost seven hundred T-years; there were firing slits in the walls flanking them, and the left-hand panel was pitted with jagged bullet holes. Honor's knowledge of Grayson history remained incomplete, but she'd learned enough to pause and incline her head in deep respect to those pits. The plaque beneath them listed the names of The Fifty-Three and their personal armsmen, the men who had held the Conclave Chamber to the last against the attempted coup which had begun the Grayson Civil War. In the end, the Faithful had brought up tanks, grinding down this very passage over the bodies of the Steadholder's Guard, blown the right-hand door to splinters, and thrown in an entire company of infantry in a desperate bid to capture at least some of the steadholders as hostages, but none of The Fifty-Three had been taken alive.

The last guardsmen went to one knee as she bowed to the plaque, and she straightened, drew an even deeper breath, and grasped the iron knocker.

The harsh iron-on-iron clang echoed in the hall. There was a moment of stillness; then the huge, centimeters-thick panels swung slowly open, and light spilled out through them. She faced a man armed with a naked sword, looking past him to the ranks of steadholders seated about the horseshoe-shaped chamber beyond him. The Door Warden's costume was a gold-braid-encrusted anachronism even more magnificent than her own gown, yet it was recognizably that of the regular Army, and his collar bore the opened Bible and sword of the Protector, not the patriarch's key of the Steadholders' Guard.

"Who petitions audience of the Protector?" he demanded, and despite her nervousness, Honor's soprano voice rang clear and unwavering in the words of ancient formula.

"I seek audience of no man. I come not to petition, but to claim admittance to the Conclave and be seated therein, as is my right."

"By what authority?" the Door Warden challenged. His sword fell into a guard position, and Nimitz mirrored Honor's movement as her head rose proudly.

"By my own authority, under God and the Law," she returned.

"Name yourself," the Warden commanded.

"I am Honor Stephanie Harrington, daughter of Alfred Harrington, come to claim of right my place as Steadholder Harrington," Honor replied, and the Warden stepped back a pace and lowered his sword in formal acknowledgment of the gathered steadholders' equality with the Protector.

"Then enter this place, that the Conclave of Steadholders may judge your fitness for the office you claim, as is its ancient right," he intoned, and Honor stepped forward in a swirl of skirts.

So far, so good, she told herself, trying to stop the frantic mental recitation of her lines. The fact that she was a woman had required some surgery on the millennium-old formulas; the fact that she was technically an infidel had required still more. But she was here now, she reminded herself, standing in the center of the vast chamber while the massed steadholders of Grayson looked down upon her in silence.

The door boomed softly shut behind her, and the Door Warden stepped past her. He went to one knee before the throne of Benjamin IX, Protector of Grayson, resting the tip of the jeweled Sword of State on the stone floor, and bowed over its simple, cross-shaped guard.

"Your Grace, I present to you and to this Conclave Honor Stephanie Harrington, daughter of Alfred Harrington, who comes claiming a place among your steadholders."

Benjamin Mayhew nodded gravely and gazed down upon Honor for a long, silent moment, then raised his eyes to sweep the rows of seats.

"Steadholders," his voice was crisp and clear in the chamber's splendid acoustics, "this woman claims right to a seat among you. Would any challenge her fitness so to do?"

Static crackled up and down Honor's nerves, for Mayhew's question was not the formality it would normally have been. Grayson reactionaries were more reactionary than most, and the upheavals rending their social fabric had all begun with her. A majority of Graysons supported the changes which had come upon them, if with varying degrees of enthusiasm; the minority who didn't, opposed them with militant fervor. She'd read and heard their bitter rhetoric since her arrival, and the opportunity to challenge a mere woman as unfit echoed in the silence, waiting for someone to take it up.

But no one did, and Mayhew nodded once more.

"Would any speak in her favor?" he asked quietly, and a vast, rumbling response of "Aye," came back to him. Not all of the Conclave's members joined it, but none opposed it, and Mayhew smiled down at her.

"Your claim is freely granted by your peers, Lady Harrington. Come now and take your place among them."

Cloth rustled as the other steadholders stood, and Honor climbed the broad, shallow steps of stone to the second tier of seats to stand directly before the Protector. Two small velvet cushions had been placed before his throne, and she set Nimitz carefully on one and went to her knees on the other. It wasn't as easy as one might have thought, given her encumbering skirts, but she could never have managed a proper curtsy. One or two pairs of feet shuffled as she knelt as a man would have, but no voice spoke as the Door Warden stepped past her and surrendered the Sword of State to Mayhew.

The Protector reversed it and extended its hilt to Honor, and she laid her hands upon it. She was startled, despite her nervousness, to see the quiver in her fingers and looked up at Mayhew, and the Protector's encouraging smile stilled their tremble.

"Honor Stephanie Harrington," Mayhew said quietly, "are you prepared, in the presence of the assembled Steadholders of Grayson, to swear fealty to the Protector and People of Grayson under the eyes of God and His Holy Church?"

"I am, Your Grace, yet I may do so only with two reservations." Honor withdrew her hands from the sword hilt, but there was no refusal in her clear soprano, and Mayhew nodded. He knew what was coming, of course. There'd been quite a bit of discussion over ways to deal with this point.

"It is your ancient and lawful right to state reservations to your oath," he said. "Yet it is also the right of this Conclave to reject those reservations and deny your place, should it find them offensive to it. Do you acknowledge that right?"

"I do, Your Grace."

"Then state your first reservation."

"As Your Grace knows, I am also a subject of the Star

Kingdom of Manticore, a member of its peerage, and an officer in the Queen's Navy. As such, I am under obligations I cannot honorably disregard. Nor may I abandon the nation to which I was born or my oaths to my Queen to accept even a steadholder's high office, or swear fealty to Grayson without reserving to myself the right and responsibility to meet and perform my duties to her."

Mayhew nodded once more, then looked over her head at the Conclave.

"My Lords, this seems to me a right and honorable declaration, but the judgment in such matters must be yours. Does any man here dispute this woman's right to hold steading on Grayson with this limitation?"

Silence answered, and the Protector turned back to Honor.

"And your second reservation is?"

"Your Grace, I am not a communicant of the Church of Humanity Unchained. I respect its doctrines and teachings," which, Honor was relieved to reflect, was true, despite a certain lingering sexism on their part, now that she'd had a chance to read them, "but I am not of your faith."

"I see." Mayhew sounded graver—with reason. The Church had learned by horrible example to stay out of politics, but Grayson remained an essentially theocratic world. The Act of Toleration legalizing other faiths was barely a century old, and no steadholder not of the Church had ever held office.

The Protector looked at the white-haired man standing at his right. The Reverend Julius Hanks, spiritual head of the Church of Humanity Unchained, was growing frail with age, but his simple black garments and antique clerical collar stood out starkly against the glitter and richness of the other costumes in the chamber.

"Reverend," Mayhew said, "this reservation touches upon the Church and so falls within your province. How say you?"

Hanks laid one hand on Honor's head, and she felt no patronization in the gesture. She was no member of his Church, yet neither was she immune to the obvious sincerity of his personal faith as he smiled down at her.

"Lady Harrington, you say you are not of our Faith, but there are many ways to God." Someone hissed as if at the voice of heresy, but no one spoke. "Do you believe in God, my child?"

"I do, Reverend," Honor replied, quietly but firmly.

"And do you serve Him to the best of your ability as your heart gives you to understand His will for you?"

"I do."

"Will you, as steadholder, guard and protect the right of your people to worship God as their own hearts call them so to do?"

"I will."

"Will you respect and guard the sanctity of our Faith as you would your own?"

"I will."

Hanks nodded and turned to Mayhew.

"Your Grace, this woman is not of our Faith, yet she has so declared before us all, making no effort to pretend otherwise. More, she stands proven a good and godly woman, one who hazarded her own life and suffered grievous wounds to protect not only our Church but our world when we had no claim upon her. I say to you, and to the Conclave," he turned to face the steadholders, and his resonant voice rose higher and stronger, "that God knows His own. The Church accepts this woman as its champion and defender, whatever the faith through which she may serve God's will in her own life."

Another, deeper silence answered. Hanks stood a moment longer, meeting all eyes, then stepped back beside the throne, and Mayhew looked down at Honor.

"Your reservations have been noted and accepted by the lords secular and temporal of Grayson, Honor Stephanie Harrington. Do you swear now, before us all, that they constitute your sole reservations of heart and soul and mind?"

"I do so swear, Your Grace."

"Then I call upon you to swear fealty before your peers," the Protector said, and Honor replaced her hands upon the sword hilt.

"Do you, Honor Stephanie Harrington, daughter of Alfred Harrington, with the afore noted reservations, swear fealty to the Protector and People of Grayson?"

"I do."

"Will you bear true service to the Protector and People of Grayson?"

"I will."

"Do you swear, before God and this Conclave, to honor, preserve, and protect the Constitution of Grayson, and to protect and guide your people, guarding them as your own children? Will you swear to nurture them in time of peace, lead them in time of war, and govern them always with justice tempered by mercy, as God shall give you the wisdom so to do?"

"I do so swear," Honor said softly, and Mayhew nodded.

"I accept your oath, Honor Stephanie Harrington. And as Protector of Grayson, I will answer fealty with fealty, protection with protection, justice with justice, and oathbreaking with vengeance, so help me God."

The Protector's right hand slid down to cover both of hers, squeezing hard for an instant. Then he returned the sword to the Warden, and Reverend Hanks handed him a gleaming double-handful of golden glory. He shook it out reverently, and Honor bent her head for him to hang the massive chain about her neck. The patriarch's key of a steadholder glittered below the Star of Grayson, and the Protector stood to take her hand in his own.

"Rise, then, Lady Harrington, Steadholder Harrington!" he said loudly, and she obeyed, remembering at the last moment not to tread upon the hem of her gown. She turned to face the Conclave at Mayhew's gesture, and a roar of acclaim rolled up against the crowded chamber's walls.

She stared out into the sea of sound, cheeks flushed, head high, and knew reservations still lingered behind some of those cheers. But she also knew those cheering men had risen above a thousand years of tradition and bone-deep prejudice to admit a woman to their ranks. They might have done it only under the pressure of onrushing events and the unrelenting insistence of their ruler. Many of them must resent her, not merely as a woman but as the out-worlder who was the very agent and symbol of terrifying change. Yet they'd *done* it, and despite her own fears, she had meant every word of her formal oaths.

Nimitz rose high on his own cushion, patting her thigh. She looked down and bent to gather him up once more, and a louder, more spontaneous acclamation greeted the gesture. The 'cat raised his head, preening before the ovation, and a tension release of laughter and applause answered as Honor held him higher with a huge smile of her own.

The Warden stepped forward and touched her elbow. She turned toward him, and he extended the Sword of State on his opened palms and bowed to her across it. It wasn't easy to take the weapon gracefully with an armful of treecat, but Nimitz surprised her with his cooperation. He climbed onto her unpadded shoulder on velveted true-feet and hand-feet, without the claws he would normally have used, and braced himself with exquisite care, one true-hand on the crown of her head, as she accepted the sword from the Warden.

That, too, was unprecedented. The Steading of Harrington was the newest on Grayson; as such, she would normally have retired to the horseshoe's far end and uppermost tier after giving her oath, as befitted her steading's lack of seniority. But she also wore the Star of Grayson, and that, though she hadn't known it when the medal was presented, made her Protector's Champion.

She held the sword carefully, praying Nimitz's clawless restraint would last, and walked to the carved wooden desk beside the throne. It bore both her Grayson coat of arms and the crossed swords of the Protector's Champion, and she sighed in relief as Nimitz leapt lightly down onto it. He drew himself up to his full height and sat on his rearmost pairs of limbs, curling his fluffy, prehensile tail about his clawed hand-feet and true-feet with regal grace while she laid the Sword of State in the padded brackets prepared to receive it.

The craggy-faced old man seated in the steadholder's chair behind the desk rose, bowed, and extended a slender, silver-headed staff to her.

"As you take your rightful place, Lady, I surrender my badge of office and my actions to your judgment," Howard Clinkscales said.

Honor took the staff of regency from him and held it in both hands, and her smile was warmer than protocol demanded. Benjamin Mayhew had made an inspired choice when he named Clinkscales as her regent. The old warhorse was one of the most honest men on Grayson; perhaps even more important, he was also one of the most conservative, with deep reservations about the changes his Protector demanded, and everyone knew it. Which meant his willingness to serve as her regent had probably done more to consolidate her position than anything else could have.

"Your service requires no judgment." She held the rod back out to him, and their gazes met as he grasped it. "Nor could I—or anyone else—praise you as your actions deserve," she added, and the old man's eyes widened, for her last sentence had stepped beyond the bounds of formal usage.

"Thank you, My Lady," he murmured, and bowed more deeply than before as he accepted his staff of office once more. Honor took her place before the steadholder's chair he'd vacated, and he moved to the second chair at its right. They turned back to face the Conclave together, and Julius Hanks stepped forward beside the Protector's throne.

"And now, My Lords—and Lady—" the Reverend turned to bestow a sparkling smile upon Grayson's newest steadholder "—let us ask God's blessing upon our deliberations this day."

✧ CHAPTER SEVENTEEN

PAUL TANKERSLEY FINISHED THE DAY'S final report and tossed the backup record chip into his out-basket with a groan of relief. Life seemed much duller with Honor off in Yeltsin, but Admiral Cheviot was clearly determined to keep HMSS *Hephaestus*'s newest deputy constructor from mooning over his lady love.

Paul grinned at the thought and made one more pass through his work files, double-checking to confirm that he'd caught everything. As the executive officer of Hancock Base, he'd been charged with managing all the details so smoothly his CO never noticed anyone *had* to manage them, and, in his own mind, he'd believed that would prove more than adequate preparation for his present duties.

He'd been wrong. He was only one of nineteen deputy constructors, yet his workload dwarfed the one he'd carried as Hancock Station's exec. He had direct supervisory responsibility for the construction of no less than three dreadnoughts and a superdreadnought—which didn't even count the host of refits underway in "his" quadrant of the mammoth space station. For the first time in his career, he was really aware, not just intellectually conscious, of the sheer scale of the Royal Navy's building and maintenance programs.

His terminal beeped confirmation that he'd dealt with every "Immediate Attention" flag, and he sighed in satisfaction as he shut it down. He logged his schedule for the evening in case something his own exec couldn't handle came up, then rose, stretched, and consulted his chrono. He'd run forty minutes over his watch, but that was less than he'd expected when he arranged to meet Tomas Ramirez for beer and darts at Dempsey's, and he had a good hour to kill before the colonel turned up. He rubbed an eyebrow, then shrugged and grinned. He might as well spend it getting a head start on the beer part of the evening; it wasn't as if abstaining would help against Ramirez's deadly accuracy.

It was a Wednesday, which put Dempsey's "on" Gryphon for the day. And since it was winter in Gryphon's southern hemisphere, a howling blizzard raged beyond the closed windows. The exterior temperature controls had been adjusted to match, edging the windowpanes with frost, and an impressively realistic holographic fire crackled and seethed in the bar's central fireplace.

Conversation murmured in the background, hushed and companionable with the sense of people sharing an oasis against the storm, whether it was real or not, and Paul felt relaxation creep through him as he ordered his second beer. He was drinking Old Tilman, a Sphinxian brew Honor had introduced him to, and he savored its rich, clean taste. If he nursed this stein just right, he should be just finishing it when the colonel walked in.

He took another sip, then turned his head in mild surprise as a stranger slid up onto the barstool beside him. Most of Dempsey's patrons were scattered about the booths and tables, which left the gleaming hardwood bar lightly tenanted. There were enough unoccupied stools to provide privacy, or at least solitude, and he wondered idly why the newcomer hadn't taken one of them.

"Double T-whiskey sour," the stranger told the barkeep, and Paul's eyebrow quirked. Most Manticorans preferred one of the native whiskeys from the viewpoint of familiarity and cost alike. Terran whiskey was expensive enough, even in the Star Kingdom, to make it an affectation of the very rich, and if the slim, fair-haired man beside him was well-dressed, neither the cut nor the fabric of his clothing suggested the kind of money that went with T-whiskey.

The bartender produced the required drink, and the stranger took a sip, then turned his stool to survey his surroundings. He rested one elbow on the polished bar, holding his drink with a sort of negligent grace, and there was an almost arrogant confidence in the way he scanned his fellow patrons.

Something about him bothered Paul. There was nothing concrete or overt, yet invisible hackles tried to rise on the back of his neck. He wanted to get up and move away, but the gesture would have been too pointed, too rude, and he concentrated on his beer, scolding himself for the hyper-sensitivity that made him wish he could do it without offending.

A minute passed, then two, before the stranger abruptly drained his glass and set the empty on the bar. His movements had a curious deliberation, almost a finality, and Paul expected him to leave. But he didn't.

"Captain Tankersley, isn't it?" The voice was cool, with an aristocratic accent which certainly matched a taste for Terran whiskey. It was also courteous, yet there was something else under the courtesy.

"I'm afraid you have the advantage of me," Paul said slowly, and the stranger smiled.

"I'm not surprised, Sir. After all, you've been turning up on HD and in the 'faxes since Hancock Station, while I—" He shrugged, as if to emphasize his own lack of importance, and Paul frowned. He'd been trapped into interviews a couple of times, especially after the newsies learned of his relationship with Honor, but he wouldn't have thought he'd gotten enough coverage for strangers to recognize him in bars.

"In fact," the other man went on, "I wanted to tell you how much I appreciate the job you did in Hancock."

"You don't want to believe all you read in the 'faxes," Paul replied. "All I did was sit on the repair base and hope Admiral Sarnow and Captain Harrington could keep the Peeps from blowing it out from under me."

"Ah, yes. Of course." The stranger nodded and raised his glass at the bartender to signal for a refill. Then he looked back at Paul.

"Your modesty is commendable, Captain Tankersley. And, of course, we've all read of Lady Harrington's exploits."

The way he said "exploits" brought Paul's eyebrows down in a quick frown. The word carried a slight but unmistakable derision, and he felt his temper stir. He called it sternly to heel and took a deeper pull at his beer, suddenly eager to finish the stein and be off. He was beginning to suspect the stranger was another newsie—and not one friendly to Honor—which lent added urgency to escaping without running away too obviously.

"To tell the truth," the man said, "I was surprised—awed, even—when I heard about the odds against her. It must've taken guts to stand and fight against that much opposition instead of pulling out to save her command."

"I'm just as glad she did. If she hadn't, I probably wouldn't be here," Paul said shortly, and instantly bit his tongue. Surely he should know by now that the only way (short of homicide) to deal with a newsie, especially a hostile one, was to keep your mouth shut and ignore him! Anything else only encouraged him—and what you actually said mattered considerably less than what he could make it seem you'd *meant* to say.

"I suppose that's true," the stranger said. "Of course, quite a few of her own people *aren't* here, are they? Perhaps if she'd scattered sooner more of them would have survived. Still, I suppose no officer can do his duty—or earn the medals Lady Harrington has—without sacrificing a few lives along the way."

Paul's temper surged again, and he felt himself flush. The other's tone was losing its pretense of disinterested urbanity. There was an edge to it, too pointed to be an accident, and he gave the stranger a repressive frown.

"I've never known Captain Harrington to 'sacrifice' a single life she could save," he said coldly. "If you're suggesting she risked her people's lives to go glory-hunting, I find the idea as ridiculous as it is offensive."

"Really?" The other man's eyes glinted with a strange satisfaction, and he shrugged. "I didn't intend to offend you, Captain Tankersley. And, actually, I don't believe I ever thought Lady Harrington might have sacrificed anyone for glory." He shook his head. "No, no. I never meant to imply that. But it still seems a . . . curious . . . decision to risk an entire task group's destruction to defend a single repair base. One might almost call it questionable, whatever the outcome, and I can't help wondering if perhaps she didn't have some other reason—besides her sense of *duty*, of course—for matching her command against such a heavy weight of metal. She pulled it off, of course, but why did she try it—and get so many people killed—when she already knew Admiral Danislav had arrived in-system to relieve her?"

Alarms jangled in Paul's brain, for the stranger's tone had shifted yet again. The earlier edge of scorn was no longer veiled; it glittered with scalpel sharpness, a cold cat-and-mouse cruelty. Paul had never heard a voice that could imply so much, put such a sneer of contempt into such outwardly dispassionate words, and the cultured undertone of nastiness was too open for most of the newsies who'd dogged Honor's every move. This man had a personal axe to grind, and common sense shouted for Paul to break off the conversation quickly. But he'd heard too much veiled innuendo about Honor from too many others, and his frown grew cold-eyed and dangerous as he gazed at the stranger.

"Captain Harrington," he said icily, "acted in accordance with her understanding of the situation and her own duty, and her actions led to the capture or destruction of the entire Peep force engaged against her. Given that outcome, I fail to see anything 'curious' or 'questionable' about her conduct."

"Ah, but you wouldn't, would you?" the other man murmured. Paul stiffened, and the stranger smiled with an air of false apology. "I mean, you're right about the outcome, of course. And she did save the repair base and its personnel. Including *you*."

"What exactly are you implying?" Paul snapped. He felt a wave of stillness rippling out from them, lapping at Dempsey's other patrons. He could hardly believe the effortless speed with which the confrontation had sprung up, the ease and skill with which the other man had provoked him. It couldn't have been an accident. He knew that, but he no longer cared.

"Why, only that her feelings for you—well known feelings, I might add, for anyone who can read a 'fax—may have influenced her." The stranger's voice was an ice-cold sneer. "No doubt it was all dreadfully romantic, but, still, one can't help wondering if the willingness to sacrifice several thousand lives simply to save someone *she* cared about is really a desirable quality in a military officer. Do *you* think it is, Captain?"

Paul Tankersley went white. He rose from his barstool with the slow, over-controlled movements of a man hovering on the brink of violence. The stranger was taller than he was, and he looked fit, despite his slim, wiry build, but Paul never doubted he could smash the other into pulp, and he wanted nothing more than to do just that. But the alarm bells were louder and more insistent, even through the red haze of his fury. It had happened too quickly, come at him with too little warning, for him to think clearly, yet not too quickly for him to realize it was deliberate. He had no idea why this man had set out to provoke him, but he sensed the danger in allowing him to succeed.

He drew a deep breath, longing to erase the smiling sneer from that handsome face and leave it far less handsome in the process. He stood for one tense moment, and then, deliberately, turned his back to walk away. But the stranger wasn't done yet. He only stood himself, laughing at Paul's back, and his raised voice carried clearly through the hushed bar.

"Tell me, Captain Tankersley—are you really that good a fuck? Are you so good she was willing to throw away her entire command to save you? Or was it just that she was that desperate to have someone—anyone—between her legs?"

The sudden crudity was too much. It snapped Paul's control, and he whipped back around with death in his face. The other man's sneer slipped for just an instant, and two iron-hard fists caught him before he could even move.

Paul Tankersley held a black belt in *coup de vitesse*. He managed to pull the lethality of those blows, but only by a hair's breadth and just barely in time. The first fist sank deep into the stranger's belly. He doubled up with a whoop of agony, and the second fist came up from below and snapped his head back like a cracking whip.

The stranger hurtled away from Paul. Barstools flew in all directions as he bounced back, arms flailing, and somehow, without really knowing how, Tankersley stopped himself from following through and finishing him off.

He stood back, breathing heavily, shocked by his own actions and quivering with the need to smash that hateful face yet again, as the other man slid down the front of the bar with a sobbing scream. His hands cupped his face, and blood from pulped lips and a smashed nose oozed between his fingers as he rocked on his knees. The entire restaurant was frozen, shocked into utter immobility by the explosion of violence, and then, slowly, the kneeling man lowered his hands and glared up at his assailant.

He spat a broken tooth onto the floor in a gob of blood and phlegm, then dragged the back of his hand across his gory chin, and his eyes, no longer polished and mocking, glittered with madness.

"You struck me." His voice was thick, slurred with the pain of his smashed mouth and choked with hatred. "You *struck* me!"

Paul took a half-step towards him, eyes hot, before he could stop himself, but the other man never even flinched. He only stared up from his knees, his face a mask of blood and hate that bordered on outright insanity.

"How *dare* you lay hands on me?!" he breathed. Paul snarled in contempt and turned away, but that thick, hating voice wasn't finished.

"No one lays hands on *me*, Tankersley! You'll meet me for this—I demand satisfaction!"

Paul stopped dead. The silence was no longer shocked; it was deadly, and he suddenly realized what he'd done. He should have seen it sooner—*would* have seen it if he'd been even the tiniest bit less enraged. He hadn't, but now he knew. The man hadn't anticipated that Paul would actually attack him, yet he'd set out from the beginning to goad him into a rage for just one purpose: to provoke the challenge he'd just issued.

And Paul Tankersley, who'd never fought a duel in his life, knew he had no choice but to accept it.

"Very well," he grated, glaring down at his unknown enemy. "If you insist, I'll give you satisfaction."

Another man blended magically out of the crowd and assisted the stranger to his feet.

"This is Mr. Livitnikov," the bloody-faced man snarled, leaning on the other for support. "I'm sure he'll be happy to act for me."

Livitnikov nodded curtly and reached into a tunic pocket with his left hand, supporting the other man with his right, and extended something to Paul.

"My card, Captain Tankersley." The correct, chilly outrage in his hard voice was just a little too practiced, a bit too rehearsed. "I shall expect your friends to call upon me within twenty-four hours."

"Certainly," Paul said in an equally frozen voice. Livitnikov's sudden appearance was all the confirmation he'd needed that he'd been set up, and he gave the other man a contemptuous look as he took the card. He shoved it in his pocket, turned his back, and started for the door, then stopped.

Tomas Ramirez stood just inside the entrance, his face frozen, but he wasn't even looking at Paul. His eyes were locked in shocked understanding on the man his friend had assaulted— the man he'd never thought to mention to Paul—and he watched in numb horror as Livitnikov assisted a stumbling, bloody-faced Denver Summervale away through the crowd.

✧ CHAPTER EIGHTEEN

AT LEAST THE CHAIR was comfortable.

That was more important than one might think, for Honor had spent at least eight hours a day in it for the last month, and the fatigue was building up. Grayson's twenty-six-plus-standard hour day was a bit long, even for her. The Sphinx day she'd been born to might be barely an hour shorter, but she'd spent the last three decades using Navy clocks matched to the twenty-three-hour day of the Star Kingdom's capital world. Not that she could honestly blame her present weariness on the length of the day.

She looked to her left, narrowing her eyes against the brilliant morning sun spilling in through the windows as the door closed behind her latest visitor. Her steadholder's mansion was overly luxurious for her tastes, especially in a new steading with a strained budget, but her own quarters occupied only a tiny portion of Harrington House's total space. The rest was given up to bureaucratic offices, electronic and hardcopy files, communications centers, and all the other paraphernalia of government.

James MacGuiness, on the other hand, clearly regarded the magnificence as no more than her due, and, unlike her, he seemed delighted with the pomp and circumstance which had come her way. The Grayson servants accepted him as their mistress's official majordomo, and he'd shown an unanticipated talent for managing a staff which seemed entirely too large to Honor. He'd also seen to it Nimitz had a proper perch in her office, arranged to catch the maximum amount of sunlight. At the moment, the 'cat was sprawled comfortably along that perch, all six limbs dangling in utter contentment while he basked in the golden warmth.

She gazed at him in frank envy, then tipped her huge, thronelike armchair back, resting one foot on the hassock hidden under her enormous desk, and pinched the bridge of her nose. She closed her eyes and inhaled deeply, and a soft chuckle from her right made her turn her head in the other direction.

Howard Clinkscales sat behind a smaller desk with an even larger data terminal. His desk was turned at right angles to hers so that they both faced the center of the vast, paneled room, and she hadn't been too sure about the arrangement in the beginning. She wasn't used to having her exec in the same office with her, but it worked far better than she'd feared, and his presence had been invaluable. He knew every detail of her steading, and, like any skilled exec, he was always ready with the facts his CO required.

"Tired so soon, My Lady?" he asked now, shaking his head in half-mocking reproval. "It's barely ten o'clock!"

"At least I don't yawn in front of them," she said with a grin.

"True, My Lady. At least, you haven't done so *yet*."

Honor stuck out her tongue, and Clinkscales laughed. She wouldn't have bet a Manticoran cent on the chance of her regent's actually becoming a friend. Mutual respect, yes; she would have expected that, and been content with it, as well. But their intense cooperation over the past weeks had produced something much closer and warmer.

If it surprised her, it must have been even more surprising for him. He'd resigned command of the entire Planetary Security Force to assume the regency of Harrington Steading, which he might easily have seen as a demotion. Nor should his opposition to at least half Protector Benjamin's social initiatives have made him any happier to work with—and for— the woman who'd provoked those changes. On top of which, he didn't really seem to have changed his own attitudes towards women in general by one iota.

None of which seemed to have any bearing where *Honor* was concerned. He never forgot she was a woman, and he treated her with all the exaggerated courtesy the Grayson code demanded, but he gave her the deference due any steadholder, as well. At first, she'd thought there might be a bit of irony in that, but she'd been wrong. So far as she could tell, he accepted her right to her position without even hidden reservations. More than that, he seemed to approve of her performance, and he'd even loosened up with her in private. He was unfailingly courteous, yes, but he'd come to treat her with a comfortable give and take that seemed decidedly odd in a man of such traditional leanings.

She checked her desk chrono. They had a few minutes before her next appointment, and she turned her chair to face him fully.

"Howard, would you mind if I asked you something a bit personal?"

"Personal, My Lady?" Clinkscales tugged at an earlobe. "Certainly you can ask. Of course," he smiled wryly, "if it's *too* personal, I can always choose not to answer."

"I suppose you can, at that," Honor agreed. She paused a moment, trying to think of a tactful way to phrase it, then decided there was no point. Clinkscales was as blunt and direct as she was, which probably meant it would be best simply to plunge right in and ask.

"I was just wondering how we work so well together," she said. His eyebrows rose, and she shrugged. "You know as well as I do how heavily I depend on your advice. I think I'm learning, but all of this is totally new to me. Without your guidance, I'd probably make a complete hash out of it; as it is, I think things are going quite well. I appreciate your help tremendously, but I also know you're going a lot further than the letter of your regent's oath requires, and sometimes that seems a little odd to me. I know you don't really approve of a lot of what's happening on Grayson, and I'm—well, I suppose Protector Benjamin was right when he called me a symbol of those changes. You could have made things a lot harder on me by just doing the job you promised to do and letting me learn things the hard way, and no one could have faulted you for it. I can't help wondering why you haven't."

"Because you're my Steadholder, My Lady," Clinkscales said.

"Is that the only reason?"

"It's enough of one." Clinkscales pursed his lips, fingers toying with the smaller, silver steadholder's key he wore around his neck, then gave his head a little toss. "In all honesty, however, the way you've tackled your responsibilities has something to do with it, as well. You could have settled for a figurehead role, My Lady; instead, you're working ten and twelve-hour days learning to be a real steadholder. I respect that."

"Even in a woman?" Honor asked softly.

He met her eyes and raised one hand in a small warding gesture.

"I shudder to think what you might do if I were to say '*especially* in a woman,' My Lady." His tone was so droll Honor chuckled, and he smiled briefly, then sobered.

"On the other hand, My Lady, I understand what you're really asking." He tipped his own chair back with a sigh, resting his elbows on its arms and folding his hands across his middle. "I've never hidden my convictions from the Protector or from you, Lady Harrington," he said slowly. "I think the Protector is pushing his changes too rapidly, and they make me . . . uncomfortable. Our traditions have served us well, over the centuries. They may not be perfect, but at least we *survived* following them, and that's quite an accomplishment on a world like this. More than that, I believe most of our people—including our women—were content with the old ways. *I* certainly was. Of course, I'm also a man, which may affect my perceptions a bit."

Honor's right eyebrow curved at the admission, and he chuckled sourly.

"I'm not blind to the privileged position I held, My Lady, but I don't think that necessarily invalidates my judgment, nor do I see any reason why every world in the galaxy has to ape social patterns which may or may not suit it. And, to be perfectly frank, I don't think Grayson women are ready for the demands the Protector is placing upon them. Leaving aside the question of innate capability—which, I'm surprised to say, is easier to do since I began working with you than I once expected it to be—they don't have the training for it. I suspect many of them will be desperately unhappy trying to adjust to the changes. I shudder whenever I think about the consequences for our traditional family life, and it's not easy for the Church to make the transition, either. Besides, deep down inside I can't put aside an entire lifetime of thinking one way and start thinking another way just because someone tells me to."

Honor nodded slowly. The first time she'd met Howard Clinkscales, she'd thought he was a dinosaur, and perhaps he was. But there was nothing apologetic or even particularly defensive in his tone or manner. He didn't like the changes about him, yet he hadn't responded to them as the unthinking reactionary she'd once thought him, either.

"But whether or not I agree with everything Protector Benjamin does, he *is* my Protector," Clinkscales went on, "and a majority of the steadholders support him, as well." He shrugged. "Perhaps my doubts will prove unfounded if the new system works. Perhaps they'll even make it work better, by making me a little more aware of the sensibilities we're treading upon—cushioning the blows, as it were. Either way, I have a responsibility to do the best I can. If I can preserve worthwhile parts of our tradition along the way, I will, but I take my oath to Protector Benjamin—and to you, My Lady—seriously."

He fell silent for a moment, but Honor felt something more waiting to be said and let the stillness rest unbroken until he said it. Several seconds passed, and then he cleared his throat.

"In the meantime, My Lady, I may as well add that you aren't a Grayson by birth. By adoption, yes. You're one of our own now; even many of those who most resent the changes around them think of you that way. But you weren't born one. You don't *act* like a Grayson woman, and the Protector was right in more ways than one when he called you a symbol. You're proof that women *can* be—and, on other worlds, are—fully as capable as men. There was a time when I was ready to hate you for what's happened to Grayson, but that would be like hating water for being wet. You are what you are, My Lady. Someday—perhaps far sooner than an old reactionary like me believes possible— Grayson may produce women like you. In the meantime, I've never met a man with a stronger sense of duty, nor have I met one more capable or hardworking. Which means no old- fashioned chauvinist like me can let you prove that you're more capable or hardworking than *I* am. Besides," he shrugged again, and this time his smile was completely natural, if just a bit sheepish, "I *like* you, My Lady."

Honor's eyes softened. He sounded as if the admission had surprised even him, and she shook her head.

"I only wish I didn't feel like a fish out of water so much of the time. I have to keep reminding myself I'm not in the Star Kingdom anymore. Grayson etiquette baffles me. I don't think I'll ever really get used to the idea of being a steadholder, and figuring out how to avoid stepping on people's sensibilities while I do it is even harder."

She was as surprised to hear herself admit that as Clinkscales might have been to admit his liking to her, but he only smiled again.

"You seem to be doing well enough to me, My Lady. You have the habit of command, but I've never seen you act without thinking or give a capricious order to anyone."

"Oh, that." Honor waved a hand, mildly embarrassed and highly pleased by his comment. "I just fall back on my Navy experience. I like to think I'm a pretty fair starship commander, and I guess it shows." Clinkscales nodded, and she shrugged. "But that's the easy part. Learning to be a Grayson is *hard*, Howard. There's more to it than just putting on a dress—" she indicated the gown she wore "—and making the right command decisions."

Clinkscales cocked his head and regarded her thoughtfully.

"May I give you a word of advice, My Lady?" Honor nodded, and he tugged at his ear once more. "Then I'd advise
you not to try. Just be yourself. No one could fault the job
you're doing, and trying to make yourself over into a 'proper'
Grayson while we're all busy trying to redefine 'proper' anyway would be pointless. Besides, your holders like you just
the way you are."

Both of Honor's eyebrows flew up in surprise, and he
laughed.

"Before you took your seat in the Conclave, some of your
people were worried about what would happen with 'that
foreign woman' holding steading over them. Now that they're
getting to know you, they're rather proud of your, um,
eccentricities. This steading's been attracting people who were
more eager than most for change from the beginning, My Lady;
now a lot of them seem to hope some of your attitudes will
rub off on them."

"Are you serious?" Honor demanded.

"Quite. In fact—"

Honor's chrono beeped, announcing the imminent arrival
of her next caller, and Clinkscales cut himself off. He glanced
down at his own data screen, then shook his head wryly.

"This should be interesting, My Lady. Your next appointment is with the engineer I mentioned to you."

Honor nodded and straightened her own chair as the quiet
knock on the door came—exactly on schedule.

"Enter," she called, and an armsmen in the green-on-green
colors she'd chosen for her steading opened the door to admit
the engineer in question.

He was a young man, and there was something vaguely
untidy about him. Not slovenly, and no one could have been
more painfully clean, but he seemed uncomfortable in his
formal clothing. He would, she thought, have looked far more
natural in coveralls, festooned with micro-comps and the other
tools of his trade, and his nervousness was palpable as he
hesitated in the doorway.

"Come in, Mr. Gerrick." She put as much reassurance into
her voice as she could and stood behind her desk, extending a hand in welcome. Protocol called for her to remain seated
throughout, as befitted her high office, but she couldn't—not
when the youthful engineer looked so unsure of himself.

Gerrick blushed scarlet and scurried across the office, covered
with all too obvious confusion, and it occurred to her that
he'd probably boned up on the way things *ought* to go. Well,

it was too late for that, and she smiled and left her hand out as he came to a halt before her desk.

He paused a moment, then reached out hesitantly, as if unsure whether to shake her hand or kiss it. She solved his quandary by grasping his firmly, and some of his uncertainty seemed to flow away. He smiled back—shyly—and returned her grip with something like assurance.

"Sit down, Mr. Gerrick." She pointed at the chair before her desk, and he obeyed the gesture quickly, clutching his brief-case in his lap with a residue of his original nervousness. "Lord Clinkscales tells me you're one of my senior engineers," she went on, "and that you have some special project you wish to discuss with me?"

Gerrick blushed again, as if he felt calling him a senior engineer might be a veiled irony, given his obvious youth, but she only waited, hands folded on her blotter. Her attentive expression must have reassured him, because he drew a deep breath and nodded.

"Yes, My Lady, I do." He spoke quickly, but his voice was deeper than his undeniable scrawniness might have suggested.

"Then, tell me about it," Honor invited, leaning back in her chair, and he cleared his throat.

"Well, My Lady, I've been studying applications of the new materials the Alliance has made available to us here." He ended on a slight upward note, as if asking a question, and she nodded in understanding. "Some of them are quite remarkable," Gerrick went on with greater confidence. "In fact, I've been particularly impressed by the possibilities of the new crystoplast."

He paused, and Honor rubbed the tip of her nose. Crystoplast wasn't really all that new, though it might be to a Grayson engineer. The armorplast routinely used in spacecraft was far more advanced; in fact, it had relegated the cheaper crystoplast almost exclusively to civilian industry, where design tolerances could be traded off against cost savings, and it took her a moment to fix the differences between the two of them in her mind.

"All right, Mr. Gerrick," she said. "I'm with you. May I assume this project of yours employs crystoplast?"

"Yes, My Lady." Gerrick leaned forward, the last of his nervousness fading as eagerness took over. "We've never had anything with that much tensile strength—not on Grayson. It offers a whole new range of possibilities for enviro engineering. Why, we could dome whole towns and cities with it!"

Honor nodded in sudden understanding. Grayson's heavy metal concentrations made simple atmospheric dust an all too real danger. Provision for internal over-pressure and filtration systems were as routine in Grayson building codes as roofs were on other planets, and public structures—like Protector's Palace, or her own steadholder's mansion—were built under climate-controlled domes as a matter of course.

She rubbed her nose again, then glanced at Clinkscales. The regent was watching Gerrick with a slight smile, one that mingled approval with a hint of waiting for the other shoe to drop, and she turned back to the engineer.

"I imagine you're right, Mr. Gerrick. And, under the circumstances, I suppose Harrington Steading would be a good place to start doing it. We could incorporate city domes from the ground up, as it were, couldn't we?"

"Yes, My Lady. But that's not all we could do. We could build entire *farms* under crystoplast!"

"Farms?" Honor asked in some surprise, and Gerrick nodded firmly.

"Yes, My Lady. Farms. I've got the cost projections here—" he started digging into his briefcase, his face alight with eagerness "—and once we take long-term operational expenses into consideration, production costs would be much lower than in the orbital habitats. We could cut transportation costs, too, and—"

"Just a moment, Adam," Clinkscales interrupted with surprising gentleness. Gerrick looked quickly at the regent, and Clinkscales gave a slight headshake as he turned to Honor.

"I've seen Adam's—Mr. Gerrick's—figures, My Lady, and he's quite right. His domes would provide a marked decrease over the orbital farms in cost-per-yield. Unfortunately, our farmers are a bit . . . traditional, shall we say?" His eyes twinkled at his own choice of words, and Honor hid a smile. "So far, Adam hasn't been able to interest anyone with the capital for it in funding his project."

"Ah." Honor leaned further back in understanding, and Gerrick watched her anxiously. "Just what sort of costs are we looking at here?"

"I've designed and costed a six-thousand-hectare demonstration project, My Lady." Gerrick swallowed, as if expecting her to protest the size, and went on quickly. "Anything much smaller than that would be too little to prove the concept to the agri-corporations, and—"

"I understand," Honor said gently. "Just give me the figure."

"Ten million austins, My Lady," the engineer said in a small voice.

Honor nodded. Given the current exchange rate, Gerrick was

talking about a seven-and-a-half-million-Manticoran-dollar price tag. That was a bit steeper than she'd thought, but—

"I realize that's high, My Lady," Gerrick said, "but part of it's the original soil decontamination cost, and we'd have to work out a lot of hardware for the pilot project, too. Not just the air cleaners, but water distillation, irrigation systems, contamination monitors. . . . That drives costs up, but once we get all of it down the first time and start mass production, the amortization over follow-on projects would—"

He reined himself in, gripping his briefcase painfully tight, as Honor raised a gentle hand and glanced at Clinkscales.

"Howard? Can we afford it?"

"No, My Lady." There was genuine regret in the regent's voice, and he smiled compassionately at Gerrick as the engineer sagged. "I wish we could. I believe other steadings would buy into the idea if we demonstrated its practicality, and The Tester knows we could use an export industry. If we made the initial investment to produce the crystoplast and support machinery—not just for farms, but for the city domes Adam's suggested—we'd be in a position to dominate the field, at least initially. That would mean jobs and the revenues to go with them, not to mention a head start on domes of our own. Unfortunately, we're too deeply committed to other projects. It's going to be at least another year—probably two—before we could fund Adam's."

Gerrick sagged further. He made a valiant effort to hide his disappointment, and Honor shook her head.

"If we wait that long, one of the other steadings is likely to get in first, traditional opposition or not," she pointed out. "If that happens, *we*'ll be in the position of buying the technology from someone else."

"Agreed, My Lady. That's why I wish we could afford to do it now, but I simply don't see a way we can."

"What about the Privy Purse?" Honor asked. Gerrick brightened at the sign of her interest, but Clinkscales shook his head again.

"We're already heavily committed there, My Lady, and even if you withdraw no personal income from it, it would only increase our funding resources by two or three million a year."

"Could we underwrite loans for it?"

"We're close to our credit limits already, My Lady. A private commercial investment would work, but until we pay down some of our start-up costs, our public borrowing capacity is limited. Much as I would like to see Adam's project tried, I can't advocate further public sector borrowing. We have to maintain some reserve against emergencies."

"I see." Honor drew invisible circles on her blotter with her forefinger, feeling Gerrick's eyes on her while she frowned in thought. Clinkscales was right about their fiscal position. Grayson was a poor planet, and the costs of establishing a new steading were enormous. If she'd known about Gerrick's idea, she would cheerfully have waived the construction of Harrington House, despite Clinkscales' argument that it had been an unavoidable necessity, if only as the steading's administrative center. As it was, Harrington Steading was in the black, barely, for the first time in the two local years since its founding, and that wasn't going to last.

She looked back up, then shook her head.

"Forget about the Privy Purse, then," she said. "And while I'm thinking about it, Howard, make a note that I want all of my income reinvested. I don't need the money, and the steading does."

"Yes, My Lady." Clinkscales sounded both surprised and gratified, and Honor cocked her head at Gerrick.

"As for you, Mr. Gerrick, how would you like a partnership with an off-worlder?"

"An off-worlder, My Lady?" Gerrick looked puzzled. "What off-worlder?"

"Me," Honor said simply, and laughed at his dumbfounded expression.

"It happens, Mr. Gerrick, that I'm a modestly wealthy woman back in the Star Kingdom. If you want to build your demonstration project, I'll bankroll it."

"You will?!" Gerrick stared at her in disbelief, and she nodded.

"I certainly will. Howard," she looked back at Clinkscales once more, "Mr. Gerrick is about to submit a letter of resignation to the steading. At the same time you accept it—with regrets, of course—I want you to draw up a permit for a privately held corporation called, um, Grayson Sky Domes, Ltd. Mr. Gerrick will go on salary as chief engineer and development officer, with a suitable salary and a thirty percent interest. I'll be chairman of the board, and you'll be our CEO, with another twenty percent interest. My agent on Manticore will be our chief financial officer, and I'll have him cut a check immediately for a few million austins for start-up costs."

"Are—are you *serious*, My Lady?" Gerrick blurted.

"I am, indeed." She rose again, extending her hand once more. "Welcome to the private sector, Mr. Gerrick. Now go out there and make it work."

✧   ✧   ✧

Yeltsin's Star had long since set, but Honor and Clinkscales had hardly noticed as they worked through their demanding schedule. Nimitz was on the corner of Honor's blotter now, amusing himself by dismantling an old-style stapler, when she finally pushed back her chair with a sigh.

"I know we're not done yet, Howard, but I've *got* to take a break. Will you and your wives join Nimitz and me for supper?"

"Is it that—?" Clinkscales checked his desk chrono and shook himself. "I see it *is* that late, My Lady. And, yes, we'd be honored to join you. Assuming," he regarded her suspiciously, "that your steward promises not to serve fried squash again." He shuddered in memory, for Manticoran squash was subtly different from the vegetable of the same name on Grayson, and he'd suffered a violent allergic reaction when MacGuiness introduced him to it.

"No squash," Honor promised with a smile. "I don't know what's on the menu, but Mac and I took that off it for the rest of our stay here. In fact, he's been taking lessons in local cuisine, and—"

A buzz from her com console interrupted her, and she grimaced.

"I may have invited you too soon," she muttered, and pressed the acceptance key.

"Yes?"

"I'm sorry to disturb you, Ma'am," a Manticoran voice said.

"I was about to com *you*, Mac. What is it?"

"We've just received word from Air Traffic, Ma'am. There's an inbound pinnace, ETA twelve minutes." Honor's eyebrows rose. The arrival of a pinnace, especially this late in the evening, was unusual to say the least. And why was MacGuiness informing her of its arrival instead of her Grayson security chief?

"A pinnace? Not an aircar?"

"No, Ma'am. A pinnace . . . from HMS *Agni*. I understand Captain Henke is aboard in person," MacGuiness added.

Honor stiffened. *Agni* here? The Manticoran element might explain why Mac was making the call instead of Colonel Hill, but why hadn't Mike written to warn her she was headed for Yeltsin's Star? For that matter, why come down in a pinnace instead of screening her from orbit? If *Agni* was in small craft range of Grayson, she could have sent a message on ahead hours ago.

"Did Captain Henke say anything about why she's here?"

"No, Ma'am. All I have is an official request for immediate access to you. Your security force passed it to me for clearance."

"Clear it at once," Honor said. "I'll be in my office."

"Yes, Ma'am." MacGuiness cut the circuit, and Honor sat back in her chair with a pensive frown.

Someone rapped once, lightly, on the office door, then opened it without awaiting permission. It was Michelle Henke, with James MacGuiness at her heels instead of the regular Grayson armsman.

"Mike!" Honor cried in delight, and started around her desk, both hands extended. She expected Henke to grin at the absurd sight of Honor Harrington in a Grayson gown, but she didn't. She only stared at her, her face that of a woman who'd just taken a pulser dart, and Honor came to a stop, hands falling to her sides, and braced her shoulders in sudden, formless dread.

"Honor." Her name came out in a tight, painful parody of Henke's normal tone, and Honor reached for her link to Nimitz. Reached for it and gasped at the anguish writhing behind Henke's tormented face. Her emotions were too intense, too painful, for Honor to sort out, but they hit Nimitz like a club. The dismantled stapler thudded to the floor as he rose up, ears flattened against his skull, and hissed in sibilant challenge, and Honor reached out again in quick compassion, stunned by the ferocity of her friend's pain.

"What is it, Mike?" She forced her voice to remain level and gentle. "Why didn't you screen me?"

"Because—" Henke drew a deep breath. "Because I had to tell you in person." Each word seemed to cost her physical agony, and she ignored Honor's hands to grip her shoulders.

"Tell me what?" Honor wasn't frightened yet. There hadn't been time, and she was too concerned for her friend.

"Honor, it's—" Henke drew another breath, then pulled her close, hugging her fiercely. "Paul was challenged to a duel," she whispered into Honor's shoulder. "He— Oh, *God*, Honor! He's dead!"

✦ CHAPTER NINETEEN

THERE OUGHT TO BE A BETTER way to do this, but Georgia Sakristos couldn't think of one, and at least she was cautiously pleased with the contact she'd finally decided upon. She had to contact *someone,* and her choice should get it to the right people without letting anyone who knew about her own part in the operation guess she was the leak; if she hadn't been sure of that she wouldn't be doing this at all.

Unfortunately, that didn't mean no one on the *other* side could ever connect her to it. That would be almost as bad as having her employer discover she'd talked, and making personal contact added measurably to her risk, yet time was short, and she had to convince the other person her information was reliable. The absence of any documentary evidence would make that hard enough without fumbling around through time-wasting intermediaries.

It was a risk, but her com was plugged through enough layers of cutouts to make it effectively untraceable. The filtration devices should make her voice unrecognizable, and she intended to screen her contact's private and unlisted civilian number. Her ability to find that number should encourage its owner to take her seriously; more importantly, civilian exchanges incorporated antirecording security circuits which could be overridden only with a court order. All of which *should* make her risk minimal, but Georgia Sakristos, née Elaine Komandorski, hadn't stayed out of prison by relying on "should."

On the other hand, she thought, her lovely face (the best biosculpt money could buy) grim, some things were worth risking prison to escape, and she'd kept her own name, face, and voice out of the transaction. She'd handled the entire thing through blind drops . . . and deliberately chosen a specialist who would insist on knowing exactly who his ultimate client was.

She ran over her plan in her mind once more. The newest Earl North Hollow had an almost childish faith in his office's security systems, and they really were good. Sakristos knew; she was the one who'd installed them for his father. The only way through them from the outside would be by brute force, and that would destroy all those other lovely records and the power they represented. No, what she wanted was to remove one, specific file—hers—without damaging the others. It was a tall order, but there was one thing Pavel Young didn't know about his own security. When she'd set it up, the computers had listed him as his father's executor, authorized to enter the system in the event of the old earl's death. Pavel knew that; what he *didn't* know was that Georgia Sakristos had been listed as the backup, with command code authority if he were unavailable, incapacitated . . . or dead.

It had taken only one night, and the bruises that went with it, to convince her that even prison would be better than an unending sentence as Pavel Young's "lover," and she was still his chief security officer. In anyone else, that combination would have been too stupid to believe; in his case, Sakristos understood exactly how it worked, and her lips worked with the desire to spit. No one else was quite real to Pavel Young. That was especially true for women, but it applied to everyone else around him, as well. He lived in a universe of cardboard cutouts, of human-shaped *things* provided solely for his use. He had no sense of them as people who might resent him— or, indeed, who had any *right* to resent him—and he was too busy doing things to them to even consider what *they* might do to *him* if they got the chance.

It was a blind spot he couldn't even recognize, much less cure, despite the outcome of his vendetta against Honor Harrington, and that same sublime arrogance blinded him to the danger in forcing his own security chief to play sick sex games. Georgia Sakristos called up the security files on her terminal once more, and her smile was ugly as the verifying code blinked. The idiot hadn't even accessed the files to see who had command authority in the event of his death. Of course, he was a young man by Manticoran standards. No doubt he thought he had plenty of time to put his affairs in order.

She reached out and punched a com code into her terminal with rock-steady fingers.

✧　　　✧　　　✧

Alistair McKeon stared down into his drink without seeing it. The ice had long since melted, floating the whiskey on a crystal clear belt of water. It didn't matter. Nothing much seemed to matter just now.

Andreas Venizelos and Tomas Ramirez sat with him, equally silent, eyes fixed on nothing with equal intensity, and the small, private compartment in *Hephaestus*'s officer's club was silent about them.

Coming here had been a bad idea, McKeon thought emptily. The suggestion had been his, but it hadn't been a good one. His quarters aboard *Prince Adrian* were like a tomb, crushing in on him, and he'd known it had to be at least as bad for the others. Especially for Ramirez. It wasn't their fault, yet all of them shared the same sense of guilt. They hadn't been smart enough or quick enough to stop it. Perhaps it hadn't really been their job to stop it, but they hadn't, and in failing, they'd failed not just Paul Tankersley but Honor Harrington, as well. McKeon dreaded meeting her again, but Ramirez had acted as Paul's second. Unlike McKeon or Venizelos, he'd been right there on the field with Paul when Summervale killed him . . . and they all knew he was going to have to tell Honor how it had happened.

McKeon had hoped they could lend one another some comfort. Instead, they'd only reinforced their collective misery, and he knew he ought to break this up. But he couldn't. Grinding though this shared grief might be, it was still better than facing his demons alone.

The admittance chime sounded, and a spark of anger glittered inside him. He'd left orders not to disturb them, and whatever steward had violated them was going to regret it.

He hit the button, turning his chair as the hatch slid open. He could feel that first spark of anger growing into a blaze of rage, and he didn't even try to resist. He could regret the savage tongue-lashing it was about to spawn later; just now his pain needed that relief, however unfair it might be.

"What the *hell* do you—?!"

The furious question died an abrupt death as the hatch slid fully open. Two people waited just outside it: a tall yet delicate-looking, black-haired junior-grade captain he'd never laid eyes on and an admiral in a counter-grav chair whom he recognized instantly from the 'faxes.

"*Admiral Sarnow?*"

McKeon shot to his feet, followed an instant later by his companions, and confusion filled him. Mark Sarnow was a patient in Bassingford Medical Center, the huge Fleet hospital on Manticore, recovering from his wounds. It would be weeks before he was well enough to leave it; everyone knew that.

"Sit down, gentlemen. Please."

McKeon sank back into his chair. Sarnow's normally melodious tenor was husky and frail, and a hospital pallor overlaid his dark complexion, but there was no weakness in his green eyes. A light blanket was tucked over the stumps of his legs, and as the captain maneuvered his chair into the compartment, McKeon saw a complex med panel rigged on its back. He'd seen panels like that before. Sarnow's conveyance might not be a full life-support chair, but it was mighty close to one.

"I'm sorry to disturb you," Sarnow went on as the captain parked him beside the table and folded her hands behind her, "but Captain Corell here—" he gestured over his shoulder at the black-haired woman "—has something to tell you. She's doing so under my authority. As such, I should be here to assume responsibility for it."

McKeon closed his mouth on the questions quivering in his throat. What could be important enough to get Sarnow out of the hospital? For that matter, how had he even known where to find them? And—

He inhaled deeply. Sarnow was an admiral; if he wanted to find someone, he could damn well find them. What really mattered was *why* he'd found them, and McKeon glanced at Ramirez and Venizelos. Surprise had drawn all three of them out of their fog of misery, but the others looked as confused as he felt. Sarnow smiled at their expressions. It wasn't much of a smile, and it looked out of place on his grim, strained face, but there was a ghost of true amusement in it, and he waved a hand at Captain Corell.

"Captain McKeon, Colonel Ramirez, Commander Venizelos." The fine-boned woman nodded to each of them in turn, her brown eyes dark. "I'm Admiral Sarnow's chief of staff. As such, I became very close to Lady Harrington in Hancock, and I was shocked when I heard of Captain Tankersley's death. I was even more shocked when I learned who his opponent had been, but there didn't seem to be anything *I* could do about it, so I tried to put it out of my mind.

"This afternoon, however, I received a com call. There was no video, and the audio was heavily filtered for anonymity, but I'm virtually positive it was a woman's voice. It also came in on my private, unlisted com. Not on an official channel; on my *civilian* circuit. My civvy combination's known only to my closest friends, and it's flagged for extra precautions, both with the Service and the civilian exchanges, because of my security clearances, but whoever called me still had the reach to find out what it was."

She paused, and McKeon nodded understanding, though his mystified expression hadn't changed.

"The caller," Corell continued carefully, "informed me that she would neither answer questions nor repeat herself. That, as I'm sure she intended, assured my full attention. There wasn't time to get a recorder on it, and I can't repeat her exact words, but there wasn't much room for confusion in them.

"According to my caller, Denver Summervale was, indeed, hired to kill Captain Tankersley." Air hissed between teeth around the table. None of them were surprised, but the confirmation still struck like a fist. "In addition," Corell went on very levelly, "he's been retained to kill Dame Honor, as well."

Alistair McKeon's chair fell to the deck as he rose with a murderous snarl, but Corell didn't even flinch. She only nodded, and he made himself bend down to set the chair upright once more, then forced himself to sit back down on it.

"As you all know, Captain Tankersley wounded Summervale," Corell said. "It wasn't a very serious wound, unfortunately, and he used his need for medical attention as an excuse to leave the field, then disappeared on the way to the hospital. For your unofficial information, Marine Intelligence is work-ing on the assumption that he was paid for the job, though neither they nor the Landing Police have been able as yet to turn up any evidence to that effect. In light of that, I had assumed, as the authorities also did, that he intended to remain out of sight, avoiding official scrutiny until the public furor died down, or even that he'd left the system. According to my caller, however, he's simply lying low until Dame Honor returns. He and whoever hired him assume she'll challenge him on sight, at which time he's to kill her, too."

"But . . . *why?*" McKeon looked appealingly at the admi-ral, then back at Corell. "Are you saying Summervale killed Paul just to get *Honor* on the field? Killing him was only bait to draw her out where he could kill *her?*"

"I don't think so. Or, at least, I don't think that's the only reason," Corell said after a moment, her voice low. "The fact that it will get her to go after Summervale is a classic defense for a professional duelist, of course. He won't have challenged her; *she'll* have challenged *him*, leaving him no choice but to defend himself. I think they also figure she'll be mad for vengeance, which may make her careless, and God knows she doesn't have any experience in something like this to begin with. All of that's true, and no doubt that would be enough from their viewpoint, but they want her to *hurt*, Captain McKeon. They want to know that before they kill her they've done the cruelest thing they possibly can to her."

"They have," Tomas Ramirez whispered. His face was as wrung with pain as his voice, and his hands were clenched in a double fist on the table before him.

"I know they have," Mark Sarnow's voice was flint, "and I won't allow anyone to get away with doing something like this to her if I can help it." He looked at Corell. "Tell them the rest, Ernie."

"Yes, Sir." Corell looked McKeon in the eyes. "According to my caller, Summervale has already recovered from his injury. It was only a flesh wound, and it's responded well to quick heal. He's waiting out Dame Honor's return in seclusion, until the proper time for him to 'accidentally' encounter her."

She reached into a tunic pocket and withdrew a folded sheet of old-fashioned notepaper. She laid it on the table, pressing it down with her fingers, and let her eyes sweep over all three of the seated men.

"At this moment, according to my caller, he's in hiding in a hunting chalet on Gryphon. I've checked. There *is* a chalet where she said it was, and the entire facility's been chartered by someone who's provided his own staff for his stay. Its coordinates are listed here, along with the number of fellow 'guests' and 'staff' acting as his bodyguards. Most of them, I suspect, are Organization professionals."

She stepped back from the table, and Sarnow spoke once more.

"Gentlemen, I can't tell you what to do. At the moment, I doubt the authorities could do anything, legally, with this information, and there isn't anything at all *I* can do—" a small gesture indicated the covered stumps of his legs "—except place it in your hands. I have my own suspicions about who's behind it, but I could be wrong. Dame Honor has certainly made enough enemies in the last few years, and too many of them have the resources to arrange this, either alone or collectively. That makes guessing about their identity—or even who Ernie's caller was, or why she commed—worse than useless at this point. But given how far they've already gone, just keeping Dame Honor away from Summervale, even assuming that were a possible task, isn't going to stop them. Even if he were to be eliminated, they'd just drop back and try another tack.

Which is why I remind you all of your Tac classes at Saganami Island and ATC: in order to plan your defense effectively, you must first identify the enemy, his probable intentions, and his resources."

He held Alistair McKeon's eyes for one long, hard second, then glanced at Ramirez and Venizelos. They looked back in silence, and he nodded.

"I believe that's all I can tell you, gentlemen." He looked up at Corell. "You'd better get me back to Bassingford before Doctor Metier comes looking for me, Ernie."

"Aye, aye, Sir." Corell stepped back behind the chair and turned it toward the hatch. The door hissed open as they approached it, but Sarnow raised one hand. Corell stopped instantly, and the admiral looked back over his shoulder.

"Dame Honor is my friend, too, gentlemen," he said softly. "Good luck . . . and good hunting."

✧ CHAPTER TWENTY

MICHELLE HENKE STEPPED OUT OF the lift and straightened her shoulders as she started down the passage. The hatch at its end was flanked by two guards, one a Royal Manticoran Marine corporal, the other a Grayson armsman in the green livery of the Steading of Harrington. Armed foreign nationals weren't normally allowed aboard a Manticoran warship, but the white-faced, mechanical parody of a human beyond that hatch was a visiting noblewoman as well as an RMN captain. Henke doubted Honor would have requested or even authorized her armsman's presence under normal circumstances; as it was, she probably didn't even know the Grayson contingent was on board.

She reached the guards, who saluted in perfect unison.

"At ease," she said, and her mouth tried to smile, despite her depression, as the Marine dropped into parade rest and the armsman, not to be outdone, assumed the Grayson equivalent. But the fragile smile vanished even more quickly than it had come, and she looked at the Marine.

"I'd like to see Lady Harrington. Please tell her I'm here."

The corporal started to reach for the button, then drew his hand back when the armsman turned his head to give him a level look. Henke pretended not to notice but sighed mentally. No doubt if she'd said she wanted to see *Captain* Harrington the armsman would have let the Marine have his way, but her choice of title let him assume she wasn't here on RMN business. The fierce protectiveness of Honor's Grayson attendants had startled her—until she discovered they not only knew about Paul's death but the verdict in the Young court-martial, as well. None of them ever discussed either incident, but their very silence only underscored their distrust in Manticore's ability to protect her . . . and Henke couldn't disagree with them.

She gave herself a mental shake, cursing the way her own mind savaged her with memories of her cousin, as the armsman pressed the button.

"Yes?" It was James MacGuiness' voice, not Honor's, and the armsman cleared his throat.

"Captain Henke to see the Steadholder, Mr. MacGuiness."

"Thank you, Jamie."

A soft tone sounded and the hatch began to open. The armsman moved aside, and Henke stepped past him. A worn-looking MacGuiness met her just inside the hatch, his swollen, bloodshot eyes weary. The sleeping cabin across the main compartment was sealed, and there was no sign of Nimitz.

"How is she, Mac?" There was no way Honor could hear her in the sleeping cabin, but Henke kept her voice low, almost a whisper.

"No change, Ma'am." MacGuiness met her look with one that dropped its own barriers to reveal the depth of his anxious grief. "No change at all. She just *lies* there, Ma'am."

The steward wrung his hands in uncharacteristic helplessness, and, despite the vast difference in their ranks, Henke put an arm around the older man and squeezed tightly. He closed his eyes for just a moment, then she felt him draw a deep breath and released him.

"Nimitz?" she asked in that same quiet voice.

"The same." MacGuiness shook himself and stepped back, gesturing her toward a chair as if just remembering his manners. "He won't eat," the steward said as Henke sat. "Not even celery." His mouth quivered in a fleeting, sad smile. "He just lies on her chest and purrs to her, Ma'am . . . and I don't think she even hears him at all."

Henke leaned back and rubbed her face with both hands in a futile effort to scrub away her own fear. She'd never seen Honor like this—never imagined she *could* be like this. She hadn't shed a single tear when Henke told her. She'd only swayed, white-faced, her brown eyes those of a maimed animal that didn't understand its own pain. Not even the heartbreaking keen of Nimitz's lament had seemed to touch her.

Then she'd turned to Clinkscales, still without a tear, expressionless as a statue, no longer human but a thing of ice, and her voice hadn't even quivered as she gave her orders. Nor had she seemed to hear him when he tried to speak to her, tried to express his sympathy. She'd simply gone right on in that terrible, undead voice, and he'd darted one agonized glance at Henke and bent his head in acceptance. Fifteen minutes later, Honor had been in Henke's pinnace, headed for *Agni.*

She hadn't spoken to Henke—hadn't even turned her head when Henke spoke to her. She might as well have been on another planet, not in the seat just across the pinnace aisle. She'd simply sat there, dry-eyed, clutching Nimitz to her chest while she stared straight ahead.

That had been two days ago. *Agni* had been delayed breaking orbit by the need to take on reactor mass, and Lord Clinkscales and Protector Benjamin had insisted on holding her another six hours while they transferred up an entourage for Honor. The Protector hadn't said so in so many words, but his tone conveyed a message Henke would never have dared ignore: Honor Harrington would return to the Star Kingdom only in a way that made Grayson's support for one of its own unmistakable.

Honor hadn't even noticed. She'd retired to her sleeping cabin, a silent, white-faced ghost with eyes of agony, and Henke was terrified for her. If not even Nimitz could reach her, perhaps there was nothing left to reach. Mike Henke was probably the one human in the universe who knew how desperately lonely Honor had been, how much courage it had taken to let Paul into her heart at all, and how much she'd loved him once she had. Now Paul was gone, and—

Henke's worries broke off in mid-thought, and her head snapped up as the sleeping cabin hatch opened.

Honor wore her captain's uniform, not the Grayson gown in which she'd come aboard, and Nimitz rode her shoulder. She was perfectly, immaculately groomed, but not even the 'cat's fluffy coat could hide his gauntness, and Honor was even worse. She was drawn and ashen, her lips bloodless in a hollowed face. She wore no makeup, and the strong bones of her facial structure, graceful no more, poked at her skin like eroded mountain crags.

"Honor?" Henke stood slowly, as if afraid of frightening some wounded wild thing, and her soft voice ached with pain of her own.

"Mike." No expression crossed Honor's face, and her eyes were worse than dead. They were brown flint, frozen and cold, like steel quenched in agony, but at least there was recognition in them once more. Recognition and something more— a frightening something. They moved to MacGuiness. "Mac."

Henke felt her own eyes sting. That flat, emotionless soprano could have been a computer's. There was no life in it, no feeling but a pain deeper than the stars.

Honor said nothing more. She simply started for the main hatch. She went through it with a slow, measured tread, and both sentries snapped to attention. She didn't even see them as she walked past.

MacGuiness looked at Henke, his eyes raw with appeal, and she nodded, then hurried after Honor. She didn't say anything more. She was afraid to. She only walked beside her friend, and Nimitz was hunched and silent on Honor's shoulder, his tail hanging down her back like a forlorn and lifeless banner.

Honor punched a destination into the lift control panel, and Henke's eyes widened, then narrowed, as she recognized it. She started to speak, but she didn't. She simply folded her hands behind her and waited.

The journey seemed to take forever, yet the lift door slid open at last, and Honor stepped out into the light cruiser's armory. The senior chief master sergeant who served as *Agni*'s Marine armorer looked up from a service manual's display, then snapped to attention behind the long, high counter.

"Is the range clear, Sergeant?" Honor asked in that same, dead voice.

"Uh, yes, Milady. It is." The armorer didn't sound happy to confirm that, but she didn't seem to notice.

"Then issue me an automatic," she said. "Ten millimeter."

The sergeant looked over Honor's shoulder at his captain. He was a man who'd spent a lifetime with weapons, and the thought of putting one into the hands of a woman who spoke like that frightened him. It frightened Henke, too, but she bit her lip and nodded.

The sergeant swallowed, then reached under the counter and produced a memo board.

"Please fill out the requisition while I get it, Milady," he said.

Honor began tapping keys. The sergeant watched her a moment, then turned away toward the weapons storage, only to stop as Honor spoke again.

"I need filled ten-round magazines. Ten of them. And four boxes of shells."

"I—" The sergeant cut himself off and nodded. "Yes, Milady. Ten charged magazines and two hundred rounds in the box."

He vanished into the weapons storage, and Henke stepped up to Honor's side. She watched the long fingers tapping memo keys with slow, painful precision, and her own face was troubled. The Star Kingdom's military hadn't used chemical-powered firearms in over three T-centuries, for no firearm ever made could match the single-hit lethality of the hyper-velocity darts of a pulser or pulse rifle. A man hit in the hand by a pulser dart might—if he was very, very lucky—survive with the mere loss of his arm, and that made auto-loading pistols antiques, yet every Manticoran warship carried a few of them, precisely *because* their wounds were survivable. They were always available, and always in the traditional ten-millimeter caliber, yet never issued for duty use; they had only one function, and as long as duels were legal they were carried for those who wished to practice with them.

But they could be used for other purposes.

Honor finished filling out the requisition form and thumb-printed the scan pad, then slid the memo board back across the counter. She stood there, hands at her sides, waiting, until the sergeant returned.

"Here you are, Milady." He laid the heavy, holstered pistol and a set of ear-protectors on the counter, his reluctance obvious. He followed them with a second pair, their connector strip adjusted to something approximating the size of a treecat's head, though Honor hadn't requested them, then placed an ammunition carrier beside them with even greater reluctance.

"Thank you." Honor scooped up the pistol and attached its magnetic pad to her belt, then reached for the protectors with one hand and the ammunition with the other, but Henke's hand snapped out. It came down on the ammunition carrier, pinning it to the counter, and Honor looked at her.

"Honor, I—" Henke began, but her voice died. How could she ask her best friend the question she *had* to ask? Yet if she didn't, how could she live with the consequences if—

"Don't worry, Mike." There was no life, no expression, in Honor's voice, but her mouth moved in a cold, dead travesty of a smile. "Nimitz won't let me do that. Besides," the first trace of feeling touched her face—an ugly, hungry twist of her lips, more sensed than seen and somehow more frightening than anything she'd done or said yet, "I have something more important to do."

Henke stared into her eyes for a moment, then sighed and lifted her hand. Honor slid the ammunition carrier off the counter, looping the strap over her left shoulder and settling the heavy pouch at her side. She nodded once to Henke, then looked at the armorer.

"Program the range, Sergeant. Standard Manticoran gravity on the plates. Set the range gate for forty meters. Human targets."

She turned without another word, and stepped through the firing range hatch.

✧ CHAPTER TWENTY-ONE

"*PRINCE ADRIAN*, THIS IS *HEPHAESTUS* CENTRAL. Stand by for final departure clearance."

Captain Alistair McKeon nodded to his helmsman to stand ready and pressed the com stud on the arm of his command chair.

"*Prince Adrian* copies standby for final departure clearance, *Hephaestus*. Holding."

"Understood, *Prince Adrian*." There was a moment of silence while the controller double-checked his board. Then— "You are cleared, *Prince Adrian*."

"*Prince Adrian* copies clearance. Undocking," McKeon responded, and looked back at the helmsman. "Disengage mooring tractors."

"Disengage mooring tractors, aye, Sir." The helmsman depressed half a dozen buttons. "Tractors disengaged, Sir."

"Check our zone, Beth."

"Checking zone, aye, Sir." The tactical officer made a quick sensor sweep, and McKeon waited patiently. He'd once seen what happened when a battlecruiser failed to do that and a shuttle pilot had strayed into the departure zone. "Zone clear, Sir. Five small yard craft at two-one-eight zero-niner-five, range two-five kilometers. *Apollo* bears zero-three-niner, same plane. Range seven-point-five klicks."

"Confirmed on maneuvering plot, Sir," the helmsman reported.

"Very good. Forward thrusters."

"Engaging forward thrusters, aye, Sir." The heavy cruiser trembled as she eased out of her berth, and McKeon watched the cavernous docking bay move back and away on the visual display.

"Hold her on her present heading," he said. The helmsman acknowledged, and McKeon switched his visual display to starboard just as *Apollo* slid stern first out of her own berth. Their courses diverged sharply, pushing them apart to clear the safety perimeters of their impeller wedges, and McKeon depressed an intraship com stud.

"Colonel Ramirez," a deep voice answered.

"Departure on schedule, Colonel. Our ETA looks good."

"Thank you, Sir. We appreciate the assistance."

"Least we can do, Colonel," McKeon replied, and leaned back in his chair as he cut the circuit.

Colonel Tomas Ramirez and Major Susan Hibson had been shocked by their latest readiness tests. While no one could fault the willingness of HMS *Nike*'s Marine detachment, the entire battalion was sadly out of training. The influx of replacements and corresponding transfer out of experienced personnel had only made bad worse, and Colonel Ramirez and his able exec had concluded that Something Had To Be Done, whether *Nike* was operational or not. After all, Royal Manticoran Marines shouldn't stand around and lose their edge just because the sissies who ran the Navy broke one of their ships!

A quick memo up the chain of command earned the endorsement of no less a personage than General Dame Erica Vonderhoff, Commanding Officer, Fleet Marine Force. Of course, COFMF couldn't issue orders to the Navy; the best she could do was authorize Ramirez to request troop lift support on an "as available" basis with her blessings.

The Navy had been sympathetic, but Colonel Ramirez's request to Training and Support Command had been greeted with regrets; the Fleet would need at least a week to free up the lift for a battalion-level training drop. Training and Support would be happy to schedule them ASAP, but in the meantime, why not carry out high orbit insertions from *Hephaestus*? After all, the space station orbited Manticore itself, and the Star Kingdom's capital planet offered suitable training areas in abundance. What about, say, Camp Justin in High Sligo? That was about hip-deep in snow just now, which ought to offer plenty of scope for toughening *Nike*'s Marines back up. Or, if Colonel Ramirez would prefer desert, how about Camp Maastricht in the Duchy of West Wind?

But the colonel had his heart set on Gryphon. Troops as appallingly out of fighting trim as his were needed *really* challenging terrain, and few things in life were as challenging as Gryphon in winter. Not only did the planet's extreme axial tilt make for . . . interesting weather patterns, but half of it was still virgin wilderness.

Unfortunately, they couldn't get to Gryphon from *Hephaestus*. The components of the Manticore Binary System were just past periastron, but the G0 and G2 companion stars were still almost eleven light-hours apart. *Nike*'s pinnaces would have required two and a half Manticoran days to make the trip, which was twice their maximum life-support endurance with full troop loads.

It had seemed Colonel Ramirez would have to settle for Camp Justin after all, but Fate works in mysterious ways. He mentioned his problem to Captain McKeon over a round of drinks one evening, and the captain saw an opportunity to help improve interservice relations. He and Commander Venizelos of HMS *Apollo* were due to participate in a defensive exercise in Manticore-B, and, with a little crowding, their ships could lift *Nike*'s full Marine detachment plus its pinnaces to Gryphon with just a short hop through hyper.

Colonel Ramirez had accepted the offer with the Corps' thanks, and so it happened that HMS *Prince Adrian*, HMS *Apollo*, and just under six hundred additional Marines departed HMSS *Hephaestus* for Gryphon right on schedule.

"Now why would you want to come along, Scotty?" Susan Hibson asked.

Lieutenant Scotty Tremaine, HMS *Prince Adrian*'s assistant tactical officer, who doubled as the heavy cruiser's boat bay control officer, watched her unwrap a fresh stick of gum. Tremaine considered gum-chewing one of humanity's more disgusting vices, but he made allowances for the major. He'd known her quite a while and seen her do some very good things during the Blackbird Raid. Besides, it wasn't her fault she spent so much of her time inside a suit of battle armor. That was probably enough to warp anyone a little, and there weren't a lot of other things a person could do for relaxation with the equivalent of a pre-space main battle tank wrapped around her. There were, after all, only so many targets one could blow up, shoot into very tiny pieces, or tear apart by brute strength.

Now she slid the gum into her mouth and chewed rhythmically, and he shrugged under the weight of her eyes.

"The Colonel needs a pilot, Ma'am."

"He's *got* a pilot," Hibson pointed out. "A reasonably competent fellow he brought all the way from *Nike* with him."

"Yes, Ma'am. But I'm worried about his nav systems." He met Hibson's gaze with total innocence. "Chief Harkness and

I have run a complete diagnostic series without managing to isolate a fault, but I'm pretty sure there is one."

"Oh?" Hibson leaned back and popped her gum thoughtfully. Lieutenant Tremaine hadn't been briefed for the operation, but that didn't seem to have kept him from figuring things out. "Is it bad enough to downcheck the boat?"

"Oh, I wouldn't say that, Ma'am. It's just that the Chief and I would feel better if we were along to ride herd on the systems. And, of course, if something *did* happen to go wrong, he and I would be on the spot to make repairs . . . and verify the fault for the record."

Hibson raised an eyebrow. "Have you mentioned your concern to Captain McKeon?"

"Yes, Ma'am. The Skipper says the pinnaces are your and Colonel Ramirez's responsibility, but if you'd care to ask for a little Fleet technical support just in case, he's willing to detach the Chief and me for a few days."

"I see." Hibson popped her gum a couple of more times, then shrugged. "I'll take it up with the Colonel, then. If he says you can tag along, it's all right with me."

"Now hear this. Now hear this. Drop point in thirty minutes. Ninth Battalion, man drop stations. Ninth Battalion, man drop stations."

Men and women looked up as the announcement rattled from the speakers in HMS *Prince Adrian*'s Marine Country. The two companies of *Nike*'s Marines scheduled to make the drop in heavy assault configuration were already armored up; their more fortunate fellows put down coffee cups, playing cards, and book viewers and began climbing into their skinsuits while they invoked traditional and time-honored maledictions upon the designers of their equipment. Navy skinsuits were designed primarily for vacuum, with an eye to allowing their wearers to engage in delicate repair work and similarly intricate activities over what could be very lengthy periods indeed. *Marine* skinnies, on the other hand, while undeniably more comfortable than powered battle armor, were heavier, bulkier, and generally far more of a pain in the ass than Navy gear, because they incorporated light but highly effective body armor and were intended for hostile planetary environments as well as vacuum. As long as the wearer's efficiency wasn't impaired, comfort ran a poor second to toughness under the Marine design philosophy, but even the Corps' most accomplished bitchers had to admit that the worst a Gryphon—or even a Sphinx—winter could offer would do little more than inconvenience a skinsuited Marine. Which, given the mission brief's weather reports, was probably a very good thing.

Orders rapped out as *Nike*'s Marines formed up in *Prince Adrian*'s boat bays. Some of the heavy cruiser's own Marines ambled by to see them off, with looks that varied from commiseration to comfortable enjoyment of someone else's misfortune. *Nike*'s Marines responded with pooh-pooh expressions and false enthusiasm, comforting themselves with the reflection that their hosts would find themselves in similar situations soon enough. What went around, came around; that was one of the Corps' imperishable truths. Besides, scuttlebutt said this particular operation was in a more worthy cause than most.

Scotty Tremaine settled himself in the copilot's seat of Nike One, Colonel Ramirez's command pinnace. Major Hibson would ride in Nike Two, ready to take over if something happened to the colonel's com systems; Captain Tyler, operating from *Apollo*'s boat bay in Nike Three, would be equally ready to back up the major. Coxswain Petty Officer First Class Hudson regarded the lieutenant with hooded eyes, then bent forward to bring his internal systems on-line. He'd just detached the pinnace umbilicals when a senior chief with a prize fighter's battered face poked his head into the cramped cockpit.

"Looking good so far, Mr. Tremaine," Horace Harkness announced, then winked. "Still got a tiny glitch in the nav systems, though. I've logged it."

"Good, Chief. I'll keep an eye on things from up here," Tremaine replied with no expression at all.

"Yes, Sir."

Harkness disappeared, and Tremaine's earbug crackled with Colonel Ramirez's voice.

"How's it looking, Hudson?"

"Hatches sealed . . . now, Sir," Hudson replied as a red telltale flicked to green on his panel. "Docking tube retracted. Ready to launch, Sir."

"Good. Inform the duty control officer and proceed on his release."

"Aye, aye, Sir," Hudson acknowledged, and switched from intercom to his intership link.

Seven pinnaces separated from the heavy cruiser and her light cruiser consort. Thrusters blazed at full power, but they left their impeller wedges down as they arrowed toward the blue and white marble so far below. This was a full dress rehearsal; they not only ran silent to avoid any betraying scrap of com chatter but killed *every* readily detectable system, even their internal grav plates, and scorched down on the huge, curdled weather system assaulting Gryphon's southern hemisphere at their maximum safe reentry speed.

Noses and leading edges of wings and stabilators began to glow as they hit atmosphere. Their passengers had been briefed on the flight conditions they could expect and clung grimly to their equipment as the pinnaces began to buffet. However rough the ride was now, it was going to get worse.

Howling winds and driving snow awaited them, and their pilots were in airfoil mode, without even counter-grav as they drove into the teeth of the winter storm. Pinnaces were made for such conditions, but no one had yet found a way to reengineer human stomachs. A few passengers grinned at their neighbors with the cheerful brutality of the immune; others fought grim battles to hang onto their lunches, and a handful of unfortunate souls lost them.

Turbines howled louder than the storm, slicing down to get below the worst of the weather and close on their designated LZs, and Captain Alistair McKeon smiled at his tracking reports. Six of the pinnaces were dead on course; the seventh had already vanished from his scanner area, veering off into some of the worst weather on the planet.

Senior Chief Petty Officer Harkness poked his head back into the cockpit with a toothy smile.

"Yes, Chief?" Tremaine never looked up from his instruments. PO Hudson was doing a dynamite job, but these weren't the weather conditions for anyone's attention to wander on the flight deck.

"Just thought you'd like to know, Sir. The nav systems must've just packed up completely, 'cause they say we're over thirty degrees off course."

"Scandalous, Chief. Just scandalous. I suppose you may as well shut the recorders down. No point logging an erroneous course, after all. PO Hudson and I'll just have to do the best we can."

Tomas Ramirez patted his equipment with an absent hand, checking his gear out of ingrained habit even as he watched his display. Nike One was further off course with every second—because of the storm, no doubt. The colonel smiled thinly, then looked up as someone appeared beside him.

"Why aren't you strapped in, Marine?" he began, then stopped, and his eyebrows knitted in an ominous frown before he shook his head with a sigh.

"Sar'major Babcock, would you mind telling me just what the *hell* you think you're doing here?" His tone was more resigned than his words might have suggested, and Iris Babcock snapped to attention.

"Sir! The Sergeant-Major respectfully reports that she seems to have become confused, Sir! I was under the impression this was one of *Prince Adrian*'s pinnaces, Colonel."

Ramirez shook his head again. "Won't wash, Gunny. *Prince Adrian* doesn't even have the Mark Thirty yet."

"Sir, I—"

"Hold it right there." The colonel turned to glare at Francois Ivashko, his own battalion sergeant-major. "I don't suppose you happened to log Sar'major Babcock as an observer supernumerary, did you, Gunny?"

"Uh, no, Sir," Ivashko said. "But—"

"Well, in that case, get her logged now. I'm surprised at you, Gunny! You know how important the proper paperwork is. Now I'm going to have to clear this retroactively with Major Yestachenko and Captain McKeon!"

"Yes, Sir. Sorry, Sir. I guess I just dropped the ball, Sir," Ivashko said with a sudden, huge grin.

"Don't let it happen again," Ramirez growled, then shook a finger under Babcock's nose. "As for *you*, Sar'major, get back in your seat. And stay where I can keep an eye on you to make sure you behave dirt-side. Understood?"

"Aye, aye, Sir!"

"Nike Flight, this is Nike Two," Susan Hibson said into her com, her voice clear and composed. "Nike Two has lost track on Nike One and is assuming command until Nike One reestablishes contact. Two clear."

She leaned back in her seat and smiled down at her panel with a trace of regret. *Life's a bitch*, she told herself, *but someone has to mind the store . . . and the Colonel outranks me.*

"Snowfall" was too passive a word for what was happening around the isolated hunting chalet. A sixty kilometer-per-hour wind drove the flakes before it like a solid wall, screaming around the chalet's eaves so violently no one could have said where the ground ended and the white hurricane began, so one might reasonably have expected any sane person to be safely indoors.

One would have been wrong. Five men and women huddled in the lees of walls and exterior stairways, cursing their employer and themselves for ever taking this job while they peered halfheartedly out into the night. Their cold weather gear was excellent, but the wind was hitting gust speeds of up to a hundred KPH; even at max, the heating systems were losing ground to that sort of cutting bite. All of which only went to prove they were out here on a fool's errand. Exterior security might have made sense under most conditions, but only a lunatic would be out in weather like this!

None of them saw the huge, swept-wing shape come slicing in from downwind, turbine scream lost in the gale. PO Hudson threw it into vertical hover at three meters while his landing legs deployed, and it bucked and staggered in the gusting wind. Then it dropped like a rock, and massive shock absorbers soaked up the impact as it touched down on the flat sheet of rock Hudson's belly radar had mapped for him. The pinnace rocked drunkenly for a moment, but he brought up the ventral tractors, killing the oscillation and locking the craft immovably in place, then began powering down his flight systems, and Scotty Tremaine patted him on the shoulder.

"That, PO Hudson, was good. It was better than good—it was outstanding!"

"Thanks, Sir." Hudson grinned, and Harkness stuck his head back into the cockpit.

"All them grunts are getting ready to jump ship, Sir," he said to Tremaine. "Reckon we better go keep an eye on them?"

"In this weather?" Tremaine hit the button to slide his seat back from the controls. "Chief, it's the Navy's job to look after the helpless. We couldn't possibly trust a bunch of Marines to find their way home without us on a night like this!"

" 'S what I thought, too, Sir," Harkness agreed, and extended a stun rifle to his lieutenant. "Hope you wore your warm undies, Sir."

The first warning any of the shivering exterior guards had was a brief glimpse of *something* materializing out of the snow. They didn't get a chance to identify it. Colonel Ramirez's official ops plan had called for his HQ platoon to play the role of a local quick-reaction defensive force against the rest of his Marines, and, just to make things interesting for the "raiders," he'd armed all the HQ types with stunners instead of the laser-tag rifles and sidearms their fellows carried.

The entire outside security force was down and unconscious before it even realized it was under attack.

"What do we do with 'em, Sir?" Sergeant-Major Ivashko asked over his suit com, prodding one limp body with a toe.

"I'd like to let them freeze, but that wouldn't be neighborly."

Ramirez looked around through the howling snow, orienting himself against the map *Prince Adrian* had plotted from orbit before the weather closed in. "There's a storage shed over there, Gunny. Stack them in there."

"Aye, Sir." Ivashko checked the small tactical display inside his helmet and picked two nearby beacons. "Coulter, you and Malthus have babysitter duty. Get these sleeping beauties tucked away."

Senior Chief Petty Officer Harkness didn't like Marines. It was an instinct he'd never questioned, but he was willing to make exceptions tonight. He padded along at Lieutenant Tremaine's heels, watching over his lieutenant with one eye while the other watched Colonel Ramirez's people in action.

With the exterior guards down, the Marines threw a perimeter about the chalet, located and disabled the emergency landline, and took out the building's satellite up-link with their jammers, all in less than four minutes. While most of them dealt with that, the HQ section formed up around Colonel Ramirez while he parceled out the doors each of them should make for.

Lieutenant Tremaine attached himself directly to the colonel, and Harkness hadn't even realized Sergeant-Major Babcock had joined the show until he saw her padding along behind Ramirez. He shook his head. The Skipper had to be up to his neck in this whole thing, which meant there wasn't a lot he could do to the gunny—officially. But Harkness suspected he was going to tear a long, bloody strip off her in private.

The colonel led the way to the chalet's front entrance and tried the latch gently. It was locked, but that didn't stop Ramirez. He shifted his stun rifle to his right hand, holding the heavy weapon like a pocket pistol, and drew a small, flat box from his equipment harness. He pressed it to the door and touched a button, and the latch sprang.

Ramirez toed the door open, and someone said something sharp and indignant as cold wind blasted through it. The massive officer didn't even blink. He just squeezed the stunner trigger and stepped through the door before whoever had complained hit the floor.

"One down," he murmured over the com as Babcock followed him.

"Make that two," someone else said over the same circuit.

"Three," a second voice said, followed a moment later by yet a third. "Four," it said quietly.

Tremaine followed Babcock into the paneled interior, with Harkness bringing up the rear. The others were inside now, as well, advancing with quick, efficient stealth and taking out the chalet's inhabitants as they went. Things were going well, Harkness reflected, when he heard someone behind him.

"What the he—?!"

Harkness spun. A beefy, over-muscled type gawked at him, one hand reaching for a shoulder-holstered pulser in bemused reflex, and the chief swore under his breath. The bastard was too close for Harkness to get the muzzle of his stun rifle around, so he brought the butt up in a crisp, flashing arc that landed neatly on the other man's jaw and sent him crashing to the floor.

"Aw, *shit!*" someone muttered as the impact shook the hall. Harkness flushed, but there was no time to feel properly embarrassed, for other doors were opening as "guests" in the bedrooms off the hall roused.

The chief dropped one with a quick shot, then whipped back around to the front just as Lieutenant Tremaine stunned a third man. A single pulser shot whined, and Ramirez took three—two men and the woman who'd fired—with a wide-angled shot, less efficient but just as effective at this range.

But Sergeant-Major Babcock had been directly in front of a door when it jerked open, and the man and woman inside it had clearly been engaged in something besides sleep. They were minimally clothed but wide awake, and the woman grabbed Babcock's stunner before she could even begin to react.

Harkness cursed and tried to get his own weapon up, but the sergeant-major was too close to them. He couldn't get a clear shot—and a moment later, he didn't need one. Babcock let the woman tighten her grip on her stunner, and then both the Marine's feet left the floor at once. She pivoted on the firmly held weapon like a gymnast, and the other woman flew back with a gurgling grunt as two size-eight Combat Boots, Marine skinsuit, Mark Seven, hit her in the belly. The impact flung her into her fellow, who opened his mouth to shout—just as Babcock touched the floor once more and her left elbow struck his skull like a hammer. He went down without a sound, and the Marine stepped back, still holding her stunner, and calmly shot the woman before she stopped whooping for breath.

It was all over in a heartbeat, and Harkness gawked at Babcock's swift, silent efficiency. The sergeant-major glanced into the room her victims had come from and gave the man an insurance stun bolt of his own, then looked over her shoulder at the chief.

"Next time, bring a goddamned drum and bugle band along!" she snarled over the com.

"Can it, Gunny!" Ramirez snapped. The colonel stood stock-still, running his skinsuit's external sound pickups up to max, then relaxed. "No damage done, I think." He did a quick count of the unconscious bodies littering the hallway. "Twelve, repeat, total twelve down," he said over the com, and turned to dart his own look at Harkness. The chief expected something severe, but the colonel only shook a finger at him and turned back to his front.

Maybe, Harkness reflected, Marines weren't all *that* bad after all.

Five minutes later, the Marines had accounted for what should be every guard in the place, assuming their information was correct. Tomas Ramirez wasn't especially fond of assumptions, however. He positioned his people to cover the access routes to the central staircase, then led Babcock, Ivashko, and Tremaine up the stairs. Harkness wasn't invited, but he wasn't about to stay behind, either, and found himself bringing up the rear beside Babcock.

The door at the head of the stairs was closed and locked. The colonel tried his magic box again, but whoever was on the other side of that door didn't trust powered locks. He'd used an old-fashioned mechanical key, as well, and the colonel shrugged.

He handed his stunner to Ivashko. They couldn't afford to put *this* one to sleep for a couple of hours, and that meant he had to do things the hard way. Which didn't exactly disappoint him.

He stepped back to the edge of the landing, balanced on the balls of his feet, and then launched himself at the door. He had room only for three running strides, but the chalet door that could stop Tomas Ramirez had never been built, and he went through the rain of splinters like a boulder.

The man sleeping on the other side had the reflexes of a cat. He jerked upright in bed, one hand sliding under his pillow before his eyes had fully opened, yet he was still far too slow. Ramirez reached his bedside just as his fingers closed on the pulser's butt, and a hand like a power scoop gripped the front of his expensive pajamas.

Denver Summervale flew out of bed like a missile, and his gun hand hit a bedpost as he passed. He cried out in pain as the pulser was torn from his grip, and Ramirez released him as he reached the top of his arc.

Summervale sailed across the bedroom and barely managed to get an arm up to protect his head before he hit the opposite wall like a cannon ball. He bounced back, and even taken totally unawares in a sound sleep, he managed to land on his feet. He fell into an automatic defensive stance, shaking his head to clear it, and Ramirez let him. The colonel simply stood there, giving him time to recover, and waited for his charge.

It came. Summervale disliked physical combat. He was a specialist, a surgeon who removed unwanted problems with a gun, but he'd killed more than once with his bare hands. Unfortunately, he was nowhere near as fast—or as strong—as Tomas Ramirez, and he was in pajamas, not a Marine skinsuit.

Ramirez brushed aside a killing blow with his left hand and drove his right like a wrecking ball into Summervale's belly. The smaller man folded over it with a wailing grunt, and the colonel brought his left up in a vicious slap. The assassin flew backward, but he didn't hit the wall again. Ramirez caught him in midair, spun him like a toy, slammed him belly-down over the edge of his own bed, jerked one wrist up behind him, and locked an arm of iron across his throat.

Summervale fought to writhe free, only to scream in pain as Ramirez, his face totally without expression, rammed a skin-suited knee into his spine.

"Now, now, Mr. Summervale," the colonel said softly. "None of that."

The killer whimpered—a sound of involuntary anguish poisoned by his humiliation as it was forced from him—and Ramirez glanced over his shoulder at Ivashko, who laid a small recorder on the bed.

"Do you recognize my voice, Mr. Summervale?" Ramirez asked. Summervale gritted his teeth and refused to answer—then screamed again as stone-crusher fingers twisted his wrist. "I asked a question, Mr. Summervale," the colonel chided. "It's not nice to ignore questions."

Summervale screamed a third time, writhing in agony, then threw his head back as far as he could.

"Yes! *Yes!*" His aristocratic voice was ugly with pain and hate.

"Good. Can you guess why I'm here?"

"F-Fuck you!" Summervale panted past the arm about his throat.

"Such language!" Ramirez said almost genially. "Especially when I'm just here to ask you a question." His voice lost its pretense of humor, cold and hard. "Who paid you to kill Captain Tankersley, Summervale?"

"Go to—hell, you—son-of-a-bitch!" Summervale gasped.

"That's not nice," Ramirez chided again. "I'm going to have to insist you tell me."

"Why—the fuck—should I?" Summervale actually managed a strangled laugh. "You'll just—kill me—when I do—so fuck you!"

"Mr. Summervale, Mr. Summervale!" Ramirez sighed. "The Captain would have my ass if *I* killed you, so just answer the question."

"Like hell!" Summervale panted.

"I think you should reconsider," Ramirez said softly, and Scotty Tremaine turned away, his face white, at the sound of his voice. "I only said I wouldn't *kill* you, Mr. Summervale," the colonel whispered almost lovingly. "I never said I wouldn't *hurt* you."

✧ CHAPTER TWENTY-TWO

"Tractor lock."

"Cut main thrusters," Michelle Henke responded. "Stand by attitude thrusters. Chief Robinet, you have approach control."

"Cut main thrusters, aye," *Agni*'s helmswoman repeated, and her fingers tapped keys, killing the last thrust from the light cruiser's auxiliary reaction engines. "Main thruster shutdown confirmed. Standing by for attitude thrusters. I have approach control, Ma'am."

"Very good." Henke leaned back in her chair and watched the ugly, comforting bulk of HMSS *Hephaestus* filling the forward visual display. *Agni* was well inside the safety perimeter of her own impeller wedge; she'd been on conventional thrusters for the last twenty minutes, but *Hephaestus'* tractors had her now, drawing her hammerhead bow steadily into the waiting docking bay. All Henke's ship had to do was insure the correctness of her final docking attitude, which required a finicky degree of precision the space station's tractors simply couldn't provide.

She watched silently over CPO Robinet's shoulder. Robinet probably could have picked up her moorings in her sleep, but the ultimate responsibility was Henke's, whatever happened. That thought jabbed uneasily at the back of her mind, as it always did at moments like this, for she'd never really liked docking maneuvers. She was a competent shiphandler, but she would never have Honor's total, almost innocently arrogant self-confidence. She knew perfectly well that it was that very lack of confidence which kept her from performing with Honor's bravura flair—which, in turn, kept her from feeling confident!

She snorted in familiar self-criticism, but the fact was that she vastly preferred a simple parking orbit that let small craft and tenders make rendezvous with *her*. All the same, she was glad *Hephaestus* had an open berth, for *Nike*'s repair slip was barely five minutes by personnel tube from *Agni*'s intended mooring. Henke had already commed Eve Chandler to warn her of Honor's arrival, and Chandler had responded with a warning of her own: the newsies were waiting in force.

Henke felt her mouth twist, then forced it to relax with deliberate, conscious effort and squared her shoulders. There was no way—no *way!*—those vultures were getting at Honor. Which was why *Hephaestus* Central had copied a flight plan for a cutter to deliver Countess Harrington and party to the main concourse. Falsifying flight plans was a moderately serious offense, and there might be repercussions when no cutter materialized to match the concourse arrivals board, but Henke thought she'd detected a certain knowing note in the senior controller's voice when he receipted her bogus flight plan. His casual mention that the newsies would no doubt be waiting for Lady Harrington only reinforced her suspicion—and her feeling that she'd done the right thing, even if she caught a reprimand for it.

A soft, musical tone sounded, and Chief Robinet nodded to herself.

"On docking station, Captain."

"Engage mooring tractors."

"Engaging mooring tractors, aye, Ma'am."

"Jack," Henke turned to her com officer, "request umbilical lock and see how fast they can get the boarding tubes run out to us."

"Aye, aye, Ma'am."

"Thanks." Henke pushed herself up out of her command chair and glanced at her exec. "Mr. Thurmond, you have the watch."

"Aye, aye, Ma'am. I have the watch."

"Good." She rubbed her temple for just a moment, then sighed. "If anyone needs me, I'll be with Lady Harrington."

Honor's cabin had no view port, but she'd patched her com terminal into *Agni*'s forward visual sensors. Now she sat silently, hands loose in her lap, and gazed at the flat screen as the ship nosed into her berth.

She felt . . . empty. Emptier than the wind or space itself, sucked clean by the silent undertow of entropy. She heard MacGuiness moving about behind her, felt Nimitz as he stretched along the back of her chair and radiated his love and concern, and there was only stillness and silence within her. The pain waited, but she had sheathed it in an armor of ice. She could see it in her mind's eye, razor-edges glittering within its crystalline prison, yet it couldn't touch her. Nor would it be able to, for it would destroy her too soon if she let it free. And so she'd frozen it, not in fear but with purpose, imprisoning it until she chose to shatter the ice and loose it upon herself, and that would have to wait until she had found Denver Summervale.

Her mind ticked smoothly away, considering ways and means. She knew Mike was frightened for her, but that was silly. Nothing could hurt her now. She was a glacier, a thing of ice and stone grinding implacably toward its appointed end. Like the glacier, nothing would be allowed to stop her . . . and, like the glacier, there would be nothing left of her at all at journey's end.

She hid that thought deep, so deep even she could barely sense it, lest Nimitz read it in her, but there was a clean, clear logic to it. It was inevitable, and it was justice, too.

She shouldn't have let herself love Paul, she thought distantly. She should have known better. Part of her wished she'd been allowed more time before the trap sprang, but the end had been ordained. It was his love for her which had doomed him; she'd known that the moment she browbeat Mike into telling her the final insult Summervale had used against him. Mike hadn't wanted to tell her. She'd fought against it, yet she must have known Honor would find out eventually. And so she'd told her, looking away, unable to meet her eyes, and Honor had known. She still had no idea why a total stranger had picked a quarrel with Paul, but *she* had been the chink in his armor. *She* was what Summervale had used to reach him, goad him . . . kill him.

Just as she would kill Summervale. Her wealth would serve a purpose after all, for she would spend it all if she must to find him.

A colder, more savage ache went through her, and she embraced it. She built it into her armor, raising the icy walls higher and thicker to hold the pain at bay just a little longer. Just long enough to do the last thing that would ever matter to her again.

Honor looked better, Henke told herself as she stepped into her friend's cabin, and it was true . . . as far as it went. Her face had lost that shattered, broken look, yet it remained a mask. Henke's heart ached every time she thought of what hid behind it, and she only had to look at Nimitz to guess what that hidden thing was. The 'cat was no longer gaunt and hunched, but the quick, eager mischief had gone out of him. His ears never rose from their half-flattened position, and he seemed to radiate a strange, dangerous aura, like an echo of the hunger Henke knew filled Honor. It was cold, as she was cold, and alien to everything Henke had ever sensed from him in the past. Still worse, perhaps, was the way he watched Honor. He sat quiet and still on her shoulder whenever she left the cabin; within her quarters, he refused to let her out of his sight, and his grass-green eyes were quenched and dark.

"Hello, Mike. I see we've arrived."

"Yes." Henke's reply came out awkwardly, in the tone of someone who didn't know exactly how to respond. There was no obvious stress in Honor's voice; indeed, the reverse was true, but its very lifelessness, its flattened timbre and deadness, made it a stranger's. Henke cleared her throat and managed a smile. "I've run a little interference with the newsies, Honor. If we can get you aboard fast enough, you may make it clear to *Nike* before they realize you aren't coming in through the main concourse after all."

"Thank you." Honor's lips formed a smile that never touched her eyes. Those dark, ice-cored eyes that never warmed, never seemed to blink even on *Agni*'s range. Henke had no idea how many rounds Honor had fired, but she knew she'd spent at least four hours a day there, every day, and her absolute lack of expression as she punched bullet after bullet through the hearts and heads of human holo targets had terrified Henke. She'd moved like a machine, with a dreadful, economic precision that denied any human feeling, as if her very soul had frozen within her.

Honor Harrington was a killer. She'd always been one; Mike Henke knew that better than most, yet she'd also known that killer streak was controlled by the compassion and gentleness which were far more important parts of Honor. It was channeled by duty and responsibility and, in a sense, it was the complement and consequence alike of her compassion. Honor *cared* about things; that had made her capacity for violence even greater, in many ways, but it had also made it something she could use at need, not something that used her. It had threatened to break free a time or two, yet it never had. If the whispers from the Blackbird Raid were accurate, it almost had that time, but she'd managed, somehow, to stop it.

This time she didn't even want to, and Henke sensed her terrifying aptitude for destruction as never before. Henke had feared for her sanity; now she knew the truth was almost worse than that. Honor wasn't insane—she simply didn't care. She'd lost not only her sense of balance but any desire to regain it. She wasn't berserk. She was something far more danger-ous, for her killer self was in command, inhumanly logical and cruel as a Sphinx winter, utterly devoid of her usual compassion and not at all concerned with consequences.

Honor stood silently, watching her best friend from within her icy walls. She felt Mike's fear for her through her link with Nimitz, and a tiny piece of her heart longed to comfort that fear. Yet it was no more than reflex, too small and lost to be more, and she'd forgotten how to offer comfort, any-way. Perhaps she would remember, someday, but it hardly mattered. All that mattered now was Denver Summervale.

"I suppose I'd better be going," she said after a moment. She held out her hand, and Mike took it. Nimitz let Honor feel the tears burning behind her friend's eyes, and that lost fragment of the woman Paul Tankersley had loved longed to feel her own eyes burn. But she couldn't, and so she squeezed Mike's hand, patted her gently on the shoulder, and left without ever looking back.

The side party came to attention and saluted when Honor caught the grab bar and swung from the boarding tube's zero gee into *Nike*'s internal gravity. Bosun's pipes wailed, Honor's own hand rose in automatic response, and Eve Chandler stepped forward and held out her hand in welcome. Honor took it, and the diminutive redhead's eyes were dark with compassion and more than a little shock, even fear, as she absorbed her commanding officer's expression.

"Captain," she said quietly. It was a simple greeting, without the condolence she sensed Honor didn't want to hear.

"Eve." Honor nodded to her, then to the side party, and beckoned one of her armsmen forward. "Commander Chan-dler, this is Major Andrew LaFollet, commanding my Grayson security team." That cold ghost of a smile touched her lips again. "Protector Benjamin sent him along to keep me from doing anything foolish." LaFollet's mouth tightened, but he shook Chandler's hand without comment. "Please introduce him to Colonel Ramirez as soon as convenient. I think they'll find they have quite a bit in common."

"Of course, Ma'am," Chandler murmured.

"Thank you." Honor turned to MacGuiness. "See to getting my gear transferred, please, Mac. I'm going directly to my quarters."

"Yes, Ma'am." Chandler had never heard the steward sound

so weary—or worried—and her heart went out to the exhausted, sad-eyed man.

Honor moved forward out of the entry port, headed for the lift, and LaFollet cleared his throat behind her.

"Armsman Candless," he said quietly, and James Candless came briefly to attention and padded off on Honor's heels. Chandler looked at the major, and he shrugged. "I'm sorry, Commander, but I have my orders."

"I see." Chandler gazed at him a moment longer, and then her expression softened. "I *do* see," she said more quietly, with a different emphasis, "and we're all concerned for her. We'll work something out, Major."

"I hope so, Commander," LaFollet murmured, watching the lift carry his Steadholder away. "I hope to God the Tester we do."

The cabin hatch closed, sealing Honor away from Candless and her normal sentry. She felt a vague sense of guilt for failing to introduce the two men to one another or explain Candless's presence to the Marine, but there was too little of her left to spare for things like that.

She stood looking around the cabin, and dry-eyed agony twisted despite her armor as her gaze touched the holo cube on her desk. Paul smiled at her from it, laughing, wind whipping his ponytail while he held his flight helmet in the crook of his arm and the needle nose of a Javelin gleamed behind him.

She crossed to the desk. Her hand trembled as she lifted the holo cube, staring down at it, longing for the tears that would not come. Her mouth quivered, and her fingers tightened, but still her frozen soul refused to weep. All she could do was close her eyes and press the cube to her breasts, rocking it like the stony heart of all her loss and pain.

She never knew how long she stood there while Nimitz huddled against the side of her neck, keening softly and stroking her cheek with a delicate true-hand. She only knew she couldn't do anything else—and that she lacked the courage to open her sleeping cabin's hatch. There was too much agony beyond it, too many treacherous reminders of joy. She couldn't face that. Not now. It would break her, and she dared not break before she did what she had to do, and so she stood, a black-and-gold-uniformed statue frozen at the corner of her desk, until the admittance chime sounded behind her.

She inhaled sharply, nostrils flaring. Then she set the holo cube gently back on her desk. She ran a fingertip down Paul's smiling face like a kiss and pressed the com key.

"Yes?" The quaver in her voice surprised her, and she crushed it in a grip of ice.

"Colonel Ramirez, Ma'am," her Marine sentry said.

"I don't—" She stopped herself. She didn't want to face Ramirez. He'd been Paul's second, and she knew him too well. Knew he blamed himself and expected her to share his self-condemning verdict. She didn't, but dealing with *his* guilt would open her own wounds wider, threaten her armor. Yet if she refused him admittance it might seem she did blame him. He deserved better of her, and when she had so little left she *could* give her own conscience refused to let her withhold it.

She drew another deep breath and straightened with a sigh.

"Thank you, Private," she said. She touched the button to open the hatch and turned to face it.

Tomas Ramirez looked even worse than she'd feared, and she braced herself as he stopped just inside the hatch and it closed behind him.

"Dame Honor, I—" he began, but she raised a hand.

"Don't, Tomas," she said as gently as the ice about her heart allowed. She knew she sounded mechanical, uncaring, and crossed to him. She rested one hand on his arm, trying to break through to herself in order to reach out to him and knowing she'd failed. "You were Paul's friend. I know that, and I know it wasn't your fault. Paul wouldn't blame you for what happened . . . and neither do I."

Ramirez bit his lip. A tear glittered at the corner of his eye, another of those tears *she* couldn't shed, and he bent his head for just a moment. Then he drew a deep, shuddering breath and looked up once more. Their eyes met, and she saw the understanding in his, the knowledge that this was the very best she could do and his acceptance of it.

"Thank you, Ma'am," he said softly.

She patted his arm and walked around her desk. She sank into her chair and gestured for him to take one facing her while she eased Nimitz down into her lap. The 'cat curled tightly, burying his muzzle against her while he radiated his love for her. It hurt, like a hammer chipping at the anesthetic shield of her detachment, but she stroked his spine slowly and gently.

"I realize you've just returned, Ma'am," Ramirez said after a moment, "and I apologize for intruding, but there's something you need to know before you . . . do anything else."

Honor smiled without humor at his choice of words. Tomas Ramirez had been with her on Blackbird. If anyone in the galaxy knew what "anything else" she intended to do, it was he.

"Last week," the colonel went on, "Major Hibson and I carried out a training exercise on Gryphon." Honor felt a slight stir of interest and raised an eyebrow, wondering how they'd gotten to Gryphon with *Nike* still in dock.

"Captain McKeon and Commander Venizelos were kind enough to assist us by transporting the battalion to Manticore-B," Ramirez went on, and she felt a stronger stir of interest, a sharpening as something about his tone probed at her icy cocoon. "The exercise was a general success, Ma'am, but we suffered a nav systems failure aboard my command pinnace. I'm afraid we landed several hundred klicks from our intended LZ—there was a severe blizzard in the exercise area, which probably contributed to our navigation error—and it took me some hours to rejoin the rest of the battalion."

"I see." Honor tipped her chair back with a slight frown as Ramirez paused. "May I ask why you're telling me this?" she said finally.

"Well, Ma'am, it just *happened* that our actual landing site was very close to a hunting chalet. Naturally, my party and I proceeded to the chalet in hopes of discovering exactly where we were so that we could rejoin the exercise. It was pure coincidence, of course, but, well, Ma'am, it seems Denver Summervale was vacationing at that same chalet."

Honor's chair snapped upright, and Ramirez swallowed at the sudden, savage glitter of her eyes.

"Is he still there, Colonel?" she half-whispered, her half-mad gaze ravenous on his face, and he swallowed again.

"I don't know, Ma'am," he said very carefully, "but in the course of our conversation, he . . . volunteered certain information." He reached into his tunic pocket and laid a recording chip on Honor's desk, refusing to look away from her frightening eyes.

"He said—" Ramirez paused and cleared his throat. "Ma'am, he said he was hired. He was paid to kill Captain Tankersley . . . and you."

"*Paid?*" Honor stared at him, and a silent tremor ran through her. Her chill armor shivered, cracking ever so slightly as heat flared suddenly within her. She'd never heard of Denver Summervale before he killed Paul. She'd assumed he must have acted for some personal reason of his own, but this—

"Yes, Ma'am. Paid to kill *both* of you," Ramirez reemphasized. "But he was hired to kill Captain Tankersley first."

First. Someone had wanted Paul killed *first*, and the way Ramirez said it echoed and reechoed through her, battering at the ice. It hadn't been the uncaringly cruel act of an impersonal universe to punish her for loving. It had been *deliberate*. Someone wanted her dead, and before she died, he wanted to hurt her as hideously as he possibly could. Someone had paid for Paul's legal murder as a weapon against *her*.

Nimitz snarled upright in her lap, fur bristling, tail belled and claws bared, and she felt her armor crumbling in ruin, felt the terrible heat of her own fury blasting away her detachment. And even as her rage roared higher within her, she knew. She *knew* who it had to be, the only person who was sick and sadistic enough, who hated *her* enough to have Paul killed. She knew, but she only stared at Ramirez, willing him to confirm it.

"He was hired, Ma'am," the colonel said softly, "by the Earl of North Hollow."

✧ CHAPTER TWENTY-THREE

TOMAS RAMIREZ COCKED HIS CHAIR back in his small shipboard office and studied the green-uniformed man across his desk. Major Andrew LaFollet returned his gaze with equally measuring gray eyes, and there was a subsurface tension between them; not anger or distrust, but the sort of wariness two guard dogs might have exhibited on first meeting.

"So, Major," Ramirez said at last, "am I to understand you and your men are permanently assigned to Lady Harrington? I'd gathered from what Commander Chandler told me that this was in the nature of a temporary assignment on Protector Benjamin's authority."

"I'm sorry about the confusion, Sir." LaFollet was tall for a Grayson, with a solid, well-muscled physique, but he was still a head shorter than Ramirez and looked almost puny in comparison. He was also ten years younger than the colonel, though they looked very much the same age thanks to Ramirez's prolong treatments, yet there was no lack of confidence in his face or posture. He ran a hand through his dark, auburn hair and frowned, obviously considering the best way to make himself understood to this foreigner.

"At the moment, Colonel," he said in his soft, slow Grayson accent, raising his eyes to examine some point above Ramirez's head, "the Steadholder doesn't seem to be thinking very clearly." The look in his eyes when he lowered them once more warned the colonel that anyone who tried to make his statement into a criticism would regret it. "I suspect she thinks we *are* a temporary fixture."

"But she's wrong," Ramirez suggested after a moment.

"Yes, Sir. By Grayson law, a steadholder must be accompanied by his—or, in this case, her—personal guard at all times, on Grayson or off."

"Even in the Star Kingdom?"

"On Grayson or off, Sir," LaFollet repeated, and Ramirez blinked.

"Major, I can appreciate that you didn't make the law, but Lady Harrington is also an officer in the Queen's Navy."

"I understand that, Sir."

"But what you may not understand is that general regs prohibit the presence of armed civilians or foreign nationals on a Queen's ship. To put it plainly, Major LaFollet, your presence here is illegal."

"I'm sorry to hear that, Colonel," LaFollet said politely, and Ramirez sighed.

"You're not going to make this any easier on me, are you, Major?" he asked wryly.

"It's not my intention to cause difficulties for you, the Royal Manticoran Navy, or the Star Kingdom, Colonel. It *is* my intention to do my duty, as my oath requires, and protect my Steadholder."

"The Royal Marines protect the captains of Her Majesty's starships," Ramirez said, his deep voice a bit flatter and harder.

"Meaning no disrespect, Colonel, that's beside the point. And," the major's eyes were very level, "while I understand that nothing which happened was your fault, or the Royal Marines', Lady Harrington has suffered enough."

Ramirez's jaw clenched for a moment, but then he drew a deep breath and forced himself to sit back. LaFollet's voice could not have been more respectful, and a part of the colonel agreed with his quiet accusation. He thought for a moment, then decided to try another tack.

"Major, Lady Harrington may not return to Grayson for years now that Parliament has voted to declare war and we're resuming active operations. Are you and your—what, ten men? Twelve?"

"There are a total of twelve of us, Sir."

"Twelve, then. Are all twelve of you ready to spend that long off Grayson when the Corps is prepared to guarantee Lady Harrington's safety?"

"She won't be aboard ship for that entire time, Sir. Whenever she leaves it, she leaves her Marine sentry behind. And in answer to your question, we *aren't* off Grayson as long as we're with our Steadholder." Ramirez couldn't quite stop his eyes from rolling upward, and LaFollet allowed himself a small smile. "Nonetheless, Sir, I take your point, and the answer is yes. We're prepared to spend however long we have to off Grayson."

"You can speak for all of your men?"

"Could you speak for yours, Sir?" LaFollet held the colonel's eye until Ramirez nodded grudgingly. "So can I, Sir. And, as I understand is true for your own Marines, every member of the Harrington Guard is a volunteer."

"May I ask why *you* volunteered?" In the wrong tone, that question could have been insulting; as it was, it was honestly curious, and LaFollet shrugged.

"Certainly, Sir. I was assigned to Palace Security prior to the Maccabeus coup attempt. So was my older brother, as a member of Protector Benjamin's personal guard. He was killed, and Lady Harrington not only took over his duty to guard the Protector but killed his murderer with her bare hands—before she went out to protect my entire planet." He met Ramirez's gaze very steadily. "Grayson owes her its freedom; my family owes her life debt for completing the task my brother couldn't and avenging his death. I volunteered for the Harrington Steadholder's Guard the day its formation was announced."

Ramirez leaned further back, his eyes probing. "I see. Forgive me for asking this, Major, but I know from my own reading of the 'faxes that not all Graysons are pleased to have a woman as a steadholder. Given that, are you confident all your men share your feelings?"

"They all volunteered for this specific assignment, Colonel." An edge of frost crept into LaFollet's voice for the first time. "As for their personal motivations, Armsman Candless' father died aboard *Covington* at the Battle of Blackbird. Corporal Mattingly's older brother died aboard *Saul* in the same battle. Armsman Yard lost a cousin and an uncle in First Yeltsin; another cousin survived Blackbird only because Lady Harrington insisted that every Grayson life pod be picked up, despite the risk that *Saladin* would return before they were found. His transponder was damaged, and our sensors couldn't find him; *Fearless*'s could . . . and did. There isn't a man in my detachment—or the entire Guard, for that matter—who didn't join because he owes Lady Harrington a personal debt, but that's only part of it. She's . . . special, Sir. I don't know exactly how to explain it, but—"

"You don't have to," Ramirez murmured, and LaFollet glanced at him. Something in the colonel's eyes made his shoulders relax, and he lowered his eyes once more, staring intently down at his hand as he ran it over the arm of his chair.

"It's . . . not proper for a Grayson to say this, Sir," he said quietly, "but we joined her guard because we love her." He stopped rubbing the chair arm and looked back up into Ramirez's eyes. "More than that, she's our *Steadholder*, our personal liege lady. We owe her exactly the same duty you owe your Queen, Colonel, and we intend to discharge it. I understand the Protector has instructed our ambassador to convey that same information to your Prime Minister."

Ramirez rubbed an eyebrow slowly. He recognized intransigence when he saw it, and the matter of the Captain's legal status as a foreign noblewoman raised questions he was more than pleased *he* didn't have to settle. More importantly, LaFollet had a point—possibly an even better one than he knew—about the Captain's security, for it was unlikely North Hollow would simply give up if Denver Summervale failed to kill her. Ramirez's Marines couldn't guarantee her safety once she left her ship, but from what he'd seen so far of Andrew LaFollet and his men, it would take nothing short of a tactical nuclear weapon to get past them.

He wondered how much that was affecting his judgment. Probably more than he ought to allow. No, scratch the probably. It was *certainly* carrying more weight with him than it should, and he didn't very much care.

"All right, Major," he said finally. "I understand your position, and, just between us, I'm glad to see you. Until and unless competent authority directs me to enforce the regs against your bearing arms aboard ship, you keep your sidearms. I'll also arrange for one of your people to join the Captain's regular Marine sentry at all times, and you'll be informed whenever she leaves *Nike*. More than that will have to be worked out between you and Dame Honor, but I know the Captain, and I don't think you're going to have much luck getting a guard posted inside her quarters, whatever Grayson law says."

"Of course not, Sir." LaFollet blushed brightly at the suggestion, and the colonel hid a smile behind his hand. Then he sobered.

"I'm afraid there's another thing you're going to have to accept, though, Major LaFollet. Not from me or the Navy, but from Dame Honor herself." LaFollet raised an eyebrow, and Ramirez sighed. "You know, of course, about Captain Tankersley's death?" The armsman nodded, and Ramirez shrugged, not entirely happily. "The Captain knows who did it. I expect she'll be doing something about that, and you won't be able to protect her when she does."

"We realize that, Sir. We don't like it, but frankly, Colonel, we wouldn't try to stop her if we could."

Ramirez couldn't quite hide his surprise at LaFollet's coldly vicious response. Grayson mores were ironclad, and the notion of unmarried people carrying on sexual relationships violated about a third of them. LaFollet smiled thinly at his surprise but said nothing, and the colonel began to realize just how much the Captain's Grayson subjects truly cared for her.

"Well, in that case, Major," he said, rising and extending his hand, "welcome aboard. Come with me and let me introduce you to the rest of my officers and my senior noncoms. After that, we'll see about finding you and your people some quarters and adjusting the guard roster."

"Thank you, Sir." LaFollet's hand was almost lost in Ramirez's huge paw, but he squeezed back firmly. "We appreciate it."

Honor's eyes opened. For the first time in far too long she woke to something more than frozen emptiness. The pain was still there, still locked away in its armored cocoon, for nothing had changed in at least one respect: she dared not set it free until she had dealt with its cause. But there was a new, poisonous certainty in her heart. An old and familiar venom. She knew her enemy now. She was no longer the victim of something she couldn't understand, but rather of something she understood only too well, and somehow that cracked the ice about her soul.

Nimitz rolled off her chest as she sat up in bed and brushed hair out of her eyes, and she felt the difference in him, as well. The 'cat had hated Denver Summervale from the beginning, and not simply for the pain he'd caused Honor. That would have been enough, but Nimitz had learned to love Paul Tankersley in his own right. And perhaps that was the difference in him, as it was the difference in her. They knew the author of their pain, and the reason for it, and the conflict between them— between Honor's urge towards dissolution and Nimitz's fierce determination to keep her alive—had vanished into a shared and implacable resolve to destroy their enemies.

She swung her feet to the decksole and let her hand rest lightly, lovingly, on the space where Paul should have lain. She could do that, now; could face the pain, even if she dared not let herself feel it to the full just yet. It was odd, a corner of her brain thought. She'd heard so many tales about the way love could save one's sanity; no one had ever told her hate could do the same.

She pushed herself up and padded into the head to brush her teeth, and her memory replayed the record chip Ramirez had left her. She was certain the colonel had edited it a bit, yet she had no doubt of the recording's truth. It was unfortunate that it would never be admissible in a court of law, even had she dared submit it to one. Ramirez had been more than simply reticent about the circumstances, but the curious, pain-shadowed breathlessness of Summervale's voice when he abruptly began speaking told her all she needed to know about how he'd been convinced to "volunteer" the information.

She finished brushing her teeth, and if the face in her mirror remained wan and wounded, at least she recognized it again, and in its eyes she saw wonder. Awe, perhaps, that so many people would risk so much for her.

She rinsed her toothbrush, unplugged it, and put it away, all without taking her eyes from her mirrored image. All those people, involved in something which could easily have cost them their careers. Which still might, for there was no way their operation could remain secret forever. Summervale wouldn't complain. Any investigation was likely to turn up the record chip, and, legally obtained or not, it would ruin a man in his profession. It might even get him killed before he could talk about one of his other "clients."

Yet even if he never said a thing, rumors would leak sooner or later. Too many people knew too many of the bits and pieces. Eventually, someone would let a word too many slip over a beer or in a bull session, for the story was simply too good to keep sealed. She doubted any of it could ever be *proven*—she knew Alistair and Tomas too well to believe they would have left themselves uncovered—but that didn't mean no one in authority would believe it.

They had to know that as well as she did, yet they'd done it anyway. They'd done it for her, and perhaps, just perhaps, that meant it *wasn't* simple hate which had broken her zombielike state. Their willingness to accept that risk for her had done as much as her hatred, and that willingness sprang from its own sort of love.

Her eyes stung, and she closed them tightly, lips trembling as the tears came at last. They slid down her cheeks, silent as snow and oddly gentle. They couldn't wash away the armor she held stubbornly in place to protect her purpose, yet they cleansed it. They . . . purified it in some mysterious way, made it only armor and no longer ice, and she leaned her forehead against the mirror and let them come. Nimitz hopped up onto the lavatory and stood on his true-feet to clasp her upper arm in his true-hands and press his muzzle against her shoulder. His soft, inaudible croon vibrated into her as he welcomed her tears, and she turned and swept him into her arms.

She was never certain how long she wept, and it didn't really matter. It wasn't something to be measured by clocks, cut up into minutes and seconds. Trying to would have cheapened it. She only knew that when she dried her eyes again she was . . . different. Mike had feared for her sanity, and she knew, now, that she'd been right to fear. But the madness had passed. The lethal purpose remained, yet it was as sane as it was cold, as rational as it was obsessive.

She blew her nose, then dressed without buzzing MacGuiness. She knew where he hid her uniforms, and he deserved to sleep late. God knew he'd put in too many thankless hours hovering over her with nothing to show for it but dead-eyed silence from her.

She adjusted her uniform with precision and gathered her shoulder-length hair in a simple braid. It didn't reach very far down her back, but it was enough, and she tied it with a black silk ribbon, the color of mourning and vengeance, before she turned to her terminal.

The messages she'd dreaded waited, headed by a tearful recording from her mother and father. She couldn't have faced that without breaking before she'd heard Summervale's recorded voice; now she could listen and recognize the love in her parents' voices. More than recognize; she could *feel* it now.

There were others, even more than she'd feared, headed by a personal recording from Queen Elizabeth herself. Duke Cromarty had sent her a stiffer, more formal message, but the sympathy in his voice was genuine, and there were others—from Admiral Caparelli on behalf of the Lords of Admiralty, from Lady Morncreek, from Paul's CO, from Ernestine Corell and Mark Sarnow . . . even from Dame Estelle Matsuko, Her Majesty's Resident Commissioner for Medusan Affairs, and Rear Admiral Michel Reynaud, Astro Control Service CO in Basilisk.

They hurt. They hurt terribly, each one reminding her of all she'd lost, but it was a hurt she could bear now. She had to stop to dry her eyes more than once, yet she worked her way to the end, and two-thirds of the way through, she looked down to find a steaming cup of cocoa at her elbow.

She smiled at the offering in mingled tenderness and pain and turned her head before MacGuiness could vanish back into his pantry.

"Mac," she said softly.

He froze and turned back to face her, and her heart twisted. He wore a ratty old robe over his pajamas, the first time, day or night, she'd ever seen him out of uniform, and his face looked old and worn—and fragile. So fragile. His eyes were almost afraid to hope, and she held out a hand to him.

He came closer and took it, and she squeezed his fingers hard.

"Thanks, Mac. I appreciate it." Her voice was so soft he could barely hear her, yet it was *her* voice again, and he knew she was thanking him for far more than a cup of cocoa. His red-rimmed eyes gleamed with suspicious moisture, and he ducked his head and squeezed her hand back.

"You're welcome, Ma'am," he husked, then cleared his throat, gave himself a shake, and wagged one finger at her. "You stay right where you are," he commanded. "I'll have your breakfast in fifteen minutes, and you've missed too many meals as it is!"

"Yes, Sir," she said meekly, and the twitch of his mouth as he fought not to smile warmed her soul.

Honor finished the last of a huge breakfast and blotted her mouth with her napkin. It was odd, but she couldn't remember a single meal between her last one on Grayson and this. There must have been some, but her memory was completely blank when she tried to recall them. She felt a fresh pang of guilt for the way she must have treated MacGuiness, but Nimitz made a soft sound, almost a chiding one, from across the table, and she gave him a small smile.

"That was delicious, Mac. Thank you."

"I'm glad you enjoyed it, Ma'am, and—"

The steward broke off and turned away as the com terminal hummed. "Captain's quarters, Chief Steward MacGuiness speaking," he acknowledged.

"I have a com request for the Captain, Chief," George Monet's voice replied. "It's from Admiral White Haven."

"Put it through, George," Honor called as she stood. The com officer waited until she entered the terminal's visual range, and she thought she saw him sag a little in relief when he saw her expression, but he only nodded.

"Of course, Ma'am. Switching now."

His image disappeared, replaced by the admiral's. White Haven's blue eyes were intent, but his face was calm and he nodded courteously to her.

"Good morning, Dame Honor. I'm sorry to disturb you so early on your first morning back."

"It's not a disturbance, Sir. How may I be of service?"

"I commed for two reasons, actually. First, I wanted to

express my condolences in person. Captain Tankersley was a fine officer and a fine man, a loss not simply to the Service but to everyone who knew him."

"Thank you, Sir." Honor's soprano was just a bit husky, and he pretended not to notice when she cleared her throat.

"The second reason I screened," he continued, "was to inform you that, during your absence, Parliament finally voted out the declaration of war. We resumed active operations against Haven as of zero-one-hundred hours last Wednesday." Honor nodded, and he went on. "Since we're attached to Home Fleet, our own operational posture won't be materially affected, at least in the short term, but it's more important than ever to expedite your repairs."

"Yes, Sir." Honor felt her cheekbones heat. "I'm afraid I haven't brought myself up to date just yet, Sir, but as soon—"

"Don't rush yourself," White Haven interrupted almost gently. "Commander Chandler's done an excellent job in your absence, and I'm certainly not trying to pressure you. This is for your information, not for any action I expect out of you. Besides," he allowed himself a smile, "it's in the yard dogs' hands, not yours or mine."

"Thank you, Sir." Honor tried to hide her humiliation at being caught uninformed about the state of her command, but her flush darkened, giving her away, and White Haven cocked his head.

"As your task force commander," he said after a moment, "I am instructing you to take some time getting yourself back into harness, Dame Honor. A day or two won't do the Service any harm, and—" his eyes softened "—I know you missed Captain Tankersley's funeral. I imagine you have quite a few items of personal business to attend to."

"Yes, Sir. I do." It came out harder and colder than Honor had meant it to, and the admiral's face went very still. Not with surprise, but with confirmation . . . and perhaps a trace of fear. Summervale was an experienced duelist, one who had killed many times in "affairs of honor." White Haven had never approved of dueling, legal or not, and the thought of Honor Harrington dead on the grass chilled his heart.

He opened his mouth to argue with her, then closed it without a word. Anything he could have said would have been useless; he knew that, and he had no right to presume to argue with her, anyway.

"In that case, Captain," he said instead, "I'll have orders cut giving you three days more of official leave. If you need more, we'll arrange it."

"Thank you, Sir," she said again, and her voice was much softer. She'd recognized his first impulse, and she was grateful for the second thoughts that left the arguments unvoiced.

"Until later, then, Dame Honor," he said quietly, and cut the connection.

✧ CHAPTER TWENTY-FOUR

THE TRIO OF MEN WHO POPPED out of the cross corridor had "newsie" written all over them, and their leader was keying his shoulder-mounted HD camera before Honor even saw him.

"Lady Harrington, would you care to comment on—"

The newsie's voice broke off on an odd note as Major Andrew LaFollet stepped in front of his steadholder. The major wasn't a large man by Manticoran standards, but neither was the newsie. LaFollet probably out-massed him by a well-muscled thirty percent; more to the point, the major's expression was not amused. Everything about him, from his close-cropped hair to the cut of his uniform, proclaimed that he was a foreigner, and the look in his eyes suggested he might not give much of a damn for the traditions of the Manticoran media.

He stood there, regarding the newsman with cold dispassion. He didn't say anything, and he made absolutely no threatening gesture, but the newsie reached up with one hand, moving very carefully, and deactivated his camera. LaFollet's nostrils flared with bitter amusement, and the covey of reporters parted magically to clear the passage.

Honor gave them a courteous nod, as if nothing at all had happened, and stepped past them, followed by Corporal Mattingly. LaFollet waited a moment longer, then fell in behind. He overtook his charge and took his proper place at her right elbow, and she turned her head to look down at him.

"That's not quite how things are done in the Star Kingdom, Andrew," she murmured. He snorted and shook his head.

"I know it isn't, My Lady. I spent some time viewing the garbage the Manties—beg pardon, My Lady. I meant I've viewed the *Manticoran* coverage of the Young court-martial." His tone made his opinion of that coverage clear, and Honor's lips quirked.

"I didn't say I didn't appreciate your efforts. I only meant that you can't go around threatening newsies."

"Threaten, My Lady?" LaFollet's voice was innocence itself. "I never threatened anyone."

Honor started to reply, then closed her mouth. She'd already discovered that arguing with the major was a losing proposition. He listened with infinite, unfailing courtesy, but he had his own ideas about what was due her, and he was even stubborner than she was. No doubt he would have obeyed her if she'd ordered him out of the newsie's way, but only a direct order would have moved him.

She sighed mentally, torn between wry amusement and resignation. She hadn't realized until this morning that her Grayson armsmen had become a permanent fixture in her life. Which, given her recent mental state, probably wasn't surprising but still bothered her. She ought to have been paying more attention, and, if she had been, she might have been able to nip it in the bud.

Now it was too late, and she suspected adjusting to their presence wasn't going to be the easiest thing she'd ever done. Not that she seemed to have a vote. It was clear LaFollet had been briefed on her, because he'd been ready not only to cite chapter and verse from the relevant Grayson law codes but to trade shamelessly on her own sense of duty. She'd detected Howard Clinkscales' hand behind the major's shrewd choice of tactics, and the discovery that LaFollet was ex-Palace Security only reinforced her suspicions.

Be that as it may, her chief armsman had politely demolished—or ignored as unworthy of demolition—every argument she'd advanced against his presence, and she hadn't even been able to fall back on Manticoran law. A special writ from the Queen's Bench had arrived in the morning mail, granting a Foreign Office request that Steadholder Harrington (who just happened to live in the same body as Captain Harrington) be authorized a permanent armed security detachment—with diplomatic immunity, no less! The fact that Tomas Ramirez had obviously signed on to the conspiracy, coupled with MacGuiness' patent approval, had given LaFollet an unfair advantage, and her last resistance had crumpled when Nimitz insisted on tapping into the major's emotions and relaying his deep concern for and devotion to her.

LaFollet had allowed no trace of triumph to color his expression or voice, but Nimitz's link had still been open and she'd sensed his intense satisfaction. She was thirteen T-years older than he, but there was something uncannily familiar about his emotions where she was concerned. Somehow, without realizing it was happening, she'd acquired a MacGuiness with a gun, and she suspected her life would never be quite the same again.

She and her bodyguards stepped into one of *Hephaestus'* personnel capsules, and her mind shook off its consideration of her armsmen. She had other business this morning, and her brief amusement faded into focused purpose as she watched the location display creep toward Dempsey's Bar.

The slender, fair-haired man helped himself to another pretzel and nursed his half-empty stein while the early lunch crowd filtered in. He sat with his back to the doors, paying the bustle about him no obvious attention, but his opaque eyes watched everything in the mirrored wall behind the bar, and it was just as well his expression gave no sign of his thoughts.

Denver Summervale was a passionate man. He'd trained himself, over the years, to hide that passion behind a facade of icy control, and he did it so well that even he often forgot the fires that drove him. He was well aware of how dangerous personal fury could be in his line of work, but this time his control had frayed, and he knew it. This assignment was no longer a mere transaction, for he wasn't accustomed to being mauled. It had been too many years since anyone had dared lay hands on him, given the aura of fear his reputation provided. That aura had always been a pleasant thing, yet he hadn't quite realized how much he truly relished and relied upon it . . . or how infuriated he would be when enemies refused to cower before it.

He chewed on his pretzel, face expressionless, and felt the hatred washing about his mind. His path had crossed Honor Harrington's before, though she didn't know it. Her activities at the time had cost him a lucrative if highly illegal income, but he'd been able to accept that—more or less—as the breaks of the game. This time was different. He hadn't hated any-one this much since the Duke of Cromarty had refused to lift a finger to stop the Royal Marines from cashiering his distant cousin.

He snarled mentally as he remembered what Harrington's allies had done to him. His beating at Tankersley's hands had been degrading and humiliating but tolerable, since it had helped him get on with the job at hand, and he'd settled *that* account with interest. The single round the captain had gotten off had come frighteningly close to being more than a flesh wound, yet that, too, was acceptable. Like his sense of personal vengeance, it had actually lent an added, sensual edge to the adrenaline rush when he saw his target fall.

But what happened after that, on Gryphon . . . there'd been no adrenaline rush in that, no sense of power, no awareness that he was the very angel of death. There'd been only fear and pain—fear that had become instant terror when the pain blossomed into agony—and shame that was worse than any pain. Tomas Ramirez was a dead man. No one would have to pay for the colonel; this one would be a freebie, almost an act of love. He'd have to wait for the right moment, when no one, especially any of his previous sponsors, would have any reason to suspect his reasons, but that was fine. The wait would only make the final kill sweeter, and, in the meantime, he would *hurt* Ramirez.

The first hint of an expression, an ugly little smile, touched his face. He banished it the moment he saw it in the mirror, but inside he gloated. He knew how to punish Ramirez. The stupid fucker had told him how to do it himself . . . and he'd already been paid for the job.

He checked the date/time display and settled himself more comfortably on the bar stool. He'd hoped and expected to see newsies in Harrington's face from the moment of her arrival, for the way she handled them would have given him more insight into her state of mind, but there'd been a strange dearth of coverage on her since her return from Yeltsin's Star. Everyone knew she was back, yet she'd managed to elude the media with remarkable success.

It was disappointing, but he knew all he really needed to know, for he'd studied her record carefully. Given what he knew about her, it was inevitable that she would come looking for him, burning for revenge, and when she did, he would kill her.

He smiled again, almost dreamily. She was a naval officer, and a good one, with a skill and competence in her chosen field which he would never have challenged, but this was *his* area of competence. He was willing to concede that she had guts. And, unlike many naval officers, who thought in terms of the sanitary mayhem of deep space warfare, she'd proven she was willing to meet her enemies and kill them face-to-face when she had to. But she'd never fought a duel, and Tankersley's death would be the perfect goad. At this moment, nothing in the universe would matter more to her than spilling his blood, and that was good. He could no longer count the men—and women—who'd stepped onto the field with him, filled with the passionate need to destroy him, yet he was still here . . . and they weren't. Righteous fury was his ally, for it made his enemies rash, and an enraged amateur stood no chance against a professional.

He didn't even have to hunt her. All he had to do was wait. He could already hear her savage challenge, and he knew exactly how he'd respond, for, as the challenged party, the terms would be his to set.

He washed down his pretzel with a sip of beer and sneered inwardly. Some members of Parliament had tried for decades to outlaw the Ellington Protocol; perhaps they might even succeed some day, yet it was legal enough for now. Society frowned upon it, and the alternate Dreyfus Protocol was much more acceptable, but it would be child's play to manipulate a bereaved lover into using language intemperate enough to justify his insistence upon it. The Dreyfus Protocol limited the duelists to a total of five rounds each and allowed only the exchange of single shots. Perhaps even more importantly, the Master of the Field was charged with convincing both parties that honor had been satisfied after each exchange . . . and any duel ended with first blood.

Under those rules, he'd have to make certain his first shot did the job, but the Ellington Protocol was different. Under the Ellington rules, each duelist had a full ten-round magazine and was free to fire without pause until his opponent went down or dropped his own weapon in surrender, and Denver Summervale knew his own speed and accuracy with the anachronistic firearms of the field of honor. They were specialized tools, not something a naval officer would be familiar or comfortable with, and he could put at least three shots into her, probably more, before she fell.

He pictured the agony on her face as the first round hit her, watching her in his mind's eye as she tried to fight past the shock, her stubborn hatred keeping her on her feet while he shot her again. And again. The real trick was to make the last round instantly fatal, leaving the medics nothing to save, but he could make her suffer before he delivered it . . . and her precious friends would know he had.

He smiled again, and raised his stein to his mirrored image as he promised himself the treat to come.

Honor paused two meters from the swinging doors that served no real practical purpose aboard a space station and drew a deep breath. A prickle ran up and down her nerves, glittering in her blood like sick fire, but none of it touched her own ice-cold control as she glanced at her armsmen, and she was glad she'd left Nimitz aboard *Nike*.

"All right, Andrew. Simon. I'm not going to have any problems with you two, am I?"

"You're our Steadholder, My Lady. Your orders to us have the force of law," LaFollet said, and Honor felt a sudden, inappropriate amusement at his sober tone. He actually sounded as if he believed that, but his next words gave him away. "We don't like the idea of your risking yourself, but we won't interfere as long as this Summervale offers you no physical violence."

"I don't like qualifications from my subordinates, Andrew." Honor's voice was quiet, but the urge to laugh had vanished, and her tone held a snap LaFollet had yet to hear from her. He didn't—quite—blink, and she frowned. "I won't try to tell you your duty under normal circumstances, but when I tell you that you will do nothing, *whatever* happens between Summervale and me, that's precisely what I mean. Is that understood?"

LaFollet's shoulders straightened in involuntary reflex, and his face went utterly blank. The fact that he hadn't heard it from her yet didn't keep him from recognizing command voice when he did hear it.

"Yes, My Lady. I understand," he said crisply, and Honor nodded. She cherished no illusion that the major would abandon his polite intransigence in all things. Hard as it might be for her intellect to accept, the overriding concern in Andrew LaFollet's life was to keep *her* alive. She wasn't used to the concept, yet she could accept that it would put them at loggerheads from time to time. She didn't look forward to those occasions, but she respected him for his willingness to argue when they arose, and what mattered at the moment was that now both of them knew there was an uncrossable line and where it lay.

"Good." She inhaled again and straightened her own shoulders. "In that case, gentlemen, let's be about it."

The doors behind him opened, and Summervale saw a black-and-gold uniform in the mirror. He didn't even twitch, but recognition of his target was instant. She was paler than her pictures, and they hadn't done justice to her beauty, yet she was unmistakable. Anticipation stirred as he watched her scan the midday diners, but another, unexpected element tugged at his attention.

Two men in unfamiliar uniforms flanked her, and their postures sounded a mental alert. They were bodyguards, and good ones. They faced slightly away from one another, dividing the restaurant and its patrons into sectors of responsibility almost by instinct, and the pulsers at their hips were as much a part of them as their hands or feet. He didn't know where she'd gotten them, but they were far more than mere hired muscle, and that bothered him. Who *were* they, and what were they doing with Harrington? Was more going on here than his patron had seen fit to mention?

The armsmen's presence drew his attention away from his target. They challenged him as he tried to figure out where they fitted into the equation, and he realized how they'd distracted him only when he discovered Harrington was already halfway across the room toward him.

He gave himself a mental shake. Whatever they were, they were a secondary consideration, and he switched his attention to his target. A tiny, anticipatory smile touched his lips, but it faded into something else as he truly focused on her for the first time.

There was no expression on her face. That was the first inconsistent note, for there was none of the fury he'd antici- pated, and inner alarms sounded as he watched her reflec- tion cross toward him. People got out of her way—not obviously, not even as if they realized what they were doing, but almost instinctively, as if they recognized something in her he was accustomed to seeing only in himself—and he felt a sudden urge to swallow.

She walked straight up to him, the only sign of emotion a slight twitch at the right corner of her mouth, and it was suddenly hard to keep his back to her. His spine itched, as if she were a weapon trained upon it, and it was all he could do to remind himself that he'd planned for this. That she was doing exactly what he wanted her to do.

"Denver Summervale?" Her soprano voice was an icicle, not the fiery challenge he'd expected. It was leached of all emo- tion, and it took more effort than he'd expected to put the proper curl into his lip as he turned to her.

"Yes?" Years of experience honed his voice with exactly the right note of insulting dismissal, but her eyes didn't even flicker.

"I'm Honor Harrington," she said

"Should that mean something to me?" he asked haughtily, and she smiled. It wasn't a pleasant smile, and Summervale's palms felt suddenly damp as he began to suspect how terri- bly he'd underestimated this woman. Her eyes were leveled missile batteries, untouched by any human emotion. He could feel the hate in her, but she was using that hate, not letting it use her, and every instinct shouted that he'd finally met a predator as dangerous as himself.

"Yes, it should," she said. "After all, I'm the woman Earl North Hollow hired you to kill, Mr. Summervale. Just as he hired you to kill Paul Tankersley." Her voice carried clearly, and shocked silence splashed out across the restaurant.

Summervale stared at her. She was insane! There had to be fifty people within earshot, and she was accusing a peer of the realm of paying for *murder*? He floundered, stunned and unable to believe she'd actually said it. No one—*no one!*—had ever accused him to his face of taking money to kill someone else's enemies. They'd known what would happen if they did—that he'd have no choice *but* to challenge and kill them. Not just to silence them, but because he would become an object of contempt whose challenge no man or woman of honor would ever have to accept again if he let their charge pass.

Yet she hadn't stopped there. She'd actually dared to identify the man who'd paid him to kill her! He'd never counted on that, and he cursed himself for his complacency even through his shock at hearing the words. No one had ever before known who'd hired him. The anonymity of his employers had been one of his most valuable wares, the ultimate protection for both of them. But this target *did* know. Worse, she had his own recorded voice identifying North Hollow, and his mind raced as he tried to sort out the implications.

No prosecutor could use it against him, given the circumstances under which it had been obtained, but private citizens weren't bound by the same constraints as the legal establishment. If he or North Hollow brought charges for slander, they'd have to prove her allegations were untrue. Under those circumstances she could damned well use it in her defense, and where it came from or how it happened to be in her possession wouldn't matter. What would matter was that she *had* it, and those were only the legal consequences. It didn't even consider what would happen if his other employers realized he'd talked and—

"We're all waiting, Mr. Summervale." That icy soprano cut through his whirling thoughts, and he realized he was staring at her like a rabbit. "Aren't you a man of honor?" There was emotion in her voice now, contempt that cut like a lash. "No, of course you're not. You're a hired killer, aren't you, Mr. Summervale? Scum like you doesn't challenge people unless the odds and money are both right, does it?"

"I—" He shook himself, fighting for control. He'd expected her to challenge him, not for her to goad him, to force him to challenge *her*, and shock had him off balance. He knew what he had to do, what his only possible response was, but it was as if the stunning speed with which she'd upset all his plans had blocked his motor control. He couldn't—literally could not—get the words out, and her lip curled.

"Very well, Mr. Summervale. Let me help you," she said, and slapped him across the mouth.

His head snapped to one side, and then it snapped back again as the same hand struck on the backswing. She crowded him back against the bar and slapped him *again*. Again and again and *again* while every eye watched.

His hand shot up, clutching desperately for her wrist. He got a grip, but it lasted only an instant before she broke it with contemptuous ease and stepped back. Blood drooled down his chin and spotted his shirt and tunic, and his eyes were mad as someone manhandled him yet *again*. He tensed to attack her with his bare hands, but a tiny fragment of sanity held him back. He couldn't do that. She'd driven him into the same corner he'd driven so many victims into, left him no option but to challenge her. It was the only way he could silence her, and she *had* to be silenced.

"I—" He coughed and drew a handkerchief from his pocket to wipe his bleeding mouth. She only stood and watched him with icy disgust, but at least the gesture gave him a moment to drag his thoughts back together.

"You're insane," he said finally, trying to put conviction into his voice. "I don't know you, and I've never met this Earl North Hollow! How dare you accuse me of being some—some sort of hired assassin! I don't know why you should want to force a quarrel on me, but no one can talk to me this way!"

"*I* can," she said coldly.

"Then I have no choice but to demand satisfaction!"

"Good." She let an emotion other than contempt into her voice for the first time, and Denver Summervale wasn't the only person who shuddered as he heard it. "Colonel Tomas Ramirez—I believe you know him?—will act as my second. He'll call on your friend—Livitnikov, isn't it? Or were you going to hire someone else this time?"

"I—" Summervale swallowed again. This was a nightmare. It couldn't be happening! His hand clenched in a fist around the bloody handkerchief, and he drew a deep breath. "Mr. Livitnikov is, indeed, a friend of mine. I feel confident he'll act for me."

"I'm sure you do. No doubt you pay him enough." Harrington's smile was like a flaying knife, and her eyes glittered. "Tell him to start studying the Ellington Protocol, Mr. Summervale," she said, and turned on her heel.

✧ CHAPTER TWENTY-FIVE

WORK SCHEDULES SCROLLED DOWN Honor's terminal as she worked her methodical way through the mountains of paperwork which had risen like crustal folds in her absence. Fortunately, Eve Chandler was as outstanding as an exec as she'd been as a tac officer. Most of Honor's responsibility was limited to signing off on the decisions Eve had already made, but it still left an appalling amount of data to wade through, and, for once, Honor was just as happy it did. It deprived her of free time she might have spent fretting.

She finished the current report and took a break to nibble a cheese wedge from the plate MacGuiness had left at her elbow. *Nike* would be ready for trials and recommissioning within another four weeks, five at the outside, and that woke a stir of satisfaction even through her somber mood. The first reports were coming back as the Star Kingdom assumed the offensive, and half a dozen Peep bases had already fallen into Manticoran hands. Twice that many sorely needed ships of the wall had surrendered intact, and the public was delighted, but it was unlikely the run of cheap successes would last long. The Peoples' Republic of Haven was simply too huge, and the Committee of Public Safety had secured control of too many of the core systems, major fleet bases, and home defense squadrons. The Peeps had spent something like eighty T-years building up their military; they'd still have plenty of firepower once they got over the shock of the Star Kingdom's renewed operations.

Which meant, given the Fleet's eternal need for battlecruisers, that the Fifth Battlecruiser Squadron's assignment to Home Fleet probably wouldn't last long. Battlecruisers combined too much firepower, cruising endurance, and mobility for that. Honor could already see half a dozen places where they were needed, and she was impatient to report her ship's availability for duty.

Yet for the first time, she was torn between professional eagerness and another need. Ramirez and Livitnikov had completed the arrangements for her to meet Summervale in another two days, but Summervale was only the first step. She had no intention of leaving Pavel Young alive behind her when she took her ship into action again, which meant she had to deal with him before new orders took her out of the home system. She frowned at the thought and leaned back, crossing her legs, and clasped her hands on a raised knee while she brooded, only to look up at a soft sound from the perch above her desk.

A smile banished her frown as Nimitz hung from the perch on his prehensile tail and chittered at her. He sent himself swinging back and forth as soon as he had her attention, and his true-hands made snatching motions at her tray of *hors d'oeuvres*. He could have sneaked down and stolen one without a sound if he'd chosen to, but that wasn't what he wanted. He shared her determination to kill Summervale and North Hollow, and his confidence in her ability to do just that was absolute, but he wasn't about to let her fret herself back into her earlier, killing depression in the meantime.

He chittered again, louder, and his pendulum motion increased. She knew what he intended, and her hands darted out to snatch the tray away, but it was too late.

He gave himself a last swing and released his tail-hold, flipping himself through the air, and his true-hands flashed with unerring accuracy as he sailed across the tray. He grabbed up a pair of stuffed celery sticks, and his four rear limbs took the impact as he landed on the corner of her desk. His mid-limbs' hand-feet gripped the edge of the desk, pivoting him through a neat forward somersault, and he hit the deck with a thump. He vanished under the coffee table in a streak of cream-and-gray fur, and she heard his exultant bleek of triumph as he absconded with his prizes.

"All right, Stinker, you got me," she told him, getting down on her hands and knees on the carpet to peer under the table. His buzzing purr was complacent, and he crunched celery at her. Cheese stuffing clotted his whiskers, and one hand-foot combed them clean as she shook a finger at him. "On the other hand," she continued ominously, "we both know what this is going to do to your appetite for supper, so don't blame me if—"

She broke off and started to jerk upright as her com chimed. Her head, unfortunately, was still under the edge of the coffee table, and she yelped as her skull clipped it hard. Her short braid absorbed a good bit of the impact, but not enough to keep her from sitting down rather abruptly on the carpet.

The attention signal chimed again, and she rose on her knees, rubbing the back of her head, just as MacGuiness padded in from his pantry. The steward paused, and the faint, perpetual worry he couldn't seem to banish faded for just an instant. He and Nimitz knew one another of old, and it didn't take a genius to realize what had been going on.

He cleared his throat and shook his head before he continued to the com, and Honor stayed on her knees a moment longer, smiling fondly at his back, then pushed herself to her feet as he pressed the acceptance key.

"Captain's quarters, Chief MacGuiness speaking," he announced with another long-suffering glance at his captain.

"Com officer of the watch," another voice said. "Is the Captain available, Chief? I have a com request for her from the flagship."

"She'll be with you in a moment, Lieutenant Hammond," MacGuiness replied, and stepped aside as Honor arrived, still rubbing the back of her head. The lieutenant on the screen saw her and cleared his throat.

"Com request from the flagship, Skipper. It's the Admiral."

"Thank you, Jack." Honor brushed a few stray strands of hair into place and gave her uniform a quick pat-down check, then seated herself and nodded. "Put it through, please."

"Yes, Ma'am."

Lieutenant Hammond's face blinked out in favor of Admiral White Haven's, and Honor smiled at him.

"Good afternoon, Sir. What can I do for you?"

"Captain." White Haven nodded to her, then glanced at MacGuiness, just visible at the edge of the com's visual field. The steward took the hint and vanished, and the admiral returned his attention to Honor.

He studied her in silence for a moment, and what he saw both pleased and worried him. The stark, wounded look had faded, but her calm attentiveness didn't fool him, for the truth showed in her eyes: those huge, expressive eyes that gave away her true thoughts to anyone who knew to watch them, however masklike her expression might be. There was a hardness in them, a glitter that lurked just beneath their surface. He saw it, and wondered how she was going to react to what he had to say.

"I'm not comming on official business, Dame Honor," he said. An eyebrow curved, she cocked her head to one side, and he drew a breath he hoped she didn't notice and plunged in without further preamble.

"I'm sure you must realize that everyone knows about your meeting with Summervale." Her eyes hardened a bit more, and she nodded. "I realize the details of these affairs are supposed to be confidential, but the challenge was issued rather . . . publicly," he went on. "I've just been alerted that the media have picked up on it and that newsies from all the major services plan to be in attendance."

Honor said nothing, but he saw the hand on her desk clench as he continued.

"In addition, there's what I can only call a furor over the remarks which passed between you in Dempsey's, Dame Honor. There's some confusion over the exact wording, but there's general agreement that you deliberately provoked him into challenging you."

He paused, and she nodded again, silently. He wasn't certain whether it represented agreement or simple acknowledgment, and he rubbed an eyebrow in an unusual nervous gesture. This was going to be harder than he'd feared, and his baritone was quietly intense when he spoke once more.

"Dame Honor, I don't believe any reasonable person can or would fault you for that. Both Summervale's reputation and the fact that he set out to goad Captain Tankersley into striking him are well known, yet I can't say I'm happy about your meeting him. I don't approve of duels in general, and I don't like the thought of your tangling with a professional killer on his own ground, but that's your option under the law." Her eyes seemed to soften a bit, and he braced himself for her reaction to his next words.

"Unfortunately, a few members of the media have also picked up on the charges you leveled against Earl North Hollow." He paused, and his blue eyes invited—no, demanded—a response.

"I can't say I'm surprised by that, Sir," she said. He frowned and rubbed his eyebrow again, and she felt the intensity of his measuring gaze.

"I don't doubt that you aren't surprised, Captain," he said after a moment. "What I want to know is whether or not you *meant* for them to."

Honor considered for a moment, then shrugged.

"Yes, Sir, I did," she said quietly.

"Why?" he asked bluntly, his voice harsh with either worry or anger, but she didn't flinch.

"Because the charges are accurate, Sir. Pavel Young hired Summervale to kill Paul Tankersley and me. He specifically directed that Paul be killed first—apparently because he hated him for 'betraying' him by siding with me, but also because his real motive was to punish me."

"Do you realize what you're saying, Dame Honor? You're accusing a peer of the realm of hiring an assassin."

"Yes, Sir, I am."

"Do you have any evidence to support that charge?" he demanded.

"I do, Sir," she replied with no discernible emotion at all, and his eyes widened.

"Then why haven't you presented it to the authorities? Duels may be legal, but paying a professional duelist to kill your enemies certainly isn't!"

"I haven't approached the authorities because my evidence wouldn't be legally admissible in a criminal prosecution, Sir." He frowned, and she went on quietly. "Despite that, it's absolutely conclusive. Summervale admitted his complicity before witnesses."

"What witnesses?" His voice was sharp, but she shook her head.

"I'm sorry, Sir, but I must respectfully decline to answer that question."

The admiral's eyes narrowed, and Honor found it difficult to maintain her calm expression under their weight.

"I see," he went on after a brief, pregnant pause. "This evidence—I'm assuming it's a recording of some sort—was obtained under less than legal circumstances, and you're shielding whoever obtained it, aren't you?"

"Sir, I respectfully decline to answer that question."

White Haven snorted, but he didn't press it, and she inhaled in relief, only to stiffen as he leaned towards his pickup with a stony expression.

"Do you intend to challenge Earl North Hollow, as well, Dame Honor?"

"I intend, My Lord, to see justice done." Her voice was equally quiet, with the tang of distant ice, and he closed his eyes briefly.

"I want you to . . . think very carefully about that, Captain. The situation in the House of Lords remains extremely delicate. The Government managed to find a majority to support the declaration, but just barely, and its working majority is still very, very narrow. More to the point, North Hollow played a pivotal roll in getting the declaration voted out. Any hint of fresh scandal attached to his name, especially one which involves you, could have disastrous consequences."

"That, My Lord, is not my concern," Honor said flatly.

"Then it ought to be. If the Opposition—"

"My Lord—" for the first time in her life, Honor Harrington interrupted a flag officer, and her voice was hard "—the Opposition means very little to me at the moment. The man I loved was killed—murdered—at Pavel Young's orders." White Haven started to speak again, but she went right on, all pretense of detachment vanished. "I know it—and, I believe, *you* know it—but I can't prove it to the satisfaction of a court of law. That leaves me only one option, and that option, Sir, is my legal right in this Kingdom. I intend to exercise it, regardless of any *political* considerations."

She jerked to an incandescent halt, appalled at herself for speaking to an admiral—*any* admiral, but especially this one— in such fashion. Her veneer of self-control was far thinner than she'd realized, and electricity jittered in her nerves, yet she met his eyes unflinchingly, and her own were agate hard.

Fragile silence hovered for a moment, then, finally, White Haven squared his shoulders and drew a deep breath.

"My concern, Dame Honor, is not for North Hollow. It's not even for the Government—or, at any rate, not directly. It's for *you* and the consequences of any action you may take against him."

"I'm prepared to accept the consequences, My Lord."

"Well I'm not!" His eyes snapped with anger for the first time, anger directed squarely at her. "Duke Cromarty's Government will survive, but if you challenge Pavel Young to a duel—worse, if you challenge him and *kill* him—the Opposition will explode. You thought it was bad before and during the court-martial? Well, Captain, it'll be a thousand times worse after this one! The Opposition will demand your head on a platter, and the Duke will have no choice but to give it to them! Can't you *see* that?!"

"I'm not a politician, My Lord. I'm a naval officer." Honor met his gaze without evasion, but there was a pleading note in her voice which surprised even her. The hurt of White Haven's sudden anger cut deep. It was suddenly the most important thing in her world that he understand, and she raised one hand at her com screen in an imploring gesture. "I know my duty, my responsibilities, as a Queen's officer, but doesn't the Kingdom have some duty to *me*, Sir? Didn't Paul Tankersley deserve better than to be killed because a man who hates me *paid* for it? Damn it, Sir," her quiet, intense voice shook with passion as she stared at him, "I *owe* Paul—and myself!"

White Haven flinched as if she'd struck him, but he shook his head slowly.

"I sympathize, Captain. I truly do. But I once told you direct action isn't always the best response. If you pursue this, you'll destroy yourself and your career."

"Then what's the point, Sir?" The anger had gone out of her voice, and despair softened the hardness of her eyes, yet she held his gaze with a forlorn pride that cut him to the heart. "All I ask of my Queen and my Kingdom—all I've *ever* asked—is justice, My Lord. That's all I have a right to ask for, but I have a *right* to it. Isn't that what's supposed to separate us from the Peeps?" He winced, and she went on in that soft, pleading voice. "I don't understand politics, Sir. I don't understand what gives a Pavel Young the right to destroy everything he touches and hide behind the importance of compromise and political consensus. But I understand duty and common decency. I understand *justice*, and if no one else can give it to me, then just this once I'll take it for myself, whatever it costs."

"And you'll end your career." It was White Haven's turn to plead. "You're right; duels are legal, and there won't be any criminal charges. You won't be court-martialed. But you'll be relieved of your command. It doesn't *matter* how justified your actions are. If you kill him, they'll take *Nike* away from you, Honor. They'll put you on the beach and let you rot there, and there won't be anything I or anyone else can do to stop them."

It was the first time he'd ever used her given name without any other title, and she knew, at last, that the rumors were true. Whether it was because of his friendship with Admiral Courvosier or simply because he believed in her she didn't know, but White Haven *had* made her career his personal project. Perhaps that meant she owed him agreement, or at least the careful consideration of his arguments, but this time—just this once—that was more than she had to give.

"I'm sorry, Sir," she said softly, her eyes begging, almost against her will, for his acceptance. "If my career is the price I have to pay, then I'll pay it. I'm out of options, and this time someone is going to call Pavel Young to account."

"I can't let you do that, Captain." The earl's voice was hard, harsher than she'd ever heard it, and anger glittered in his eyes. "You may be too pigheaded to realize it, but your career matters more than a dozen Pavel Youngs! Just because we're rolling the Peeps up right now doesn't mean we'll go on doing it forever, and you know it as well as I do! We're in a war for the very survival of this Kingdom, and the Navy's invested thirty years in you. You're a *resource*, Captain Harrington—a weapon—and you have no right—no right at all!—to throw that weapon away. You talk about duty, Captain? Well, your *duty* is to your Queen, not to yourself!"

Honor jerked back, her face bone-white, and opened her mouth, but his furious voice rolled over her like a hurricane.

"The Navy needs you. The Kingdom needs you. You've proven that every time you made the hard call, every time you pulled off one of your goddamned miracles! You have no *right* to turn your back on all of us to pursue your own, personal vendetta, whatever Pavel Young did to you!" He leaned even closer to his pickup, his eyes hard as stone. "The fact that you can't see that doesn't make it any less true, Captain, and I am ordering you—*ordering* you, as your superior officer—not to challenge the Earl of North Hollow to a duel!"

✧ CHAPTER TWENTY-SIX

THE SHUTTLE GROUNDED AT Capital Field, Landing's main space-to-ground facility. The hundred-meter polished granite spire commemorating the landing of the sublight transport *Jason*'s first shuttle of colonists loomed up nearby, sparkling with blood-red reflections of the rising sun, but Honor had no attention to spare it.

She rose from her seat, and there was nothing within her but stillness. Every human emotion had been banished, leaving only the stillness as she turned to the hatch and stepped out into the warm, hushed morning. Andrew LaFollet, James Candless, and Tomas Ramirez followed at her heels; aside from them, she was alone as she walked to the waiting ground car.

It was odd. Nothing seemed quite real, nothing impinged directly upon her, yet everything about her was preternaturally clear and sharp. She moved through the quiet, apart from it yet immersed in it, and her face was calm as LaFollet opened the ground car's door for her.

Her detached, focused purpose was hard come by and dearly won. The confrontation with Admiral White Haven had shaken her more than she dared admit, even to herself. His fierce insistence had stunned her, and it hadn't gotten any better. She couldn't give him what he wanted, and her inability had infuriated him. She'd tried to explain, but he'd only snapped out a repetition of his order and cut the circuit, leaving her to stare at a blank screen.

The cruelty of his anger at such a time had cut soul deep. She needed confidence and focus; the *last* thing she needed on the brink of a fight for her very life was a personal quarrel with an officer she respected deeply. Why couldn't he understand that this was something she *had* to do? How could he bark out orders—*illegal* orders—he knew had to upset her at a time like this?

She didn't know. She only knew it had hurt, and that it had taken her hours to regain the honed, steely edge of her purpose. She regretted the breach between them, but she couldn't let it deflect her. If White Haven couldn't or wouldn't understand that, there was nothing she could do about it.

She shifted slightly in the contoured car seat, feeling the lightness of her right shoulder, and a deeper pang pierced her detachment before she could banish it once more. Nimitz hadn't wanted to stay behind with MacGuiness. For the first time she could remember, he'd fought her decision—actually hissed and bared his fangs at her while anger boiled through their link—but she'd refused to relent. He couldn't be with her on the field itself, and she had no doubt what he'd do if she'd let him join the spectators and the worst happened. He was blindingly fast and well armed, but Denver Summervale would have researched treecats when he planned his vicious campaign; he'd know as well as she did how Nimitz would react, and it was unlikely his magazine would be empty when she went down.

She sighed and raised one hand, touching the pad on which he should have ridden, and closed her eyes to concentrate on what was to come.

Tomas Ramirez sat in the jump seat facing the Captain, the pistol case heavy in his lap, and wished he could feel as calm as she looked. But this was the second time he'd made this trip in less than a month, and nausea twisted his stomach as he remembered the last time.

At least the Captain knew what she was doing, he told himself. Paul had been less focused, as if he'd been more baffled by events . . . or because he was less of a killer than the Captain. Ramirez had seen her in action. He had no doubt of her determination; it was only her skill he questioned, for Denver Summervale had killed more than fifty people on fields just like this.

He turned his head and glanced at the Grayson armsmen flanking her on either side. Candless was trying hard to hide his own anxiety, but LaFollet looked almost as calm as the Captain herself. A part of Ramirez hated the major for that nearly as much as it envied him, but he shook it off and made himself remember what LaFollet had said when he expressed his own concern.

"I don't know about duels, Colonel," the armsman had said.

"Grayson law doesn't allow them. But I've seen the Steadholder on the range."

"On the range!" Ramirez had snorted, fists bunching with muscle on the table between them. "This won't be a target match, Major, and the Captain's a Navy officer, not a Marine. The Navy doesn't train its people with small arms, not even pulsers, the way the Corps does. Summervale knows *exactly* what he's doing, and he's a crack shot with those damned antiques!"

"I presume that by 'antiques' you're referring to the pistols?" LaFollet had asked, and Ramirez had grunted frustrated agreement, then blinked as LaFollet barked a laugh. "I can't say anything about this Summervale's ability, Colonel, but believe me, he can't be any better with them than Lady Harrington. I know."

"How can you be so positive of that?" Ramirez had demanded.

"Experience, Sir. What you call antiques would have been first-line issue for Palace Security two years ago. We didn't have the tech base to build grav-drivers small enough to make pulsers practical."

Ramirez had frowned at him, longing to believe the younger man knew what he was talking about, but almost afraid to let himself.

"She's that good?" he'd asked, and LaFollet had nodded.

"Colonel, I was a small arms instructor for my last two years with Security. I know a natural shot when I see one, and Lady Harrington is just that." It had been his turn to frown, and he'd run a hand through his hair. "I'll admit I didn't expect her to be particularly good with something that old-fashioned myself, but I discussed it with Captain Henke, and she said something that stuck in my mind. She said the Steadholder's always tested very high for kinesthesia, that it's something your Navy looks for. I hadn't heard the term before, but I think it's what you or I might call situational awareness. She always knows where she is—and where anything else is in *relation* to her." He'd shrugged. "Anyway, trust me. Any shot of hers will go exactly where she wants it to."

"If she gets one *off*," Ramirez had muttered, thumping the tabletop with his fist. "God, I know she's fast. Her reflexes are at least as good as mine, and mine are better than almost any native Manticoran I've ever met. But you have to *see* Summervale to believe how quick he is, and he's been here before." He'd shaken his head, hating himself for doubting the Captain but unable to stop himself. "I don't know, Major. I just don't know," he'd sighed.

Now he looked away from the Grayson officer and stared out the window while he prayed LaFollet's confidence was justified.

The ground car slowed, and Honor opened her eyes as it glided through the gate in the vine-grown stone wall and crunched to a halt on the graveled drive. The sun hung just above the eastern horizon, the last of its blood-red color fading into white and gold, and the emerald carpet of smooth, close-cropped Terran grass glittered with dew like diamond dust.

She followed LaFollet out of the car, flaring her nostrils to inhale the smell of growing things, and a square-shouldered, brown-haired man met her. He wore the plain gray uniform of the Landing City Police with a black brassard and a heavy military-issue pulser, and he bowed to her.

"Good morning, Lady Harrington. I'm Lieutenant Castellaño, LCPD. I will be serving as Master of the Field this morning."

"Lieutenant." Honor returned his bow, and something like embarrassment flickered in his eyes as she straightened. She raised an eyebrow, and he waved a hand at the crowd of people clustered down one side of the field.

"Milady, I'm sorry about this." Chagrin deepened his voice, and he glared at the spectators. "It's indecent, but I can't legally exclude them."

"The media?" Honor asked.

"Yes, Milady. They're out in force, and those . . . *people* up there—" he jabbed a disgusted finger at a smaller cluster atop a small hill at the far end of the field "—have telephotos and shotgun mikes to catch every word. They're treating this like some sort of circus, Milady."

"I see." Honor surveyed her audience for a moment, brown eyes bleak, then touched Castellaño lightly on the shoulder. "It's not your fault. As you say, we can't exclude them. I suppose—" her lips twitched with dour humor "—the best we can hope for is a stray shot in their direction."

Castellaño twitched, unprepared for even that biting a jest, then gave her a small, humorless smile of his own.

"I suppose it is, Milady." He shook himself. "Well, then. If you'd come with me, please?"

"Of course," Honor murmured. She and her companions fell in behind him, their feet leaving dark blotches in the silver dew as they crossed the grass. A simple fence, no more than a white wooden rail on uprights, ran around an absolutely level stretch of grass at the center of the field, and Castellaño paused with an apologetic glance at LaFollet and Candless as they reached it.

"Excuse me, Milady. I was informed about your guardsmen, of course, but the law prohibits the presence of any armed supporters of either party at a meeting. If they wish to remain, they'll have to surrender their weapons."

Both Graysons stiffened in instant rebellion, and LaFollet opened his mouth to protest—only to close it with a snap as Honor raised a hand.

"I understand, Lieutenant," she said, and turned to her armsmen. "Andrew. Jamie." LaFollet met her eyes for just a moment, hovering on the brink of refusal, then sighed and drew the pulser from his holster. He handed it to Castellaño, and Candless followed a moment later.

"And now the other one, Andrew," Honor said in that same quiet voice.

LaFollet's eyes widened, and Ramirez glanced at him in surprise. The Grayson's jaw clenched and his entire body tensed, but then he sighed again. His left hand made a strange little motion, and a small pulser popped out of his sleeve into it. It was short-barreled and compact, designed as a weapon of last resort but no less deadly for that, and he grimaced as he passed it over.

"I didn't know you knew about that, My Lady."

"I know you didn't." She smiled and punched his shoulder lightly.

"Well, if you figured it out, someone else can," he muttered. "Now I'm going to have to find someplace else to hide it."

"I'm sure you'll think of something," she reassured him as Castellaño took the small weapon without expression, but Ramirez was still looking at LaFollet—and wondering if the armsman would have mentioned that hideout to him if he hadn't agreed to let him openly retain his weapons on shipboard.

"Thank you, Milady," Castellaño said. A policewoman appeared magically at his side, and he handed the weaponry to her, then raised his hand to wave toward the fenced-off grass. "Are you ready, Milady?"

"I am." Honor shrugged her shoulders as if settling their weight, then glanced at Ramirez. "All right, Tomas. Let's be about it," she said quietly.

Denver Summervale stood on his killing ground and watched his latest victim cross the wet grass toward him. He wore the dark clothing of the experienced duelist, without a trace of color to give his opponent a mark, and he hid a smirk as he studied Harrington. The captain was in uniform, its gold braid glittering in the sunlight. The three golden stars embroidered on her left breast made a nice aiming point, and he decided to put at least one bullet through the middle one.

Castellaño escorted her toward him, and Summervale's mouth curled. The Master of the Field's neutrality was required by law, and Castellaño was oppressively honorable and conscientious. He couldn't show partiality—not openly—but he hated and despised Summervale. That was why he'd chosen to greet Harrington in person and leave Summervale to one of his subordinates. The duelist knew it, and it amused him.

Honor and Ramirez stopped two meters from Summervale and Livitnikov, facing them while the morning breeze plucked at their hair. Castellaño nodded to the uniformed officer who'd accompanied Summervale, then turned to face both duelists and cleared his throat.

"Mr. Summervale, Lady Harrington. It is my first and foremost duty to urge a peaceful resolution of your differences, even at this late date. I ask you both now: can you not compose your quarrel?"

Honor said nothing. Summervale only eyed the Master of the Field contemptuously and said, "Get on with it. I'm meeting someone for breakfast."

Castellaño's face hardened, but he swallowed any retort and raised his right hand, fingers crooking as if to grasp something. "In that case, present your weapons."

Ramirez and Livitnikov opened their pistol cases, and matte-finish blued steel gleamed dully in the sunlight. Castellaño chose one pistol at random from the pair in each case and examined them with quick, skilled fingers and knowing eyes. He worked each action twice, then handed one weapon to Honor and the other to Summervale and looked at the seconds.

"Load, gentlemen," he said, and watched as each of them loaded ten fat, gleaming rounds into a magazine. Ramirez snapped the last old-fashioned brass cartridge into place and handed the magazine to Honor as Livitnikov handed its twin to Summervale.

"Load, Mr. Summervale," Castellaño said, and steel clicked as Summervale slid the magazine into the butt of his pistol and slapped it once to be sure it was seated securely. He made the simple task an almost ritualistic gesture, rich with confidence, and smiled thinly.

"Load, Lady Harrington," the Master of the Field said, and she loaded her own pistol without Summervale's flamboyance.

Castellaño regarded them both with grim eyes for a moment, then nodded.

"Take your places," he said.

Ramirez laid a hand on Honor's shoulder and squeezed briefly, smiling confidently even as his eyes worried, and she reached up to pat his hand once before she turned away. She made her way to one of the white circles on the dark green grass and turned to face Summervale as he took his place on the matching circle forty meters from her. Castellaño stood to one side, exactly halfway between them, and raised his voice against the morning breeze.

"Mr. Summervale, Milady, you may chamber."

Honor pulled back the slide, jacking a round into the chamber. The harsh, metallic sound echoed back to her as Summervale followed suit, and she was searingly aware of the hushed stillness. Tattered snatches of conversation came to her, faint and distant, enhancing the quiet rather than breaking it, as vulture-like newsies huddled over their mikes, and Summervale's sneering eyes glittered at her across the shaven grass.

Castellaño drew his pulser and raised his voice once more.

"You have agreed to meet under the Ellington Protocol." He drew a white handkerchief from his pocket and held it up in his left hand, fluttering in the breeze. "When I drop my handkerchief, you will each raise your weapon and fire. Fire will continue until one of you falls or drops your weapon in token of surrender. Should either of those things happen, the other will cease fire immediately. If he or she fails to do so, it will be my duty to stop him or her in any way I can, up to and including the use of deadly force. Do you understand, Mr. Summervale?" Summervale nodded curtly, and Castellaño looked at Honor. "Lady Harrington?"

"Understood," she said quietly.

"Very well. Take your positions."

Summervale turned his right side to Honor, his arm straight down beside him, pointing the muzzle of his weapon at the grass. Honor stood facing him squarely, her own pistol aimed at the ground, and his mouth wrinkled into a snarl of pleasure at the proof of her inexperience. This was going to be even easier than he'd hoped, he thought. The idiot was giving him the entire width of her body as a target, and he felt an ugly little shiver of lust at the thought of pumping his hate into her.

Honor twitched her left eye socket's muscles, bringing up the lowest telescopic setting on her cybernetic eye to watch his face. She saw his snarl, but her own expressionless face mirrored the hollow, singing stillness at her core as white cloth fluttered at the edge of her vision. Tension crackled in the morning air, and even the newsies fell silent as they stared at the motionless tableau.

Castellaño opened his hand. The handkerchief leapt into the air, frisking in the playful breeze, and Denver Summervale's brain glowed with merciless fire as his hand came up. The pistol was an extension of his nerves, rising into the classic duelist's stance with the oiled speed of long practice while his eyes remained fixed on Harrington. His target was graven in his mind, waiting only to merge with his weapon's rising sights, when white flame blossomed from her hand and a spike of Hell slammed into his belly.

He grunted in disbelief, eyes bulging in shock, and the fire flashed again. A second sledgehammer slammed him, centimeters above the agony of the first shot, and astonishment flickered through him. She hadn't raised her hand. *She hadn't even raised her hand!* She was firing from the *hip*, and—

A third shot cracked out, and another huge smear of crimson blotted his black tunic. His pistol hand was weighted with iron, and he looked down stupidly at the blood pulsing from his chest.

This couldn't happen. It was impossible for *him* to—

A *fourth* shot roared, punching into him less than a centimeter from the third, and he screamed as much in fury as in agony. No! The bitch *couldn't* kill him! Not before he got even one shot into her!

He looked back up, staring at her, wavering on his feet, and his gun was back at his side. He didn't remember lowering it, and now *hers* was up in full extension. He stared at her, seeing the wisps of smoke blowing from her muzzle in the breeze, and bared his teeth in hatred. Blood bubbled in his nostrils, his knees began to buckle, but somehow he stayed on his feet and slowly, grimly, fought to bring his gun hand up.

Honor Harrington watched him over the sights of her pistol. She saw the hate on his face, the terrible realization of what had happened, the venomous determination as his pistol wavered up centimeter by agonized centimeter. It was coming up, rising toward firing position while he snarled at her, and there was no emotion at all in her brown eyes as her fifth bullet smashed squarely through the bridge of his nose.

✧ CHAPTER TWENTY-SEVEN

THE EARL OF NORTH HOLLOW hunched in his armchair, face white, and clutched a glass of Terran whiskey. Quiet music played from his luxurious suite's hidden speakers, yet he heard nothing but the terrified thudding of his own heart.

God. *God!* What was he going to *do*?!

He threw back a swallow of the expensive whiskey. It burned like raw lava and exploded in his belly, and he closed his eyes and scrubbed the cold glass across his sweating forehead.

He couldn't believe how wrong things had gone. That traitorous bastard Tankersley had gone down exactly as planned, and he'd exulted as he savored his triumph over the bitch. He'd hurt her this time. Oh, yes, he'd *hurt* her, and he'd tasted her pain like sweet, sweet wine. He'd known when *Agni* departed to take her the news, and he'd counted the hours and treated himself to supper at Cosmo's and a celebratory night with Georgia on the day he calculated word had reached her, then waited in tingling anticipation for her return.

But then she *had* returned, and the disaster had begun.

How? How had the bitch guessed he'd hired Summervale? Even the media hostile to North Hollow had handled that part of her initial confrontation with the assassin with unwonted care—possibly from an unwillingness to let the bitch use them against him, but more probably from the monumental damages any court might award for libeling a peer. Yet her charges had leaked anyway, and when it reached North Hollow's ears, he'd reviled himself with every curse he could think of for having met personally with the bungling incompetent.

Someone must have seen them. Someone must have known and given—or sold—the information to the bitch or one of her ass-kissing friends. He'd known it was dangerous, but

261

Georgia had assured him Summervale was the best, and his record had certainly seemed to support her claim. When you wanted the best, you had to play by their rules, even if there was an element of risk. That was what he'd told himself when Summervale demanded to meet him face-to-face to close the deal, and he'd done it.

Damn it. Damn it to *Hell*! He'd been certain someone had seen them and whispered the news in Harrington's ear, but now it might be even worse than that, and the icy breath of space blew through his bones at the thought.

He'd watched the duel. He'd regretted the newsies' failure to get to Harrington sooner, for he'd looked forward to seeing her face and savoring her pain. But he'd told himself it was even better this way. Her elusiveness had been the last ingredient the media needed to whip up a hurricane of speculation and innuendo. They'd played the avenging lover angle to the hilt, turned her into some sort of tragic heroine as she prepared to go up against the fearsome duelist who'd killed the man she loved. North Hollow had laughed out loud at their tear-jerking coverage, because underneath all their emotional blather they'd been working the story for all it was worth. They'd actually taken crews out to the dueling grounds, and he'd leaned back with a glass of fine brandy to watch her destruction in full, glorious color.

But it hadn't worked out that way, and he shuddered as he recalled what *had* happened. Summervale had moved like a striking serpent while the bitch hadn't seemed to move at all. She'd simply stood there, facing her killer—and then she'd fired before Summervale's gun was halfway into position.

North Hollow's jaw had dropped, his face blanching, as Summervale staggered. The whole thing had happened with blinding speed, yet time had crawled, as well. He'd heard each shot, each separate, explosive burst of sound. He'd seen his highly-paid killer jerking like a marionette as the bullets slammed home, and his eyes had been wide and shocked as Summervale's head exploded with the last round.

It was impossible. It couldn't have happened. Harrington was a *Navy* officer, for God's sake! Where in hell had she learned to *shoot* that way?

The question had boiled through his brain, but then one of the news services had replayed the entire event even as the medics hurried forward to do their useless best, and he'd seen something that replaced his shock with terror. One of the cameras had been focused on Harrington, bringing her face so close it filled the HD tank, and North Hollow had seen her expression. He'd seen the icy control worse than any raw hatred, the implacable purpose drained of all emotion, and known he looked upon the face of Death itself.

He'd sat there, trembling, trying to understand, and then the newsies had swarmed onto the field like scavengers. They'd boiled about her, shouting questions and thrusting microphones at her despite the best efforts of the police and her own fucking bodyguards, and she'd handed her pistol to the Marine colonel at her side and looked squarely into the cameras and held up her hand like some sort of goddamned queen.

The newsies' babble had died into silence, and her eyes had seemed to leap out of the HD. They'd stared straight into his soul, and her voice had been just as cold, just as hard, as those liquid helium eyes.

"I'm not taking any questions, ladies and gentlemen," she'd said, "but I do have a short statement."

Someone had tried to shout another question, but even his own fellows had hushed him, and then she'd said it.

"Denver Summervale killed someone I loved. What's happened here today won't bring Paul Tankersley back to me. I know that. *Nothing* can bring him back, but I can seek justice from the man who had him murdered."

The camera focused on her face had twitched, and confusion had hovered almost visibly over the newsies.

"But, Lady Harrington," someone had said at last, "Captain Tankersley was killed in a duel, and you've just—"

"I know how he died," she'd cut the speaker off. "But Summervale was hired—paid—to kill him." Someone had hissed in surprise. Someone else had uttered a muffled oath as he remembered the reports of her initial exchange with Summervale, and North Hollow had heard his own, frightened whimper hanging in the silence of his luxurious suite.

"I accuse," she'd said, "the Earl of North Hollow of hiring Denver Summervale to kill not merely Paul Tankersley but myself, as well." She'd paused, and her thin smile had frozen North Hollow's blood. "As soon as possible, I will so accuse the Earl in person. Good day, ladies and gentlemen."

The Duke of Cromarty groaned as he watched the ghastly newscast yet again. Just when he'd thought things were settling down, *this* had to happen! His switchboard was already swamped by calls from Opposition leaders, all furiously demanding that he *do* something about Captain Harrington's slanderous accusations, but there wasn't anything he *could* do. The woman was a lunatic! Didn't she know what would happen when she accused a peer of the realm of hiring a professional killer?!

He switched the HD off and buried his face in his hands. He couldn't feel any sympathy for Denver. He didn't even want to. If anyone ever deserved to die it was Denver, and part of the duke felt only relief that he was finally gone, but having a member of the Prime Minister's family, however disgraced, in the middle of something like this was a serious blow to the Government.

He shuddered at the very thought of how the Opposition might use that once it realized what a weapon it held, but how would North Hollow himself react? The man was fundamentally stupid, yet he had a certain cunning and an instinct for the jugular. The Young family were little more than well born, wealthy thugs, yet they'd acquired an indisputable taste for using their power. Pavel Young was less intelligent—and even more arrogant, hard as that was to believe—than his father had been, but he was certainly ambitious. He'd plunged into the game of schemes and maneuvers with the courage of invincible ignorance, unfettered by any hindering principles, and, so far, his gutter instincts had served him well. He'd astonished far more astute and experienced political tacticians by the way he'd positioned himself in the Lords as a voice of sweet reason, willing, in order to rally the Kingdom in this time of national crisis, to overlook the way the Government had allowed the Navy to vilify him. Cromarty didn't doubt he'd wax too ambitious and destroy himself in time, but he'd played his chosen part to perfection so far, which only made this mess even worse.

The duke straightened in his chair. The logical thing for North Hollow to do was sue for slander, since the law forbade duels between the parties to any litigation. But what if he couldn't sue? What if Harrington was right? What if he *had* hired Denver—and she had proof of it?

Cromarty frowned, rubbing his palms slowly together before him. If that were the case—and the earl was certainly capable of something just that vicious—then he wouldn't dare resort to the courts. All Harrington had to do was present her evidence to refute the charge of slander, and North Hollow could kiss any possible political power goodbye forever.

But if he didn't sue, what else could he do? There was no mistaking Harrington's threat, and the brutal, astonishing efficiency with which she'd demolished Denver was chilling proof she could make good on it. That she *would* make good on it the instant she came close enough to North Hollow to challenge him.

Was it possible the earl would refuse the challenge? Cromarty gnawed his lip for a moment, trying to second-guess the imponderables. North Hollow was a coward, but would even that let him refuse to meet her? Proving his cowardice to the entire Kingdom would be as fatal to any career in politics as being proven a murderer, but he might believe that if he met her—and survived the experience—he could survive the scandal, as well. Certainly the Opposition 'faxes would back his efforts to put it behind him; they'd have to, for they would be tarred by their own association with him if the scandal destroyed him.

But he wouldn't live through it. The very thought was ridiculous after watching her cut Denver down, and the *way* she'd done it was horrifying. That meeting had been an execution, not a duel. Denver had been totally out of his class without ever realizing it; she'd shot him so many times not because she'd had to, but because she'd *wanted* to.

And if she ever got Pavel Young onto a dueling field, she'd do exactly the same thing to him.

The Duke of Cromarty couldn't remember the last time he'd been physically afraid of someone, but Honor Harrington terrified him. He doubted anyone who saw the record chips would ever forget her expression—her *non*-expression—as she shot Denver down, and if a Queen's officer took down a peer of the realm the same way—

The duke shuddered, then drew a deep breath and turned to his com. There was only one person who might be able to prevent disaster, and he punched her code into his terminal and waited for the liveried receptionist to answer.

"Mount Royal Palace. How may I—? Oh, good afternoon, Your Grace."

"Good afternoon, Kevin. I need to speak to Her Majesty."

"Just a moment, Your Grace." The receptionist looked down, checking the schedule stored in his database, then frowned. "I'm sorry, Your Grace, but she's closeted with the Zanzibaran ambassador."

"I see." Cromarty leaned back in his chair, steepling his fingers under his chin in thought. "When will she be free?" he asked after a moment.

"Not for some time, I'm afraid, Your Grace," the receptionist said, then paused as the duke's expression registered. Elizabeth III didn't pick idiots to screen calls on her private line. "Excuse me, Your Grace, but is this an emergency?"

"I don't know," Cromarty said, and his own admission surprised a wintry smile out of him. It vanished as quickly as it had come, and he lowered his hands to his desk. "It certainly has the potential to become one, at any rate. I think—" He paused again, then nodded. "Interrupt her, Kevin. Tell her I must speak with her as soon as possible."

"Of course, Your Grace. Do you want to hold?"

"Yes, please."

The receptionist nodded and disappeared, replaced by the Star Kingdom's coat of arms, and Cromarty drummed nervously on his desk. Some prime ministers had made themselves monumentally unpopular with their monarchs by disturbing them with things that could have waited. Cromarty knew that, and the fact that he made a practice of not interrupting his Queen unless he absolutely had to was a not inconsequential factor in their close working relationship. It also meant that Elizabeth normally accepted his calls with minimal delay, and he sighed in relief as she appeared on his screen in less than five minutes.

"Allen," she said without preamble.

"Your Majesty."

"I hope this really is important, Allen. The Ambassador is nervous about the notion that our new deployments will pull the picket squadron out of Zanzibar. It's taking more stroking to settle him down than we'd expected."

"I'm sorry, Your Majesty, but I think we may have a situation."

"What sort of 'situation'?" Elizabeth's voice sharpened and her eyes narrowed. "You know I always hate to hear that word from you, Allen!"

"I'm sorry," he repeated, "but I'm afraid it's accurate. Have you seen a news broadcast in the last hour or so?"

"No. I've been tied up with the Ambassador. Why? What's happened?"

"Lady Harrington just killed my cousin Denver." Elizabeth's eyes widened, and Cromarty shook his head. "No, I'm not upset about it. Or, rather, I am, but not because she killed him. You know how he's hurt the family for years, Your Majesty. He took a positively sadistic pleasure in doing it."

"Yes, I do know." Elizabeth's voice was quiet, and she nibbled her lower lip. "I knew they were going to meet, of course. I imagine everyone in the Kingdom did. And, given what you've just said, I won't scruple to tell you that I'm as relieved as I am surprised that she won."

"I think we were all wasting our worry on the wrong party this time, Your Majesty," Cromarty said flatly. "She hit him four times before he could fall, then put a fifth bullet right through his head."

Elizabeth's eyes widened still further, and she pursed her lips in a silent whistle.

"That, however, is the least of our problems," the duke went on. "The media were there in force. They've splashed every gory moment of it over the services on a system-wide hookup—and they've also been carrying Lady Harrington's statement, as well."

"Statement?" The Queen sounded puzzled, and Cromarty nodded.

"Yes, Your Majesty, her statement. She's formally accused the Earl of North Hollow of paying Denver to kill Tankersley—and her."

"My God," Elizabeth whispered, and the duke felt a sort of masochistic satisfaction at her obvious shock. He watched her eyes narrow and waited patiently as the wheels began to turn. It took her less than thirty seconds to run through all the permutations he'd already considered and look squarely back out of the screen at him again.

"Did he?" she asked, and Cromarty shrugged.

"I have no evidence one way or the other, Your Majesty. It's certainly possible, and I very much doubt that Lady Harrington would accuse him unless she had some sort of proof to back it."

Elizabeth nodded, rubbing her cheekbone with a knuckle. "If she does have evidence, she'll act on it." She might have been speaking to herself, but her eyes never looked away from the Prime Minister's. "For that matter, she never would have told the media unless she planned to kill him." She nodded to herself, and her voice sharpened. "How bad will the fall-out be if she does?"

"Bad, Your Majesty. Possibly very bad. If she kills him the same way she did Denver, it may even be disastrous." The Prime Minister shivered. "You haven't seen it yet, Your Majesty. I wish I hadn't. If she takes North Hollow out the same way, the Opposition will go mad. We may be looking at a crisis even worse than the declaration fight."

"Damage control?" the Queen asked crisply.

"Difficult, but not impossible—maybe. We'll probably lose the Conservative Association, whatever happens, but we've brought in almost enough Progressives to offset that, and the New Men are on our team, at least for now. The Liberals are almost certain to join the Conservatives in demanding Harrington's head. Even if we give it to them, they'll probably go even further into Opposition. If we *don't* give it to them, the Progressives will go with them. Even in the best case, this is going to hurt us badly, Your Majesty."

"But your majority will survive?"

"If we give them Harrington it will, Your Majesty. Or I think it will, at any rate. I can't be certain. At this point, I can't even begin to guess how the Commons will react. Harrington's been almost a patron saint to them ever since Basilisk, but with something like this—"

He shrugged, and Elizabeth frowned. He let her think about it for several seconds, then cleared his throat.

"I see only one optimum solution, Your Majesty," he said.

"Really?" The Queen chuckled without humor. "I fail to see *anything* 'optimum' about this one, Allen!"

"I happen to know that Earl White Haven has already ordered Lady Harrington not to pursue a challenge to North Hollow," the duke began, "and—"

"*Ordered* her?" Elizabeth's face hardened, and a dangerous sparkle crept into her eyes. "He *ordered* her not to challenge him?"

"Yes, Your Majesty, he—"

"He violated the Articles of War is what he did!" Elizabeth snapped. "If North Hollow were still a serving officer he would have been within his rights, but he doesn't have a leg to stand on in this case! Dame Honor would be fully justified in filing charges against him."

"I realize that, Your Majesty." Cromarty realized he was sweating and made himself not wipe his forehead. He recognized the signs, and Elizabeth III in a temper was *not* something he cared to confront. "I believe," he went on carefully, "he was concerned with the consequences to her career. And while he undoubtedly exceeded his authority, his concern was certainly justified."

"And Hamish Alexander has always been willing to ignore the rules when he thought he was right," the Queen added in a flat voice.

"Well, yes, Your Majesty. But he generally *is* right, and I don't think, in this case, that we—"

"Oh, stop defending him, Allen!" Elizabeth brooded in silence for a long minute, then shrugged. "I don't like it—and you can tell him so for me—but you're probably right. It's not my affair unless Dame Honor *does* elect to file charges."

"Yes, Your Majesty." Cromarty managed to hide his relief and leaned toward his pickup. "But the point I was going to make is that he *was* right, both about the effect on her career and about the political fallout." Elizabeth nodded unwillingly, and the duke put on his most persuasive expression. "Since he was right, and since Dame Honor clearly has no intention of accepting his arguments or his order, I thought perhaps—"

"Stop right there." The hardness was back in Elizabeth's eyes. "If you're going to suggest that *I* order her to drop it, you can forget it."

"But, Your Majesty, the consequences—"

"I said I won't do it, Allen."

"But perhaps if you simply *spoke* to her, Your Majesty. If you explained the situation and just *asked* her not to—"

"No." The single word came out flat and cold, and Cromarty closed his mouth. He knew that tone. The Queen looked at him for a moment, her eyes harder than ever, but then her face softened and a strange expression crossed it, one almost of shame.

"I won't pressure her, Allen." Elizabeth's voice was very quiet. "I can't. If I asked her not to, she probably wouldn't, and it would be utterly unfair to her. If we'd done our job in the first place, North Hollow would have been convicted of cowardice. We wouldn't have cashiered him, Allen; we would've shot him, and none of this would have happened."

"You know why we couldn't, Your Majesty," Cromarty said softly.

"Yes, I do, and it doesn't make me feel one bit better. We failed her, Allen. It's already cost her the man she loved, and it's our fault. My God, if this Kingdom ever owed any of its subjects justice, it was her, and we didn't give it to her." She shook her head. "No, Allen. If this is the only way Dame Honor can finish the job *we* should have done, I won't stop her."

"Please, Your Majesty. If not to avoid the political consequences, think of the effect on *her*. There won't be any way we can protect her. She'll lose her career, and *we'll* lose one of our most outstanding young captains."

"Do you think Dame Honor doesn't know that?" Elizabeth asked softly. Her eyes demanded the truth, and Cromarty shook his head silently. "Nor do I. And if she knows the price and she's willing to pay it, I'm not going to tell her she can't. And neither are *you*, Allen Summervale. I forbid you to pressure her in any way, and you tell Earl White Haven the same goes for him."

✧ CHAPTER TWENTY-EIGHT

ADMIRAL SIR THOMAS CAPARELLI put on a pleasant expression as his personal yeoman opened his office door. The Earl of White Haven walked past the petty officer with a courteous if absentminded nod, and Caparelli rose behind his desk to extend a hand.

White Haven gripped it, then took a chair at a gesture. Caparelli settled into his own chair and tipped it back while he regarded his guest and made a mental bet on the reason for this visit. He and White Haven seldom met except on professional matters, for there was little love lost between them. The First Space Lord respected the earl, but he'd never liked him much, and he was well aware White Haven felt the same way about him. Which made it unlikely the other man was here for social reasons.

"Thank you for seeing me on such short notice," White Haven said, and Caparelli shrugged.

"You're the second in command of Home Fleet, Admiral. When you ask to see me, I assume you have a reason. What can I do for you?"

"I'm afraid it's a bit complicated." White Haven ran a hand through his dark, white-streaked hair, and Caparelli blinked. One of the things he most disliked about White Haven was his unflappable (and usually justified, damn it) self-confidence. He wasn't used to seeing the earl uncertain or nervous. Angry, yes, and sometimes savagely sarcastic with slower thinkers, but nervous?

The First Space Lord made himself wait, saying nothing, his courteous expression attentive, and White Haven sighed.

"It's about Lady Harrington," he said, and Caparelli nodded inside as he won his bet.

"I assume," he chose his words with care, "that what you actually mean is that it's about Lady Harrington and Pavel Young."

"You assume correctly." White Haven seemed to realize he was still running his hand through his hair and stopped with a sour twist of his lips. "I attempted to reason with her when I realized what she— No," he shook his head with a bitter self-reproach Caparelli had never seen from him, "I didn't try to *reason* with her; I lectured her. In fact," he met the First Space Lord's eyes, "I ordered her not to meet Young."

"You *ordered* an officer not to meet a civilian in a duel?" Caparelli couldn't keep his eyebrows down, and White Haven shrugged. He looked angry—at himself, not at anyone else or even at having made that admission to someone who'd never been his friend.

"Yes," he growled, and pounded the arm of his chair gently. "If I'd had a gram of sense, I would've realized that was only going to—" He cut himself off and shook his head again. "I realize I was out of line, but I couldn't just stand by and watch her destroy her career. And you and I both know that's exactly will happen if she kills him."

Caparelli nodded, wishing he could argue the point. It was just like White Haven to try ordering Harrington off Young, but in this case the First Space Lord found himself in unwilling agreement with the earl about the consequences. And while he might have been prepared to be prejudiced against a White Haven protégée on general principles, the thought of losing an officer of Harrington's caliber at a time like this was a depressing one.

"Well, it didn't work," White Haven admitted heavily, "and the way I came at it guarantees I can't go back and convince her to see reason."

"Assuming it would *be* 'reason' from her viewpoint," Caparelli said. White Haven looked up sharply, and the First Space Lord shrugged. "I've heard her allegations. Assuming they're valid— and I think they are—then I'd want exactly the same thing in her place. Wouldn't you?"

White Haven looked away. He said nothing, but his very silence replied for him, and Caparelli frowned. It looked as if the earl was trying to convince himself he *wouldn't* have wanted what Harrington did, and self-deception wasn't like him.

"At any rate," the First Space Lord said before the silence grew too uncomfortable, "I suppose you've come to me in hopes *I* can do something?" White Haven nodded unwillingly, as if he hated admitting he was asking for help, and Caparelli sighed. "I sympathize, My Lord, and I don't want to lose her either, but she's within her legal rights."

"I know." White Haven chewed his lip, and his sense of duty warred with his emotions. Cromarty had passed along the Queen's message—and its explicit warning—but he couldn't just sit by. Besides, what he had in mind wasn't the same thing as pressuring Harrington. Not quite.

"I realize that no one has the command authority to stop her," he said after a moment, "but I've been reading the background briefs on our operations beyond Santander. We're going to need battlecruisers out there any day now."

He fell silent, eyes intent on the First Space Lord, and Caparelli scowled. He didn't like what he was hearing, but he liked the prospect of watching Harrington self-destruct even less.

"Are you willing to give up *Nike*?" he asked, and White Haven grimaced.

"I'll give up the entire Fifth Squadron if I have to," he said flatly.

"But *Nike*'s still under repair," Caparelli murmured. He turned to his terminal and tapped keys, and his screen blinked obediently. "She won't even leave the yard for another two weeks, and then she'll have to work up again." He shook his head. "We're looking at a month before we could deploy her. The way Harrington's pushing this thing, I doubt that would be soon enough."

"We could transfer her to another ship," White Haven said, manifestly unhappy with his own suggestion but making it nonetheless.

"No, we couldn't." Caparelli cut the idea down in its tracks. "We have no cause to take *Nike* away from her—not yet, anyway." He met White Haven's imploring gaze sternly despite his unwilling sympathy. "What you're suggesting—what *we're* suggesting—is already highly improper, but *Nike*'s our best battlecruiser command; taking her away from Harrington could only be seen as a demotion. And even if that weren't true, it would be a dead giveaway of what we're really after." He shook his head again. "No, My Lord. I'll cut her orders for Santander ASAP, but that's as far as I'll go. As far as I *can* go. Is that understood?"

"Yes, Sir." White Haven closed his eyes, his face oddly exhausted and worn, then opened them again. "Yes, Sir. I understand. And . . . thank you."

Caparelli nodded. He wanted to mark it down as a favor the earl owed him, but he couldn't. In fact, he felt a bit uncomfortable at being thanked when he could do so little.

"Don't mention it, My Lord," he said gruffly. He rose, terminating the interview, and held out his hand again. "I'll get together with Pat Givens and have the orders cut this afternoon. I'll also have a word with Admiral Cheviot and try to get *Nike*'s repairs expedited. If his yard dogs can get her out of the slip soon enough, recommissioning her may keep Lady Harrington too occupied to do anything drastic before we get her out-system. At any rate, we'll give it our best shot, I promise."

Willard Neufsteiler shaded his eyes against the Landing sun as the air limo slid toward him. It touched down on Pad Three atop Brancusi Tower, and a man in a jade-green tunic and trousers of lighter green climbed out to scan his surroundings before he stepped aside for a tall, black-and-gold-uniformed woman. Two more bodyguards fell in at her heels, forming a hollow, protective triangle about her, and Neufsteiler waved as she started toward him.

He was frankly amazed Dame Honor had managed to make it ground-side without the media finding out, but she seemed to be developing her own way of dealing with newsies. Or perhaps it was simpler than that. After watching her in action, they might just be frightened of crowding her.

Her handshake was firm when she reached him, but he felt a pang of sorrow as he saw her face. The laughing joy of their supper at Cosmo's had died with Paul Tankersley, and even the 'cat on her shoulder was subdued and tense. She looked neither broken nor defeated, yet there was a bleakness, a sense of ice under the surface, and something else he couldn't quite put a finger on: a strange, electric shiver that defied identification. It wasn't his fault he didn't recognize it; he'd never stood on a command deck with Captain Harrington when she took her ship into battle.

He led the way to a lift and punched a destination.

"It's such a lovely day," he said, waving a hand at the golden, sunlit city beyond the transparent lift wall as it sped down the outside of the tower, "that I thought we might meet in Regiano's, if that's all right with you, Dame Honor. I've reserved an upper section to insure privacy."

Honor looked at him. He met her eyes with the half-hidden worry she'd grown too accustomed to seeing in the faces about her, and the effort he'd put into making his voice light was almost painful. She wished her friends would stop fretting. There was nothing they could do, and their concern was one more burden she longed to shed, but she made herself smile.

"That sounds fine, Willard," she said.

"Excuse me, My Lady, but that's a security risk." Neufsteiler blinked in surprise as the auburn-haired head of Dame Honor's guards protested in a soft, foreign accent. "We haven't had time to check out the restaurant."

"I think we can live with that, Andrew."

"My Lady, you've warned this North Hollow you're coming for him." There was a stubborn edge in Major LaFollet's voice. "It would solve his problem neatly if something happened to you first."

Neufsteiler blinked. Was the man suggesting what Neufsteiler thought he was suggesting?

"The same idea had occurred to me," Honor replied quietly, "but I don't plan on jumping at shadows. Besides, no one knew we were coming. Even the newsies missed us this time around."

"The fact that we *think* no one knows is no proof they don't, My Lady, and you're not exactly the hardest person to identify if someone sees you. Please, I'd feel much better if you stuck to your original schedule and met in Mr. Neufsteiler's offices."

"Dame Honor, if you think it would be better—" Neufsteiler began, but she shook her head.

"I think it might be *safer*, Willard, but that doesn't necessarily make it better." She smiled and touched her chief armsman's shoulder. "Major LaFollet is determined to keep me alive." The edge of fondness in her voice surprised Neufsteiler, and he watched her give the Grayson a gentle shake. "We're still working on how much veto right that gives him—aren't we, Andrew?"

"I'm not asking for veto right, My Lady. All I want is a little commonsense caution."

"Which I'm willing to give you, within limits." Honor released LaFollet's shoulder, but her smile didn't fade. Nimitz raised his ears, cocking his head to regard the major with bright green eyes, and she felt the armsman's frustration-tinged concern for her through her link to the 'cat. "I know I'm a trial to you, Andrew, but I've spent my entire life going where I wanted without armed guards. I'm willing to admit I can't get away with that any longer, but there are limits to the precautions I'm willing to take."

LaFollet opened his mouth, then hesitated, visibly reconsidering his words, and sighed. "You're my Steadholder, My Lady," he said. "If you want to go to a restaurant, we'll go, and I hope I'm worrying about nothing. But if anything *does* happen, I expect you to take *my* orders."

He gave her a mulish look, and she nibbled her lower lip as she gazed back down at him. Then she nodded. "All right, Andrew. If something happens, you're in charge. I'll even put up with your telling me 'I told you so.' "

"Thank you, My Lady. I hope you don't have to," LaFollet said. Honor patted his shoulder again, then looked back at Neufsteiler.

"In the meantime, Willard, where are we on our Grayson funds transfer?"

"Um, we're doing fine, Milady," Neufsteiler had to give himself a mental shake at the change of subject, "though I'm afraid the transaction was a bit more complicated than you apparently assumed. Since you're a Manticoran subject and your major financial holdings are here, you're technically subject to Manticoran corporate taxes even on out-system investments. There are ways around that, however, and I've already transferred four million to Regent Clinkscales. I drew up the incorporation papers under Grayson law; that let us take advantage of the most-favored-nation status *and* the tax credit incentives the Crown has extended to Grayson. In combination, that was enough to get us off with no tax burden at all on this one, but it put us right at the limit for a single-investor project, unless we can get a special exemption from the Exchequer. I think we can, under the circumstances, but given your status as steadholder, it might not be a bad idea to transfer everything to Grayson. I'm still looking at your steading's fiscal structure, but there are two or three very interesting Grayson tax provisions that—"

Honor nodded, reaching up to stroke Nimitz and listening with half her attention while the lift whizzed down the five-hundred-story tower and she stared out at the Star Kingdom's thriving capital. She knew her memory would play it all back for her, word for word, when she needed to think about it. Just now she had other things on her mind, and as long as Willard was satisfied with his financial maneuvers, she could concentrate on what really mattered.

Regiano's was a high-ceilinged, airy restaurant that sprawled up and down through a five-story atrium. It fell midway between Dempsey's and Cosmo's for sheer swank, but it had a lively yet relaxed air all its own, and if its staff weren't accustomed to seeing Sphinx treecats for lunch, they'd recovered quickly. No one had suggested anything about leaving pets at the door, and they'd produced a highchair for him with commendable speed. Besides, the food was good. It was *not* the "authentic Old Earth Italian" cuisine Regiano's owners claimed—Honor had met real Italian cooking and knew the difference—but it was tasty enough for her to forgive them, and their wine cellar was excellent.

She sat back to let the waiter remove her plate and sipped a glass of the house rosé. Its pleasant little bite suggested a Sphinx vineyard, and she let it roll over her tongue while she waited for the waiters to complete their duties and disappear.

She and her companions sat on a platform of polished golden oak that floated eight meters above the floor. She couldn't decide whether the architect had used grav plates under the platform or corner tractors from the overhead. It could have been either, for there were no other platforms directly above or beneath, but it didn't really matter. The hovering effect was pleasant, and its position gave them both the privacy of isolation and a commanding lookout post for Andrew LaFollet.

She looked over her shoulder at the major and felt a pang of remorse. He and his men hadn't eaten, and they couldn't quite hide their unhappiness. The very things that made her table's position so pleasant also brought it into clear sight of everyone. LaFollet had done his very best not to wince when he looked at all the possible sightlines, but his unhappy acceptance made her feel a little guilty. She supposed any good security officer required a streak of paranoia, and she made a mental note to keep that in mind for the future. There was no point in distressing someone so obviously devoted to her well-being as long as she could compromise without feeling like a prisoner.

The last waiter vanished down the platform stairs, and she lowered her glass and looked at Neufsteiler. They'd finished all her official business over lunch; now it was time for the real purpose of her visit.

"Well?" she asked quietly.

Neufsteiler glanced around, checking for eavesdroppers out of sheer instinct, then shrugged.

"You can't get to him, Milady," he said, equally quietly. "He's holed up in his official residence, and he's only coming out to visit the Lords."

Honor frowned and ran an index finger up and down the stem of her wineglass while she berated herself. There were advantages to the approach she'd taken—at the very least, the entire Kingdom knew what North Hollow had attempted—but she'd also warned him of what *she* intended, and he'd done the one thing she hadn't counted on.

He was hiding from her, and it was proving surprisingly effective. As long as he refused to sue for slander, she might as well not even have her illegal recording, unless she chose to hand it directly to the media, and that could have disastrous consequences for the people who'd obtained it for her. And as long as he avoided meeting her face-to-face, no one could accuse him of declining her challenge. He was trying to wait her out, counting on the Navy to order her out of the home system sooner or later, and she wondered if he'd heard about the orders the Admiralty had already cut. She had five days, possibly six before *Nike* left the slip; after that, she'd either have to resign her commission or buckle down to her duties and give up on him for the present.

It was the coward's approach, but that shouldn't have surprised her. And, in the meantime, the Opposition 'faxes were playing the refrain she'd half expected. Most were doing their best to turn her into some sort of ravening monster, lashing out at her old enemy in pure hatred without a scrap of proof, but the more dangerous ones simply *oozed* sympathy for her. She'd been through so much, lost the man she loved in the brutal senselessness of a duel—a practice it was past time the Kingdom outlawed, anyway—and she wasn't thinking clearly. Who could blame her for striking out in her pain? Captain Tankersley's death had been a tragedy, and it was as understandable as it was irrational for her to want to blame someone, *anyone*, for it. Yet that didn't mean she was right to blame the Earl of North Hollow, and readers should remember all that had already passed between them and remind themselves that the earl was also a victim. The fact that *she* blamed him for it—yes, and truly believed she was right—didn't necessarily make him guilty; it simply meant she was prepared to see him as the enemy when she needed a target so desperately. In the absence of conclusive proof, he must be extended the presumption of innocence, and his own, cool-headed refusal to pour fresh fuel on the fire was to be applauded.

Nimitz bleeked softly as he caught the bitter trend of her emotions, and she drew herself back. She gave the 'cat a gentle, apologetic caress and lifted him into her lap, and he responded with a forgiving purr as she returned to her reflections with determined dispassion.

The Opposition's efforts went on and on, she thought, and this time the Government 'faxes were silent on her behalf. She couldn't blame them for that. Whatever happened, the political fallout was going to be brutal. They had no choice but to distance themselves from it, especially when the Opposition was practically praying they wouldn't, and she'd discovered she could accept that. Indeed, a part of her was glad. This was between her and Pavel Young; she didn't *want* anyone to intervene.

"Are you certain he's not coming out at all?" she asked finally.

"Positive." Neufsteiler leaned toward her, his voice even lower. "We've gotten someone inside his staff, Milady. He's only a chauffeur, but he's in a position to see all their movement schedules."

"I've *got* to get to him," she murmured. "There has to be some time—even if it's only for a few minutes—when I can catch him. All I need is long enough to issue the challenge, Willard." She paused, frowning down into her wine. "If he's going to Parliament, then maybe what we need is someone inside that end of the pipeline. He's got to be moving around the building. If we can get hold of his schedule, then maybe—"

"Milady, I'll try," Neufsteiler sighed, "but the odds are mighty long. He *knows* you're hunting him, and he's got the advantage of being planet-side all the time. Getting his schedule with enough advance warning for you to get down here and take advantage of it . . . ?" He shook his head, then sighed again. "Well, we're already spending over eighty thousand a day on it; a few more operatives won't pad the bill by that much."

"Good man. In that case, I think—"

"*Down!*"

A hand like a steel claw fastened on Honor's shoulder, and her eyes popped wide in surprise as Andrew LaFollet snatched her backward. Her chair flew across the platform and arced toward the atrium floor, and LaFollet was already hurling her under the table. She'd never imagined he had that sort of strength, and she grunted as his weight came down on top of her.

Nimitz had catapulted from her lap an instant before LaFollet grabbed her, warned by the armsman's suddenly peaking emotions, and she heard the tearing-canvas sound of his war cry as she hit the floor. Berserk rage flooded down her link to him, and she managed to reach out and snatch him close an instant before he could hurl himself to attack whatever threatened them.

It was as well she had, for her mind was still trying to catch up with what was happening when she heard the snarling whine of a pulser. Explosive darts ripped their way up the stairs the waiters had used—the stairs *Nimitz* would have used—and shredded the end of the dining platform, and Neufsteiler cried out as a jagged splinter drove into his back. Then Candless was there, jerking her financial agent out of the line of fire, and a pulser had appeared in his other hand. She tried to rise, still struggling to control a snarling, hissing treecat with one hand, and LaFollet smashed her back flat with an elbow and a snarled curse the instant she started to move. Stars spangled her vision, his weight shifted on her back, and a pulser whined in her very ear as the patrons' screams and shouts began at last.

She turned her head, dimly aware that she was gasping for breath from how hard LaFollet had hurled her down, and saw her chief armsman's solid darts rip through a human body in a spray of blood. A sawed-off pulse rifle flew through the air as LaFollet's target went down, but someone was still firing. A body fell heavily beside her, and LaFollet rolled off her and went to one knee, gray eyes merciless as he laid his pulser barrel over his forearm and blew another victim apart. Candless took a third gunman down, then a fourth, and suddenly the firing was over and there was only the bedlam of panicked human beings as they stampeded for the exits.

"*Shit!*" LaFollet was on his feet, pulser weaving like a serpent as he tried in vain to draw another bead. She started to push up to her knees, and he didn't even look at her. "Stay *down*, My Lady! There were at least two more of them. I think they're using the crowd for cover to get out of here, but if they try another shot—"

She went flat again, still clutching Nimitz. But the 'cat's fury was ebbing as he realized Honor was safe. She released him cautiously, and he whirled to check her, then leapt up on the table and crouched there, still hissing and ready to attack but under control.

Honor breathed a sigh of relief and turned quickly to crawl toward Armsman Howard. The young man's face was gray as he tried with one hand to staunch the blood spurting from his thigh, but his gun hand was still up, his pulser ready even as his eyes glazed. She felt herself beginning to tremble at last, but her mind was amazingly clear. She stripped her belt purse from under her tunic and looped the strap about his leg above the wound. It must have been another flying splinter, not a direct hit, her brain said dispassionately; he still had a leg, and he gasped as she jerked the crude tourniquet tight. Then he sighed and slumped sideways, but the arterial spurt had slowed and stopped, and she caught up his pulser and crawled over to Neufsteiler.

The financier was moaning in pain, and a raw-looking stump of wood stood out of his right shoulder like a stubby arrow. She caught his head, twisting it around to look into his eyes, then sighed in relief. They were dark with pain and terror, but clear, with no sign of shock, and she patted his cheek.

"Hang on, Willard. Help's on its way," she murmured, and looked back up as LaFollet lowered his pulser at last. The armsman surveyed the carnage that had once been a pleasant restaurant and drew a deep, shaky breath.

"I think we made it, My Lady." He went to one knee beside Howard and checked Honor's tourniquet, then felt the young man's pulse. "Good work with that belt, My Lady. We might have lost him without it."

"And it would have been my fault," Honor said quietly. LaFollet turned his head, and she met his eyes squarely. "I should have listened to you."

"Well, to be perfectly honest, I didn't really think he'd try something this brazen myself," LaFollet said, and Honor nodded. Neither of them doubted for a moment who'd been behind it. "I was just being cautious, and, for that matter, you were right, My Lady. He couldn't have had them waiting for us, or they'd have tried sooner. In fact, it was seeing them come in together and how hard they were scanning the crowd that caught my attention." The major shook his head. "He must have had them on standby, just waiting for someone to tell them where to find you. We were lucky, My Lady."

"No, Major. *I* was lucky; *you* were good. Very good, all of you. Remind me to think about raises all around when Willard's patched up."

LaFollet's eyes crinkled at the humor in her voice. It wasn't much, but it was more than most people could have managed, and he pointed an index finger at her.

"Don't worry about raises, My Lady. We're all indecently rich by Grayson standards already. But the *next* time I give you some advice, promise to spend at least a few minutes considering that I might be right."

"Aye, aye, Sir," she said, and rose to her knees in Howard's blood as the first police officers came rushing into the wreckage below with drawn weapons.

✧ CHAPTER TWENTY-NINE

GEORGIA SAKRISTOS GAZED AT THE reporters besieging the Earl of North Hollow's Landing residence and shook her head in disbelief. She'd known Pavel was too stupid to choose matching socks without help, but she'd never imagined he'd try something as blatant as a public murder! More ominously, he'd made the arrangements without mentioning them to her. That might indicate only that he'd realized she would have done her best to dissuade him, but it might also indicate he'd decided he didn't quite trust her anymore. Either possibility suggested her influence over him might be waning, and that was an unpalatable thought. A Pavel Young who couldn't be controlled was about as safe to those around him as a fusion plant with an unstable mag bottle . . . as his most recent—and spectacular—blunder amply demonstrated.

She made her way down an unobtrusive garden path between towering banks of sweet-smelling crown blossom bushes and carded an even less obtrusive security door. It let her into the underground parking area without any of the newsies' noticing, and she nodded to the security man who looked quickly her way. He nodded back in recognition, and she withdrew her ID card from the door lock and headed for the central lifts. She passed the new chauffeur along the way and hid a smile as she watched him supervising the buffer remote working on a ground car. Now how, she wondered, would he react if he discovered that she'd known exactly who he was working for when she authorized his employment?

She put the thought aside in favor of others as the lift door opened. The first part of her plan had worked out perfectly. She'd half expected Harrington's friends to simply kill Summervale once they knew who'd employed him, but what

had actually happened might actually be better. Certainly
Harrington had proven more dangerous than she'd dared hope!
That duel had been a joy to watch, and the captain was also
much wealthier than Pavel had assumed. More, she was
learning to use the power of her wealth effectively, which was
something to bear in mind, given Sakristos' own position in
the North Hollow hierarchy. If Harrington chose to respond
in kind to today's assassination attempt things could get messy,
though Georgia doubted it would happen. Unlike Pavel,
Harrington was both willing and able to do her own killing.

All in all, it looked as if Harrington intended to remove Pavel
just as thoroughly as Georgia could have hoped. Unfortunately,
Harrington had screwed up by warning him she was onto him.
Sakristos had expected better tactics than that out of her, but
perhaps that had been unfair. She might have gotten close
enough to challenge him if she'd kept her mouth shut, true,
but she couldn't have found a better way to *punish* him if
she'd considered it for years. He was ready to piss himself
in terror, and the impact on his political plans was still worse.
The Opposition might defend him in public, but only because
they had no choice; in private (and without having to consider how they would have felt if Denver Summervale's killer
were hunting *them*), they were free to express their own
opinion of his "cowardice." He'd become a laughingstock in
Parliament's cloakrooms, whatever the public appearance. Even
his brothers were disgusted with him, and Stefan, the older
of them, was already playing up to Georgia.

She grimaced. Stefan was as bad as Pavel in most ways.
She knew he was pursuing her primarily to humiliate Pavel
by taking "his" woman away—none of the Youngs had ever
seen attractive women as anything but a way to keep score,
or people less powerful than they as anything except tools—
but he was at least a little smarter than his eldest brother.
Once Pavel was gone (and once she had that file out of his
vault), Stefan should prove much easier to guide. Someone
with an imagination was always easier to manipulate, especially when he had the ambition for power and knew his
manipulator intended to share it with him.

But first, she reminded herself, Pavel had to go, and he was
too busy imitating a Manticoran turtlehound for Harrington to
get at him. Sakristos crossed her arms and leaned back against
the lift wall, pouting in thought while she wondered if there
might be some further way she could help his enemies out.
Unfortunately, nothing occurred to her. There were limits to how
much exposure she could risk, and she'd already reached them.

No, she told herself, banishing her thoughtful expression as the lift stopped and opened, she'd done all she could except sit back and wait. And at least watching Pavel squirm was the most amusement she'd had in years.

"We can't tie them to anyone, Milady," the burly LCPD inspector said unhappily. "Three of them were in our files—very bad boys, indeed—but as for who may have hired them—" He shrugged, and Honor nodded. Inspector Pressman might not be willing—or able—to say so, but they both knew who had hired her would-be assassins. Without evidence, there was nothing the police could do, though, and she rose with a sigh, cradling Nimitz in her arms.

"We'll keep looking, Milady," Pressman promised. "All four of them had just made quite large deposits, and we're trying to get a line on where it came from. Unfortunately, they made the deposits in cash, not by card or check."

"I understand, Inspector. And I want to thank you, both for your efforts here and how quickly your people responded."

"I only wish we'd gotten there sooner," Pressman said. "That young man who was hit—your . . . armsman. Is that the right term?" Honor nodded, and the inspector twitched his shoulders. "I'm glad he was there, Milady, but we don't like having to let someone else do *our* job. Especially not when they get hit that hard in the process."

"Is that a criticism, Inspector?" Honor's tone had cooled, and Nimitz twisted his head around to regard the policeman, but Pressman shook his head.

"Oh, no, Milady. Fact is, we're delighted someone was there to do it that well. In fact, I'd appreciate your passing my compliments to your people. Here in the capital, we're used to dealing with foreign security personnel; every embassy's got them, and, just like your people, most of 'em have diplomatic immunity. The thing is, we don't have any way to tell how good they are until it falls in the toilet. We worry about it— worry a lot—and pulser fire in a crowded restaurant is one of our special nightmares, but that was some of the best reactive fire I've ever seen. They took down their targets without hitting a single bystander . . . and they had the sense to *stop* shooting when the crowd started to panic and run. I know from experience how hard it is to keep thinking instead of just reacting when one of your own is down, and we could've had a real bloodbath on our hands if they'd lost their heads."

"Thank you." Honor's voice warmed, and she smiled at the

cop. "I hadn't realized quite how good they are myself, and I'll be very pleased to pass your comments along to them."

"You do that, Milady, and—" Pressman paused for a moment, then shrugged. "Don't you go anywhere without them, Dame Honor. Not anywhere. Those people were pure hired muscle, and whoever hired them—" the inspector avoided any emphasis with care "—is still out there."

LaFollet and Candless were waiting when she left Pressman's office. They flanked her, eyes nervous even in police HQ, as they moved to the lifts. Nimitz echoed their tension, fur bristling while a sub-audible snarl quivered through him, and she held him firmly—not to restrain him, but to reassure him.

Corporal Mattingly came panting up with three more of her armsmen as they stepped out of the lift at ground level. Honor was surprised by how quickly the reinforcements had arrived, and she gave all six of her protectors a smile as they took up their positions about her and headed for the exit.

"They don't have any idea who hired them, do they, My Lady?" LaFollet said quietly once he'd checked his team and set them all in motion once more.

"Not officially, anyway," Honor replied. Mattingly stepped through the main doors and scanned the street, then opened the door of the armored ground car the LCPD had laid on. The green-uniformed armsmen turned themselves into a double line of human shields to cover her as she walked quickly to the car, and a dozen heavily armed police stood obtrusively about, two of them cradling heavy military pulse rifles with electronic sights as a pointed hint to anyone with hostile inclinations. The Graysons followed her into the car, and LaFollet heaved a sigh of relief once they had her under armor and moving toward Capital Field at a rapid clip.

"I'm not surprised, My Lady," he said. Honor looked at him, and he flipped a hand in the air. "That the police couldn't ID North Hollow for hiring them. Those were thugs. Off-the-street muscle, not part of his regular staff."

"That's what Inspector Pressman said," Honor agreed, and LaFollet snorted at the slight surprise in her tone.

"It didn't take a hyper-physicist to figure it out, My Lady. Only a *complete* idiot would use his own people for something like that. And the way they came in showed they were a pickup team. They had a pretty good plan, given the short time frame they must've put it together in, but it wasn't rehearsed. They were watching each other as well as us because the entire operation was off-the-cuff and none of them were dead certain the others would be in the right places at the right time. Besides, they were all worried about getting out again. For a successful assassination, you need people who either know their escape route's almost infallible or don't care whether or not they get out. These clowns were so busy making certain their lines of retreat were open that one of them slipped up and actually let me see his weapon. That's what I meant when I said we were lucky."

"I'm impressed, Andrew," Honor said after a moment. "And not just with how you reacted when it happened, either."

"My Lady, you're a naval officer. I wouldn't even know where to start doing your job, but this is what Palace Security spent ten years training me to do." The Grayson shrugged. "Different planet and different people, My Lady, but the basic parameters don't change. Only the motives and the technology."

"I'm still impressed. And grateful."

LaFollet waved his hand again, uncomfortable with her thanks, and she settled for another smile, then leaned back, Nimitz still tense in her lap, and closed her eyes. The knees of her uniform were stiff with Armsman Howard's dried blood, and she thanked God he was going to be all right. And Willard. Neufsteiler had recovered enough to crack a few weak jokes before the ambulance took him and Howard away, but she shuddered at how close he'd come to dying.

She'd never dreamed innocent bystanders might be caught in the crossfire when she launched her charges at Young. She remembered what Pressman had said about gunfire in a crowded restaurant and shuddered again, breathing a silent but intense prayer of thanks as she considered what could have happened.

It had to have been an act of desperation. Only a terrified man would risk something like this, however well-hidden his links to the killers, and if he'd been panicked enough to try once, he was unlikely to stop trying. She folded her hands around Nimitz, partly to comfort him and partly to keep from pounding her fists on the upholstery.

If he kept trying long enough, he'd get lucky. Worse, someone else *would* get killed. He might have started this, but *she* was the one who'd brought matters to a point where other people could die, and that meant it was up to her to end it somehow. Self-preservation demanded it as much as justice or the need to protect bystanders, but how did she get close enough to challenge a man who'd crawled into a hole and pulled it in after him?

She frowned in thought. There had to be a way. *No one* could cover himself every single moment, unless he wanted to retreat to his private estates and cower there, and Young couldn't do that. He was a politician now, and hiding that obviously would be fatal to his position. Her lips tightened in contempt at the thought of Pavel Young aping the role of a statesman, but it tingled in her brain with a familiar, persistent presence.

Her brow furrowed as she probed at it, sensing its importance with the same intuitive sixth sense that plucked the critical element from a complex tactical problem. She'd never understood how it worked in combat, and she didn't understand now, but she'd learned to trust it the same way she trusted her kinesthetic sense in a high-speed approach maneuver.

He was a politician—or he wanted to be one. She could understand that. With his naval career in ruins, it was the only sort of power he could grab at, and he was a man who craved power. He needed it like a drug, but to exercise it, he had to make regular Parliamentary appearances. That was why he *had* to stay in Landing. For that matter, it was why he had to kill her. As long as she was alive and her accusations hung over his head, no one would take him seriously. He'd still have his wealth and family name, but they wouldn't help his power base. They could assure him a seat in the Lords, but that was all—

She stiffened suddenly, eyes popping open, and Nimitz's head flew up in her lap. The 'cat twisted around, staring up at her, and bright, unholy fire blazed in his eyes as they met hers.

✧ CHAPTER THIRTY

THE EARL OF NORTH HOLLOW squirmed, trying to get comfortable in the luxurious chair. He failed, but perhaps that was because his discomfort wasn't physical. Cool air drifted about him, and the quiet of the House of Lords was broken only by the woman standing to address her colleagues.

North Hollow surveyed the speaker with coldly contemptuous eyes. Lady Greenriver was thin as a rail, with a voice that was anything but musical. She was also one of the few nonaligned peers who enjoyed near universal respect, and she'd been gassing away in support of the special additional military appropriation for over fifteen minutes. Which, given her voice and looks, was fourteen and a half minutes too long.

Who cared about the appropriation, anyway? The damned Navy could piss in a vac suit, as far as North Hollow was concerned. It wasn't going to be a roll call vote, so he could vent a little spleen by voting against it without anyone knowing, and he intended to do just that. Fuck them. Fuck them all. He knew how the Fleet must be delighting in the fresh humiliation the bitch was inflicting upon him. Well, let them. He was building his own political machine, and once the bitch was out of the way—

His thoughts broke. The bitch. It always came back to her, and he could no longer lie even to himself. He was terrified of her. He felt like a hunted rabbit, dashing from one bit of cover to another, and there were jokes—jokes about *him*—in the cloakrooms. He knew it; he'd seen the way conversations broke off when he appeared, then resumed about some utterly inconsequential subject. Even *here* the bitch could reach him, destroy him. She'd already taken away his Navy career; now she was hounding him again when she should already be *dead*, damn her to hell!

He closed his eyes, and damp hands clenched into fists. She was like some monster out of myth—like a hydra. He hacked and hacked at her, until anything human would have lain down and died, and every time the bitch simply climbed back to her feet and came after him again. She wasn't a hydra; she was Juggernaut, rumbling along on his heels, pursuing him remorselessly until he stumbled and fell and she could crush him at last, and—

He clenched his fists tighter, and forced his breathing to slow until the panic attack retreated into sick, roiling nausea.

She wasn't Juggernaut, damn it! She was mortal, not mythical—and anything that was mortal could be killed. Those incompetent fuckers might have missed her at Regiano's, but sooner or later someone else would get lucky, and Georgia could go fuck herself if she thought she was going to talk him out of having Harrington killed! He wanted her dead. He wanted her rotting in the ground so he could piss on her grave, because until she was dead he was a prisoner. He could only hide in his residence or cower here behind Parliament's security while *she* walked around heaping contempt upon his name.

The bitch. The puking, baseborn *bitch*! Who the *hell* did she think she was to hound *him* this way?! Why, his family could have bought and sold hers a dozen times over before she started rolling in her fucking prize money! She was *nothing*, just one more yeoman slut, and a deeply hidden part of him hated her most of all for the contempt he'd seen in her eyes the first day they ever met. She'd been a fuzzy-haired, homely, stupid commoner, yet she'd dared to look at him without awe, without fear. With contempt.

His teeth grated, but at least Greenriver was sitting down at last. He tried to find some comfort in the blessed silence of her grating voice, then checked the huge time display above the Speaker's desk. Another three hours and he could leave. His mouth twisted afresh at the thought. Leave. The other lords could take themselves off to their clubs, to restaurants, or the theater. No madwomen were waiting to kill *them*. But the Earl of North Hollow could only scurry out to his limousine, race home to his residence, and hide there the same way he'd hidden here, and—

His thoughts hiccuped as the House doors opened. There was some sort of stir down there, and he frowned as he shifted position to watch. Someone was talking to the Sergeant-At-Arms— someone wearing the red-embroidered black of formal robes over one of the chivalrous order's scarlet and gold splendor. The Sergeant seemed confused, from the way he was shaking his head, but the newcomer waved an insistent arm, and the Sergeant gestured to the Speaker.

The unusual commotion piqued North Hollow's interest despite his frustration and fear. No one else in the House chamber wore formal robes, for this was a regular working session. Full regalia was trotted out only on ceremonial occasions like the Address from the Throne or for a new peer's maiden speech, and he couldn't remember seeing any new names on the roster.

He brought the day's agenda up on the terminal at his ornate desk, but it offered no clues. And now the Speaker himself was striding over to the door.

North Hollow's forehead creased, but at least the disruption was something different, and he could use any diversion that offered. He watched the Speaker reach the newcomer and stop dead, then wheel on the Sergeant with a quick, choppy wave of his hands. The Sergeant spread his arms, eloquently disclaiming any responsibility, and North Hollow chuckled at the comedy playing out before him. The Speaker confronted the newcomer, shaking his head adamantly, but then the headshakes stopped. He folded his arms, cocking his head to one side and listening intently, then nodded with slow, manifest unwillingness. The newcomer said something else, and the Speaker nodded again, then threw his hands up in disgust as the newcomer made some additional point.

Buzzing conversation echoed around the chamber, and some of the peers were rising and flowing toward the door. North Hollow saw the closest ones stop dead exactly as the Speaker had, then wheel back to the peers behind them, gesticulating and muttering animatedly, and some were looking back at those of their colleagues who were still seated. North Hollow had shunned any close association with his fellows ever since Harrington leveled her charges, but now his own curiosity was roused. He pushed himself up out of his seat, then stopped as the Speaker stepped out of the knot of bodies. He returned to his desk, and his spine was stiff with either outrage or anger.

North Hollow sank back into his chair as the clot around the door began to shed bodies, and the Speaker seated himself behind his desk with an angry flounce. He picked up his ceremonial gavel and pounded it on the rest under the microphone. The sharp, jarring impacts echoed through the chamber, and he leaned towards his own microphone.

"Be seated, My Lords and Ladies," his voice boomed, and North Hollow had never heard just that note from the Speaker. The gavel fell again, so hard the handle cracked and the head flew up to rattle against the mike. "Be seated, My Lords and Ladies!" the Speaker repeated even more loudly, and the sound of his voice chivvied the peers back to their places like frightened birds.

The buzz of conversation died, and the Speaker stared out at the chamber. He waited for total silence, then cleared his throat.

"My Lords and Ladies, I crave your indulgence," he said harshly, not sounding as if he craved anything of the sort. "I apologize for this interruption of your deliberations, but under the rules of this House, I have no choice." He turned his head, almost as if against his will, to look toward the robed figure at the door, then turned back to his microphone.

"I have just been reminded," he announced, "of a seldom used rule. It is *customary—*" he turned to glare at the newcomer again "—for new peers to send decent notice to this House, and to be sponsored, before taking their place among us. Under certain circumstances, however, including the exigencies of the Queen's Service, new members may be delayed in taking their seats or, as I have just been reminded, may appear before us at a time convenient to them if their duty to the Crown will make it impossible for them to appear at one convenient to the House as a whole."

North Hollow rubbed his beard, wondering what in hell the Speaker was talking about. Exigencies of the Queen's Service?

"That rule has just been invoked, My Lords and Ladies," the Speaker said heavily. "A member who wishes to make her maiden address to the House informs me this may be her last opportunity for some months due to the demands of the Service. As such, I have no choice but to permit this irregularity."

The buzzing mutter was back, louder than ever, and heads were turning to peer toward the rear of the House. No, not toward the rear, North Hollow realized. They were peering at *him*, and sudden dread gripped him as the Speaker gestured to the robed newcomer.

The stranger crossed to stand before the Speaker's desk, then turned to face the House. Her hands went up, drawing back the blood-red cowl of the Knights of the Order of King Roger, and Pavel Young lunged up out of his seat with a strangled cry of horror as Honor Harrington smiled coldly up at him.

✧   ✧   ✧

Honor's hands trembled in the concealing folds of her robes as she let them fall back to her sides, but she hardly noticed. Her eyes were locked on Pavel Young as he jerked to his feet, his face white with sudden understanding. His head whipped about, like a trapped animal searching desperately for escape, but there was none. This time he couldn't run away, not without everyone in this chamber *knowing* that he'd run. And, perhaps even more terrifying to a man like him, his only exit route would have brought him within arm's reach of her.

Hate boiled within her, battering her with the need to attack him physically, but she simply folded her hands before her and let her eyes move across the rest of the seated peers. Some of them looked as horrified as Young; others simply seemed confused, and a very few were watching her with narrow, alert eyes. The House's judicial air had shattered like so much fragile glass, and the Sergeant-At-Arms moved closer to her, as if he feared he might have to restrain her forcibly. She felt the uncertainty shudder about her, as if they sensed the hunger of the predator who had suddenly appeared among them.

"My Lords and Ladies," she said finally, her soprano rising clearly amid the quivering tension, "I apologize to this House for the unseemly fashion in which I have interrupted its proceedings. But, as the Speaker has said, my ship is under orders to depart Manticore as soon as her repairs and working up period are completed. The demands of restoring a Queen's ship to full efficiency will be a heavy burden on my time, and, of course, my departure from the system will make it impossible for me to appear before you after my ship is once more ready for deployment."

She paused, tasting the silence and savoring the terror that hovered almost visibly above Pavel Young, and drew a deep breath.

"I cannot in good conscience leave Manticore, however, without discharging one of the gravest duties any peer owes to Her Majesty, this House, and the Realm as a whole. Specifically, My Lords and Ladies, it is my duty to inform you that one of your members has, by his own actions, not only demonstrated that he is unfit to sit among you but made himself a reproach to and a slur upon the very honor of the Kingdom."

Someone blurted a chopped-off exclamation of disbelief, as if unable to credit her sheer effrontery, but her calm, clear voice was like a wizard's spell. They knew what she was going to say, yet no one could move. They could only sit there, staring at her, and she felt the power of the moment like fire in her veins.

"My Lords and Ladies, there is among you a man who has conspired at murder rather than face his enemies himself. A would-be rapist, a coward, and a man who hired a paid duelist to kill another. A man who sent armed thugs into a public restaurant only two days ago to murder someone else and failed in his purpose by the narrowest margin." The spell was beginning to fray. Peers began to rise, their voices starting to sound in protest, but her soprano cut through the stir like a knife, and her eyes were fixed on Pavel Young.

"My Lords and Ladies, I accuse Pavel Young, Earl North Hollow, of murder and attempted murder. I accuse him of the callous and unforgivable abuse of power, of cowardice in the face of the enemy, of attempted rape, and of being unfit not simply for the high office he holds but for life itself. I call him coward and scum, beneath the contempt of honest and upright subjects of this Kingdom, whose honor is profaned by his mere presence among them, and I challenge him, before you all, to meet me upon the field of honor, there to pay once and for all for his acts!"

✧ CHAPTER THIRTY-ONE

"WELL, SHE DOESN'T DO ANYTHING by halves, does she?" Bitter amusement colored William Alexander's voice, and the Duke of Cromarty fought an urge to snarl at him.

"You might put it that way, I suppose," he said instead. He shook his head angrily, then opened the balcony's sliding doors. Alexander followed him out into the breezy dark, and the two of them stood three hundred stories above the streets of Landing. Air car running lights drifted like rainbow bubbles beneath a huge moon, and black-barred banks of moon-silvered cloud gathered on the damp breath of approaching rain. Distant lightning flickered somewhere along the eastern rim of the world, and the capital's lights glittered below them. More rivers of light swept up the flanks of other towers, like the carelessly spilled jewels of some elvish queen, and the Prime Minister stared at them as if an answer hid among their beauty.

But there was no answer. Honor Harrington had snatched events totally out of his hands. Queen Elizabeth might have forbidden anyone to pressure Harrington, but Cromarty had known the fix was in. The civilian government and Navy alike had conspired to save her by keeping her from North Hollow's throat, yet she'd found her way to him despite the odds against her.

"Do you know," Alexander murmured in the darkness, "I still can't believe she had the sheer gall."

"I doubt North Hollow believed it, either." Cromarty leaned on the railing, filling his lungs with cool night air while breeze ruffled his hair.

"He wouldn't have been there if he had," Alexander agreed. The Chancellor of the Exchequer stood beside his political leader and mentor, peering down at the rivers of light, and shook his head. "Just between the two of us, Allen, she's right, you know," he said very quietly.

"Right and wrong don't come into it." Cromarty turned eyes spangled with reflected glitter upon Alexander. "She's found the one way to positively guarantee the alienation of every member of the House of Lords."

"Oh, no, Allen. Not all of us."

"All right, then," Cromarty snorted, "you and Hamish vote to support her. Hell, I'll even join you. That'll give her three votes; if you can find three more to go with them, then *you* should be the goddamned prime minister!"

Alexander bit his lip but said nothing. What, after all, *could* he say? There was no doubt in his mind that Lady Harrington's hand had been forced by the attempt on her life—just as he'd never doubted who'd been responsible for that attempt. He'd never met her, but he'd discussed her enough with his brother to feel certain she would never have used the House of Lords or her own membership in it in such fashion if there'd been any other way to get to North Hollow. And he'd watched the House recordings of her short, impassioned speech and seen no theatrics, no false drama. She hadn't played the assembled peerage of the Kingdom for fools; she'd come before them as her court of last resort, and the sincerity—and truth—of her charges had echoed in her every word.

But the House didn't see it that way. The House was affronted by her assault upon its dignity. The House was furious at the cynical manner in which she'd twisted its rules and procedures to suit her own ends. The House knew a rules mechanic when it saw one, and it was determined to punish her for daring to pervert its magisterial dignity.

"How bad is it, really?" he asked after a moment, and Cromarty sighed, more in sorrow than in anger this time.

"High Ridge has already entered a motion to exclude her. He wanted to strip her of her title outright, but a solid majority of the Commons—including almost half the *Liberal* MPs, if you can believe it!—is lined up with Her Majesty. That will protect her title and quash any move to trump up some sort of criminal charge against her, but not even the Queen can force the Lords to seat a peer they've voted to exclude. She's gone, Willie. I'll be surprised if five percent of the House opposes the vote."

"And after?" There was a core of anger and frustration under the quiet in Alexander's voice, and Cromarty's shoulders slumped.

"You mean after she kills him." It wasn't a question, and he sensed Alexander's nod in the darkness and turned away from the railing to fling himself into a lounger. He leaned back, closing his eyes, and wished he could escape the next few days as easily as he could blot away Landing's lights.

Harrington had well and truly backed North Hollow into a corner. Furious as the Lords were, she'd thrown her charges and challenge into his very teeth. He could no longer evade them, and that meant he could no longer ignore them. If he tried, he'd lose not simply his political base but everything in life that mattered to a man like him, for he would be outcast. A pariah, ignored by his one-time equals and an object of contempt to his inferiors—not merely a coward, but guilty by self-confession of Harrington's every charge.

It was ridiculous on the face of it, a throwback to the barbarism of trial by combat, yet that made it no less true. Even a gutless wonder like North Hollow had recognized that. His tenor voice had quivered with unmistakable terror when he accepted her challenge, but he'd accepted it.

And he was a dead man.

He'd held out for the Dreyfus Protocol, but after the way Harrington had cut Denver down, there was no question in Cromarty's mind that one shot was all she needed, and only an idiot could believe she'd settle for wounding him. She meant to kill him, and she would, and when she did—

·"She's finished, Willie," he said finally, his voice soft with pain, and not for Pavel Young. "When she kills him, the same bullet will kill her own career. We can't save her. In fact, I'll have to initiate her removal from command myself to hold the Progressives in the Lords."

"It's not right, Allen." Alexander turned his back to the city's fairyscape, leaning his elbows on the balcony's rail. "She's the real victim. It's not *her* fault this is the only way she can get justice."

"I know," Cromarty never opened his eyes, "and I wish to God I could do something. But I have a government to hold together and a war to fight."

"I know." Alexander sighed, then laughed softly, sadly, without a trace of humor. "Even Hamish knows that, Allen. For that matter, Dame Honor herself knows she hasn't left you any choice."

"Which only makes me feel even worse." The duke opened his eyes and turned his head to meet Alexander's gaze, and even in the darkness, the younger man saw the sorrow in his face. "Tell me, Willie," the Prime Minister of Manticore said softly, "why anyone but a madman would want my job?"

✧   ✧   ✧

Lieutenant Commander Rafael Cardones looked up as the bridge lift opened. He was officer of the watch, supervising the skeleton bridge crew of a ship in a repair slip, and he came to his feet quickly as the Captain stepped from the lift. One of her green-uniformed armsmen followed her, but the Grayson parked himself against the bulkhead, standing at parade rest and watching his steadholder as she walked to the command chair at the center of the bridge.

She moved slowly, hands folded behind her, and her face was composed and serene. But Rafael Cardones knew her too well. He'd seen that same serenity while she kicked a dispirited, hostile crew back to life . . . and when she'd taken a crippled heavy cruiser on a death-ride straight into a battlecruiser's broadside. Now he saw it again, on the night before she met a man who hated her with a pistol in her hand, and he wondered how many years she'd needed to perfect that mask. How long to learn to hide her fear? To learn how to radiate confidence to her crew by concealing her own mortality from them? And how long, how many nights of pain and loneliness, to hide the fact that she cared—cared more than she should ever let herself care—about the people around her?

She stopped beside the command chair, and one hand stroked the stored displays and readouts the way a horsewoman might caress a beloved mount. She stood there, staring into the depths of the main visual display, only her hand moving, as if it were independent of the rest of her. He saw the pain in her eyes, despite her mask, and suddenly, he understood.

She was saying goodbye. Not just to *Nike,* but to the Navy, and fear filled him. Fear for her, but for himself, as well. She might die tomorrow, he told himself, yet only his intellect spoke, for his heart, his emotions, knew better. Pavel Young couldn't kill the Captain. The very idea was ludicrous.

But even if she lived, her career would end. She'd been told that too often to doubt it, and it was a price she'd chosen to pay. Yet when she lost the Navy, the Navy would lose *her.* Someone else would command HMS *Nike* and all the other ships she might have commanded, and someone else could never replace her, be all the things she'd been. No one could, and Rafael Cardones and Alistair McKeon, Andreas Venizelos and Eve Chandler and Tomas Ramirez, would all be diminished by it. Something special and wonderful would have gone out of their lives, and it would leave them the poorer for having known and lost it.

He was ashamed of himself. Ashamed for thinking of what *he* wanted, what *he* needed from her, yet he couldn't help

it. Part of him wanted to shout at her, to curse her for aban-
doning the people who depended upon her, and another part
wanted to weep for what leaving them behind must be costing her. He was trapped between his tangled emotions, unable
to speak while his eyes burned, and then her treecat raised
his head on her shoulder, looking in Cardones' direction. The
'cat's prick ears twitched, his green eyes glowed, and the
Captain turned her head, as well.

"Rafe," she said very softly.

"Skipper." He had to clear his throat twice before the word
came out, and she nodded to him, then looked back down
and ran her hand along the arm of her command chair once
more. He could feel her need to sit in that chair one more
time, to look around her bridge and know it was *hers*. But
she didn't. She only stood there, looking down at it, her long,
strong fingers stroking its arm with delicate grace, and Cardones
raised a hand. He held it out to her, with no idea of what
he meant to do with it or say to her, and then she drew a
deep breath and stepped back from the chair. She turned and
saw his hand, and he opened his mouth, but she shook her
head.

It was a tiny movement, barely seen, yet it crystallized all
she was. It was a captain's headshake, its authority so absolute and unquestionable there would never be a need to
enunciate it. And as he recognized it, Cardones recognized
something he'd always known without quite realizing that he
knew. Her authority came not from her rank; it came from
who and what she *was*, not what the Navy had made her.
Or perhaps it was even more complex than that. Perhaps the
Navy *had* made her what she was, yet if that were true, she
had long since become more than the sum of her parts.

She was Honor Harrington, he thought. No more and no
less, and no one and nothing could ever take that from her,
whatever happened.

He lowered his hand to his side, and she drew herself to
her full height and straightened her shoulders.

"Carry on, Commander," she said quietly.

"Aye, aye, Ma'am." His voice was just as quiet, but he came
to attention as he spoke, and his hand rose to the band of
his beret in a salute that would have done Saganami Island
proud.

Pain flickered in her eyes, and sadness, yet there was more
to it than that. A measuring something that he dared to hope
was approval, as if she were passing something more precious
than life itself into his keeping.

And then she nodded and turned away and walked away without another word, and HMS *Nike*'s bridge was suddenly a smaller, a lonelier, and an infinitely poorer place than it had been only a moment before.

✧ CHAPTER THIRTY-TWO

THE RAIN WHICH HAD BEGUN late last night ended as Pavel Young's ground car passed through the gate in the vine-covered stone wall. He heard the distinctive, slurred crunch of wet gravel as the ground-effect counter-grav field died and the car settled, and the last silver beads of rain trembled down his window while hollow terror consumed him.

His chauffeur climbed out and came around to open his door, and Pavel stepped out into the gusty, wet morning. His brother Stefan followed with the pistol case, as silent as he'd been through the entire drive here, and Pavel wondered once more what he was thinking.

He shouldn't have been able to wonder that; he shouldn't have been able to wonder *anything* through his terrible, panicky horror. He tasted the fear, like vomit at the back of his throat, yet his brain raced madly down a dozen different tracks at once with a sort of fevered clarity, as if it sought preservation by disassociating itself from the moment.

Chill humidity lay against his cheek like clammy fingers, misty cloud raced low overhead, enveloping the towers of Landing beyond the dueling grounds' wall, and gusts of wind slapped like open hands at his clothing and the trees along the inner face of the wall. He heard it sucking at leaves and branches, blowing spatters of rain from them, sighing and rustling with mournful life, and he flinched as a gray-uniformed policewoman appeared.

"Good morning, My Lord," she said. "I'm Sergeant MacClinton. Lieutenant Castellaño will be serving as Master of the Field this morning, and he's asked me, with his compliments, to escort you to the field."

The Earl of North Hollow nodded. It was a choppy, spastic

movement, but he dared not trust his voice. MacClinton was a trim, attractive woman, the sort who normally started him speculating on her skills in bed. Today she only made him long desperately to live, made him want to cling to her, to beg her to make this all some nightmare that would pass and leave him unscathed.

He looked into her face, searching for . . . something, and what he saw beneath her professional neutrality was contempt overlaid by something far worse. MacClinton's eyes were distant and detached, as if looking upon a dead man who awaited only the grisly mechanics of dying to make his death official.

He looked away quickly and swallowed, and then he was following her against his will across the rainsoaked grass. The dense sod squelched, soaking his feet, and another corner of his damnably racing mind reflected that he should have worn boots instead of low-topped shoes. He wanted to scream at the utter banality of his own thoughts, and his jaws ached from the pressure on his clenched teeth.

And then they stopped, and a strangling bolus of terror choked the breath in his throat as he came face-to-face with Honor Harrington.

She didn't even look at him, and somehow that was infinitely more terrifying than hatred would have been. She stood beside Colonel Ramirez, strong face framed in a few, wind-blown curls that had escaped her short braid. Stray drops of water glittered on her hair and beret, as if she'd arrived early to wait for him, and there was no emotion on her face. None at all. He could see only her left profile from where he stood, watching numbly as Castellaño recited the useless formal plea for reconciliation before he examined and selected the pistols. Ramirez and Stefan loaded the magazines at his command, their fingers flicking, flicking on the brass cartridge cases, and the stillness—the focused, empty calm of Harrington's expression—mocked his own terror more cruelly than any sneer. Her confidence was a fist about his heart, squeezing with fingers of steel, and panic filled him like poison.

She'd destroyed him. She would complete his destruction in a few more moments, yet his death would be no more than a punctuation. His decades-long efforts to punish her, to break and humble her, had failed. More than failed, for she'd turned the tables and brought him to this shameful, degrading end after agonizing days of waiting for the axe to fall. She hadn't just made him afraid; she'd made him *know* he was afraid, exposed his shameful terror for all to see and made him *live* with it night after night, until he woke whimpering in his sweatsoaked sheets.

Hate pushed back some of the fear, but that was a mixed blessing. The paralysis eased, yet that only made the strobes of his panic sharper, more terrible in the clarity with which he perceived them. Sweat oozed down his temples in fat, oily snakes, and the air felt suddenly colder. The automatic pistol weighed his right hand like an anchor when he took it, and the fingers of his left hand were so numb he almost dropped the magazine Stefan handed him.

"Load, Lady Harrington." North Hollow's eyes were wide and fixed, showing white all around their rims, as he watched Harrington slide the five-round magazine into the butt of her pistol with a smooth precision so graceful it seemed choreographed.

"Load, Lord North Hollow," Castellaño said, and he fumbled clumsily with his weapon. The magazine tried to slip from his sweaty fingers, twisting like a live thing before he got it in place, and he flushed with humiliation while Castellaño waited for him to complete the simple mechanical task. He watched Ramirez touch Harrington's shoulder, saw the grim approval on his face before he turned away, and longed for the simple comfort of feeling the same touch from his brother. But Stefan only closed the pistol case and stepped back with cold hauteur, an expression that promised Harrington she was far from done with the Youngs whatever happened here, and in that moment, fleetingly and imperfectly, Pavel Young glimpsed the fundamental hollowness of his entire family. The futility and nihilism that infused them all. The arrogance that kept Stefan from even considering the value of one last physical contact.

It was an ephemeral awareness, swept away by his terror almost before he perceived it, yet it was enough to touch him with fresh hatred for the woman who had shown it to him. It was as if his own mind were determined to deal him one last, searing humiliation—the realization that even if he somehow managed to kill Harrington she would still have won. Unlike him, she'd achieved something, left something behind her that people would remember with respect, while he'd done nothing, left nothing but a memory of contempt beside which even oblivion was to be preferred.

"Take your places," Castellaño said, and Young turned to put his back to Harrington's. Her presence cut the wind, radiating a warmth against his spine that was sensed, not felt, and he swallowed again and again, desperately, fighting his nausea, as the Master of the Field spoke quietly.

"You have agreed to meet under the Dreyfus Protocol," he said. "At the command of 'Walk,' you will each take thirty paces. At the command of 'Stop,' you will immediately stop and stand in place, awaiting my next command. Upon the command 'Turn,' you will turn, and each of you will fire one round and one round only. If neither is hit in the first exchange, you will each lower your weapon and stand in place once more until I have asked both parties if honor is satisfied. If both answers are in the negative, you will take two paces forward upon the command 'Walk.' You will then stand in place once more until the command 'Fire,' when you will once more fire one round and one round only. The procedure will repeat until one party declares honor is satisfied, until one of you is wounded, or until your magazines are empty. Do you understand, Lord North Hollow?"

"I—" He cleared his throat and willed iron into his voice. "I do," he said more clearly, and Castellaño nodded.

"Lady Harrington?"

"Understood." The single word came out low-voiced but clear, with none of his own panic, and North Hollow fought the need to dash sweat from his eyes.

"You may chamber," Castellaño said, and the earl winced at the crisp, metallic sound behind him. The slide of his own pistol slipped in his sweaty fingers. It took him two attempts to chamber a round, and patches of dull crimson burned on his cheekbones as he lowered the weapon once more.

"Walk," Castellaño commanded, and North Hollow closed his eyes, fighting to keep his spine straight, as he took the first step and the terror roared inside him.

One shot. That was all he had to survive before he could declare "honor" was satisfied and escape. Just one shot at a full sixty paces; *surely* she would miss at that range!

Another step, cold feet wet in his soaked shoes, earthy-smelling sod squelching underfoot, wind plucking at his sweatsoaked hair, and the memory of Denver Summervale's death replaying in hideous detail behind his eyes.

A third pace, and he saw Summervale jerk from the first hit, saw the ease with which Harrington pumped bullet after bullet into him, saw his head explode with the final round, and horror gagged him. She wouldn't miss. Not at sixty paces or at six hundred. She was a demon, a monster whose sole function was to destroy him, and she wouldn't—couldn't—fail in her task.

A fourth pace, and he felt himself listing to the side as the pistol in his hand weighted his heart and soul. He blinked desperately against the mist filming his eyes, fighting to breathe.

A fifth pace. A sixth. A seventh, and with each of them the terror grew, blotting away the previous clarity of his racing thoughts, crushing him in a vise of steel. He heard a soft, endless whimper and realized vaguely that it was his own, and something happened deep inside him.

Honor felt him behind her, walking away from her, and kept her eyes fixed on the horizon. The newsies were out in force once more, huddling against the wet wind as they crouched behind their cameras and microphones, but she paid them no heed. She was focused, focused as never before, even against Summervale. She would have only one shot, so it must be perfect. No shooting from the hip, no rushing. A centered, balanced turn, careful on the treacherous wet grass. Take his fire, dare him to hit her with his own rushed shot, then capture him in her sights. Hold him there. Take up the slack. Exhale. Steady her arm and squeeze, squeeze, squeeze, until—

"Down!"

Only one voice would have shouted that word at a time like this, and for only one reason. It came out with the same hard, unwavering authority she'd heard once before, snapping into her brain like lightning, unthinkable to dispute and impossible to disobey. She didn't think. She didn't even realize until later that she'd heard or recognized the voice at all. She simply moved, hurling herself down and to the right before the first echo reached her.

Pain. Agony roaring in her left shoulder as something exploded behind her. Crimson spraying out before her in a steaming fan that beaded the sodden grass with rubies. Another explosion and something screaming past her. Another, and then she struck the ground in another crescendo of pain while a fourth and fifth explosion crashed behind her and she rolled to her left, biting back a scream of white-hot torment as her shoulder hit the grass, and the reactions of thirty-five T-years of martial arts training brought her back to her knees in the muddy, bloody grass.

Pavel Young stood facing her, less than twenty meters away, his gun hand wavering before him in a cloud of gunsmoke. Blood pumped from her shattered shoulder, splinters of bone glittered white in the wound, her left arm was a dead, immobile weight of agony, and her brain was clear as frozen crystal. The corner of her eye saw Castellaño, his face twisted in fury, his pulser already swinging down to fire. There could be only one penalty for Young's action, and the Master of the Field's gun hand flashed toward its target. But shock at the unbelievable breach of every rule of conduct had held him for a fraction of a second, and he moved so slowly. *Everything* moved so slowly, like figures in a dream, and somehow her own hand was already up before her, the pistol in full extension.

Young stared at her, wide-eyed and mad, still clutching his empty weapon, and the automatic bucked in her hand. A crimson rose blossomed on Young's chest, and she rode the recoil up, brought her hand back down, fired again. And again. And then Castellaño's pulser finally snarled. The burst of darts ripped through Pavel Young in a spray of blood and shredded tissue, but he was already dead, with three ten-millimeter rounds, in a group small enough to cover with a child's hand, where once his heart had been.

✧ EPILOGUE

HONOR HARRINGTON STOOD IN THE captain's cabin of HMS *Nike*, her cabin no longer, and watched James MacGuiness dismounting Nimitz's life-support module from the bulkhead. Most of her personal possessions had already been removed, and Jamie Candless moved past her with the sealed carry-all that held her last uniforms. Andrew LaFollet stood outside the cabin hatch with Simon Mattingly, and Nimitz bleeked softly at her from the back of a couch.

She looked down at the 'cat, trying to smile, and the tip of her index finger stroked between his ears. He looked back up at her, rising high on the couch back. One true-hand gripped her tunic for balance, and the other reached up to touch her cheek with exquisite gentleness. She felt his concern, but for once she could not respond with assurance that all would be well.

She tried—again—to shift her immobilized left arm and winced with the stab of pain that rewarded her forgetfulness. She was lucky, though it had been hard to convince Nimitz of it. He'd known the instant she came back aboard and nearly torn the sickbay hatch down, then crouched taut and anxious just beyond the sterile field, purring as if to burst, while Fritz Montoya put her under to repair her shoulder. He hadn't been able to use all original parts; the bullet had shattered her left scapula, then torn up and out through the point of her shoulder, demolishing the joint in passing and barely missing the main artery. Quick heal could do a lot, yet Fritz had been forced to rebuild her shoulder socket to give it something to work around, and his face had been knotted with disapproval while he worked.

But Honor wasn't concerned about her shoulder. Fritz Montoya, as she knew from painful personal experience, did good work, and, extensive as the repairs had been, they were all routine procedures. Yet there were wounds no doctor could heal, and she bit her lip against a pain not of her body as she touched the plain black beret on her bare desk and faced the brutal amputation of her future.

She didn't regret her actions. She couldn't, and she'd known the price going in. She'd thought it worth paying then; she thought so still. It was only that the pain was so much worse than she'd thought possible.

She didn't mind the vote excluding her from the House of Lords, or the group of news services tearing her apart for her "brutality" in gunning down a man with an empty gun. Pavel Young's life had been forfeit from the moment he turned upon her. In the eyes of the law, it mattered less than nothing whether it had been Lieutenant Castellaño's fire or hers that executed sentence upon him, but it mattered to her.

She'd expected to feel pleasure at his death, yet she didn't. Cold, merciless satisfaction, yes. A sense that justice had been done at last, a grim sense of completion that it had come at her hand and one of rightness at the sordid ignobility of his end. It was something she'd *had* to do, a scale that had to be righted, but there was no pleasure in it, and the emptiness of her tomorrows stretched bleakly before her. In a sense, Young, too, had won. He'd taken Paul from her, and she'd sacrificed the career she'd spent thirty years building, the joy of doing the one thing in the universe she'd been born to do in the service of her Queen, to destroy him.

She sighed as MacGuiness disconnected the last fitting and two ratings lifted the life-support module between them in a counter-grav collar. They carried it carefully through the hatch and down the passage, and LaFollet stepped just inside the hatch and looked at her as they passed.

"Are you ready, My Lady?" the man who'd twice saved her life asked, and she nodded.

"Mac?" she said quietly.

"Of course, Ma'am." MacGuiness held out his arms, and Nimitz leapt up into them. He climbed to the shoulder pad the steward wore, the one Honor couldn't offer him until her wounds healed. MacGuiness was a native Manticoran, and the 'cat's weight was a heavy burden for anyone reared on the Kingdom's capital planet, but he held himself up with a curious pride. He raised one hand to Nimitz, and the 'cat brushed his head against its palm as he would have against Honor's, then sat upright and still, his eyes on his person.

She looked back for a moment, then lifted the black beret from her desk. She faced the mirror, adjusting it one-handedly on her head, accepting the loss of the white one a starship's captain wore. She settled it to her satisfaction, determined to go into exile with her appearance perfect, and turned back to the others.

"Lead the way, Andrew," she told LaFollet, and the major started through the hatch and down the passage, then stopped. His spine stiffened in surprise, and he came to attention as a broad-shouldered man a centimeter taller than Honor rounded a bend in the uniform of an RMN admiral.

"Dame Honor," Hamish Alexander said quietly.

"Admiral." Honor's eyes stung, and she bit her lip harder. She'd hoped to avoid this. She'd even refused to return two com calls from White Haven, despising her own cowardice but unable to face the man who'd tried to save her career from herself. Her feelings were too raw, too ambiguous, the memory of his anger too painful. She'd come to suspect in recent weeks just how deep an interest he'd taken in her career, and the thought that he might believe she'd failed him by throwing it away was too much to bear on top of everything else.

"May I have a word in private, Dame Honor?" White Haven's voice was soft, and she felt a tingle of shock as she realized it was almost pleading. She longed to tell him no, that she had no time. She actually started to, but then she stopped. He must know she'd ignored his calls, yet he'd come to her in person. However he might despise her, she owed him at least the courtesy of the meeting he sought.

"Of course, My Lord." Her voice was flat with her effort to keep emotion from it, and she nodded to her henchmen. "Wait for me in the passage, please."

MacGuiness nodded, and he and LaFollet stood outside the hatch as it closed behind White Haven. She turned to face him, knowing her face was a mask, and he looked around the stripped cabin. There was an awkwardness about him, a strange sense of imbalance, and he cleared his throat.

"Have you decided where you're going?" he asked finally.

"Back to Grayson." She shrugged her good shoulder, and the fingers of her right hand stroked the captain's uniform she wore. She was still entitled to that, just as she was still entitled to take MacGuiness with her, though she would have left him behind, had he asked. They hadn't been able to cashier her despite the scandal; all they could do was send her the letter which "regretted to inform her" that Their Lordships could find no command for her at this time. She was on the beach, reduced to half-pay, and part of her wondered why she hadn't ended the agony by simply resigning.

"Grayson," White Haven murmured. "That's good. You need to get away for a while, put it all in perspective."

"I'm going to Grayson because at least I can still do something useful there, My Lord, not to put things in *'perspective.'* " Honor heard the bitterness in her own voice, and this time she couldn't stop it. He turned back to her, and she faced him, slim and tall, defiant and yet oddly vulnerable in the silent cabin which had once been hers.

"You were right, My Lord," she went on harshly. "You told me what would happen. I—" She swallowed and looked away, then made herself go on. "I know I've disappointed you, Sir. I . . . regret that. Not what I did, or why, but that I disappointed you."

"Don't," he said quietly, and her eyes snapped back to him in astonishment. "Dame Honor, do you know the real reason I was so furious with you when you rejected my illegal order to you?" he asked after a moment.

"Because you knew what would happen. That I'd end my career," she said around the lump in her throat.

"Bushwah!" White Haven snorted, and she twitched in fresh surprise and an echo of pain. He saw the hurt in her eyes and reached out quickly. "What?" he asked much more gently, and she gave her head a little toss and inhaled deeply.

"That was what the Admiral—Admiral Courvosier—always said to me when I came up with the wrong answer, Sir," she said softly.

"Really?" White Haven smiled crookedly, and this time he touched her, resting his hand on her good shoulder. "I'm not surprised. It's what he used to say to me, too." His hand tightened gently. "He was a good man, Honor. A good teacher and a better friend, and he always had the eye. He knew the stars when he saw them, and I think—" he looked directly into her eyes "—that he might be prouder of you now than he ever was before."

"*Proud*, Sir?" This time her voice did break, and she blinked on stinging tears.

"Proud. The reason I was so angry with you, Honor, was that you made me forget the very first principle of command: never give an order you *know* won't be obeyed. The fact that it was an illegal order only aggravated my anger, and I took it out on you. That's what I came here for—to tell you that . . . and to apologize."

"Apologize?" She stared at him through the spangles of her tears, unable to understand, and he nodded.

"You did the right thing, Honor Harrington," he said softly.

"You're catching hell for it now, but it was the only thing you could do and still be *you*, and what you are is a very fine thing indeed, Captain. Never doubt that. Never let the bastards snapping at your heels convince you otherwise."

"Is this some sort of pep talk now that the damage is done, Sir?" She was shocked by the vicious note in her own voice and raised her hand half-apologetically, but he only shook it off with a toss of his head.

"It is not. You're on half-pay now. Well, you're not unique in that. *I've* been on half-pay more than once, and never for a reason as good as yours. This war is going to last a long time, Captain. Peep resistance is already stiffening, and they still have the tonnage advantage. We'll cut deeper before they can stop us, but then it's going to be stalemate while each of us looks for a fresh advantage. I think we'll find one in time, but it's going to *take* time, and, as Raoul once told me on an occasion somewhat like this one, 'This, too, shall pass.' We need you, Captain. I know that, the Admiralty knows it, Her Majesty knows it, and one day the Kingdom will remember it."

Honor's mouth trembled with the need to believe him and the fear of more pain to come if she let herself, and he squeezed her shoulder again.

"Go to Grayson, Honor. Take your medicine. You don't deserve it, but no one ever said life was fair. But don't think this is the end. The scandal will die down eventually, the Navy will know it needs you, and, in time, even the House of Lords will realize it. You'll come home, Lady Harrington, and when you do, there'll be a command deck under your feet again."

"You're not just—? I mean, do you mean it, Sir?" She stared into his eyes, begging for honesty, and he nodded.

"Of course I do. It may take time, but it'll come, Honor. And when it does, I'll welcome you under my flag any day, anywhere, for any mission." He shook her lightly with each phrase, and she felt her trembling mouth firm. It blossomed in a smile—a shy smile, and fragile, but her first since Pavel Young's death—and he nodded. Then he released her and stood back with an answering smile.

"Thank you, Sir," she said softly.

"Don't thank me, Dame Honor. Just go out there and spit in the eye of any bastard who looks at you sideways, hear me?"

"Aye, aye, Sir." She blinked her misty eyes, nodded to him, and turned back to the hatch, and Hamish Alexander watched Dame Honor Harrington walk down the passage between Andrew LaFollet and James MacGuiness with her head high.

FIELD OF DISHONOR

HONOR BETRAYED

The People's Republic of Haven's sneak attack on the Kingdom of Manticore has failed. The Peeps are in disarray, their leaders fighting for power in bloody revolution, and the Royal Manticoran Navy stands victorious.

But Manticore has domestic problems of its own, and success can be more treacherous than defeat for Honor Harrington. Now, trapped at the core of a political crisis she never sought, betrayed by an old and vicious enemy she thought vanquished forever, she stands alone.

She must fight for justice on a battlefield she never trained for in a private war that offers just two choices: death . . . or a "victory" that can end only in dishonor and the loss of all she loves.

❦

David Weber is the new Big Name in science fiction, and his dauntless Honor Harrington has conquered not only the enemy but the hearts of thousands of readers everywhere, who have been relentlessly demanding Honor's exploits in a more permanent form. And we're happy to oblige.